The Comp

The Competition

Caroline Miley

The Competition by Caroline Miley
Published by Australian eBook Publisher
www.AustralianEbookPublisher.com.au
© Caroline Miley

The moral right of the author has been asserted. All rights reserved. Without limiting the rights under copyright restricted above, no part of this publication may be reproduced, stored in or introduced into a retrieval system, or transmitted, in any form or by any means (electronic, mechanical, photocopying, recording or otherwise), without the prior written permission of both the copyright owner and the publisher of this book.

1st Edition 2016, pbk.
ISBN: 978-1-925516-33-3
Book design by: Julia Lefik

National Library of Australia Cataloguing-in-Publication Entry:

Creator:	Miley, Caroline, author.
Title:	The Competition / Caroline Miley.
ISBN:	9781925516333 (paperback) 9781925516340 (epub) 9781925516357 (kindle)
Subjects:	Art, Competitions, Great Britain, Fiction. Historical fiction. Great Britain, Social customs, 18th century, Fiction.
Dewey No.:	A823.4

Also available as an ebook from major ebook vendors.

Find the author at www.carolinemiley.com

Acknowledgements

I would like to thank the Clifton Hill Writers for their support and advice in the writing of *The Competition*, and especially Judith Lukin-Amundsen, Trish Bolton and Annette Dutton for their unfailing help and encouragement. Many thanks also to Varuna, the Writers House, for a Fellowship which helped bring the manuscript to completion.

Preface

The ascent was to take place from the pleasure gardens of the Mermaid public house at Hackney, but we arrived late and were trapped on the outskirts of the crowd. I could see only the billowing top of the immense silk balloon, decorated in the King's colours. It quivered above the trees as though alive, sinking and rising as it was inflated. I hadn't thought it would be so exciting, although I'd hoped so. The people cheered. I climbed on the wheel of a public coach that had stopped nearby and gave Campbell a hand up after me. Now we could see over the heads. A banner proclaiming the 'Daredevil Aeronaut' was draped across the front of the house. I took out my book and began drawing rapidly, capturing the main lines of the apparatus, making notes of the colouring and its size compared to the tavern, which it dwarfed. I could draw the house and gardens at leisure after the crowd had gone.

The aeronaut came out, followed by another man and a dog. The dog, a small yellow specimen, was wagging its tail and looking about with a self-important expression. It obviously thought it was the reason for the cheering. The Italian wore a cocked hat and a silk scarf. He mounted the ladder, bowing and waving with every appearance of coolness. His companion handed up the dog then followed him. Another roar and the silk bubble wavered, trembled, and lurched upwards. It seemed far too large and weighty actually to float, but as I watched it rose, faltered, rose again, hesitated, then broke free of the earth, trailing ropes behind it. At last it swayed above the heads of the crowd, hundreds of gasping faces, including my own, turned up to adore it. The sun shimmered on the canopy as it made its way with incredible lightness into the empyrean, diminishing rapidly as the breeze caught it and it swam away over the Thames. Near me a lady fainted and another was being fanned by her companion, while a white-faced man leant against the coach, his hands trembling as he pulled out a flask and administered a strengthening draught. 'By God,' he kept saying. 'By God, I've never seen anything like it.'

Chapter One

I'd first met Campbell, a lean, sandy native of Edinburgh, ten years ago when we were drawing in the Antique School at the Royal Academy, struggling with grubby studies of the Dying Gladiator or the Apollo Belvedere and throwing bread at each other when the master's back was turned. I had always been fond of the Gladiator. He seemed to me a tragic figure and much more real than the posturing gods and emperors who filled the room. I used to picture what his life must have been, while I was drawing his sagging muscles and bowed head.

The Painting Master then had been Fuseli, an old gnome with a powerful accent—'Dot is goot, Mr Armiger'. By perseverance, enthusiasm and native talent, Campbell and I had made our way from the Antique to the Life School and eventually to our Diploma works and freedom. It was the love of art that had drawn us together. I had real ability, the masters said, if only I would 'restrain my eccentricity and apply myself to the proper canons of taste'. We met from time to time at Old Slaughter's, the coffee house artists frequented, or the colourmen's shops, especially since we both favoured Middleton's. On occasion we dined together; now and again we clubbed together to hire a model.

Love of drawing had brought me to the Academy. My father, now gone, God rest his soul, to lie beside my mother, had not wanted me to be an artist, but the drawing master at school thought I had ability and I persecuted Father until he relented. It had been difficult. Ever since he'd nearly lost everything through investing in the Virginia tobacco trade just before the American wars, he'd become averse to anything in the nature of a risk—he, previously the most carefree of men. My earliest memories were of his despair when the Colonials refused to pay British investors for their property. I later discovered that it was only my uncle's intervention that had saved him from bankruptcy, but there were many years of my childhood when he hid in his dark study grappling with bills, head in hands, and of a frugality in the running of the house that my mother hated.

He'd married her in the good times in a reckless excess of emotion and she, from an old family, never stopped reproaching him, even when he at last got back on an even keel. It was he who used to read to me—I remembered *Rasselas* best—I loved the Happy Valley and the prince's adventures. Those were our best times. Perhaps he could see the desire for adventure in me when he agreed to my going to the Academy to study. Perhaps he could see that I would never make anything but an artist.

Drawing to me was like life itself. To take a sheet of paper and a pencil and make something where before there had been nothing; to feel the paper under my fist and the sound of the crayon's whisper across the page; to bring to life on the blank surface line, light and shadow: a tree, a cloud, a river, men, horses, dogs—a landscape—a whole world. That was drawing to me. And after that, painting: all that drawing had to offer, with the addition of colour. Colour; all the hues of nature in my gift, and the perfumes of turpentine and oil, and the feel of the brush in my hand and the way the paint glided from the brush to the canvas and gave it life. That was art, to me.

Ten years ago I'd set out on my own as a landscape painter

with lodgings near the Academy, a few pupils and a moderate practice. In bad times I painted inn signs; in good, lived well in some gentleman's house while I painted his property; but what I really liked was roaming about London's great parks and painting them in their various moods. Although I had hopes of getting a big commission or finding a wealthy patron and becoming very comfortable, I could see a lifetime stretching ahead in which a modest success would be accompanied by a modest income, and so it would go on until I died, and twelve months later no-one would have heard of me.

The ten years had passed without my really thinking about them. The struggle to get set up had occupied the foreground, but since my thirtieth birthday I'd been aware of an inner disquiet. It was nagging, persistent, but I wasn't sure what it was.

For some time I attributed it to the lack of love. Unlike painting, it was a field in which I was conspicuously unsuccessful, not for want of trying. When I was just turned twenty-one and full of the joys of manhood I proposed to a girl I was in love with—Belinda. I could say her name now. I think I really loved her; certainly I believed so at the time. I got up my nerve, asked, and was rejected out of hand. Not long afterwards she married someone else. Some of the words she'd used when she refused me were still burned into my heart—the words, and her look when she said, with all the decisiveness in the world, that 'she could not possibly think of it'. It was as though she had snapped a book shut in my face. For more than six months afterwards I made a detour to avoid passing down her street and I could not go to the places where we had met. Eventually it wore off a little and I was able to resume work, and as time went by I was able to go about as before.

Subsequent relationships had not got so far. My affairs, such as they were, seemed to proceed in a muddled medley of desire (mine), beauty and charm (hers) and a modicum of conversation, and mixed in with a good measure of propinquity. Then I never quite understood how they declined, except that the propinquity and the conversation grew less and eventually ended altogether. When I was young and in love I'd been considered far too young to marry, and now at thirty-one I felt as though I'd soon be too old.

I was not ill-looking, or so my friends told me; at least I had the advantage of being tall, with thick waving hair and a presentable countenance, but I had not the sort of looks or address that would encourage women to throw them away on me. Then there was money. There was my father's legacy in the three per cents and a certain amount at my banker's, the results of my own diligence, which I had managed to save. Together they did not amount to the sort of fortune to attract a young lady of fashion or even of fashionable pretensions. But I wanted female companionship, even love. I had not altogether given up hope that one day there would be someone for me to pour out my affection on and get some in return. Now there was only Laura. We had met a year or two ago and our relationship had jogged along, each satisfying the other's desire, but that was all. She was lonely, too.

APART from Laura, Campbell was my closest friend, so when he went down to Bath for the season and invited me to stay I accepted gladly. I had no trouble in getting away since my pupils were mostly out of town on their own jaunts. I packed some clothes, my folding easel and paint boxes, and took the Bristol Mail.

The journey over the rolling chalk was a holiday in itself. The landscape was picturesque, the weather fine and I sat outside on the box to better enjoy the view. By the second day the novelty was gone and with the aid of half a crown I persuaded the coachman to let me take the reins. I loved driving but hardly ever had the opportunity in London.

There were a lot of reins for the four horses but I managed to gather them all between my fingers. The horses tossed their heads, feeling a new hand, and set off. We rattled along the turnpike at a good trot. It was thrilling to be in charge of such a large equipage. Once we'd got well under way I gave the horses a flick with the whip. The coachman put out a restraining hand, but it was already done.

"Road goes downhill here, sir—shouldn't ha' done that!"

He was right. The horses, getting along at a fine clip, breasted a slight rise and I saw the road disappear in front of their heads. The coachman gripped the rail as the coach tipped downwards and the horses increased their pace, necks stretched out, ears back. My hands prickled and I felt the hair on the back of my neck bristle. My breath stopped in my throat, my heart pounded. The road ahead was rutted but straight. They broke into a fair canter and the coach rocked from side to side, rattling as though a wheel was about to come off. The wind grabbed at my hat but I wouldn't stop now for the world. The coachman tried to wrestle the reins from my hands but I was enjoying myself too much to give them up. A lurch as a wheel hit a stone. I'd never gone so fast on such a big carriage.

"Give 'em to me, sir—give 'em here! Pull up, for God's sake!"

The reins were slipping through my fingers, but I still had enough control to give them a pull. The horses slowed to a trot, then a walk. I gathered up the leathers and handed them reluctantly to the coachman, who took them, his broad face red with annoyance.

"Much obliged to you," I said, cramming my hat onto my head and getting my breath back. "Most stimulating."

He didn't speak to me for the rest of the journey, but I didn't care. I'd felt the blood rushing through my body and my heart thumping. I'd felt alive.

It was not long before Bath came into view and we pulled up at the White Hart and I got down, still exhilarated.

BATH was a handsome place, built of honey-coloured stone and full of smart modern buildings. It was good to see Campbell and we explored the place together. I'd been there a day or two and we had visited the Pump Room and attended both the theatre and the concert, when Campbell started talking about the Competition. We were sitting in the Sidney Hotel drinking ale.

"A Competition? I haven't heard about it. When was it announced?" I pricked up my ears. Something new—a challenge.

"It hasn't been, but everyone is talking about it." Campbell's freckled complexion flushed. Everyone at Bath, I supposed. "The Royal Academy is putting up a prize and there are rumours of a big commission to follow. The man who gets it will be made."

It sounded wonderful—if true. "How do you know?"

"Hallett told me the other day."

"And you believed him?"

"Aye, I know. It sounds like one of his stories."

"It certainly does. What was he doing down here?"

Campbell looked acid. "I think this is where his natural daughter is—tucked away with some chaperone." His Presbyterian soul disapproved of such goings-on. His father was an Edinburgh doctor, his mother a pillar of the Ladies' Guild.

"Oh. I suppose he told you that he personally had been approached to be in the Competition, or judge it, or something of the sort."

"He did indeed. He told me he'd been invited to enter, but of course I took it with some salt. But it happened that the next day I ran into Toby Quayle in Milsom Street and he confirmed it."

"Quayle! Is he here too?"

"As dapper as ever. He's come down for the season. Of course some of his clients will be here and his patron, Lord Arbuthnot, has taken a place in Great Pulteney Street—we passed by it. A vast place. I think he's staying with him."

I pulled a face. Quayle was staying with Lord Arbuthnot; Campbell and I were sharing lodgings over the baker's in Trim Street.

Campbell was clearly elated by the prospect and I felt a rising tide of apprehensive excitement too. 'The man who gets it will be made'. Campbell was right. Membership of the Academy would naturally follow—if it didn't go to one of the existing members. My heart sank. Of course it would. I had no chance. But I must try. If I could get it, my life would be transformed. Patrons would seek me out. And the 'big commission' to follow must mean a big fee with it.

"I suppose everyone will go in for it." I tried to sound careless.

"Well, Quayle, obviously, and all that sort of people."

"Hallett evidently fancies his luck."

"Aye, he always does, and he'll do everything he can to get it. It would be infuriating if he won. But of course that depends a great deal on the theme, which we know nothing of at present."

We speculated on the subject. In some ways there was not much to speculate on. It must be a history painting, the queen of genres. It was only what period in history or event would be chosen. We rejected the obvious topic, an allegory of the reign of our present King, since his health was so bad as to make the subject an embarrassment, and much of the country still blamed him for losing the American colonies.

"Military subjects will be *hors de combat*, I imagine," I suggested.

"Since Benjamin West's magnificent treatment of the 'Death of Lord Nelson', only a few years ago, the Academy will hardly call for a rival to it, even though it was so popular. Competing with the President of the Academy can't be intended."

"I'm sure you're right. Viscount Wellington's campaign in the Peninsula, perhaps?" That had interesting possibilities and would be topical, for once.

"No—too current and too political. It'll probably be a safe classical subject—the 'Death of Socrates', or 'Caesar at the Rubicon'."

Dull, but probably correct. "Will you go in for it?" I inquired.

"I suppose so, although I don't know that I have much chance. It'll go to one of the usual people. I don't have enough connections."

Exactly what I felt, but still! It was far too big a prize to let it go without making all possible effort. Both of us needed something to bring us onto the stage with some *éclat*, advance our careers with a bound instead of a crawl. A 'big fee'? If I won, I'd have money—I could pay my debts—travel—perhaps even marry!

"But what about you?" Campbell asked.

"There's no possibility of my entering. A landscape won't be considered."

It always rankled with me that painting nature was rated so low, but of course the Greeks and after them the great Italians had long established that man represented nature in its apogee. It followed that all other forms of nature were inferior. Campbell concentrated on portraiture, which was next in line after history painting, but he knew my ambition, which was to paint nature with the heroism of Claude. I loved the countryside and nature in all its permutations, but I felt that there was something unsatisfactory in treating it only as so many lights and shades, formed by trees, streams and meadows. I had seen some Claudes at Angerstein's house in Pall Mall. There was an artist who had the courage to treat nature as embodying something great and noble. Mere imitation of Claude was obviously unacceptable; he had plenty of imitators already and I had to develop a style of my own to be taken seriously. And I didn't want to imitate any man, however great: I wanted to strike out in my own direction. But even Claude himself would never do for the Competition.

"Aye—unfortunately for you. But you have genius. You'll think of something to please them."

"Thank you. But I wish I didn't have to please them."

"That's how it is."

I knew he thought this attitude of mine nonsensical. I sighed. "I suppose you're right. It's not often that you can make a living doing what you like."

He clapped me on the shoulder. "Aye. Now, shall we walk to the Pump Room?"

I decided that while I was in Bath I would take the waters, which were bought by the glass from an old woman ensconced behind a rail. They were very hot and had a strange flat, dull taste, disagreeable in a way that was hard to specify, but not very foul. I didn't know whether they would do any good, judging by the number of fat dowagers and gouty old squires assiduously downing their three pints a day. The Pump Room was the place to go to see and be seen. A band played there much of the time and people, including a number of pleasing young ladies, walked up and down. The town was full of soldiers, I supposed on their way to, or from, Spain.

The next day Campbell was occupied with a sitting for the portrait of Miss Hall. When I dressed I noticed that the waistband of my breeches was too tight. The life of an artist was not conducive to maintaining a good figure, since it consisted largely of standing in front of the easel, sitting around in a coffee house or inn, or walking slowly around looking at the view or other people's paintings. And all the sitting around in coffee houses and inns was accompanied by large quantities of madeira, sherry wine or chocolate, as the case may be, and beefsteaks, mutton chops or game pies. I decided to climb up to Beechen Cliff, the vista and vantage point *par excellence* of Bath, put on boots instead of shoes and slipped a sketchbook into my pocket.

I set off past Westgate Buildings and through the south gate and soon gained the base of the cliff. I was surprised at how steep the road was and by how many ladies as well as gentlemen were making the ascent on foot. A group of ladies passed me, shading themselves with their parasols as I stopped to rest halfway up. I should take more exercise if a walk of a couple of miles could put me out of breath.

When I got to the top it was well worth the effort. The cliff was clothed with a hanging wood of beeches, but from the road I could see the whole city of Bath, spread out in a sort of basin between the foot of the cliff and the Avon. In the distance low, wooded hills formed a pretty frame. The whole effect was of a maze of warm amber stone cushioned by verdure of different colours and textures; a point of focus was provided by the Abbey, with behind it Pulteney Bridge and a silvery glimpse of the river. The view of the Abbey was of the side of the nave. The carved stonework caught the sunlight handsomely. Other steeples dotted the town, but none to compete with the Abbey's bulk and square tower. I wondered if I could climb it—it would give an excellent prospect. After resting on the grass gazing with pure enjoyment for some time and picking out the landmarks, I got out my book and began to draw.

I passed a pleasant afternoon drawing the view from various perspectives and amusing myself by altering it in one sketch or another, to conform more or less to the rules of the Picturesque as laid down by Gilpin, then trying one in the manner of Claude. A few lady amateurs were similarly occupied. I caught one in the act of coming up behind me and craning over my shoulder. She turned away quickly, tucking her book in her reticule and hastening off. Another came up but pretended to be completely uninterested.

"Pray, sir, do not put me in it."

I had no intention of doing so. She went away.

I walked home under a mackerel sky of rose shot through with faint turquoise, whose hues dimmed, while just above the horizon the rose intensified to a bright coral, before the whole brindled scheme dissolved into a violet-tinted dusk.

As I neared the Abbey I saw Campbell walking about the piazza with a lady and gentleman. He signalled violently with his hand behind their backs and I went over, to be introduced to a florid corpulent man in a snuff-coloured coat which did no favours to his complexion, and a plump young lady enough like the gentleman to make them relations.

"Mr Hall, may I present my friend Mr Armiger? Mr Armiger is an artist like myself. Mr Joshua Hall, Miss Anne Hall, Mr Edward Armiger."

We bowed to each other. Campbell had shortened the lady's nose a trifle and lengthened her neck, but his portrait was a speaking likeness.

"Miss Hall felt somewhat fatigued after the sitting, so we thought we would take a turn around the square before returning home," Campbell explained. I nodded gravely and fell into step. "Have you had a profitable afternoon?"

I took his hint. "Indeed. Beechen Cliff is most picturesque. I have made a number of sketches of the town and the Abbey, which I plan to work up into a series of views in watercolours and perhaps some in oils."

Campbell turned to Mr Hall, who was listening while he stared about him at the architecture. His daughter hung on his arm, smiling occasionally at Campbell. He might have made a conquest there. I noticed him smiling back.

"What style would you say the church is in, Mr Campbell?" he asked in a bass voice.

You had to know Campbell well to notice him wince. "It is Gothic—in the later style. A fine example. Of course parts of the building are much older. You can see it is Gothic by the pointed arches."

A discussion of clerestories and crockets ensued and I saw that one of Campbell's tasks was the education of Mr Hall. It was especially heroic of him as I knew he was not interested in architecture.

"And this?" Mr Hall indicated the Pump Room.

"Classical—definitely Classical. You see the pediment and the Corinthian columns?"

I thought it was time to help. "Are you very interested in architecture, Mr Hall?"

"Aye, that I am. I'm building a place up home."

I didn't know where 'home' was, but his broad speech suggested it was in the north of the country.

"And I thought to look about at the various styles while I was here. I've heard tell that Bath has much in the latest fashion. Would you say so?"

"Most certainly. The Pump Room here, Sidney House, for instance, and many of the houses in Pulteney Street are excellent examples of current fashion."

Campbell cut in. "Mr Armiger paints views of architecture which are very much sought after in London. I don't know whether you would be interested to see some?"

"Aye, Mr Campbell. Perhaps Mr Armiger would accompany you to my daughter's next sitting and I can look at his work while Anne is occupied."

I bowed gracefully. A date was fixed and we parted, they towards Milsom Street and we to a chop-house which we had discovered behind our lodgings, where they served a very creditable rabbit pie and gooseberry tart, with porter, for one and sixpence. All in all, a very good day.

Chapter Two

Campbell's next sitting was fixed for Wednesday, so I had to set to work immediately on the production of views that might attract Campbell's client, whom he was so willing to share with me. We worked together in the sitting room of the lodgings, he roughing in the background of Miss Hall and I working up some of my sketches into watercolours of different sizes. While we painted Campbell talked about the Halls.

"They come from the Midlands—somewhere near Rochford. He is in the process of building a seat there in the country outside the town."

"He doesn't have the look of a country squire—a townsman, I would have thought, and a small town, at that."

His clothes were good quality but not well cut, although Miss Hall's, which were in the height of fashion, had probably been bought in Bath.

Campbell stood back from his easel and considered his work. "No, he's one of the new men. He made all his money, of which I understand there is a great deal, from factories. Wool, I think." He stepped forward and began to mark in the shadows in the fold of crimson curtain he had put behind Miss Hall. He favoured a touch of the Grand Style, especially for the more conservative clients. I pulled a face.

"No need to be so choosy," he remarked. "When you have Lord Arbuthnot or his friends and relations as your patron, you can afford to turn your nose up at tradesmen, but I for one haven't reached that stage yet."

"I'm grateful to you for the introduction, I really am, and as you see I'm working towards pleasing him. But I'm concerned at what his taste will be. Do you have any idea?"

"As far as the portrait's concerned, a very good likeness which flatters the lady is what's called for. Nothing too adventurous." He grimaced in his turn. "If this comes off, I hope to do the rest of the family."

"Are there many of them?"

"Mrs Hall and another daughter, whom I haven't seen, but who is supposed to be remarkably pretty."

SINCE I planned to make some interior studies of it, I went to attend Matins at the Abbey. It was a spacious, airy building, lately repaired and handsome, although distinguished more by its antiquity than its architecture. I made a satisfactory view of the nave with the light streaming through the great west window and touching the pew ends. However, it was dull work. I'd rather have been developing my ideas about noble landscape, which I had had time to think about while at Beechen Cliff. I planned to work up one of the views from up there in a more Claudian manner and see whether Mr Hall liked it. It would be splendid if he did—and I began dreaming about a patron who would encourage me in the sort of work I really wanted to do. And about the Competition—if there really was one.

Perhaps the Competition was the opportunity for me to branch out as I'd been longing to. If I could create something exciting, a huge landscape with figures, with nobility and grandeur—if I could invent my own genre, instead of following the accepted fashions—I was becoming tired of picturesque views. And I wanted to experiment with the new pigments that were coming out. Last time I was at Middleton's he showed me a new yellow he called chrome, a very good bright colour. Lawrence had used in his portrait of a gentleman in a fur coat—it brightened the shadows of the necktie. As long as it didn't go black in sunlight, the way Turner's yellow did, and Ackermann's yellow was not much better, despite his promoting it so highly. I would use it to get a brighter green in some of the views, and maybe touch it in in the sunlight in the Abbey picture. Not too much, I didn't want to frighten the client, although a large oil of the scene, with more impasto to give real solidity to the light flooding the nave—so that one could really feel the light, the warmth, not just observe it—perhaps when I got back to Town. New materials and techniques, now that would give weight to my Competition piece, and mark me out as an up-and-coming man. So I worked away, and the morning passed.

Campbell met me for dinner at the Sidney Hotel, where we ran into Hallett, tall, lean and surrounded by hangers-on, including a pretty, vulgar girl who smiled whenever he looked her way. He wore a cocked hat and a frogged coat with epaulettes. His neckcloth was brilliant white and tied in an extraordinary style. He appeared, as always, conspicuous but entirely at ease. He ran a flickering eye over Campbell and myself, both in buff breeches and green (Campbell) or blue (myself) broadcloth.

I couldn't resist. "Off to storm the barricades, Hallett?"

He smirked. "Afraid I can't stop—I have to meet someone. Wait a moment," as I opened my mouth to speak. He conferred with the girl while Campbell and I ordered drinks.

"Come on, Hallett, tell us about the Competition."

He shook his head.

"I promised I would say nothing. No-one is supposed to know about it."

"You know about it."

"Yes, but it was told me in confidence" and he broke off again to talk to his friends and consult his watch. "Look at this," and he held it out. It was unlike any timepiece I had ever seen and had lubricious scenes enamelled on the cover. "Got it in Paris, a little shop in the Palais Royal."

In the end Campbell and I gave up. Probably Hallett knew no more than we had already discovered, for all his claims of inside information. It was maddening. It would be typical of him to have already started work on some great piece before it was announced, while disclaiming all knowledge of the subject. But it looked as though it really did exist.

"The only consolation," Campbell remarked while we ate some cutlets, "is that he's so occupied with his numerous friends and projects that he works terribly slowly."

"He works fast enough when it's something he really wants to do, though." We finished the cutlets and called for wine. "Hallett's a man born out of his time. If he'd been here twenty or thirty years ago he would have been all powder and patches and an immense wig."

Campbell laughed. "Aye, and a generation before that, he would have been Beau Nash." A statue of the eccentric old Master of Ceremonies lorded it over the Pump Room.

It was true that Hallett had been the last among us to leave off powder when the fashion changed two or three years ago. The more malicious of his friends said he had been caught between the conflicting demands of being at the front of fashion and of concealing his creeping baldness, which powder did so well. In the end fashion triumphed and he now appeared in a Titus cut, short and brushed forward over his temples, with the hair artfully standing up over his crown in a sort of cock's comb.

All the same, he seemed to have a finger in every pie and gain advancement without apparent effort.

After dinner I walked out into the fields around the town to make some more sketches. The Competition would have to wait until I had finished the work in hand. A prospect of the town from the north with Beechen Cliff in the background would be useful, if I could find a suitable vista. In the end I made only one or two sketches, knowing in my heart that I had better views already at home. I determined on a large study of the Sidney Hotel and one of Pulteney Bridge from the town side. That would have to do, if I was going to have enough time to work them up.

At the end of the afternoon I turned for home. I was tired and thirsty, but had some useful drawings. I went round the Orange Grove and saw a man lying asleep under the church wall. Something about him made me stop. He lay half curled on his left side, his back against the wall in a niche in the architecture. His head was cushioned on his left arm and the hand, very dirty, was stretched out. He was neither young nor old and looked strong, but his clothes were threadbare and his light hair matted. He had clogs on his feet, well worn and with square toes turned up, quite different from the pattens the ladies clattered about Bath's dusty streets in. A great brown dog lay against him, fitting its body to his, its head resting on its paws. I stopped to look and saw that the dog was not sleeping. Its large brown eyes were open but it made no movement. I took a step towards them and at once the dog reached out a paw and placed it quietly over the man's outflung wrist.

I stayed watching them for some time but neither stirred. There were plenty of beggars in London but this man was different. I could not fathom how, but he was. Perhaps he was not a beggar but simply itinerant, but why and how he slept during the day I didn't know. The path ran close by him and was well travelled, many people walking past and speaking loudly while I stood there, but he slept on regardless. A man could sleep anywhere, it seemed. Quayle was staying with Lord Arbuthnot; Campbell and I were at the baker's; this man and his dog were behind the Abbey. I thought of drawing them but felt as though it would be indelicate. At last, oddly perturbed, I went on.

When I got back to the lodgings the man and dog were still on my mind, so I took a large new sheet of cream wove paper, sat down at the table by the window and began to draw them from memory. Drawing was always a pleasure. I started with a fine grey point to lay in the main forms, but soon put it down in favour of a softer black lead. The paper had a good tooth and the pencil dragged across it raising a slight fuzz, the lead lying just on the surface except where I pressed firmly, when it left a greasy sheen. The matt surface was cool and the picture took shape quickly. There was a dark shadow behind the man's back that threw up the texture of the stone wall of the Abbey and brought his body into relief. I hadn't noticed it at the time, but it was strong in my mind's eye. The thing I most remembered consciously was the expression in the dog's eyes and the way their depths shone golden where the sun struck them. I couldn't get it adequately with the pencil, so after a while I put it down and opened my box of watercolours.

The work went well and it was only when Campbell came in and stood behind me that I felt the crick in my back and realised that the light was going.

"What on earth is that?"

"A man I saw coming back from my walk. Who do you think he is?"

"I have no idea. Some beggar, I suppose. Or gipsy, with that big dog. But why paint him? I suppose he would make a good foreground to a picturesque landscape—a peasant resting under a tree, that sort of thing."

I continued touching in some tufts of grass at the base of the wall.

"I must say, you are giving it the treatment!" There was a note almost of disapproval. "What are you going to do with it?"

My interest in the subject had not lessened while I worked. I tried to imagine the man's life, where he had come from, what he was doing there, how he and the dog had met. For some reason I didn't think he was from Bath.

"I'd like to do it in oils." The thought had been at the back of my mind.

"Oils! But you could never show it. What would be the point?" He looked at me curiously.

"I know. But I just think it's... interesting. I get tired of views and scenes."

"There's no market for that sort of thing."

"I know that, too. I can't imagine who would buy it. I suppose it would just be for the pleasure of the thing."

Campbell inspected it. It was more or less finished, except where I needed to touch in some highlights with white body colour. "Well, I must say, it's nae bad. I feel I know the man—and the dog. It's full of life. I didn't see you as a figure painter, but perhaps you should do more. 'Scenes of Rural Life'? Gainsborough did very well with that sort of thing."

I hunched my shoulders. Campbell meant to be encouraging, but Gainsborough's ragged peasant children hovering around tumbledown cottage doors were not at all what I wanted. I had admired them when I was a student and they were of course excellent of their kind, but they were based entirely on the idea that the rags, and the children, and the cottage, were only so much 'foreground interest'. I looked at the dog's paw resting on the man's wrist. It had enormous dignity. That was what I wanted.

By Wednesday Campbell had made suitable progress on the portrait and I had assembled a variety of conventional views which I hoped would please Mr Hall. I included a few more interesting pieces in which I had tried to make the landscape and buildings speak of something more than their mere existence and contours.

"You're not going to show Mr Hall that beggar, are you?" Campbell said while I was packing up my pieces.

"Oh yes, I thought it might appeal to him." I wasn't averse to giving Campbell an occasional jolt.

"Don't. Where is it? I don't want you alarming him with one of your wild schemes. You'll put him off me as well."

"Don't worry, it's only views. Look, there's the beggar," and I turned it up in my folio.

"That's all right, then."

"Don't fret, I'll behave myself!"

The Halls had taken a house in Milsom Street, the fashionable quarter near the best shops. Campbell had nothing to lose, but putting my work before a new audience made me anxious. Failure, even disastrous failure, was inevitably a fear. If the client liked my work, he might buy a few pieces; he might commission some more; he might recommend me to his friends. If he rejected them, it was painful—shuffling the unwanted productions back into the decent obscurity of a portfolio; trying to maintain my composure; resisting the impulse, when I got back to my studio, of consigning the embarrassing reminders of fiasco to the fire. I'd done that more than once in my earlier days. But it was a risk one had to take, and if successful, the money would come in exceptionally useful. Although I was holidaying very economically, thanks to Campbell's generosity, it was still turning out much more expensive than I had bargained for. It always does, what with the coaches, buying food and drink and treating Campbell from time to time.

A footman answered the door and showed us into the room where Campbell was used to working, where he had left a large easel set up near a window overlooking the street. Like everyone else, he favoured a good light coming from the left to illuminate the sitter. Mrs Hall was there, a round sort of a body with a mass of brown curls escaping from her cap and a wealth of ill-arranged lace around her neck. Campbell seemed rather a favourite with both of the ladies, who fussed about with tea and plates of little cakes until eventually Miss Hall was seated in her place and Campbell took up his palette.

"Now then, young man, are you going to show me your pictures?" Mr Hall boomed.

I arranged them carefully on some tables, wishing it was possible to hang them. I interposed the more adventurous works here and there, hoping that they might recommend themselves that way, rather than striking the viewer all in a lump at the end. The light was not particularly good. I stood away, gazing carelessly out the window, while the examinations took place. The alternative was hovering anxiously and recommending this or that one to the client, which was altogether too much like a stall-holder suggesting you try the winkles.

But Mr Hall was having none of it. "What's this, then?" indicating the perspective of the Abbey interior with a broad red finger.

I explained it to him.

"I like that sunlight there. Come and see this." He held it up to show his wife, turning it this way and that to catch the light. "I like that one. You'll find I'm a straightforward sort of man, Mr Armiger. If I like something I'll say so, and if I don't like it you'll know it too. And what's this, here?"

He picked out one of the views of the town from Beechen Cliff, with clouds overhead and quite a nice effect of the winding Avon. "This would look grand in the hallway. You've got the likeness of the church."

As we went on, he pointing to the works he liked and me explaining the principles of art, I began to like him. Campbell had described him as 'not a bad sort of fellow' and I saw what he meant. He did indeed seem as straightforward as his own description made out and although it was obvious he knew as little about art as he did about architecture, he took an unaffected pleasure in the work that was pleasing. I also discovered that it would be a mistake to underestimate him.

"I know nowt about art, young man, since I made all my money in trade. I'm not ashamed to own it. It's a poor thing in my opinion for a man to be ashamed of what gives him a living. But now I've a deal of brass, I want my family to enjoy it." He looked across at his wife, who smiled fondly, looking up from her netting. "We don't come from Rochford but from Coldbrook nearby, though my factories are all in Rochford and I must be there much of the time. But I'm building a big house at Coldbrook for my wife and my girls, where I can be when I don't have to be overseeing the work, and I mean for it to be in the best style." Mrs Hall was nodding at each sentence. "I'm not a university man myself but I like to learn from those who know more than I do. 'To ask, 'tis a moment's shame. Not to ask, 'tis a lifetime's shame'. That's always been my creed and it's stood me in good stead. Mr Campbell here has been teaching me a thing or two, and now you've taught me a bit more. Eh?"

I rubbed my nose to cover my confusion. I had a feeling that he had read my mind, including my notion that he looked a great deal as a side of beef would look if dressed in a suit and wig. Thankfully, he seemed to take it in good humour.

"Now then, I suppose you'd like me to choose some pictures, eh?"

I was pleased and relieved, especially by the plural. The

work of the afternoon was done, and successfully. I had begun to hope, but I had spent many afternoons with people admiring my work and then going away saying they would 'think about it'. That guaranteed that I would never see them again. It is always gratifying when someone likes your work, however pedestrian his taste. Perhaps Mr Hall had more discrimination than I had given him credit for. But he paused, then rang the bell. The footman entered.

"Has Miss Francesca come in? Ask her to come down." He turned back to me. "My younger daughter. She is the artistic one in the family, and I'd no more think of buying pictures without consulting her than I'd get in a new type of frame without the advice of my foreman."

I wasn't quite pleased with the analogy, but was happy enough with the sale. I was drinking a glass of wine to congratulate myself when the door opened and a young lady walked in. One look and I put the glass down. An inexpressible sensation seized me, a sort of sick, fainting, distress at the heart, which I had learned long ago to identify as desire. At least, that is what I believed it was. I felt it when I saw the silks Quayle had brought home from India. He had thrown them out one at a time on the table—a very rich wine red, brick where the light struck it and claret in the shadows; next to it a peacock blue that would make the angels weep. He saw my expression and with a slight smirk flicked open a bolt of brilliant orange, which he cast on top of the heap, and finally a pale green the colour of elm leaves just springing, with a papery texture and strange silvery lights. I could remember them, and the sensation, as sharply as when I saw them then. Now, as I looked at the girl who had just entered the room, my throat constricted and my heart felt paralysed.

"My younger daughter, Miss Francesca," Mr Hall mentioned. He pronounced her name in the Italian manner, which delighted me.

She was dark, which was the first thing I noticed; of medium height, which was the second, and smiling, which was the third. Her hair was not black but a very dark chestnut tending to umber, her mouth red and full and her eyes, which were black, were lively. She dropped a curtsey, looking up under her lashes as she did so. Campbell and I were introduced; I managed to bow. I tried not to stare.

"I'm going to buy some pictures of Mr Armiger's for the hall, my dear, and thought you would like to help me choose."

"Oh, yes, Papa. Where are they?"

She tripped across to the table and I came to stand beside her. Her head reached my shoulder. I wished I was better looking. A faint perfume came from her hair.

She studied them for a few minutes while I studied her. She was exquisite. Nothing in the rest of the family had prepared me for her beauty. Her mother and father were plain; her sister Anne was a pleasant-looking young lady with her mother's curls, only fairer.

Her father seemed to read my mind again.

"My younger daughter is the beauty of the family, Mr Armiger. She is very like my own mother, so much so that she always puts me in mind of her—eh, my dear?" She gave him a dazzling smile. "While I take after my father—a very worthy man, but no picture to look at. Fetch down your grandmother's picture for Mr Armiger," and she went to the mantelpiece and returned with a miniature portrait framed in black velvet. Our hands almost touched as she gave it to me. It was the work of a minor artist, but he had captured the lively expression as well as the dark features of a lady in the powdered hair and stiff bodice of fifty years ago.

"She is indeed beautiful, Mr Hall. You are very fortunate in both your mother and her grandchild."

"I think so," he remarked complacently, taking the picture from me and gazing at it affectionately.

We went back to looking at my paintings and a new agony seized me. Mr Hall had been easy to please, but by his own confession he knew nothing about art. But his daughter was expert, according to him, and he relied on her judgement. What if she didn't like them? I began to scan them anxiously as she picked them up. The large tree on the left in this one was feebly drawn. I should have put in more shadow, eliminated that overhanging branch. She pointed to a perspective of Pulteney Bridge and I saw that the effect of sunlight on the side of the last shop on the right was not quite correct. Pray God she didn't notice.

"Look at this one, Mama!"

Lord, she had noticed. I hurriedly prepared to explain, to offer to redo it. Mrs Hall came up.

"It's just like it! See, this is the shop where I bought that pretty bonnet!"

"It is, indeed, my dear, and very well you look in it."

"Oh, I do like this one, Papa."

Relief. An almost palpable sensation of subsiding. By the time she had looked over the rest I was calm enough to discuss them with her, and found she knew about screens and perspectives, first and second distances and the ideas of the Picturesque. She told me she had read Gilpin and was pleased when I recommended Price's work, which she hadn't. She admired Gainsborough, but thought him a little old-fashioned. She liked my work. She was perfect.

By the time a half-dozen large watercolours had been selected, I hardly cared which, Campbell had packed away his brushes and paints and it was time to take our leave. I had Mr Hall's bank draft in my pocket and my folio under my arm, having been charged with getting the selection framed. Best of all, I was to call with Campbell and take tea. As we walked back down Milsom Street, encumbered with his equipment, he clapped me on the shoulder, smiling.

"A satisfactory afternoon, then?"

"My God, why didn't you tell me how exquisite she is?"

"I'd never seen her before," he reminded me. "She always happened to be out."

"Well, I saw her first!"

"Aye, I can see you're smitten."

"D'you think she'd have me?"

"I don't know. Her father would be the obstacle, I'd think, even if she favours you. He strikes me as a man who likes value for his money. And he's rich as Croesus."

That pulled me up. "I suppose she has all manner of wealthy suitors."

"I haven't heard of any, nor seen them, but I imagine so. But don't you think you're setting your cap a bit high?"

I stopped dead in the street. "Do you think she's too good for me?"

Campbell shrugged. "It's nae for me to say, but I would nae think you've much of a chance."

It was horrible, at the very outset, to encounter such pessimism. "Look here, Campbell," I caught his sleeve, "I'm desperate for her. Will you help me?"

"You've only just met her. If you really want my opinion, you'd do better to forget her. You'll only come to grief. Money always wants to go with money."

He walked on and I followed, thinking hard. Perhaps he was right. Gloom descended. Of course she was far too good for me. I had no chance. Even if she could like me, her father would never permit it. He would be looking for a rich man, to add to his fortune. Rich men liked other rich men. What chance did a poor painter have? But all the time I was thinking these prudent and rational thoughts, my heart was still reeling from her beauty, her charm. I trudged along, downcast, by Campbell's side, until we were nearly home. Then I made up my mind—or rather, gave in to my heart.

"Campbell."

He stopped and turned to me.

"I must have her. You're probably right, but I must try. If she can care for me, she might persuade her father. And if I win the Competition, and it is a big prize, I'll be in a better position to address her. But although I've only just seen her, I know I can't forget her. It's not possible."

He shook his head, but kindly. "You'll hurt yourself, or she'll hurt you. But I suppose you'll say you're willing to take the risk."

"Yes. Yes, I am."

Chapter Three

A few days later we went to the ball at the Upper Rooms. I went specifically with the view of dancing with Miss Hall. We had been to tea the previous afternoon and while Campbell painted her sister, I admired her and carried on the sort of conversation one has with a young lady's parents. My campaign must be considered and careful, because I must win it.

"Some cake, Mr Armiger?"

"Thank you." I was not particularly fond of seed cake.

"Are you related to the Essex Armigers?"

"Distantly, I believe, ma'am. My father's people certainly came from the county originally, but we do not know the family."

"And your mother's?"

"My mother was a de Courcy, of the Oxfordshire family." I could never articulate this rubric without flinching. I had heard it so often, in harsh, reproachful tones as my mother castigated my father for having brought the daughter of such an ancient family so low, or in a bright, elegant voice as she explained her origins to some wealthy visitor she wished to impress. 'Never forget that you are a de Courcy, Edward. The Armigers are all very well, although it was a sad come-down when I married your father.' She sometimes deployed a handkerchief at this point.

Mrs Hall sat up, attentive. "The de Courcys are a very good family, I believe."

"That is so, ma'am." A mark in my favour.

"I think these family connections are very important. Not that Mr Hall... are they considered important in London society, Mr Armiger?"

'Not to me, particularly', I felt like saying, but I could see where she was going. "I suppose so."

"Armiger is a very old name, I think."

"Yes, and a good one, but my people are not among the famous ones." I wasn't going to lie about it.

"Perhaps you will redress that?" Mrs Hall had a disconcerting way of leaning forward when she spoke and fingering her old-fashioned bracelets. Possibly she was just short-sighted.

"I don't think any Armiger ever became famous through painting."

"But you took up art all the same?"

"It was my passion from my youth, ma'am, and my father was good enough to indulge me in it." No need to go into his numberless arguments as to why I should take up something that was, above all, financially secure; no need to list my mother's objections to anything that might lower the family in society's eyes. All that was in my past, behind me. It did not need to become part of my present, let alone the future that I was envisaging.

A pause, while Mrs Hall digested the idea that a man might encourage his son in so frivolous an activity.

"I believe the Countess of Sutherland is an artist?"

"Yes, ma'am." This was promising.

"There are not many titled people in Rochford." She nodded to herself several times as though confirming something.

I ate some more cake.

"I expect when you are in London you attend the exhibitions of the Royal Academy?" Francesca gave me a charming smile. She was sitting on a sofa next to the tea urn so that she could hand the cups.

"I do, indeed. It is the high point of the artistic year."

"Perhaps you have been in the exhibitions yourself—and Mr Campbell?"

Campbell was occupied in dabbing away at Miss Anne, but I could tell from the set of his shoulders that he was both listening and sympathising.

"We have both had that good fortune. Last year Mr Campbell showed a very fine portrait of Lady Belmore and one of Mrs Augustus Webb, with her children, while I had two landscapes." Not in the first room, but not too far below the line for people to avoid seeing them altogether. But of course we wanted to do better this year.

"So you are both members of the Academy?"

"No, I'm afraid not, ma'am." It would have been good to say I was, but again, a lie. I winced internally, and set about explaining the exhibiting process—how anyone could enter and that the works were received anonymously. "It is a very fair system and far better than they have in France, where men have to be invited to enter. Here, the public has the opportunity to see the work and judge it themselves."

"I would so like to see one of the exhibitions! Wouldn't you, Mama?"

But mention of France had turned Mrs Hall's mind to other ideas. She began plying her fan.

"It is very bad what has been going on there, do you not agree, Mr Armiger? That Bonaparte can be allowed to run roughshod over everyone! How Lord Wellington can permit it! I do not think that he exerts himself anything like enough."

She must be the only person in Europe who held that opinion, I thought, including Napoleon himself.

Mr Hall came in and took a cup of tea. "What, worrying about Bonaparte again, my dear?" He put in several lumps of sugar and stirred vigorously. "My wife frets about an invasion, Mr Armiger. Fortunately, as I tell her, we are a deal too far away from France up at Rochford to have to worry about it."

"I agree, sir, and we can be sure that the army would settle with him as soon as he got ashore."

"There, you hear, my dear, what Mr Armiger says?" He did not wink, but an expression of the sort crossed his face.

I hoped I was making some headway with the family. I needed them to like me. Mrs Hall was still fanning herself energetically and had gone quite pink. It was not a pleasing effect. I looked at Francesca, whose eyes were sparkling.

"But suppose they should come round by Liverpool?"

"I think it is hardly likely, ma'am, and remember the navy!" I said. "It is only a few years since Trafalgar. They are not likely to have recovered so soon."

"Besides," her husband put in, "I think Bonaparte is a good deal too occupied with Poland and Russia just now. The Continental Blockade has been very bad for trade, Mr Armiger. Fortunately we have some ways of getting round it."

He sat down next to me and began to explain the effects Bonaparte's embargo had had in the north. Apparently exports had fallen by over thirty per cent in some businesses since '06. I had read something about it in the papers, but it never means as much until you meet someone who experiences it personally. I had not realised that the trade embargoes were at the root of the disagreements we were having with the Americans. It wasn't the sort of thing we talked about at Slaughter's.

Francesca sat demurely in her place, occasionally twisting her fingers in her glossy ringlets or smoothing her skirt, and jumping up now and again to refill cups or hand her father a biscuit. I decided she must be eighteen or nineteen. Every movement was graceful. The man who could come home to her company at night would be in paradise. And, after the company, when we retired upstairs, alone... That would be ecstasy. If only it could be mine. I had been afraid of being bored at Bath, as I was so often at home, but since I had seen Francesca it was an impossibility.

Before we left I had found out that they were going to the ball and had secured her for two dances. It was essential: my visit was nearly at an end. I had only two more days in Bath and I knew already that the Halls were going to Clifton next day, so my chances of seeing her again before I left were slight. She had mentioned that she didn't think they would be in London this year, as her father was very much occupied with his business and building the new house. I could not imagine how I was going to see her again, so I must make a good impression at the ball.

THE portrait of Miss Hall was almost finished. I inspected it on the easel in our lodgings. Campbell had placed her so that her figure was turned slightly away to the left, while her face tilted to the right, looking directly at the viewer. She wore a low dress and held a fan in her left hand, which with some difficulty Campbell had got her to keep closed and drooping a little so as to form an elegant arabesque with her hand and arm. The crimson curtain gave depth to the picture and brought her pale complexion and light hair forward.

"Where the light falls on the throat and arms is very good, and the pose of the hand is refined," I told him. He had done his best, and altogether I thought it had come off, although not his best work. Not that there was anything wrong with the lady, but she was twenty-five or -six, and had none of her younger sister's sparkle.

He brightened and went to the cupboard where we kept a few bottles. "Did I tell you that not only am I to paint the mother, but I've just got a commission to paint an officer, a Colonel Murray, before he goes back to Spain."

I congratulated him and we drank a toast to his success.

Bath was doing well for him. He had had a bit of a triumph with his portrait of Sir Studley Everard at the annual exhibition two years back, but that had faded and he needed something to bring him to the fore again.

"It's a great thing to get among the military," he went on. "Officers all have a great circle of acquaintance among other officers, and if the portrait comes off well, he might recommend me to them. And once one has got the knack of uniforms and swords it's easy."

"A line of light in Naples yellow along the edge of the blade, a fine gleam on the gold lace of the epaulette touched in with a bit of impasto?" I suggested.

He laughed. "And it's guaranteed that there won't be an inch of white satin among the lot of them."

Lawrence always said that white satin was the real test of painting and there was a lot of truth in it. I had tried it myself to see and brought it off reasonably well, but with nothing like Lawrence's inimitable knack. I knew Campbell laboured under the weight of Lawrence's genius, since he had succeeded not only in making a style all his own, but in doing it with flair and delicacy. As poor Campbell had also committed himself to portraiture, he faced a lifetime of coming second, at very best. Fortunately there was a large clientèle, so it was possible to make a living at it regardless.

"An excellent idea. Why don't you do something a bit different for the Colonel? You could set a new style in military portraits."

He was very able, but I was always trying to get him to extend himself. I loved finding new things to see or do, but Campbell was constitutionally antagonistic to anything like an experiment. I was sure he could do something better if he would let himself go.

I was not a good dancer, so next morning while Campbell was out I spent some time practicing steps. I didn't want to put Francesca off with my ineptitude. What a perfect name for a girl who was enthusiastic about art! I could be her Paolo—we might discuss Dante. According to the *Inferno*, the Italian lovers had been brought together by the story of Lancelot and Guinevere; perhaps their story would bring Francesca and me together. What exquisite colouring she had. I must paint her portrait. I had done virtually no work since meeting her, except going to the framer's, but I justified myself with reference to how hard at it I had been up until then. I shaved carefully and put some pomade in my hair, which I had had cut especially, then put on my best clothes and my dancing shoes.

When we entered the rooms and got over the blaze of hundreds of candles and the noise and heat of the crowd, I began to look for the Halls. The salon was a long rectangle decorated with looking-glasses between pilasters along the walls and elegant chandeliers. The orchestra was fiddling away on a dais at one end, and the room was so full that it was impossible to see who was there. 'Not arrived yet', according to the Master of Ceremonies. Chairs and carriages were pulling up at the door constantly, but I didn't want to loiter about in the doorway looking as though I was waiting to pounce.

Campbell met someone and went off to the card room with him; when I next saw him, he was dancing with a young lady I didn't know. There were a lot of women both old and young sitting about on the benches, but I didn't mean to dance with anyone for fear of missing Francesca when she arrived. As always on these occasions, the hardest thing was keeping myself in countenance while standing about conspicuously with nothing to do. I stared at the dancers through a country dance and a minuet; wandered about the room pretending to look for someone; looked into the card room once or twice; got out my watch and pretended to look at it; forgot to notice the time and had to get it out again. At last I found Campbell again.

"Who was your partner?"

He grinned, his freckled face red with exertion. "Miss McPhee, the sister of my friend McPhee, whom you have heard me speak of." He had often mentioned his old school friend, but hadn't expected to see him at Bath. "But look—there's someone you'd be interested to meet." He nodded in the direction of the set just forming for a cotillion.

"Who?"

He nodded again, indicating a slender, lively-looking woman in her late thirties, dancing with a naval officer of the same age. Both had brown curls and round eyes, and she wore a blue spotted muslin. Naval officers reminded me of Laura, which made me recoil slightly. I had somewhat forgotten her since meeting Francesca. The two spoke together, laughing; they seemed on excellent terms and when the cotillion ended he steered her back to where an older woman and another younger lady sat out.

"Who are they?"

"The lady in blue is, I believe, Miss Austen."

The name conveyed nothing to me.

"The authoress of your new novel, which you were extolling to me only the other day."

"What! Not *Sense and Sensibility*?" I stared at her as well as I could without her noticing. I don't know what idea I had formed of the author, but not what I saw. However, observing her intelligent, appraising look and the quickness of her expression as she looked around the room, I began to feel that it was quite possible, and to wish that I could meet her. I had been struck by the quiet realism of the book. I was partial to

Mrs Radcliffe's tales, but they were too Gothic to be taken seriously. *Sense and Sensibility* was something else altogether. I suspected, too, that it contained some enjoyable, although restrained, satire at Mrs Radcliffe's expense.

"Have we any acquaintance who could introduce us?"

Campbell scanned the room. "I'm afraid not. I don't know anyone who knows them. They were pointed out to me just now by McPhee, who doesn't know them either." We both scrutinised her regretfully.

"*Miss* Austen? Who is the officer then—not her husband?"

"A brother, I believe. And as I understand, her mother and sister."

The band began again and Miss Austen took the floor with another gentleman.

"Do you think I could go up and say 'Miss Austen, we haven't been introduced, but I am a great admirer of your book—may I have the pleasure', *et cetera*?"

"No."

"No. Well, it's something to have seen her."

It was, indeed. I thought about her long after. She was an artist, too.

THE Halls finally arrived, the mother fussing about her gown and finding fault with the chairmen. Mr Hall looked broader than ever in evening dress. I had to wait my turn, since it appeared that Francesca had already promised some dances, but at last she was—not exactly in my arms, but at least holding my hand. She danced exquisitely, floating lightly and twirling gracefully at the turns. She wore a tamboured muslin and flowers in her hair. Her low dress showed her shapely bust to advantage. I managed to avoid treading on her dress or her feet. Her hand barely rested on my arm. I wished it had been much heavier, so that I could really have felt its pressure. The thought made me breathless.

"I am so glad you like dancing, Mr Armiger. I adore it. But I was afraid that artists would be very serious men, always thinking about their theories and so on. I imagine that is what you and Mr Campbell always talk about?"

"Well, some of the time, at least."

"I do love art so much. Papa has promised to take us all to Italy some time. It must be wonderful to see the works of the Italian masters, and of course the beauties of the countryside and the architecture. Have you been to Italy?"

"When I finished at the Academy I spent a few months in Rome. It is indeed a fascinating place, Miss Hall." It was also exceptionally hot and humid and one was plagued with an inordinate number of beggars. But the art was magnificent.

"I should so like to travel. Mama is not fond of travel. Imagine, I have never been to London. Now you will think me a complete ignoramus." She turned gracefully, her light dress swirling around her delicate little ankles and feet. She wore white satin slippers. My feet looked clumsy in comparison. "I suppose you go to all the art exhibitions?"

She was an easy conversationalist and I found myself telling her about the Academy's annual show, the works I had seen at Angerstein's and the sculptures at Mr Townley's, where I went to draw occasionally. I had rarely met a girl who was so interested in art.

"Do you think this dress is well? It did very well for Rochford, but I am afraid it would not do for London, although they say that the fashions here at Bath are as advanced as at London, or Paris, almost."

I assured her she had nothing to worry about.

"I do worry about appearing in society, what the manners are in London. Are all the ladies very accomplished? I am afraid I can only sing. But you have been to Paris and Rome! You must tell me if I go amiss."

Her mother and sister appeared at her elbow. “It is supper time, dear.”

I hadn’t heard the announcement. “May I escort you to supper?”

“Thank you, Mr Armiger, but Francesca has already danced with you twice. Captain Bethune will take us in,” and they disappeared with a smirking officer into the crowd streaming towards the supper room.

It was impossible to compete with the glamour of the scarlet coat and gold braid and the atmosphere of danger and devil-may-care that those fellows brought with them.

Campbell saw my scowl. “Did you hear about the time one of those coves wore boots to a ball? The Master of Ceremonies drew himself up and said ‘I beg pardon, sir, but you have forgotten your horse’.”

“Quite right, too! Must maintain the proprieties!”

He had made me laugh and we went to get a drink. The card room was full of officers, old squires and some younger blades, and the fug of cigar smoke. Mr Hall didn’t play.

‘I have too much respect for my money to be giving it to wastrels.’

I was hardly able to get near Francesca for the rest of the evening. Her card was full, as one might expect. I hung about making conversation with her mother in the intervals and was able to snatch a few words with her, and took pains (dancing with Miss McPhee) to get next to her in a Scotch reel, but that was all. There always seemed to be several men around her, laughing and talking. At one stage, rather annoyed, I went off and got myself introduced to some girls and danced gaily with them, hoping Francesca would notice. It was puerile and I felt ashamed of myself later. It was the first time I had seen her in company, and it brought home to me what an immense amount of competition I had. Any man who saw her couldn't fail to be struck. What hope did I have? Perhaps she was already engaged. I tried to keep an eye on her, and couldn't see that she stood up with anyone in particular for more than the two dances she had allotted me. If she had danced with anyone more than that, it would have been as good as announcing their engagement.

By the end of the evening Campbell was exhausted from his exertions and I was despondent, which made me drink more than I should have. I've always been able to put away quite a bit before it affects me, which turned out to be fortunate. We decided to go home, but I didn't want to leave before saying goodbye to the Halls.

Although gloomy and cross, I had the sense to wait until Francesca was with her parents to seize the moment to say goodbye. I hoped to convey something of my feelings for her by some pressure of my hand or look, and gauge hers in the same way.

When we came up Mr Hall was with his family and hailed me pleasantly.

"I wanted to see you again before you left, Mr Armiger." He bowed to Campbell.

I reciprocated, a little surprised by his warmth.

"I understand you're leaving us on Saturday."

"I must get back to my pupils." The Academy term started again next month and I, or rather they, had to get some work in before then.

"Aye, a man must apply himself to his work. I like to see that in a young man." At that moment I felt rather old, but it was kind of him.

"I'm glad you don't think art an altogether pointless occupation, Mr Hall."

"I believe that whatever you do, you should keep on the road you've made and not shirk it."

I couldn't make out whether this was intended as encouragement of a specific sort or whether he was just enunciating one of his general principles. But it sounded at least favourable to me. Francesca was talking to her mother during this exchange and hardly looked my way, which was extremely provoking. I was in a fair way to advancing my cause with her father, but she didn't seem to care. I felt I was glaring and attempted to put on a more agreeable face.

"Is there anything I can do for you before I leave? I could collect the pictures from the framer's and bring them to you."

I thought this was an excellent inspiration but he looked at me from under his brows.

"Nay, nay, young man, I'll not put you to the trouble. I can do that quite well myself—but thank you." I had the distinct impression that he was not taken in by my helpfulness. He turned away for a moment to speak to his wife, and when he turned back I put out my hand and began to make my farewells.

"Nay, but there's something I wanted to ask you. I don't want to take you away from your work, but I've been thinking on it and I mean to see if you could come up north some time. You know I'm building a house at Coldbrook; I'd like to get some pictures of it while it's building, and of the land thereabouts before we get it improved. It would be grand to have some sketches of it before, and then after, if you understand me."

I was taken entirely by surprise. All my thoughts had been concentrated on the possibility of my staying in Bath or their getting to London. I had never been further north than Cambridge. I'd also decided that Mr Hall's patronage extended to no more than the half-dozen studies he'd already bought. I must have gaped, because he added:

"You'll have to see when you can get away. Suppose you drop me a line to let me know when would be convenient.

I expect you artistic men have your busy seasons and slack seasons, as in all trades. That is, if you'd like the job."

By this time we were shaking hands. I glanced across at Francesca; she was looking in my direction and when I caught her eye she gave me one of her brilliant smiles.

"I would be delighted."

Chapter Four

I dropped in at Old Slaughter's. There were always artists in the booths as well as philosophers of various sorts, astronomers, mathematicians. I was looking for Campbell. He wasn't there, but Quayle was sitting in the window where he could be seen by the passing traffic.

He hailed me from a comfortable chair, a can of coffee at his elbow.

"Armiger! Back from Bath, then? How did you do?"

I sat down beside him and ordered coffee. "Enjoyable holiday, met a few people, interesting to look around."

It was quite good to be back in the old place, although I hadn't noticed before how grimy the ceiling beams were and how scarred the furniture. The noise some of the men were making at the table behind us was annoying. One of them was Hallett's crony, Alcock, who gave me his insincere smile, which had no effect on his drab, raddled countenance. He had been at the Norwich Academy, although he usually didn't mention it. I disliked him intensely and knew the sentiment was mutual. I considered him a man of little talent, which was forgivable, but I could not stand the airs he gave himself and knew of instances of complete dishonesty on his part in his efforts to advance himself, which I could not stomach. Toby Quayle had the ambition of a Caesar, but he was urbane and made no secret of his objectives—or success.

"You look a bit off-colour."

Perhaps being away hadn't really agreed with me. His own dark good looks were as sleek as ever.

"No, I'm well."

"You didn't meet Lord Arbuthnot, did you? He's very amusing. I'm painting a big piece to go over the chimney-piece in his town house. Classical subject, of course. That's what he likes—a man of real taste—and income."

"What is it?"

"'Dido Embarking at Carthage'. But I'm treating it in a new manner. One must move along, you know, not get stuck with the same old ways, doing the same things as everyone else."

On the spur of the moment I decided to confide in him. We'd always got on all right and he certainly had the recipe for success.

"I'd like to move along. I get so bored. There's no adventure in it any more—or very little. I've been wondering whether it isn't time for a change."

"Good idea." He signalled the waiter and bought me a round.

"I'm tired of landscape. Well, not really, but not the way it's been. I want to branch out, do something different." What I'd really like was an exciting escapade, but failing that, a change in work would go some way to stifling the ennui.

"Get into classical compositions." He raised a hand. "I know what you're going to say, everyone's done them, but you just need to do it a bit differently, as I have. I've got another big commission coming up, and Lord Arbuthnot will probably want some companion pieces to Dido to go in the panelling beside the fireplace." He ran a palm over his neat black hair and pulled out a smart cigar-case.

I had known, really, that that was what he would say. In a way he was right, but I remembered that soon after I'd got my Diploma I'd been to see the great history painter Barry lying in state at the Adelphi, with a long queue waiting to pay their respects, and thinking even then that I didn't want to paint like him.

"I really don't think that would do."

He shrugged. "What do you want to paint, then?"

"I don't know, but not that stuff like Barry's. I couldn't stand it—not for a day. It makes me feel tired just looking at them. I mean, they're magnificent, of course," I hurried to add—anything else was heresy. "But not for me."

"I think you're wrong there. They're what's popular now—if you want to get the big jobs. No-one wants a 'nice landscape' for a big job. It's got to have figures in it. It's got to be a big 'machine' painting, with history—you know that. And I don't mind saying you've got the ability—you've done well so far."

"Thanks. But I prefer Copley."

"No, no. Not the thing at all." He made a brushing-away movement of the hand. "No, Barry's is the stuff to follow."

I thought of his gigantic 'Crowning of the Victors at Olympia' and the rest of it at the Society of Arts. "And spend ten years pecking away at one huge thing? History by the yard? All those writhing limbs and portentous gestures?"

"History painting's what's important. My career's been built on history painting. Are you telling me that's wrong?" His eyebrows met in a scowl.

I'd been too candid, as usual. "Yours are wonderful, of course—full of life and so on. And you're so good at them."

"That's not what you said. What's your real opinion? Not good enough for you, is that it?"

I'd really annoyed him. "It's fine if you like it, but I'd die of boredom. It'd be like shovelling coal. Every day the same as the next, the heap gets a little smaller, and in the end you get to the end of the heap—long after you've forgotten why you started on it in the first place. Then, if you're successful, there's another great heap, very like the first, waiting for you."

"I didn't know that you'd ever shovelled coal." He was far from pacified, but sounded genuinely curious. Sometimes I wondered what on earth went on in his head.

"Thank you, I have not, but I have the imagination to understand it, and I do not think that I should like it." It had all been done before. I wanted something completely new, but I realised Quayle wasn't the man to give me that.

"You don't know what you're talking about." He leant back in his seat, drawing on his cigar. "Take it from me. If you want to get ahead you've got to treat it as a job—none of your romantic inspiration and genius, that trash. Not that you tell the public that, mind. They like a touch of Byron—have you read his new thing, 'Childe Harold'? Magnificent stuff. No, you keep that under your hat, but all the same, that's the way to go about it. You have to give customers what they want."

I thanked him for his advice, which he brushed away, still aggrieved, swallowed the last of my drink and made my way into the chop-house at the back. Campbell wasn't there but Alcock was, so I went up to Rupert Street. Slaughter's wasn't what I was in the mood for anyway, and I could drop in at Middleton's for some more charcoal on the way.

As soon as I got inside the John O'Groats I spotted Campbell sitting over a plate of mutton with a tankard of porter by his side, reading the paper. He waved and I went over.

"Have ye seen this?" He held up the *London Gazette*, the page folded back, and pointed with a stubby finger: 'The President and Council of the Royal Academy are pleased to announce that they offer a Premium of One Thousand Guineas for an Art Work which best expresses the Spirit of the Present Age. Gentlemen wishing to enter should write to the Secretary... &c.' The closing date was the fifteenth of April. Seven months to produce a masterpiece.

"I'm going to start right now. I don't know what my subject will be, but my mind's on fire with it." He shoved his plate aside, spilling porter on the crumpled pages of the *Gazette.*

"A thousand guineas!" More than I'd ever had for a single work, and more than I'd ever held in my hand at once. More than two years' income. "Is it only for Academicians?"

"Nae, nae. Open to all professional artists. It'll be like the Annual Exhibition —you'll send your work in without a name on it. But of course they ken well the style of all the big names."

This sounded more like it—an incitement to strike out on a grand scale. Just what I wanted—something noble and exciting. "And a commission to follow? Does it say anything about that?"

"Aye—hereabouts." He ran his finger down the column, smudging the ink. "Aye. 'The Author of the work which gains the Premium will be invited to complete an Additional Work on an important Subject, which will likewise become the Property of the Academy. A like Sum will be attached to this Work'. A like sum! Extraordinary!"

More than four years' income for two paintings! And they couldn't fail to elect the winner. An Associate if he was not a member, full membership if he were already an Associate. 'Edward Armiger, A.R.A.' I could see it now. It might even be enough to sway Mr Hall.

"Do you think there's any chance?"

"Well, I'm going to go for it. Did you see the closing date?"

"It looks as though they plan to judge it with the Annual Exhibition and announce the winner at the same time."

"'The Spirit of the Age'. A grand subject! What say you?"

"The most notable event of our age is the Revolution in France, I suppose."

"Hardly the subject for an institution patronised by the King—or now, the Prince Regent!"

At that moment Brigstock came in, swinging his shaggy grey head slowly from side to side. He spied us and came over, taking the bench opposite. "The Royal Academy is offering a prize for a painting competition!"

Campbell held up the *Gazette*. "Aye. But the 'Spirit of the Age'. That's open to any interpretation. What is it, do you think?"

"That's obvious. It's the Mechanical Age. The great recent inventions would be an excellent subject. I went to see the steam locomotive at Abercorn when I was in Wales. I made some fine sketches of it, which everyone admired." Brigstock was not a professional artist, but had studied under a drawing master for some time and liked the company of artists. "I can imagine a huge canvas with the engine carrying its passengers into the future. It would be a magnificent subject and completely representative of the theme."

Campbell raised his eyebrows. "A painting of an engine? No-one would take such a thing seriously. And it's at Abercynon, not Abercorn. Any road, if I were going to paint an engine, it'd be the steam boat that's just been launched on the Clyde. That's really new. But the 'Spirit of the Age' must be to do with the whole age, not just a few engineers."

"'Dido embarking at Carthage', for instance?" I suggested.

"Aye, an allegory—something of the sort. A splendid theme. Is that your choice?"

I shook my head. Wily Quayle had stolen a march on the lot of us by pretending that his great piece was for Lord Arbuthnot. I had to admire his cunning, worthy of such an experienced campaigner. Perhaps it had started out for his Lordship, but his Lordship might get a surprise when he came to claim the work—although I wouldn't put it past Quayle to have his assistant blocking in a copy, which would be produced for his patron. I wondered whether the noble gent was aware of it.

Brigstock was still rambling on about steam engines. I had been wondering for some time exactly what animal he resembled. Quayle, for instance, despite his guile, was not so much a fox as a hound: a really well-bred, handsome pointer with a glossy black coat, excellent at scenting game, bounding ahead energetically to fetch it for his master, tail wagging, looking up to him for praise. But not above foraging off on his own on occasion, and ignoring calls and whistles. Campbell, of course, was a terrier: earnest, determined, working away steadily to enlarge the burrow and get at those rabbits. A little coarse-haired, perhaps, but a fine, sturdy, loyal fellow. Now I realised that Brigstock was a hedgehog. His plump little hands waved about as he spoke and his grey untidy head nodded at something Campbell said. His expression was always benevolent, if a little vague. He'd been sure there was a beetle there somewhere; now, where could it have gone? I must draw him as a hedgehog some time—I could see the sketch in my mind. And what was I? A horse, I supposed—a plodding old hunter. Or a jackass. Then I thought of Francesca, and changed the image to a spanking blood horse. Nothing less would do for her.

"Don't you think so, Armiger?" Campbell was tapping his fingers impatiently on the table.

"What?"

"Brigstock says that the Academy wants a military painting, but I'm sure this is not the moment."

"Yes—the 'Death of Wolfe', and of course the President's 'Death of Nelson'." The hedgehog nodded benignly.

"I agree with Campbell." There was, however, an idea in the back of my head. Perhaps Brigstock had stumbled onto something. "What do you think of a modern subject?"

"Modern?" Campbell scratched his head.

"Well, it's supposed to be about 'the Age'."

"Aye, but an allegory, not a description, surely."

"Yes and no, I think. For instance, look at de Loutherbourg's 'Coalbrookdale'."

"We agreed that a landscape wouldn't do—even one with a furnace in it!"

"Yes, of course. But it's a modern subject. Something about modern life—a history painting, certainly, but about today." Now I was getting excited in my turn. Campbell looked doubtful. "Something like that mural of Barry's—'The Triumph of Navigation'?"

"No."It was a detestable work, exhibiting all that I most disliked about traditional history painting: Old Father Thames lounging in the centre looking despondent, with Mercury poised over his head, doing quite what, I had never been able to work out, and some men heaving up a lighthouse in the background. "There's nothing modern about it but the subject, and navigation isn't all that new."

I couldn't quite imagine what I might do, but the idea of a modern history painting on a big scale appealed enormously. Something really new, that would take the Academy by storm. Canvasses by Loutherbourg and West flashed into my mind. No—no—no. It was something else I wanted.

That was it. "Wright of Derby. Something like that." He had painted pictures of philosophers with air-pumps and other scientific subjects last century.

"Air-pumps?" Brig was at sea.

Campbell amplified for his benefit. "Theatrical lighting—impressive. Very good finish and a great man for composition. A wee bit old-fashioned now."

It wasn't quite what I was groping for, but it was on the right track. I must enter the Competition. I would find a startling new subject in modern life, noble enough to stand against all the Didos and Olympias. Something with real meaning. I didn't know what I was going to paint, but I could hardly wait to begin.

Passing Slaughter's on the way back, the scene had changed entirely. I glimpsed a crowd poring over the newspapers, arms waving, heads nodding, men clapping on their hats and making for the door. The news had reached the art world.

In the intervals of work, and often during it, I thought about Francesca. She was so lovely, I longed to hold her in my arms. My heart ached for her. I would see her again when I went up to Rochford. I had not yet settled the date with her father, but I was hoping to go soon, in October or November. But before that I had to do something about Laura. It was not fair to her to keep her in ignorance of what was going on in my mind—or, more to the point, my heart. I thought about writing to her, but I knew it was no good. Our relationship had never been what it ought to be, which was of course mostly my fault, but breaking with her by letter would be too bad.

Having put it off once or twice I eventually sent her a note to say I would call, and went over at the time named. Although I'd been mulling over how to break it to her, I hadn't been able to think of anything that wouldn't be hurtful to her and in consequence make her angry. I would do anything I could to avoid a row, but it was inevitable, I suppose. Since a boy I had never been able to endure raised voices and anger. Somewhere inside me I recalled my mother's overbearing tirades, as violent as they were capricious, shouting her rage against my father or me. When she was in that mood, anything could start her off, and she knew no moderation or tolerance. It wasn't manly, but it seemed to have left me so over-sensitive to wrath that inside I flinched like a beaten dog at a lifted hand. The best I could do was to maintain a dignified exterior. The only alternative seemed to be to attack in return. I didn't know how other men managed these things. Many seemed not to notice—they were fortunate.

And of course attack was out of the question with Laura.

I thought I would soften the occasion a little by taking her out for a drive, something she liked but we did rarely. I went to the expense of hiring a gig and drove it up to her door. It turned out a mistake, as it strengthened her assumption that my visit was from a special desire to see her. She had put on a pretty dress and ribbons in her fair hair in my honour. I should have just turned up.

"I thought you might like to go for a drive." I'd also hoped that once in the Park, I would gradually introduce the topic more easily than just sitting at home.

"Oh. All right, if you wish," pouting a little. Not a good start. She came to the door and eyed the carriage. "It's not very smart." She liked things to be fashionable.

"I thought it was quite nice."

"If we go, you won't drive fast?"

"Not if you don't want me to."

"Because you always do, you know."

"I like driving, and I've never upset a carriage yet." Not even careering down the road towards Bath! How enjoyable that had been—but I hadn't told Laura of it.

"But you want to go too fast. No, I think I'd rather stay home. Come in. We can have some tea. Susan, bring some tea."

As soon as she had dismissed the maid I began, breaking in awkwardly as she was pouring the tea and telling me about a friend's visit and a walk in the gardens.

"Laura, I'm afraid there is something I must tell you."

"Oh, what a serious face!" she pouted. Then an idea suddenly crossed her mind and she put her hand to her mouth. "Not—not about Henry?"

"No—no. I haven't heard anything at all." Her husband was the last person I wanted to discuss. "It's about you and me."

She frowned. "What about us?"

"Laura, it can't go on. It was never right to start with, and I feel we should finish it now."

Well, at least I had got it out. Either she would start to cry or get angry. It was too much to hope—as I had intermittently fantasised—that she would calmly agree. She began to cry, gazing at me forlornly, tears rolling down her cheeks. I went to sit next to her on the sofa, feeling a terrible pang.

"Please don't. I'm a worthless fellow and you shouldn't upset yourself over me." I felt a complete fraud, since I'd been happy enough with our affair until I met Francesca, whom I was determined to keep out of the whole debacle. Obviously I had always known it was wrong, but as she hadn't minded, I had calmed my conscience.

She took my hand and tried to dry her eyes. I gave her my handkerchief.

"Is it something I've done? I'm sorry I haven't written more often." She gazed up into my face.

This was awful. "No, it's nothing you've done. It's me. Things have changed with me. My life has changed. I'm going to be away a lot. It was never right to start with and it must stop now," I reiterated, feeling a coward.

She dabbed at her eyes and then sat up. "Changed! Yes, you have changed! You used to want me, say you couldn't wait to see me again!"

It was true.

"I suppose you've met someone else! That's it, isn't it?"

Now I was for it. I should have realised she'd guess straight away. Women are very acute in such matters. I thought I might as well make a clean breast of it.

"Yes. I've met someone else and I didn't want to keep on seeing you under false pretences. I'm sorry, really I am, but it's for the best."

Then the fireworks really began. "Some daughter of a wealthy mill-owner, I suppose! And very pretty!"

She really was uncommonly perceptive, but she couldn't know how unique Francesca was. She made it sound so commonplace.

"Is it?"

I had to nod.

"I knew it!" Then she threw herself down on the sofa, sobbing. I tried to take her hand, but she snatched it away. "Oh, go away! I hate you! You play with me and then you throw me away because you've met someone younger and prettier! You've ruined me! You're a beast! Heartless! I'm ruined!"

Things went on along these lines for some time. I tried to reason with her, pointing out that as far as being 'ruined' was concerned, my breaking with her would be an improvement on our continuing to see each other. She dismissed this contemptuously. I tried to comfort her and administer tea and wine, but she pushed me away haughtily. Then she started sobbing again and clung to me, kissing me and trying to beguile me. When I put her away gently she fired up again and showered me with insults, some of an intimate nature which made me squirm for a long time afterwards. At one point she threw herself at me, hitting my chest and arms with her hands as hard as she could.

"You're nothing, anyway! I don't know why I ever bothered with you. Who are you? Who was your father? Nobody! If my father were here he wouldn't even speak to you—he visits with all the county, and who do you visit—just artists, and low people, in taverns and things. No," striking me particularly hard on the neck, "I was always too good for you. Go! Go away and leave me!"

It was all very bad, and at the back of my mind was the cowardly fear that she would tell Campbell, and then there would really be a row of almighty proportions. She had been at least as committed to keeping our secret as I was, for obvious reasons, but in her rage she might blurt it out to him. I wasn't concerned about Captain Tennison—'Henry'. He was still in the Adriatic and anyway, she would never tell him in a thousand years.

I stayed for a lot longer than I had wanted to and in the end we parted on bad terms. I had hoped that there might have been some sort of *rapprochement* and that we could remain friends, but according to her that was impossible with such a paltry excuse for a man who had no idea how to behave. I told her that if an event should occur, she must write to me and I would help her. It wasn't likely, I supposed and hoped, because nothing had happened in the two years we had been seeing each other, nor in the time she had been married, but still... She sniffed, and slammed the door behind me.

I felt I had handled the whole thing badly, but was relieved to have at last escaped. I reflected as I drove slowly down the familiar street, presumably for the last time, that she had protested a great deal too much about my 'ruining' her, considering that I would never have thought of making the first approach if she hadn't encouraged me, and I knew as a fact that I was not the first. Captain Tennison should not have left a pretty young wife like her alone for so many years at a stretch. I cringed at the thought of some of her remarks. She had always known how to hurt me when she was in a temper. All the same, it was a shame. I was fond of her and we had had many good times together.

But at least I was now free to address Francesca.

Before I could go to Rochford I had to transfer some of my Bath studies to canvas and complete some views of London I had started earlier, that I wanted to put in the Water-Colour Painters' Society exhibition in April. But the Competition was what I thought of continually. I began to have a glimmering of an idea. It must, of course, have figures in it, and most probably they must be classical. But I couldn't bear to create one of those huge set-pieces full of posturing men in Roman dress and a few women drooping gracefully at the sides. Besides, it would be ridiculous. I had no reputation as a history painter. In my recent work I had been striving to bring some of the greatness of Claude into my landscapes. If only it were possible to combine Claude and the other great master whom I idolised—Rembrandt. The Dutchman's shadowy tonalities and evident compassion for his subjects, tenderly articulated in rich browns and touches of impasto, were my *beau idéal.* The few paintings of his I had seen were not large but intensely moving, and his gift for capturing the essential moment was beyond anything. Landscape, with him, was part of the picture, but not the main subject. Claude's colouring and recessions were magnificent, but his figures were only staffage. If, somehow, the richness and imagination of the two could be brought together... Rembrandt's figures in Claude's paysage, the two united in one work? Surely that might produce a work of grandeur without posturing. That was what I wanted.

I was not there yet, but I began to see a figure confronting nature. Nature—the elements—would be as much a character as the man. There must be confrontation, to create tension, and to bind the two together into one harmonious whole. A man standing on a rock, shaking his fist at the sky. Stormy clouds swirling about—or perhaps a sunset? The Competition work must have grandeur, and it must express the Spirit of the Age—whatever that was. Mere rage would be inappropriate. A scene from the present war? No, we'd already ruled that out. Besides, the landscape must dominate—a heroic landscape. And it should be universal, which meant classical. I decided to re-read Homer.

Chapter Five

As soon as I had a moment I got out my *Odyssey*. I needed to find a theme and get started without delay. In London alone there were two and a half thousand artists, or men who called themselves artists, and every one of them would enter the Competition. I had to find something exceptional. I filled a glass with madeira, lit a cigar, put my feet up on the sofa and settled down to read.

The great epic was full of wonderful ideas, but the hero was unsuitable for a great theme such as the Competition demanded, since he was the type of a trickster. I soon realised this, but ploughed on. I had got as far as the tale of Polyphemus in Book Nine and was about to give up, when my eye was caught by the lines where Odysseus introduces himself to the monster:

'We boast ourselves of Agamemnon's train,
The son of Atreus, at this hour the Chief
Beyond all others under heav'n renown'd'.

'At this hour the Chief'—a splendid phrase, and it brought in the idea of the 'present age'. I read it over and liked it more. But who would Agamemnon be in my allegory?

I thought about it through luncheon, absently ingesting a piece of bread and cheese and a pot of ale at the chop-house, and afterwards walking through the park to try to clear my mind. I sat in the shade for a while, enjoying the greenery, although the leaves had the dusty, worn look of late summer.

At home again, I went back to the book. 'At this hour the Chief'. The man whom Agamemnon would figure must be the Chief of all, which was obviously the Prince Regent. My allegory would be of the Prince leading the many tribes of Britain—yes, that was good—Scots, Welsh, Irish, and of course Englishmen—into the future, and a very effective compliment in the last line. I'd write the verse under the picture—it had lately become fashionable, and there was no source as august as the *Odyssey*. That would let them know I was serious! I sprang up and flung my fist in the air.

Agamemnon had caught my fancy. I had an insistent image of him in my mind that would be just right for my grand picture, standing on a hilltop with hand raised, dark beard and hair whipping away in the wind. It was time for dinner, so I copied out the lines and put the book away.

I had no opportunity next day to work on it, as I had pupils preparing for the examinations to get their tickets into the Academy Schools. It seemed a lifetime ago when Campbell and I, among others herded into a dim room, spent our day on, if I remember right, a leg of the Discobolus. Although a prospective student was judged on his day's work, previous study would help him to a good performance. I didn't have a cast of the Discobolus, and had them at work instead on the torso of the Apollo Belvedere. I had four pupils, only one of whom, in my opinion, had a chance. The worst seemed to have no eye at all or natural instinct. I was sure I could draw better when I was ten and scribbling sketches of my dog on the backs of old letters. Still, along with my 'views', this was what paid the rent.

I didn't like teaching in my studio. The big shabby room at the top of the house was the reason I'd taken these lodgings. An artist had set it up a generation ago so it had that primary requisite, good controllable light, in the form of a row of high windows along the street front fitted with folding shutters. Apart from that it was just a room, but in the five or six years I'd been here it had become my nest, my eyrie. Canvasses and folios were stacked round the walls, my easels were at one end near the windows, my work-tables (one large, one small, which doubled as a writing-desk) with the palettes and pots of brushes, were placed conveniently. I had an old cupboard for my materials and a battered press full of drawings and unused paper. On the walls I'd pinned pictures and prints, some of mine, some of Campbell's and other friends, some I'd bought. When I wasn't working—or was undertaking the form of work, not to be underrated, that consists of thinking—I lay on a comfortable sofa covered with worn green plush. Books, props, casts and the odd ornament stood on shelves. It was my home, and having pupils there invaded its comfort.

I set the boys work then left them to it and began to make some little studies on scraps of paper. It occurred to me that all we artists were putting ourselves up for examination like the boys. It never finished.

I met Campbell by arrangement at the plaster shop in Drury Lane, where I hoped to find a bust of Agamemnon.

"There's nothing available, sir," the assistant told me, rubbing his hands together.

"Why not?"

"There's no call for them."

"Well, I'm calling for one."

He assumed a weak smile. "Ha ha, very good, sir. But even so."

Annoying, but not essential. It would give me more scope to be original. I waited for Campbell. The sepulchral ranked casts, standing in dusty white rows in the shop's gloomy interior, evoked a mausoleum. They were dead, all dead. I was glad I wasn't going to copy one for my picture. I realised that what I wanted it to have more than anything was life.

When Campbell arrived I hurried him out.

"I can't stay in there another minute. Let's go and look in the print shops."

There were several of de Loutherbourg's. His 'Avalanche' was truly sublime. I inspected a print of his 'Destruction of Pharaoh's Army'. The triangular composition was well handled and the boiling clouds and sea impressive. I bought a small one of his, a beggar with a wooden leg, holding his hat out. It was nothing like, but it reminded me of the sleeping beggar at Bath and had a little of the compassionate quality of Rembrandt. There were several beggars in the street when we left, as usual. One wore a soiled red coat so had been a soldier, or pretended to have been one. He was disgusting, with filthy hands and a large oozing ulcer on his cheek, but I gave him twopence. Campbell looked at me curiously.

"Have you heard from Mr Hall?"

I had, and his letter was keeping warm in my breast pocket. "Yes. I wrote to him as soon as I got back. I'm to go up next week for three weeks. I can't see that I'll get away with the coach for less than two guineas there and back, what with the inns and the shillings for porters and so on, but I must hope that he'll be pleased with my work and that'll more than make it worthwhile."

"Not to mention the opportunity to see the beautiful younger Miss Hall."

"Not to mention, indeed." I planned to do a portrait of her, if at all possible. I'd made one from memory in watercolours, which was on the chimneypiece in my room, but it came nowhere near capturing her liveliness and charm, nor even the exquisite symmetry of her features. I thought about her a lot, including in bed at night, which made me hot and restless, and think of Laura.

"When you get there, notice how my pictures are hung and how they've had the one of Mrs Hall framed, and if they're not well placed, see if you can get them moved."

"Of course, and of course I'll recommend you to all their friends and neighbours. But before that, I want to go and see the balloon ascent in Hackney on Saturday. Come with me?"

Campbell screwed up his face. "If I come, you won't..."

"Won't what?" I knew what was bothering him, but I refused to acknowledge it. He was such an old woman where some things were concerned.

"Nothing—just—you're not planning any kind of..." He was clearly afraid of putting an idea in my head.

"What?"

He shook his head. "I mind me how when we went to St Albans to see the Semaphore, you insisted on climbing up onto the roof of the clock tower and making them show you how it worked."

I smiled at the memory. It had certainly been entertaining. "I can't promise anything, but I assure you that I have no plans, other than to see the balloon and make some studies of it." What Campbell didn't grasp was that I never 'planned' anything; it was just that from time to time I was so crippled with *ennui* that I felt I would throw myself off a cliff to prevent it. And I'd been longing to see a balloon ascent for ages.

"Don't you ever get bored, Campbell?"

"Not really—well, occasionally. But then I go down to Slaughter's and drink some coffee and look at the papers, or talk to some of the fellows. A change of scene."

The sort of boredom I experienced wasn't cured by an hour of gabbing about the latest scandal, who was bankrupt and who had been detected in an affair. In fact it was at some of those times that I felt most inclined to jump on a table and start to sing, dance, or anything, to relieve the tedium. It was better to be alone in my studio, concentrating on work and lost in musings of my own creation.

"Well, are you coming to Hackney with me, or not?"

"All right. I can take a day off work."

I had to call at the Academy to make arrangements for my pupils. I thought at the same time I'd look at whatever modern-life paintings might be on display. As I took the familiar road down the Strand towards Holborn I always stopped to admire the vista of the handsome Italian church of St Mary-le-Strand, set askew in the middle of the road. But as I neared, the imposing classical façade of Somerset House hove up on the right, casting its shadow over the crowded street. It made a symbolic choice, almost too obvious. Which to enter? Church or business? Religion or art? The spiritual or the worldly?

I turned into the great temple of art, under the dark stone archways into the enormous courtyard, surely the largest in London. It was like a sort of St Mark's Piazza, but under grey English skies instead of brilliant Italian. I stopped at the lodge for my usual exchange of pleasantries with Strowger the porter, who I'd made friends with when I was a student. The whole Great Room could be filled with pictures of him, since when he was a model he'd been drawn and painted by everyone who'd ever been though the Schools. We joked that his portrait had been painted by more famous artists than the Prime Minister—as well as by many lesser men. He was just as well-known, in his own way.

THE balloon ascent was magnificent and I was still thrilling from the experience when Campbell and I went to Slaughter's for a meal afterwards. It had come up to all my expectations.

It had been novel, inspiring, an aesthetic as well as an intellectual pleasure. When the vast silken bubble rose weightless into the brilliant sky, apparently of its own volition and free of all constraint, my heart rose with it. I could hardly speak, think. It had been a sublime moment. If only I could have been with it! It would transform my life. I had watched it float into the distance with longing, as for a departing ship carrying a loved one, and it was all Campbell could do to get me away.

"It was a Scotchman who made the first ascent in Britain—James Tytler." Campbell remarked. He'd been impressed, too, although more by its scientific aspects. "It was the talk of Edinburgh when I was a boy."

"I thought it was the Italian, Lunardi."

"Nae, nae, a Scotchman."

"If only all modern contrivances were as dazzling."

"I believe Bonaparte had a Balloon Corps in Egypt."

"That would have been something to see!" I imagined a squadron of them rising over the Pyramids while below, tribesmen on maddened camels raced across the sand. I felt the urge to get out of London, have adventures, do something exceptional. Galloping across the desert on a camel would be a start. Rising above the earth, leaving everything worldly behind, fuelled only by invisible air, seeing the globe spread out beneath me—that would be bliss. I wondered how much it would cost and what the world would look like.

"Do you think it would be possible to get a passage in one?"

"To where?"

"Nowhere. Just to be up there."

"I would nae think so."

We were still discussing the balloon when Hallett and Alcock arrived and sat themselves down. They would talk of nothing but the Competition.

"Are you entering?" The question was directed at Campbell.

"Aye, I am. Are you?"

Alcock scuffed his feet. "Possibly—depends—I have a lot of work on hand."

He was a portrait painter of average ability, but his father, Ebenezer Alcock, RA, was an agreeable old man who in his day had been a painter of classical scenes in the grand manner of the great Reynolds, whom he had followed closely. Reynolds' friendship had helped him to his place in the Pantheon, and he in his turn was exerting all his influence to get his son a seat.

"Something exceptional for the judging?" I suggested.

He grimaced, knowing that I was referring not so much to the Annual Exhibition next May, as to the next election of Associates, which took place annually in November. Despite having produced a laborious Diploma piece, he had missed out among an unusually large field of candidates for the four vacancies last year and was generally supposed to be working night and day to secure interest to get him in this time.

"I hear de Loutherbourg isn't very well." He gave his ambiguous smile, which his prominent eye-teeth made wolfish. The more RAs who died, the more vacancies there would be.

I gave him the most malevolent look I could summon and turned to Hallett. "What about you?"

Hallett, stylishly dressed as usual, in an extremely tall beaver hat of an extraordinary shade of chestnut, was talking to another of his cronies. It was rare for him to have a conversation *tête-a-tête*; he preferred several to be going on at once. He turned round. "I didn't know he was still alive."

"No, are you going to enter the Exhibition?"

"Oh, don't know, might do. I'm off to Paris again next week and then I have to go to Amsterdam to see about printing some things I've had engraved."

If they had to be published in Amsterdam they must be *risqué* in the extreme. Campbell raised an eyebrow. He disapproved of anything licentious. "Do you like this hat? I've found a Frenchman in Bow who makes them for me. He's making me a green one, which I plan to…"

"Aren't you afraid of travelling to France at present?" I interrupted. I got tired of hearing about Hallett's wardrobe. "I thought practically all travel to France had been suspended."

"It's alright as long as you know someone. I have friends there whom I stay with. And I have extraordinary adventures *en route*. Listen to this. Last time, I was on a fishing smack and it was the dead of night. We were cruising along at a great rate when without warning a lugger loomed up on the port bow. The master of the smack wanted me to hide, but I had my pistols and I…"

One of the servants came up. "Excuse me sir, a young... person asked me to give you this." He handed over a folded note.

"One of your many lady friends?" I asked. I'd noted the servant's evident distaste.

Hallett glanced towards the bay window, through which a feminine form could be seen hovering. "Ha ha, yes, just a friend—have to go now," and putting the note in his pocket he strode off, ruffling his frilled shirtfront and cuffs. At least we were spared another of his implausible anecdotes.

Campbell was frowning. "Who is that girl, Alcock?"

Alcock shuffled. "Just a friend, I think."

"Friend? A girl by herself? Walking in the street with him?" He looked his most Scotch, as I thought of it—his long, dour face.

"Well, actually, she's one of his models. I use her myself from time to time. A fine figure, especially behind, although the front is good too. You've seen my 'Muse of Poetry', haven't you—that's her."

Campbell seized my arm. "Let's go!"

He dragged me to the door and we ended up at the John O'Groats with Brigstock, who regaled us with a wealth of probably inaccurate gossip about who was lobbying whom for influence over the judging committee. According to him, Hallett and Quayle were both going to be among the judges.

"If that's so, Brig, neither of them will be able to enter."

"Oh. I hadn't thought of that."

As long as Hallett didn't win, I thought. If Brigstock was a hedgehog, Hallett was too obviously a popinjay, strutting about and flaunting his plumage—an object of admiration, but underneath, was he any different from other birds? I liked fine clothes as much as the next man, and had just bought a smart new coat to go to Rochford, but I didn't think it was quite respectable to be as infatuated with one's dress as Hallett. I supposed it was different for women, it was more of an occupation with them. But as long as a man was clean, neat and well turned out, it should suffice. Anything more seemed to suggest having nothing to think about than the tie of a cravat.

"If there's any justice in the world, Alcock will never become an RA." His remark about one of my favourite painters, and an interesting and able man, still rankled.

Campbell shook his head. "You already ken that there's nae justice in this world."

INSPIRATION arrived next day. I'd been preoccupied with the idea of Agamemnon standing on his hill and found that I kept thinking of his daughter, Iphigenia, and saw in my mind's eye a whole strand covered with ships and men. *Iphigenia in Aulis*, that was it. I'd seen Herr Gluck's opera of it in Paris on my way back from Rome and liked so much I'd been twice. I rummaged around and found my old Potter's translation of the Euripides. I soon came on a magnificent description of the Greeks gathered at the Bay of Aulis—'the countless fleet, a wonder to behold'.

Just reading it inspired me. There were plenty of reference to Nelson and Trafalgar, if I could manage the picture well enough. I began to get a vision of a crescent-shaped bay with a broad beach. Agamemnon on his hill must dominate the composition—that and the landscape.

I let the book fall into my lap. It must be closely connected to the theme: 'the Spirit of the Present Age'. But what was that, exactly? I'd discussed it with any number of people, but I couldn't remember that we'd ever arrived at any conclusion.

'We're at war, but that's hardly new,' Hallett had commented when the topic was aired at Slaughter's. Contemporary politics were best left alone, most thought.

'We've avoided the Revolution in France and the appalling effects of the overthrow of established order, although there are some, not all of them ranting Jacobins, who think some amelioration in social conditions would be beneficial,' one of the philosophers cut in, leaning over our table. Some of his fellows took him up on the subject as they strolled away:

'Britain's in the forefront here, too: it's only a few years since Wilberforce's anti-slavery bill finally got passed.'

'There are a great many beggars in the streets.'

'There always have been, and there's plenty of work in the new factories for any who want it.'

'The Empire's expanding; trade with India's excellent.'

'Our philosophers and men of science are advancing knowledge in every arena. Mr Humphrey: Mr Dalton; why, only the other day Mr Davy was demonstrating...'

Really, considered all round, the 'Spirit of the Present Age' was one of constant improvement, with Britain at the head, like Agamemnon leading his armies.

So he would be on a hilltop, addressing his men, before

they set off. They would all be in armour and would make a magnificent spectacle. For a moment I had a misgiving—he'd offended Artemis and the wind had failed to blow for the fleet—that would never do. I read on rapidly and found that the difficulty was, of course, overcome. Agamemnon had sacrificed his daughter—or perhaps the goddess had whisked her away—and made the winds move again. That was why I had been thinking of Iphigenia.

There was my theme! All the fractured parts fell together in an instant and I seized a piece of paper and sketched it out. A curve of the bay—sand shaded in, in a graceful crescent—the fleet and armies scribbled and dotted over the crescent. A big sky filled with lowering clouds being driven from left to right, with all sorts of dramatic effects—yes—and in the foreground, not of course central, but a little to the left, to balance the massive clouds—Agamemnon, triumphant, with hand raised in command on the cliff-top, issuing the rallying-cry to the assembled troops. 'The Triumph of Agamemnon', I would call it. His triumph over the recalcitrant gods and the forces of nature would be an allegory of our nation's triumph over other nations and over nature—we had harnessed the air, too, in the form of balloons and steam, and made it 'fill the sails' of our industrial progress.

I sank back on the sofa, more pleased with myself than I could remember for a long time. I knew it would work, and it would do everything I wanted it to. I poured myself another large glass of wine and went down to dinner.

Chapter Six

Fantasy castles of carved snow rode low on the horizon as the coach jogged over the spine of England. Banked Alpine peaks shimmered above, while the undersides of the floating mountains were flat and dark. Higher up in the blue drifted insubstantial wisps of wool, incredible as being of the same stuff. Sitting on top of the coach, the view was exhilarating. Swathes of moorland interspersed with patches of rock breaking into forest made a completely new landscape. I had not seen mountains like this since I was in Italy, where they bore the same name, Apennines. The air was cold and fresh and the journey wholly delightful. It was the second day of my trip north; for the first, we had crossed the rolling waves of chalk hills covered with arable that were a common sight from Oxford to Bath. Now I was entering an unfamiliar world.

The coach heaved up a rise and the horses paused for rest. Getting down to stretch my legs, I glimpsed a lovely old house crouched under a grassy hill clothed in a hanging wood of ancient oaks. A clutter of barns and stables at a short distance showed it was a farm of some size. The timbered gables and small mullioned windows, whose diamond panes reflected the afternoon sun in a hundred fragments, indicated it was of the age of the Henrys. Raised at one end was square castellated tower of later date, but the passage of time had given it a patina which harmonised with the grey slate roofs and clustered chimneys of the older parts. Advised by the coachman, I had been looking out for Coldbrook for some time. Was this it?

The coachman pointed his whip. "I see you're admiring the old hall, sir. Coldbrook Manor, that is. All this land here's part of it," and he gestured widely, taking in broad fields of tawny stubble, grazing cattle, massive hedgerows bright with hips and more distant woods in full autumn leaf.

"It's handsome. Is it Mr Joshua Hall's place?" I craned my neck to take it in as the horses began to trot down the rutted slope. I hadn't been sure what to expect, but this was really magnificent and I itched to get out my sketchbook straight away. It slid from view behind a stand of fine old oaks and beech.

The coachman laughed shortly. "No, master, that it ain't. That's the old Manor, belongs to Squire Ashby. Mr Hall's place, further on, why I suppose that'll be new hall—when it's finished."

He raised his whip and the horses gathered pace.

The coach stopped at the village inn of Coldbrook, then once more, so that by the time it rattled through Rochford's south gate the sun was lowering and broad streaks of yellow had begun to appear over the western horizon. The city had been momentarily visible from a hill two miles distant as a smudgy haze populated by a mass of dark towers or steeples. It disappeared as we descended into lower ground, not to reappear until we were almost upon it. Then it sprang up suddenly in a confusion of noise, smoke, multitudes of people in the streets mixed with dray horses, carts, bales and buckets, baggage of all description being pushed hither and thither. The houses were of brick and grey stone and the streets were cobbled, some almost too narrow for more than one wagon to get through at a time, and the coachman was occupied in cracking his whip and bawling to clear our way. Eventually, less than half an hour after the advertised time, we pulled up outside the George and Dragon, which made one side of a large square. I got down, stretching and yawning, and looked around for my baggage.

A smartly-dressed manservant came up, touched his forelock and inquired if I was Mr Armiger. I told him I was, and within ten minutes we were walking up the front steps of a large, dirty stone house not far from the inn, and close to a long dark building of two storeys with many small windows clad with iron bars.

"What's that?" I pointed, surprised by its looming bulk.

"That's the mill, sir—Hall's Mill."

Then the door opened and Francesca stood on the step, looking like an angel with golden light streaming around her, and I forgot everything else.

A clattering racket outside, as of an army approaching, woke me early next morning with a start. I got out of my snug bed and looked out the window into a grey dawn. The street was filled with an immense crowd of men, women and children making towards the factory. It sounded like a troop of horse, but I could see none. Yawning, I returned to my cocoon.

I got up again and went down to breakfast. It was delightful to have my tea poured by Francesca's own hand. She looked as charming first thing in the morning as at any other time: her dress was fresh, there were coral-coloured ribbons in her dark hair and her skin was as warm as a peach. I had dreamed of her—spicy, ardent dreams—and felt embarrassed in case my desire showed in my face.

I did not have far to look for Campbell's portraits, which faced me over the chimneypiece, one on each side of a huge gilded glass in the Grecian style, which consorted oddly with the rest of the furniture. There was a bit of everything, all well-made and heavy, but in an odd mixture of styles. However, the portraits looked very well. Mr Hall sat at one end of the mahogany table, reading the newspaper and regaling us with tidbits.

"Mr Bullock, of Liverpool, has set up a Museum in London. Do we know him, my dear?"

"I don't believe so. Jeffreys, more tea for Mr Hall. Some toast, Mr Armiger?"

"'Curiosities from Africa and the Americas, amphibious animals, fishes, insects, shells, minerals and botanical subjects—including items brought home by Captain Cook'. Cook was a Middlesborough man, you know, Mr Armiger. Have you seen it?"

"No, I'm afraid not, although I would very much like to." I had heard something of its going to be set up, in Piccadilly. I should go and draw from it.

"Oh, Papa, could we not go to London? There is so much to see there. There is nothing in Rochford."

"Less complaining, if you please, Miss; there is plenty to do in Rochford. We have our own Assembly Rooms, Mr Armiger—not as fine as at Bath perhaps, but we may attend a ball while you're here." He turned to Francesca, who was buttering a piece of toast with a disconsolate expression. "Would that satisfy you, young lady?"

"Oh, yes, Papa. And we must take Mr Armiger to the concert and to the theatre."

"Riots at Nottingham. The lace-makers have been doing badly. Parishes unable to pay their Poor Rates. That's bad, very bad. We don't want any of that here. The Poor Rates must be paid. Something must be done for the deserving poor. But rioting—definitely not."

"Have you enough milk, Mr Armiger? Anne, ring for Jeffreys." Mrs Hall fretted constantly. Perhaps she would be more at ease when the novelty of my presence wore off.

Mr Hall turned the pages, crackling. "Are you interested in politics, Mr Armiger?"

"In a general way. I'm afraid you will think me ill-informed. What has caused these riots?"

"Stocking-knitters, by all accounts. Business has been bad since the Orders in Council against trade with the Americans, and the men don't like to have their wages reduced, or to be laid off."

I thought that I wouldn't like to have my wages reduced or be laid off, no matter what the Orders in Council said, but judged that Mr Hall would not share my opinion. I was on my very best behaviour, which included suppressing my ideas in favour of trying to make myself agreeable as a son-in-law. It would be uphill work but so far, so good.

"Mr Hall is a magistrate," his wife confided, leaning towards me.

He folded the paper crisply and took out his watch. "Time for work. Would you care to see the mill, Mr Armiger?" He smiled, as one offering a treat.

I had hoped to spend the morning with Francesca and even start on her portrait, which would give many occasions for sitting and chatting to her, but that would obviously have to wait.

"Delighted." It should be interesting, anyway.

The moment we entered the building I was confronted by a vast room filled with such a jumble of machines and men and clacking din that for several minutes I could make nothing out. Under it all there was a distant, heavy, panting, ominous but far-off, as of some huge animal crouched in waiting. I could see the amusement on Mr Hall's face.

"Aye, young man, it's something to see, isn't it! You were never in a mill before?"

I could hardly hear him. "No, indeed, and I had no idea that it was anything like this."

"I'll explain it to you." He beamed with proprietorial enthusiasm and began to lead me around, stopping now and then to point out special traits of the machines in question.

"In this room we keep the scribblers. It has three parts in the one frame. It's what you might call a kind of carding engine, with rollers in place of the cards, and doffs the wool for the carding itself—there's another engine for that."

'Carding' was the only word I grasped, and I hung on to it. "It prepares the raw wool for spinning?"

Hall nodded. "Aye, it makes it up into rowans."

Seeing my blank expression, he led me across the room, threading our way between the machines and the men bent over them, who were so occupied that they did not look up even as their master passed by. Children ran to and fro, picking up wool from the machines; he called a boy over and took in his hands a long hank of wool and showed it to me.

"This is as it goes to the spinners."

It was soft and greasy to the touch and stank of sheep. We returned to the main hall, full of clacking and whirring like a thousand starlings fighting.

"This is what we call a gig mill."

The room was full of them, with their attendants. To my eye it looked like a vast loom, with a piece of cloth passing through it while I watched; eerily, since the machine worked by itself, the operative tending to the machine rather than working the cloth, as I had first thought. I could not make out what was happening, but it turned out to be simple.

"The mill raises the nap—we call it 'roughing'—by passing

the cloth over a roller while teazles are applied to it."

Each mill had a kind of belt at one side which went round a great wheel above the machine, through which ran a stout axle parallel with the floor, which in its turn, as I followed its course, had a cog wheel on the end which engaged with a larger wheel set at right angles to it. This was attached to a sturdy beam set into the floor. I was not in the least mechanically minded, but even I could see that the motive power was supplied by something which drove the large cog wheel and then transmitted it by means of the smaller cogs, axles, wheels and belts to each of the gig mills in the hall.

"What is it that drives them?"

As I asked, I realised what the answer must be. Hall led me through the room, between the rows of operatives, to a small door at the far end. This he flung open and beckoned me to follow. Inside, reared up in the darkness, lit only by high windows and an opening at one side, was a huge steam engine. The massive beam, far above my head, moved up and down with animal dexterity; it seemed as though the colossal shaft it drove would run away, but that it was tethered at its base to a kind of crank which drove a gigantic wheel. Wisps of steam escaped here and there, and men with oily rags in their hands moved about on raised platforms, dabbing at it and making adjustments. It was a scene worthy of Piranesi. Between its thumps and breathy respirations, I heard Hall explaining its workings, but I was so awestruck that I simply stood and stared. I must draw it, I thought, as the wonder began to wear off. Brigstock would like to see it, was my next idea. I'd send him a sketch. For a moment I wondered whether perhaps he was right and the industrial inventions of the age should be my subject for the Competition, but after a few more minutes I dismissed it. It had greatness, but only of size and intricacy. After that, it was simply an engine. It had no real grandeur—that was the province of nature, or man.

"I can see you're impressed," bellowed Hall, and indeed I was. "When I bought the mill it had a water wheel, but I soon saw that was not the way to go, and I got this fellow."

We went back into the main room. "I have over a mile of line shaft in the whole building," he remarked, pointing to the rods which transmitted the power via the cog wheels to each individual mill. "Here—you! Stop that!" he barked suddenly, breaking away from me. "Hidcote!"

A man in a round hat hurried up; he was evidently the overseer. Hall pointed to an operative nearby, a sallow, sullen-looking fellow. The overseer went over, examined the machine, stopped it, and began ranting at him. The man stood there, hanging his head.

"You have to keep an eye on them all the time, or they get up to God knows what mischief."

"What had he done?"

"He's not taking care of the machine—that it runs smooth. It would take too long to explain. Did you not see that the cloth was uneven? Now that piece'll have to be set again. He's always causing trouble, that one. We'll likely turn him off if it happens again—there are plenty more wanting to take his place."

I looked around; the other workers were diligently attending to their tasks, but I saw one or two flickering sideways glances at the overseer and at Mr Hall. All at once I was heartily sick of the incessant clashing and banging of the machines, the overpowering smell of wool and oil and unwashed men, the whole mill, in fact. I suggested to my host that perhaps I could see the remainder another day.

"Aye, it's a lot to take in," he said kindly. "I'll show you the shearing frames another day. They're the old type: I'm getting new ones soon; a brand new kind, and they'll be the first in the district."

CAMPBELL wrote to tell me that he had settled on his subject. We had discussed what he should do both at Bath and London, and had got as far as a group portrait, but of whom, he could not make up his mind. Now he had crystallised his idea. He had decided on 'a circle of philosophers, a round dozen of men of the age, who in their varying fields, personalities and achievements would represent the Spirit of the Present Age'. He appended a list: The President of the Royal Academy, Benjamin West, the architect John Nash, the poet William Wordsworth and Sir George Smart, professor at the Royal Academy of Music, would represent the various Arts. Philosophy was in the hands of Jeremy Bentham, while Politics and Philanthropy were to be united in the person of William Wilberforce.

'His character as a philanthropist will, I hope, make his inclusion, while other politicians are excluded for prudential reasons, acceptable', Campbell explained, 'and I consider his achievement in relation to the abolition of slavery so great that I cannot leave him out'. I agreed with him entirely. Dr Jenner would exemplify our great advances in Medicine; James Watt was the proponent of Engineering and Industry; John Dalton and Humphry Davy of Chemistry; William Herschel, as the King's Astronomer; and Sir Joseph Banks, both as Explorer and Botanist, would round off the whole. 'I intend to depict them as though in conversation, each accompanied by some attribute relevant to their achievements, Banks with a plant and a map of his explorations, for instance, while Dalton would be perhaps showing someone a diagram of his atoms'. What did I think?

I contemplated it with a sinking feeling. The group was interesting enough. I had no particular argument with his choices, and noted his shrewd inclusion of many men connected with Royal patronage. But even if Campbell managed to bring off the individual likenesses, I felt it would need a great deal of *élan* to avoid it being the sort of work that ended up being described as 'worthy but dull'. If carried out with a great deal of interesting colour, light, technique and so on, it might do, but those were not Campbell's forte. I turned over the page.

'I plan also to see if Mrs Humphrey will publish it as an engraving, as I think it would have popular appeal, so that even if it doesn't win the Competition, I may still profit from all the labour that it will take'. Canny Scotchman! His prognostication was probably correct. The market for engravings was immense. His acumen made me smile and I put the letter away with more confidence than I had started with.

In the evening my host got out the drawings for his new house and we studied them over our wine and tobacco. He had gone in for the Palladian style, with everything that could be expected in the way of a country seat. On paper it looked enormous. My visit to the mill, with its gigantic extent and expensive machinery, had started misgivings in my heart. Now these were intensified by the huge scale and ambition of the new house. These were the belongings of a very wealthy man, much more than I'd realised at Bath, and such men usually wanted other very wealthy men for their daughters. No dream could place me now or ever in that category. I probably had no chance with Francesca at all. My heart plummeted. It was hard to attend to what Hall was saying.

"I couldn't get Nash, so I have a local man, but he's copied some of Nash's plans."

He had indeed. I tried to concentrate. It was a large rectangular building of two stories in stone, with a colonnaded portico. The ends of the building had been advanced to form pavilions, each with a large bow window on the ground floor, which gave onto a terrace. A separate wing behind was in the same style, with the farthest end also advanced to form a matching pavilion.

"Servant's quarters," Hall remarked, tapping the page with his pipe. Ash fell onto the drawing, obscuring a large conservatory at the other end. "I mean to have a pinery, grapes, and all the exotic plants."

The garden front was plainer, and showed a subterranean floor of kitchens and offices.

"It's going to be very big, isn't it?"

"Aye. I mean to do it in style, and to have plenty of room for guests, and when my girls marry, why, they can have a wing each if they like."

I leapt into the opening. "Is either of the young ladies engaged?"

He gave me a sharp look. "Not at present, but you never know."

It sounded encouraging, although I couldn't make sense of his final remark. It seemed to suggest that there was someone in the offing. I hoped that it was Miss Hall who was the lucky girl. I would have liked to enquire further, but if I did so I would have to make an offer in form and it was far too early for that. My heart thumped at the thought of being united to Francesca for life, but what had become shatteringly apparent was that I would have do a great deal to work her father around to the idea. Her own inclination was hard to read. At one moment she smiled, at another seemed distant. She did like me, though. I was sure she liked me. Only that morning she had especially showed me her canary bird, which she had raised herself from a chick, and her favourite spaniel. I was touched by her tenderness towards the little creatures. Perhaps I ought to ask Mr Hall for permission to address her?

I became aware that he was frowning and that the silence had stretched out rather. I pointed to the drawings at random.

"Do you have plans for the grounds?"

"I want an arboretum, a bowling green and all those contrivances. I couldn't get Mr Repton, but I'm looking about for a man who's worked with him. I've heard tell of a fellow and I've written to him to come and look at it. There's not much there at present—all very old-fashioned. But you'll be able to give me your opinion tomorrow, when we go over there."

THAT night I spent much time thinking about Francesca and my chances, but had also to devote some consideration to Agamemnon, conscious that I mustn't lose the enthusiasm I had felt when I first thought of the idea and aware that I had done nothing at all since. But I also had to start work on the views for my host. I compromised by reading through the Euripides again. It was awkward not having a studio. If I'd been at home I could at least have begun on some sketches of the composition.

IN the morning we were off smartly after breakfast, packed into a barouche with a large picnic hamper, my drawing gear and a footman behind. After an hour we arrived at a large meadow, acres of grass yellowing in the crisp autumn sun, the sky a beautiful pale blue. A white building stretched naked on top of a small hill. A fine wood of oaks and beech stood a short distance away in a dell. Nearby, a group of huts and tumble of stones suggested men at work. The carriage turned off across the meadow, following the trail of crushed grass and muddy ruts which marked the progress of previous visitors and the contractors' drays.

I jumped out when we arrived and assisted the ladies, managing to retain Francesca's hand for a moment. She dimpled at me and went off, twirling her parasol daintily, to sit with her mother and sister on a rug the footman was spreading. Mr Hall was speaking to the workmen and I spent a few minutes enjoying the sun, the smell of the grass and the twitter of birds. Then it was time for work.

"As you see, Mr Armiger, the first storey is near done."

We strolled up to the edifice, covered in part with scaffolding and the usual debris of construction. Even in autumn the stone glared white.

"I see you've chosen to place it at the top of the hill." I hoped it wasn't windy—but while I thought it, a sharp breeze whipped at my hat.

"Aye, and grand views it has, don't you think? I'm very fond of a view, and so is Madam."

The vast expanse of field ran away before us, unbroken by anything save a little brook, some sheep, and in the distance, the smoke and chimneys of Rochford. Far, far away, larger hills made a blue-grey blur. There was not much here to make a perspective of. It would take all my ingenuity and a certain amount of imagination to make this barren plateau look like a gentleman's residence. Mr Hall had placed the house so that the view he commanded was of the ugly town—but then, it was the source of his wealth, so I imagined there was a constant satisfaction in gazing at it. I walked round the other side; the vista wasn't much, farmland and meadows, but if it had been mine, I would have turned the house, and my back, on the smokes of Rochford. I looked at the oak wood I'd noticed as we drove in; there were some fine old trees in it. If I could get among them I might use them to frame the building. I climbed up on a stone and noticed a steeple just beyond them to the right.

"Is that a village?"

"Aye, Coldbrook village."

"It makes a pleasing object. If you were to place a folly, or summer-house, or something of the sort, just there," I pointed to a low rise, "it would command it."

"Aye, maybe. I'll mention it to the architect. But see here—the colonnade—it's to have pairs of columns—only the bases are in place at present, but you can see how it will be."

It would be huge. I began to walk around, looking for vantage points. To the left, under the hill, stood what I took to be builders" huts. The group was very picturesque in its tumbledown condition. I walked towards them.

"What is this, Mr Hall?"

He caught up with me. "Oh, only the old farm that we're pulling down, but the men use it to store their bits and pieces."

As we came up I saw that it had been an ancient farmhouse with outbuildings, some half-ruined with the roofs falling in, and others partly pulled down by the men. The remains of a noble gable still sheltered the main part of the house, with a cobbled yard in front and roses, geraniums and lavender sprawling wild over decayed garden walls.

"What a shame!" The words were out before I could think how tactless they were.

Hall looked at me and raised his shoulders. "Old things must go, young man, and make way for new. The farm was falling away for years. Fellow who had it could never make it pay. I did him a favour by buying it." He turned back to the house.

I paused, looking up at the rich russet roof tiles and the sky reflected in a few shattered panes of glass. As I, too, turned to go back a rose branch caught my sleeve. There were a few pink blossoms left on it. I took out my penknife and cut the spray, and carried it to where the ladies were sitting.

"A gift for you from the old farm," I said, and bowed as I presented it to Francesca.

She took it in her little hand and bent her face to it, her parasol behind her head and the sun filtering down through the branches to dapple her dress. It was a picture that would draw all eyes at the Academy—if I could paint it.

"Thank you, Mr Armiger. Look, Mama. Oh! They have no perfume." She put the spray down, but smiled at me all the same.

"You know, Mrs Hall, I would like to make a sketch of Miss Francesca while I am here, if you do not object. Mr Campbell is the proper person to do a portrait in oils, if you think of such a thing, but if I might perhaps make an essay in watercolours?"

Francesca clapped her hands. "Oh, yes, Mama! After all, you have a picture of Anne—why shouldn't it be my turn?"

"Well, well, I don't know. We'll have to ask Mr Hall. Now I think he's looking for you, Mr Armiger."

It was a step in the right direction, and she had liked the idea. I returned to my host and my work with a springier gait.

While luncheon was being laid out I put up my portable easel and after eating set to work. I would make a perspective of the half-built, staring monster from each side, or rather, three-quarter views across the meadows. Later, vistas from the hilltop itself, looking towards Rochford. God knows how I would be able to contrive them to look anything but bare. I supposed I would have to emphasize the sweep of pasture and so forth, and suppress the smoke smudge on the horizon.

In the event, I managed rather better than I had thought. With a fine sheet of Large Post paper I'd prepared with a light bluish wash, I sketched in the façade from the right. From the angle I'd chosen I was able to incorporate the old farm and outbuildings on the left hand side, disappearing into shadow. I worked out the details of the edifice itself with a fine pencil, then began to apply a series of washes to block in the main areas of colour, reserving areas of paper in the sky for clouds. Later, I could wash out parts of the pale blue background if it was not bright enough, or touch it up with body white. I began to hum quietly to myself as I worked. The afternoon was pleasantly warm, the meadow smelled delightful, bees vibrated in the tall grass and birds chirped drowsily in the oaks. The afternoon sun sloped across the half-built house and I caught it in long shadows, throwing the squared stonework and tree clumps into relief, while beams palely streaked the grass. If I glanced around I could see Francesca, resting with her mother and sister in the shade; once or twice she came up to inspect my progress, and once absently brushed my arm with her shawl. London and the Academy seemed far away.

Chapter Seven

Mr Hall put down his cup and turned the pages of the paper. His wife looked up at the sound of his grumbling.

"My dear?"

"According to the *Mercury*, it is getting completely out of hand. 'By the latest letters from Nottingham, Derby, and Leicester, we learn, that in the neighbourhood of Loughborough, three frames had been destroyed, but that during the middle of the week, the counties were tolerably tranquil...' Aye, I'd heard of it."

"Well, that is something to be thankful for! But that is so close to us! Actually destroyed! What is being done?"

"Nothing like enough! And of course the work will fall upon us magistrates, as usual."

Francesca darted me a merry glance and made a wry face. She'd told me that she thought these concerns of her father's were an exact parallel of her mother's anxiety about Rochford being stormed by French soldiers.

"You see, I'm right. 'Government are adopting more effectual measures to suppress these riots. The *Gazette* on Saturday night contains a Proclamation directed to the Magistrates, and all civil officers in the towns where any Riotous Proceedings have taken place, directing the apprehension of any Person concerned, and offering Fifty Pounds to be paid upon the conviction of each and every offender.' You see? And just when I'm bringing in these new frames myself. Couldn't be at a worse time."

"What would you like to see done, sir?" I inquired. "Fifty pounds seems a lot to me."

"Nay, young man, it's not the fifty pounds, it's catching the rogues. Of course the reward will help to get information on the scoundrels, but their supporters in the towns hide them and no-one knows who they are. Why, some of them may even work in the mills they're helping to ruin!" He was getting red in the face and his neck bulged over his collar.

"What should be done, then?"

"They should bring up a troop of dragoons—nay, several troops—and station them at every mill where they think there might be trouble, instead of leaving it to the civil authorities. What can we do, without soldiers?" He threw down the paper and got up. "I will not be in until dinner, my dear, I have a deal to do."

"You've not forgotten that we have dinner guests?" He blinked.

"Eh? No, of course not. But I won't be much before them." He left, but returned briefly to say to me:

""I know you wanted to see the shearing frames, but I have to attend to business. However, Hidcote will show you round and answer any questions you may have."

Any possibility that I was to be spared the totality of the mill's workings evaporated. I did not really mind. I had found thc world of engines interesting, if no more, and had spent some time before sleep reviewing my recollections of my first visit. The busy jumble, the clatter of the machines, the earnest operatives bent over their work, and most of all, the gigantic engine in its separate chamber, had made powerful impressions on me. It was like something from a Gothic novel, only translated to the modern day. Although I'd dismissed 'the Mechanical Age' out of hand, I began to think what a fascinating subject the mill would make. If I could manage to bring grandeur and drama to a modern subject—but what? And how? I needed to think about it a great deal more.

I worked on my views all morning, transferring the water colour sketches onto boards and drawing in details according to the notes I'd made on the spot. I'd brought some nice prepared canvasses and a good supply of materials with me. I had to explain to Mrs Hall the necessity of my having a workroom with a good light, where I could leave my paintings set up and work on them at any time of the day or night. The good soul had thought that artists worked as Campbell did when he painted her portrait—appearing out of nowhere with his canvas and his colours ready made up, and painting away in the drawing room. But she found me a room, the old schoolroom the girls had had, and got part of the floor covered with drapes. I made myself at home and was soon making excellent progress. I needed to get on with these so that I could start on Agamemnon as soon as I got home. I needed plenty of time to create something really new in the way of technique, as well as a powerful image.

In the afternoon I left some things to dry and went over to the factory. Mr Hall would be displeased if I didn't take up his offer. The overseer, or overlooker, as they called them, referred me in turn to one of the operatives.

"Thwaite here'll show you whatever you want to see."

The man was not tall, but gave an impression of dogged sturdiness. He wore a clean shirt, a red woollen waistcoat, grey worsted stockings and buff breeches, and stood holding his cap in his hands while he waited for Hidcote to finish speaking. When the overlooker left and we began to walk off, I heard the same clicking sound I'd thought were horses in the street on my first morning. I looked down; on his feet were clogs with leather uppers, nailed closely all round and clasped with a tin buckle. They were the same as the ones the sleeping beggar in Bath had been wearing. I stopped to think. Could that man, who had somehow touched me, have come from here? And what on earth was that clack-clack-clack, as we walked along?

"What is it that makes that sound?"

He smiled and lifted his foot behind him like a horse being shod. "I reckon you don't have these down in London?"

The sole and heel were guarded with strips of iron shaped like narrow horseshoes. Looking around, I saw that most of the workers, men, women and children, were barefoot or wore the same footgear; only the overlookers had shoes.

"You're quite right, we don't. Ours have iron rings let into the sole to keep them out of the mud, and they're a different shape." The toes on his were square and turned up in the same way as the beggar's. "Is this style peculiar to Rochford?"

"I can't tell you that, but they're the only sort I've ever seen."

We came up to the machines and he paused, pointing. "That's the shearing frame," he remarked, sourly, I thought.

I watched it for a few minutes as the attendant bent over it. It looked much less complicated than the scribbling and gig engines I had seen before—a kind of flat bed with sides, like a child's cot, or frame of a box, with rollers underneath. These drew the cloth across the top, where large shears trimmed the nap as it went past. A wheel at one side held the belt which drew power from a hub on the axle above, and so from the great steam engine. Thwaite gave me to understand that the shearing, or cropping, was a final stage in the process of producing a finished cloth from the raw wool, and the operatives were skilled men. Some had spent years perfecting the art, which entailed shearing off the surface of the cloth so as to present a fine flat finish. I hadn't realised that it didn't come from the loom in that state.

"I suppose that the standard of cloth has improved greatly, now that machines can do this finishing work to smooth it," I remarked.

He gave a barking laugh and the operative grimaced. "Nay, master! 'Tis the other way around."

He moved off and I followed him. "How?"

He faced around, looking about him as though to see who was listening. "Before engines came, all the work were done by men—croppers, or shearmen—cloth dressers." Croppers were the best-paid workers in the cloth trade, he said, because of the skill needed to do the shearing by hand. "I were a cropper, master, before the frames came." His face lengthened.

"Did you have your own..." I hardly knew what to call it "...business?"

"Aye, a few of us worked together in the finishing shop, with a boy to clean the teazle boards. That's how it were—is, for them as still has their trade."

"Tell me about the work—if you don't mind."

"Mind! Mr Hidcote told me to tell you anything you wanted. But I don't mind, because I can see you want to know. Most folks don't want to know, as long as they have clothes to their backs."

Then, dark eyes brightening, he expanded. Their first task, it seemed, was to raise the nap of the cloth, which he called 'roughing' it, and was done with teazles. This in itself was skilled work—"and now it's gig mills do it." Then the cloth was fixed to a board and laid over a sort of bench, or horse, and the shears were worked over it to dress the nap flat. The shears were not unlike those in common use, but specially made with curved blades and of gigantic proportions, like everything else, it seemed, in this trade. They were four feet long and immensely heavy, he told me, extending his arms to indicate the size. They were also very expensive—more than two guineas each, not to mention the other equipment required.

The cropper pushed one blade toward the other, a work which gave them a huge callous on the right wrist, so that, with the developed musculature of the arm, croppers were distinctive in appearance. He showed me his wrist, which was remarkable. I asked him to roll up his sleeve and he willingly obliged. He would make a wonderful model, I thought, with a physique as good as old Strowger at the Schools, who had been in the Life Guards in his time.

"Aye, a lad could never do it, not even lift the shears. 'Tis a grown man's work."

This laborious process was repeated several times, according to the quality and kind of the cloth. A good dresser could improve the value of a cloth by as much as twenty per cent. I looked at the material of my coat with new respect and felt it between my fingers.

Thwaite laughed. "By your leave, master." He took it in his fingers as I had. "Aye, a good piece of cloth, but not of the finest, begging your pardon."

I grinned. "I knew that already!" But I let him see that I was impressed by his expertise. I realised that these rough-looking men could value the coat on the back of every man they saw walking down the street, just from the finish of the cloth. It struck me with some force that they would never be able to wear cloth of the quality they could make. I was still ruminating over this obvious fact when I left the mill.

There was something wrong with that. A cook cooks the same for herself as for her master, and often eats the same food, in the way of leftovers. A maid cleans her own room with the same skill as her employer's. A carpenter makes his own furniture with the same art that he employs in the workshop. But in the cloth trades, men and women worked to make things that they could never afford, and were condemned to wear garments infinitely inferior to those they could make and to know them to be inferior. No wonder he was disgruntled.

I got back to the house in the late afternoon, thoughtful and longing to make drawings of all I'd seen, just in time to dress for dinner. Guests were coming, but it was to be a sedate gathering, at the not very fashionable hour of six.

The visitors were announced—the local clergyman, a Mr Robson, and his wife; Hall's architect Mr Innes, whom I had not yet met, and his sister Miss Innes; and a Mr Shirlow. Shirlow was a man in his late thirties, a neighbouring mill-owner, who apparently was an old friend of the family. I was not sure whether the guests had been invited to meet the great artist from the capital, or to relieve my hosts of the tedium of spending yet another evening *en famille* with me. I was rather annoyed that Mr Shirlow took Francesca in and I was left with Miss Hall.

The soup and fish passed while we were becoming acquainted with each other. I was seated between Miss Innes, a dried-up looking spinster of about forty, who kept house for her brother, and Miss Hall. Francesca sat opposite between Mr Shirlow and Mr Innes. While Mr Hall carved an immense joint of beef and the footman handed round the roast ham, Mr Innes talked about the house.

"I hope you were pleased with it, Mr Armiger? Of course, coming from London, you will be familiar with all the latest developments in architecture. Mr Ruffield is building a modern house in Regent's Park in the style of Mr Nash, I believe. Have you seen it?"

I admitted that I had strolled past, but not stopped to inspect it. It was covered in scaffolding.

"How unfortunate! Still, I expect you are a busy man. And I understand that Mr Nash has completed his plans for connecting the Park with Charing Cross. What a magnificent project that is! I expect it is the talk of London. I do hope Parliament will approve it."

He was a small man with eyeglasses, which he removed

to eat his dinner, then replaced every time he addressed me across the table. I was able to assure him that the designs had been much discussed in the clubs and coffee houses, and that I among others thought it an excellent idea.

"Of course, we have clubs and coffee houses here, too," he added wistfully, "but you do not see the great names in them as you do in London. Have you seen Mr Nash at all?"

"I don't think so, but I have seen Sir John Soane on many occasions at the Academy, and I shared a table with Mr Smirke last time I was at Old Slaughter's."

"Oh! Mr Smirke. I have an engraving of his Royal Mint. I think the coat of arms on the pediment very fine. Do you think there should be something of the sort on Mr Hall's house?"

"Tell me, Mr Innes, what's the building to be called? Such a grand edifice must surely have a name. I've been wondering."

He flushed and replaced his eyeglasses. "Ah, yes. The problem is that there is already an old building in the neighbourhood called Coldbrook Manor, otherwise that would be the obvious title."

"I've seen it."

"Yes, it's old—no more than a hodge-podge of bits and pieces. Nothing more than a farm, really, but it has the name, which is unfortunate. And then…" he fidgeted in his seat.

"Then?" It was mischievous of me, but I'd already heard some rumours.

"Well, you know, a place is usually named after the owner, but in the case of Mr Hall... a fine name, a very worthy name, but..."

The owner of the name caught its mention. "What are you saying, Innes?"

"I was asking about the name of the house," I put in.

Mr Hall laughed. "Aye, I know there's been talk about it. I can't call it 'Hall Hall', and 'Hall Manor' doesn't do either.

So we're at a standstill, unless you can think of something."

'New Hall' flitted through my mind, but I thought it might be tactless. The copse of ancient trees which I thought the finest thing on the estate, that Mr Hall wanted to cut down, sprang into my mind.

"'Oakwood House'? It has a fine sound, and there is that wood near the house."

"Aye—'Oakwood House'. I like that. What do you think, my dear? But I'd have to keep the trees then. I can see what you're about, young man!' But he smiled genially.

His good temper always struck me. Nothing about his station in life, or his low origins, bothered him in the slightest. It was his most agreeable characteristic, especially noticeable when I had spent so much of my life enduring people like Hallett and Alcock making them out to be bigwigs, or Quayle bragging about his connections.

The cloth was removed and the nuts and apples brought in, with a lot of little cakes, since this was a smarter dinner than usual. I was waiting for the wine and cigars, since I found small talk trying. I was not good at it, and frequently wondered how people could spend so much time on it. I was also getting into a frenzy watching Shirlow helping Francesca to the best peach and cracking walnuts for her.

At last the ladies disappeared. The clergyman, who I noticed now had the red nose of a toper, got a decanter in front of him and began to discuss church architecture with Mr Innes. Mr Shirlow drew his chair up to the host's and they started on the subject of the frame-breaking at Loughborough and Mr Hall's new frames.

"There are hundreds, perhaps thousands, throughout the county on Parish Relief," ventured Mr Robson, drawing the madeira towards him.

"What's the reason?" I asked.

"Don't want to work," replied Shirlow smartly.

"Nay, it's not only that," Hall said, leaning back in his chair and filling his pipe. "Price of bread has gone up, there's no doubting that."

Robson agreed. "It's the highest it has been in my memory, and I've been in my parish thirty years."

"Why is it so high?"

"The crops have been failing. Last year was bad, but this harvest just past was even poorer."

"I see." It was what I had understood from the newspapers, but it was different to hear it from men who lived among farmers and workers.

"Aye, and when the damned blockades are added in, trade is bad and we have to lay off men. There's no keeping men on when I can't sell the cloth I have. And now this business with the Americans!" Hall added.

"Yes—if we can't sell to them, it will be hard to keep trade up. I blame the war in Europe for the fall-off in general. What business had we getting involved in Spain—or Portugal?" Shirlow said.

"Surely we had to help when the Spaniards came to ask for our assistance? And Wellington is the only general who has been able to beat Napoleon, and has even pushed him back—more than the Austrians or the Italians were able to do." I'd been interested in the Peninsula War since it began, and followed the military dispatches in the *Gazette* eagerly.

"We should have minded our own business and let the foreigners fight it out among themselves."

Shirlow's mouth turned down at the corners in a disagreeable way when he was annoyed, and I had the idea that opposing his view always annoyed him. His mouth was rectangular and the teeth in his lower jaw ran straight across it, so that his eye teeth stood like sentinels at the corners. His smile lifted his upper lip, exposing his top teeth. The effect was forceful and manly, but neither graceful nor charming.

If Brigstock was a hedgehog, Shirlow was a bulldog—quite a good-looking bulldog, to be sure, with dark brown hair and eyes, but a bulldog all the same.

"Aye, but your contract with the army for uniforms and blankets has done you no harm, I'm thinking." Hall winked at me, but his face was serious.

"Yes, the army contract is useful, I'll grant you that, but it doesn't make up for the loss of European trade in general. You've had to cut back, I know that—we all have. And in my opinion these rioters are a lot of damned Jacobins. We never had this trouble before the Revolution in France. When I bought the factory fifteen years back there was none of this cant about 'workers' rights'. I blame that radical Tom Paine. 'Down with the aristocracy'! Country's going to the dogs."

Shirlow was keyed up, but Hall looked thoughtful. "I don't have any great feeling for the aristocracy, not being one of them, and old things have to change—I've told you that, haven't I, Mr Armiger? But rioting and disturbing the peace, and breaking frames—we can't have that. That's downright crime."

"Sometimes I wonder if the Dissenters aren't behind it", Robson suggested. His features had become a fine shade of puce. "They're more educated than ordinary working men, and I think they go about and stir them up."

Hall snorted and Shirlow shook his head. "They're just as likely to be your own flock, from what I can see. Some of your colleagues are on their side, giving them aid when they're turned off. That just encourages the rogues."

There was something about all this I didn't comprehend. "If I understand what you say, your business is bad and there's already a great deal of unemployment in the cloth trade. So why buy new machinery?"

"I wouldn't expect an artist to understand," Shirlow replied, "since it's outside your line. But you have a point in a way. Business is bad, but it's bound to improve. True, you have to lay out money for the new frames, but the new frames save wages. Every day you have them working, you save the wages you'd be paying. And then as soon as trade picks up again, which it's bound to do, you'll be in front of those who don't have them. That's why I'm getting them in, as well as my friend Hall here."

I poured myself another glass before I spoke, annoyed by his condescending manner. "I see. But if trade is bound to pick up, as you say, why lay off the workmen, so that they have to go on the parish? Why not keep them on, even at a lower rate?" Shirlow frowned. "You don't understand it at all, Mr Armiger. Things are probably very different in London. I think you'd be best advised to keep to your own line of work."

He glared, my hackles rose, and I was saved from an argument that would have put me in my host's black book, by the appearance of Jeffreys with the message that Madam wondered when the gentlemen would be finished with their wine. Mr Hall took the hint and in a few minutes we were in the drawing room listening to Miss Hall playing the pianoforte and Francesca singing. Shirlow turned the pages for her—I was not quick enough. He was too old for her, and he was going bald, as I could see when he stood near the candelabra and bent his head. It was worrying to arrive here and discover him on the scene, smiling and making up to her. I would just have to make myself so agreeable I would cut him out. In the end, though it all came down to Francesca. If she loved me, I had nothing to fear from Shirlow or anyone else.

At last I began my portrait of Francesca. In deference to Campbell, whom I regarded as the Hall's 'official' portrait painter, I would do it in water colours. I had a fine set of new colours ready made up into cakes, which worked very well, and some nice sable brushes. We discussed her pose at length, which was delightful, and eventually decided that she would be seated next to the drawing-room window which gave onto the garden. All her poses were naturally graceful, and I let her settle herself on the sofa, only stopping her in an especially happy position, with her head just turned from the light. Again with respect for Campbell, it was to be only a small work—but privately, of course, I intended to copy it in oils as soon as I got the chance.

I was no great portraitist, but I could usually get a likeness. I thought I would enhance the work by some interesting treatment of the pigments, starting with laying down some broad washes which I might blot out later for lights. At my request she wore the coral ribbons again, which I would touch in with expensive vermilion, and which would give force to her natural warm colouring. I threw the room behind her into semi-darkness with a mixture of Prussian blue and umber, so that I could blur the ugly furniture and model her figure with the light from the window.

The washes went well and she sat like an angel. I was not good at chatting while I work—one of Campbell's gifts—and was afraid that she would become bored; however, her sister offered to read to her, which was perfect. The choice of both ladies was 'Marmion', and I had to say Miss Hall had a pleasing voice and read with more expression than I would have imagined. I had got as far as the preliminary lines of the figure when the footman came to say that Francesca was wanted to answer a note.

"Only if Mr Armiger can spare me!" She gave me such a droll look from under her lashes.

Her departure gave me the opportunity to walk about and then to alter a few lines. Miss Hall put down her book and came to stand beside me, watching me for a few minutes as I pushed the colours around with a soft brush.

"My sister is very beautiful", she remarked. I was struck by her tone and turned to look at her. Her expression was as reticent as ever.

"Yes, she is, indeed." I applied a little more colour to the dress. "I hope I can capture something of it."

"She has always been very much admired."

"I'm not surprised to hear it."

She continued to stand quietly beside me while I worked away. I felt she had some motive in doing so, but couldn't fathom it. Perhaps I wasn't enthusiastic enough? "A young lady of her charms..."

Miss Hall broke in. "Yes—charm—that's it. She is very charming, don't you think?"

"Most certainly." What did she want from me? A declaration?

She frowned, her eyes cast down. She seemed about to speak again, looked at me, hesitated. "You have a real genius for art, Mr Armiger."

I was startled at her tone. Previously, she had not seemed to show much interest.

"I feel it is much more than merely a profession with you."

"Thank you. I hope it is—I hope you are right."

She looked straight at me. "It must be difficult sometimes to find..." she was deliberating over every word, "... the right person. I mean to say, that there are some people who do not truly appreciate art."

"That's very true." How lucky I was to have found Francesca!

"People are so different in their... ways of being. I suppose art is the same."

"Indeed." I was completely at a loss.

"Some pictures appeal at first glance, others take some study to really understand. Don't you think that people are somewhat the same?"

"Certainly—I mean, I suppose so."

She gave me an earnest look. I felt that I was on the verge of understanding her meaning when Francesca re-entered the room and took up her place again in the most graceful manner, arranging her skirt and tilting her head into exactly the right position. Miss Hall went back to her chair and took up her book, and I my brush. While I worked I thought of our conversation, so uncharacteristic of her. At first she had seemed to want to recommend her sister to me, then to draw back from it. But when she said that some people did not appreciate art, she clearly could not mean Francesca. The whole conversation was so odd. The only meaning I could draw from it was that she was jealous of her sister. I looked at the two of them together, the one sparkling with life, showing her beautiful white even teeth in a smile, her glossy dark ringlets hanging down on her peach-bloom neck; the other, amiable enough, brown-haired and blue-eyed, but with her habitual expression of reserve, as she read on in even tones. If she was jealous, I was sorry for her, but there was nothing I could do about it. I was head over heels in love with her sister.

Chapter Eight

There is nothing in the world harder than to get a girl alone in order to have an intimate conversation with her. I'd thought that when I was staying in the house it would be easier, but it turned out not so. Her mother and sister were always about. I began to think of them as naval corvettes, which are never out of sight of one another. You think that there is only one, and begin to make your way towards your objective when lo! one of its colleagues looms up on the horizon. It made me feel like a French privateer attempting to seize a Spanish prize.

With this in mind I accompanied the ladies on their errands whenever possible. We were hurrying through the plaza in front of the Exchange late one morning, held up by rain, when a cart happening to pass just in front of us, the horse suddenly threw itself aside with a wild neigh and a scrape of iron tyres on the cobbles. Nostrils red and flaring, eyes showing the whites, it staggered sideways and fell heavily on the wet stones, breaking a shaft with a sharp crack.

Francesca stopped dead. "Oh, look, the poor thing!" Dropping her umbrella, she ran over to it.

The carter got down and stood next to the heaving animal, whose ribs stood out under its rough coat.

"Come away, Francesca!" her mother commanded. "Leave it be!"

She had dropped to her knees, disregarding the wet, and

was stroking the quivering animal's head.

"Stand away there, Miss, you can't do no good." The carter took up his whip and lashed the animal across the ribs, cursing it at the same time. It struggled to rise. I saw its knees were broken and blood ran into the mud it lay on.

"Come away," I said, going to help her. She turned her face up to me and I saw it trickled with tears. The hem of her dress was wet.

"Can't you stop him? Please stop him!"

The poor horse groaned and flailed feebly, striking a spark from the cobbles. I turned Francesca away towards her mother and went up to the man.

"Look here, don't do that. It's not doing any good."

"What business is it of yours, master? Here's my cart full and that damned animal dropping down, how I am I to get it to the market?" He aimed a hefty kick at its rump, which struck with a dull thud.

"Don't do that," I said. "I'll help you. And mind your language."

I pulled him round to the front of the cart and got him to take the weight of the remaining shaft on his shoulder while I essayed to get the struggling animal to its feet. Pulling on the bridle one way and pushing it the other, I got it half up, forelegs scrabbling, before it fell heavily again. The carter dropped the shaft and swearing, aimed another kick at it. The horse groaned. A crowd had gathered and a young man came to help. But it was no good. The wretched animal was so exhausted it could not get up, even under the rain of blows the carter was now inflicting.

I took him forcefully by the arm and spoke into his ear.

"If you don't stop doing that, I'll hit you myself." I showed him my fist. He stopped, sullenly, while I examined the trembling beast. "Look, its leg is broken."

"Nay, that's nowt!"

A soldier stepped from the crowd. Ignoring the carter, he knelt and felt the place. "Yes, it's broken." He looked at me.

"Have you got a pistol?" I asked.

He nodded, drew it from his coat and began loading it. The carter, cursing at the top of his voice, tried to take it from him, but he calmly cocked it, put it to the horse's head and fired. A loud bang and a puff of smoke: the acrid smell of gunpowder; the animal jerked once, then collapsed onto its side, legs quivering, then still. The officer nodded to me, tucked the pistol into his pocket and sauntered off, leaving the carter raving.

Francesca ran up to me. "Oh, thank you! That horrible man! The poor horse!"

Her mother appeared behind her, frightened and trembling. "Francesca, you bad girl! Mr Armiger, you shouldn't have! Mr Hall will be so angry! Kneeling down in a public street—in front of the Exchange! Look at your dress! And that odious man! Come away home. We will forget the errands. Jeffreys can go out for them later."

She cast me a wrathful look, then turned and marched off, Francesca pale, her mother bustling her along. I trailed behind. Now I'd really torn it. But she had been pleased with me.

At home, I was not long in doubt of her father's reaction. I heard him rating her through his study door while I loitered shamelessly in the hall.

"Your behaviour is disgraceful! To think we are trying to make you into a lady, while you are determined to behave like a chambermaid! You will remain in your room until I send for you!"

The door opened suddenly and she scuttled out, turning her face away from me, but I heard her sniffing as she climbed the stairs. I only had time to move quickly to the bottom of the stairs before her father appeared, red in the face.

"And I'll thank you not to interfere, or to encourage her in her tomfoolery!" he barked. Then he disappeared back into his study, shutting the door very loudly.

I went into the billiard room and played a few solitary frames, wondering whether I had ruined my chances for ever. I was taken aback by Mr Hall's attitude. I'd never seen him angry before, except when he reproached the man in the mill, and it was not a happy sight. But what else could I have done? I felt closer to her than ever, and more than glad that she'd turned to me in her distress. That promised well for me, but it all depended on how much influence her father had over Francesca—or vice versa.

In the end no more was said about it. He was silent and preoccupied at dinner, but when Mrs Hall began to expand on how terrified she had been, and the state of Francesca's dress, he cut her off sharply. He had other things to think about than women's twaddle, he said—business troubles.

Her mother took me aside in the drawing room. "Mr Hall doesn't like to be crossed, and Francesca is so much his favourite, and he is always so concerned the girls' behaviour is proper, because of his being in trade."

That was not so promising.

Next morning I detained her a moment in the hall before breakfast and asked her whether she was recovered from the incident. I really meant after her father's tirade, and I thought she understood me.

"Oh, don't worry," she said, smiling, although I thought she looked wan. "Papa has these moods, but he dotes on me really."

I could have sworn that she had been terrified of him at

that moment, but now she was her usual self. She was a brave girl. Life was perhaps not as easy for her as at first seemed.

The effect of all this was to intensify my feelings for her.

GOING about the town on business made me familiar with the principal parts of Rochford. I had imagined it would be like London, only smaller and with less in the way of great buildings, shops, clubs and recreations. It was, although less than I had supposed. There were plenty of these facilities for leisure and instruction, in the main newly built. Fifty, even twenty years ago, the town would have had a very different character. But what really set it apart from London was the atmosphere of work. The high factory chimneys and the grime they produced dominated the city and lay indifferently on everything—buildings, trees, grass, clothing. I had thought that nothing could be dirtier than a London street, but Rochford's had all the sources of dirt that London did, with the factory filth added. There were some pleasant squares and parks, but nothing like the great stretches of nature and ancient woods to be found in London, and the soot soiled even the leaves and grass. The river Roche which gave the place its name was little more than a canal. I was told its flow was much reduced by the numerous mills which had been established upstream.

But apart from the surroundings, the people were different. I hadn't expected it. Bath was like London in miniature, only with more of a holiday atmosphere; Cambridge was similar, but much smaller and more scholarly, and with a plenitude of magnificent architecture, so that it was an outdoor gallery like Rome or Florence. But Rochford was something new. Everyone seemed to be bustling about on their business, and the streets at certain hours, in some quarters, were choked with working men, women and children rushing to work or home. Beggars were everywhere, often robust-looking men with no apparent defect, surly and demanding, not humble and supplicating like those I was used to. And the working people had a pallid, greyish look and were thin in the face. I thought of the coachman who'd brought me from London, whose ruddy features endured all weathers but seemed none the worse for it, and the stout pink legs and rosy face of the buxom dairymaid in the fields outside Bath. The working people in Rochford looked as though they had never picked berries from a hedge in their lives.

MUSING on all this one afternoon as I made my way down the High Street to the Exchange, where there was a small book dealer I wished to inspect, I all but ran into a clerical gentleman in black examining the stock. He was holding a volume in his hand while arguing with another cleric. He turned round with a sharp remark. As I apologised for treading on him, I realised it was Robson, who I'd met at Hall's.

"My apologies—I hope you have taken no hurt."

"Oh!" He twisted round to look at his foot. "Oh—Mr Armiger. No, I am well, thank you." He did not look particularly pleased to see me. I was about to walk on when I noticed his wife talking to a young woman in a green pelisse. I bowed.

"Mrs Robson—I hope I see you well?" By this time we had formed a group that was impeding the traffic, and withdrew into the shop doorway.

"This is my colleague Reverend Somers, of St Saviour's. Miss Somers. Mr Armiger."

We exchanged courtesies and Robson, rather red, returned to what he and Somers had been discussing. Somers was in his sixties, dressed in black and a broad hat, which he took off, ruffling his thin grey hair with one hand. The argument seemed to have something to do with the book Robson was waving about.

"But even if he is a disciple of Paine, surely it is worth hearing what he has to say?" Mr Somers was saying.

"You mean you find it acceptable that this sort of revolutionary trash is openly on sale in our town, where any rogue can read it?"

Somers examined the book, turning the cover to show me its title as I craned rather rudely. It was called *Enquiry Concerning Political Justice*, by William Godwin.

"At £1 per volume, I don't think many working men will be among its audience," he remarked, leafing through it. "Have you read it, Mr Armiger?"

"No, I'm afraid not. I think I've heard of it—certainly heard Godwin discussed in the coffee houses, but I have little idea what it's really about."

"Radical, sir, an out-and-out radical," Robson burst in.

"Really, I think it is a mistake to characterise..."

Miss Somers, who had been listening with attention, took her father by the arm. "Father, we are blocking the doorway, and keeping Mrs Robson waiting."

"Oh yes, my dear. Forgive me," and he moved aside, allowing a pair of old ladies to escape the building.

"Yes, we must be off." The Robsons took their leave.

Somers turned to me. "Are you from Rochford, Mr Armiger? I don't believe we've met before."

"No, from London, sir. I am here to paint some views of a gentleman's residence, which is my profession. Mr Hall, of Hall's Mill. I am staying with him."

"How interesting that must be! We are not acquainted, but I had heard that he was building a new house in the country."

We began to talk about the exigencies of an artist's life and how I found Rochford in comparison with London, before Miss Somers took out her watch.

"Father, if we are to collect the linen and be home in time..."

"Yes, indeed." He shook my hand warmly. "It has been interesting meeting you, Mr Armiger. I hope we may meet again before you return to London?"

I promised that I would come to see him if I could. I'd enjoyed the meeting, too.

THE portrait of Francesca was finished, roughly to my satisfaction, and her family were happy with it. In my room I copied it secretly, both in watercolours and an oil sketch to finish at home. It would be my treasure until I could claim the right to paint her for myself, from life.

I was more than halfway through my time with the Halls and needed to finish the paintings of the house. I'd let them languish a little, but now applied myself. It was hard to work up much enthusiasm, but I did my best. We had decided on a set of six. Four were of the house, being a three-quarter view from each corner, and one each of the view from the road front and the garden front. Next time I came, when the house was finished, I would replicate these perspectives exactly, so that the changes would be obvious.

I made up for the lack of brilliance in the subject by some experimental technique, especially in layering pigments in the shadows, somewhat in the manner of glazing in oil painting. I think it gave them a certain flair. I'd also had the inspiration of depicting each perspective at a different time of day, or in different weather conditions, so that gave them variety as well. The conceit came to me on one of my visits to the site when it began to rain lightly. Fortunately I had happened to be under one of the oaks at the time and decided I liked the pale grey flattened light that the rain and cloud gave the landscape. Other views showed the house in full sun (my first visit), in the early morning and late afternoon. I inscribed them underneath: 'Mr Joshua Hall's new house at Coldbrook in building: Early Morning' *et cetera*. He was delighted.

The passing days concentrated my thoughts on Francesca. I would have to leave in another week; should I speak before I left? I'd spent hours on tenterhooks, trying to gauge how much she cared for me. I watched her closely when Shirlow was present, which irritatingly seemed to be quite often. I could see that he hung about her a great deal, but I couldn't see whether she cared for him. He was so much older than she, and their opinions didn't coincide at all. Only last night we had been discussing literature. Her favourite novels were *The Monk*, which I had enjoyed as a melodrama, and *Camilla*.

"I am going to be quite outrageous now, Mr Armiger, and tell you that my favourite character is not Camilla at all but Indiana, because she is so beautiful. Of course I like Camilla too, and after all, she does marry Edgar in the end. No-one could like Eugenia—she is so ugly! And giving up her lover for her sister! That was quite ridiculous. But it would be so wonderful to be madly in love, as those heroines always are."

I caught her gaze and her eyes held a look of real longing that made my heart beat faster. She had not read Miss Austen's book, which I thought far superior to both, but was excited to hear that I had seen her.

"To see a real authoress! But I expect you have that sort of thing in London all the time," sighing prettily. "I expect all the ladies read, and write, and draw, and speak French, and compose poems. I wish I did." A shadow crossed her face. "Perhaps I could learn to write poems? What do you think, Mr Armiger?"

Shirlow, who was sitting next to her again, remarked in his disobliging manner: "Poems! I would leave them well alone. I thought only women read novels—I have never read one in my life, nor intend to, but I suppose it is different for artists."

"It is," I replied. I felt he didn't like me, and I didn't like him—but I looked at Francesca, and she only smiled. Shirlow took the smile for himself, and returned it with interest, but I thought it was meant for me. People who despise novels and poetry have no interest in works of imagination. I had a wager with myself that he didn't like art either—correctly, as it turned out, because I asked him on purpose later on.

I felt tolerably secure on that front, but I had learned a painful lesson with Belinda. It was not an experience I wanted to repeat, but I decided that I must speak to Francesca before I left Rochford. Her whole course of treatment of me showed that she cared, and I was not in doubt of my own feelings. Her father was another matter. But if she would accept me... then I'd go to him and hope he'd approve.

I had found a useful colourman in one of the small streets near the market and strolled there occasionally. It wasn't that I needed any supplies, but as a matter of course any colourman's shop, cast shop, print-seller or stationer in a new place had to be investigated thoroughly. I'd developed the habit as an excuse to get out of the house or just to stretch my legs. I liked walking but I had to have a purpose to it.

Today I made my way briskly toward the shop, meditating whether I could justify the purchase of a palette knife, which I probably wouldn't use until I got back to London, but it was a different type to the ones Middleton stocked. The streets near the market were unusually crowded and with men, which was odd—usually it was women and servant girls—and all going towards the square. A loud and growing murmuring sounded ahead. I could never resist a spectacle, so I followed along at a good pace. The crowd thickened near the marketplace and I had to force my way through to see what was happening. The voices rose to a roar.

"There they are!" The whole mob surged forward as one, and I with them. "Get hold of 'em!"

"Here—look out!"

"No, you don't!"

Men were shouting and I heard horses neighing, clopping hooves, the iron wheels of wagons, women shrieking. I shoved forward.

In the middle of the market square two loaded drays were stopped, a group of men, some armed with palings and stakes, holding the horses' reins. A burly, red-faced farmer stood in one and a smocked carter in the other. It looked as though they'd just arrived with their produce. Women clustered around the cart's wheels, arguing with the farmer.

"Eight shillings! That's what we want! No more!"

"Fifteen shillings! That's the price! Get away from my cart!" the farmer roared.

"Eight shillings a load! That's the right price!" A stocky ruffian with broken teeth and a pugnacious jaw lunged at him and tried to drag him from the cart. The farmer beat him off with admirable determination. I wouldn't have wanted to fall into the hands of such a fellow.

"Fifteen, you rogues! Get out of my road, or I'll call the law!" He lashed out with his driving whip at the nearest men, who jumped back, except for one young flaxen giant who rushed forward, back hunched under the stroke, caught the whip and wrenched it out of the farmer's hand.

Some in the crowd laughed, while others ran to the backs of the drays and began unloading them. I saw his cargo was sacks of potatoes. Some sacks they dragged away wholesale, or loaded them into barrows, and some they slashed open, scooping the muddy clods into buckets and baskets and making off with them. Stall-holders around the square rushed to help, while others busied themselves securing their own goods. Some took up cudgels and stood ready to defend their stalls. It could only be minutes before someone sparked a riot that would end in blood.

Next to me an old woman, toothless and wizened, crouched to pick up a few that rolled in her direction. As she stretched out her hands scrummaging people, oblivious, trod backwards on her.

"Oh! Sir!" she cried, peering up at me from the dirty cobbles.

I picked her up—she was no heavier than a child. She was clad in a mass of vile-smelling rags, so I was glad to put her down by the railings of a house. Safe, she held out her apron piteously. I didn't know whether it was her appeal, or that the madness of the crowd seized me, but I pushed in among them and gathered up as many as I could, clasping them to my chest until I could drop them in her dirty apron. I managed to get a good many.

The farmer got down onto the road and, seeing his profits vanishing down laneways, began haranguing the crowd and his carter impartially.

"Let go of my horses, you there! Damn you, Burstall, can't you stop them? Get that tailboard up! All right, thirteen shillings! I have to eat too, you know! Stop that! Put them down!" He rushed back and forth, alternately trying to shove the crowd away from his produce and to clear a road to drive on.

Passers-by had formed a small crowd some distance away, so that they could enjoy the performance but had room to flee if the violence became more general. Now two gentlemen in broadcloth (for a moment I thought of Thwaite holding my sleeve) came up to the fringe of the mob and addressed them loudly.

"What's going on here? Why are you behaving like this? Let this man drive on."

"Us can't afford to buy at these prices," one of the men holding the horses' heads answered. "All the corn's been bought up already." He gestured around the stalls. "What are we to eat? Fifteen shillings a load he's wanting for potatoes—that's near twice what it were before! And many of us are out of work." His voice dropped, exhausted.

"Stop that looting and see if we can't come to an arrangement. Come on, my good man—get your people to stop that for a moment."

"They're not my people," he said sullenly, turning away. As he released the bridle I saw the deformity of his wrist and knew him for a shearman. Perhaps he had been one of those 'let go' because of the downturn in trade.

The farmer pushed forward. "Who's asking you to interfere? Fifteen shillings is the price—I can come down a bit, but eight shillings is ridiculous! D'you want me to starve, Mr Townsman?"

Meanwhile, women were yelling: "Eight shillings! No more!"

I didn't know how it would have ended, but I felt the pressure around me lessening and saw the crowd thinning at the edges. In another minute I heard what those farther off had already done—a steady tramp on the cobbles, the clatter of hooves; and a company of soldiers burst into the street, bayonets fixed, led by an officer on a charger.

I had often heard the expression 'bayonets fixed' and it conjured up a pretty image of serried ranks, but the actuality was far from pleasing. There was a very sharp, pointed, glittering appearance to them, which made me instinctively edge away, and worse still was the soldiers' faces. They were fixed in grim contortions and their eyes were blank. They had become a single solid entity of enormous weight, which would march on regardless. Already they were trampling over dropped baskets and brickbats without breaking stride. As they closed on us the black holes of their gun-barrels pointed directly at me. My heart thumped. I turned and ran down a side street.

The soldiers came on, directed by their officer; the mob began to run in all directions, some trying to keep hold of the precious food, others dropping it heedlessly. Children clung to their mothers' skirts or, losing their grip, fell down and were separated. The steady thump of boots went on. Then a whistle blast stopped them. The sound of running feet diminished, leaving the field, or rather, square, to wailing infants, shouting soldiers, and a vast debris of scattered and trampled potatoes, sacks and baskets. I slipped around the corner of a house and found myself face to face with the man who had held the reins.

He looked me up and down, taking in my pale sweating face, his eye lingering on my coat. It was stained with earth. I took out my handkerchief, my hand trembling, and began brushing it off.

"Reckon you let yourself in for more than you'd thought, eh, master?" he asked.

"What was it about?" I needed to hear normal speech, to exchange words with a fellow human. My knees felt feeble.

"Price of bread's beyond a lot of folk now, and corn is scarce—haven't you heard tell of it, in your big house?"

"I have, yes. And that potatoes have gone up too."

"Aye, and butcher's meat, and all. And many are out of work, and can't pay, and the price goes up every week—every market day, sometimes. Folk must eat or starve, so today we thought we'd help ourselves, if they wouldn't bring the price down. And they wouldn't, so we did." He took out a short clay pipe and lit it.

"Why don't you ask the government to help—to fix the price, or something?"

He laughed grimly, exhaling smoke. "Government's all manufacturers and landed gentlemen—or in their pockets—so no government at all, in my book. When did you ever hear of government taking the part of working men?"

"But surely..."

He interrupted unceremoniously. I raised my eyebrows. "Have you never heard of the *Rights o' Man*, master?"

For a moment I could think of nothing, incongruously, but the old French warship the 'Droits de l'Homme', then I remembered Shirlow's remark at dinner—'that radical Paine'.

"Do you mean the book by Tom Paine?"

"Aye—a good book, the best. Paine says government should take care of the poor as are in distress, and beggars, and then it's a good government. But our government sends soldiers to drive away folk that are only trying to feed themselves. That's not right, is it?"

His face was earnest; he hesitated a moment, then touched his cap and walked off, leaving me contemplating being lectured on politics by a workman.

Paine's book was on the long imaginary list of books I meant to read some time. It had been talked about in the clubs and coffee houses when it first came out ten years ago. I recalled that he conflicted with Burke's view of the Revolution in France, that many decried him as a Jacobin, and that he could not enter England for fear of arrest. I was surprised to hear him quoted by a factory worker in clogs in the north Midlands. Godwin, now Paine. When I got back to London I would have to get these books and read them. I should become better informed about these currents of ideas that seemed so prominent up here. Odd that we rarely discussed them at Slaughter's or the clubs. We seemed to have other things to occupy us.

I only got back to the house in time to change for dinner, and managed to get upstairs before anyone saw the state of my coat.

DINNER was bound to be dominated by the marketplace riot. I chose not to say that I'd been there, as I felt my hosts would think me rackety. In my room I'd had time to recover from the abject fear I had felt in the presence of the soldiers. I had never experienced anything like it before. I hadn't thought that I would have been so awe-struck. Thinking about it still gave me a disagreeable sensation in the stomach. At the same time, I had to admit—in the safety of my room—that it had been exciting. I even smiled at the thought of my collecting potatoes in the street for old women. I knew Campbell would disapprove—another of my 'exploits', he'd say—but I wasn't so sure what Francesca would think. She might consider it romantic—or not.

Mr Hall started on it as soon as the soup was served. As a magistrate, he'd been informed during the afternoon in case the Riot Act needed to be read and people imprisoned.

"It'll be frame-breaking next, you mark my words," he said, taking in soup noisily, a sign that he was in a bad temper.

"Oh, no! That would be terrible!" Mrs Hall was in a flutter, twisting her napkin in her hands and picking up and putting down her spoon. "The men won't come here, will they? If only our new house was finished—we'd be able to go there and be right away from them! What shall we do, Mr Hall?"

"Do?" he grunted. "Call out the soldiers, that's what we'll do. I've asked the Lord Lieutenant for a squadron of dragoons, in view of what happened today. Where's the roast?" and he pushed his plate away.

Mrs Hall rang the bell. Miss Hall was apparently lost in her own thoughts, while Francesca made a face at me from behind the centrepiece.

Miss Hall suddenly spoke. "Didn't they call out soldiers today?"

"Yes, but they were only the militia. Dragoons is what we want."

"Did they arrest anyone, Papa?"

"Two men, that was all. Most of the scoundrels ran away."

"Cook said that there were women there, too?"

"They're as bad as the men."

"But if they haven't enough to eat, it must be dreadful."

Mr Hall attacked the roast with some vigour while Jeffreys passed it around. "There's work for those who want it, and there's Poor Relief, for which I'm paying an extra rate, and there's Parish Relief, and if they can't manage on those there's the workhouse. Rioting in the streets is out of the question and I won't see it in Rochford if I've got anything to say about it." He forked in some slices of beef sternly.

"Mr Hall is worried about his factory," Mrs Hall confided, leaning towards me clutching her handkerchief. "It would be so terrible if anything happened. Do you think it will?"

I had no idea—how could I? "I'm sure Mr Hall has everything in hand," was all I could think of. I supposed that he did.

After dinner, when we joined the ladies, Francesca said she had something to show us. She ran out then returned, holding before her a low dress of pale, flowing pink. She twirled around so that the skirt flew out and everyone could admire it. The bodice and hem were decorated with little beads that glittered where the candlelight struck them.

"Do you not like it, Mama? My new silk. It's just finished, so I can wear it to the ball."

"It will look very well, my dear. Don't you think so, Anne? Come here, my love," and she began fiddling with the sleeve. "I think I will just pin this up a trifle."

"Oh, not now, Mama. Mr Armiger hasn't seen it yet," and she danced across the room to me, pressing it to her breast in the most irresistible way and tilting her head. "Now, do you think the colour suits me? I want your true opinion as an artist."

She must have known how absolutely delightful she looked. Her youth and freshness needed no enhancement, but the colour, a pale rose, was the perfect complement to her particular beauty. I felt she was especially putting herself out to attract me, and she was succeeding. If I could get her alone for one moment I would tell her—show her—exactly what I thought. As it was, with the family all ears, I merely said that I thought she would look very well in it indeed, and hoped that my eyes would express my feelings. She smiled, looked into my eyes for a moment, then danced away, leaving my heart thudding.

I had great hopes of the ball. I had already secured two dances—she wouldn't give me more, but they were the first and the last, so I'd be able to help her with her wraps and into the carriage. But it was during the dancing that I planned to get her alone. I couldn't go on agonising about proposing. I lay awake thinking about it, I thought about it when I woke up, I thought about it while I was painting and eating. Thinking about it was interfering with my work. I still didn't know, especially now, how her father would take it, but I would never be easy until I had asked her.

I spent a long time rehearsing my approach. It was the most important of my life. At first I was inclined towards traditional formulas: 'May I solicit the honour of your hand?' *et cetera*. But they did not suit me nor the strength of my feelings, and I thought she would also find them too formal. In the end I decided to speak first of her charms, which would be easy and would engage her attention, move on to my feelings, then to the actual proposal. I thought I would leave the words to arrange themselves at the moment, while determining that they would include the expression that I was 'unable to live without her'. Campbell's warnings sounded in my head, but I had sworn I would try. All I needed now was the opportunity.

Chapter Nine

The next day, having got Hall's permission, I took my pencils and sketchbooks and went to draw in the mill. I'd wanted to do it since I arrived. I was now forward enough with the views to indulge myself.

Compared to the insipid landscapes of the last two weeks, the inside of the great works almost overwhelmed me with visual sensations. The dim interior, pierced with rays of pale sun which lit parts of machines, shafts and workers impartially, made the scene into a tapestry of light and shadow, movement and stillness, limbs and engines. At first I wandered about getting accustomed to it all. It was good to have the freedom to go where I would. I soon settled, propping my large book on an idle piece of apparatus and sketching a corner of the main room. I made two studies in the large book, then got out a smaller pocket book and drew bits of the fascinating architecture, the cogs and beams looming, the dwarfed operatives bent over their work. My pencil flew over the pages like a freed bird. I scribbled details and notes; I didn't know what I was going to do with them but I didn't want to miss this opportunity, which might never come again. The workers paid no attention, except for some of the pinched-looking children, whom the overlookers soon hustled back to their work.

At the meal time I went into the yard and ate a piece of cold ham and egg pie I had from the Hall's cook, while they unwrapped their meagre parcels of food. A little lad leant against the wall not far from me, shoulders hunched, head down, pressed close as though the rough stone could give him sustenance. He wore a man's breeches cut down and tied around his waist with string, and a dirty shirt that had no doubt been his father's. He was not an attractive object.

"Here, boy."

He looked up. I held out the remains of my pie.

He came toward me, eyes fixed on the food. "What do you want, master?"

For some reason this form of address, common in the region, annoyed me. "I'm not your master. Do you want this pie?"

Again the furtive glance, then he drew himself up. "What do I have to do?"

I was getting tired of holding it out. Another boy was sidling towards me, his eyes also on the food. They were like pigeons that had spotted a crust. In another minute there would be a dozen besieging me.

"Do?" I didn't understand. "Do? Nothing. Do you want it or not?"

He ducked his head, hand to forelock, and almost snatched it from my hand. Half disappeared into his mouth instantly, the other half into his shirt. I realised he would take it home for his supper, or perhaps for someone else.

"Thank 'ee, master," he mumbled, mouth full.

His red ears stuck out from his thin face and brown hair fell over his collar. I didn't know how old he was—perhaps eight or nine. Still swallowing, he shuffled rapidly backwards away from me, as though I was a wild beast who might spring at him. Suddenly I was profoundly horrified. One of us was a dangerous animal. I behaved as though it were him; he behaved as though it were me.

The whistle pierced the cold air and as though drawn by a string, the scattered workers massed together and vanished inside. The yard was empty. The filthy windows made pale rectangles in the grimed brickwork; odds and ends of broken barrels and frayed pieces of rope lay in corners, where stealthy dogs nosed for crumbs. I stayed on in my corner, too disturbed to go in.

At last I got up, brushed my coat and returned to the racket of the machines. I looked about for the lad, but didn't see him. He was probably one of those who worked in the scribbling room. I didn't know what to think about the incident in the yard, but I was still troubled.

In the afternoon I drew the workers, not the machines. I thought while I drew, about the riot in the market-place and the children I'd seen there, clambering up on the carts and throwing down food to their mothers. Perhaps they were some of these children or women. They were all small, I noticed. Many were barefoot on the splintered, soiled floor, scabby feet shuffling in the waste under the machines. The conversation I'd had with the man in the street about government had stayed with me and I found I was looking into the faces of the workers as though to discern their thoughts. How many of them could read? How many of them had read Tom Paine?

"I see you can't keep away from the place, master," came a voice I recognised, and I looked up to see Thwaite, who'd shown me round when I first came.

"Yes, but now I'm drawing it, so as to have some mementoes to take back with me."

"You'll be going back to London then?"

"Yes—in a few days. My work here's finished—for now, at any rate."

I was pleased to see him for a particular reason. I wanted to draw some of the workers—studies, not sketches of them at their machines, but I didn't like to ask. I was afraid of causing trouble if I took them away from their work, and after the encounter with the boy I was almost afraid of their attitude to me. But Thwaite was someone I knew.

"I'd like to draw you. Would that be all right?"

"Me! Aye—but—how? Where?" He frowned, concerned about something.

"Well—here, I suppose, and perhaps some time outside, where the light is better."

He plucked at his waistcoat. "Just like this?"

"Yes, but I'd like you to roll up your sleeves."

He laughed, shaking his head, then nodding vigorously.

"What is it?"

He wiped his mouth on his cuff, still smiling. "I don't mind you drawing me, if you've a mind to, master. But I'd heard something about artists, and about their drawing folk—that they drew them without any clothes. I didn't want to disoblige you, but I couldn't be doing with that."

I laughed, and he laughed with me.

"Yes, that's very true, we do draw people without clothes, as you say, but they're usually young ladies—or not ladies," and I winked.

"Not old, worn croppers." We were both serious now.

"That's what I want to draw at this moment. Come, will you roll up your sleeves, and stand here?"

A shaft of light from one of the grimy windows fell by the upright beam that connected the frames to the great power shaft. He stood where I told him, and I drew him emerging from the half-dark, the muscles of his arms modelled by the slanting light, his right leg relaxed, the other bearing his weight and his shoulders tilted in as perfect a contrapposto as Michelangelo could have wished for. He gripped his short clay pipe in his teeth and his dark features were thoughtful. The sketch came out well. I wanted to do an oil of this man, standing just like that next to the frame and the beam, part of the machinery that replaced him, but separate. It would make a splendid pair to the sleeping beggar. Two halves of a story. Perhaps the beggar was a shearman who'd been displaced by the new machines. What was he doing at Bath? Looking for work? There was no woollen industry there. Travelling to see friends or family who had moved there? Probably I'd never know, but I was certain now that he had come from somewhere like this. Two halves of a story—but there was a lot in between that I didn't know, and would like to paint.

I showed him the drawing—in the large book, a half-folio—and he laughed admiringly and called some of his friends over to see it.

"Happen you'll be famous now, Tom," they joked.

"I'd like to paint you as well. Is that possible?" It would have to be in the next few days.

He drew his hand over his mouth again, thinking. I waited.

At last he said: "Sunday. If you can come Sunday, I can do it then."

"Where shall I meet you?"

"You can come to the house—if you've no objection."

"I've no objection."

He told me where it was and we agreed a time. The Halls would be at church, but I would make my apologies. I was already visualising the painting, how I would pose him, and how I would work it up when I got home. I was surprised at how much I was looking forward to it.

On Sunday I saw the family off to Matins, alleging that work kept me at home. I disliked lying, but sometimes it was expedient. I supposed that was how everyone judged their actions. If I had to lie, I tried to make it as small as possible; after all, I was going to work, but I knew perfectly well that they thought it was on the views of New Hall, as I privately called the house. I would have preferred to tell them openly what I was doing but I had an idea that Mr Hall wouldn't like my fraternising with his workmen. That made me feel even worse about my deceit—but off I went, all the same, sketchbook and paintbox under my arm.

His cottage, a small neat place, was in one of the maze of alleys behind the market. He stood at the door to welcome me, pipe in mouth and a little girl hiding behind his legs, arms wrapped round one stockinged calf.

"Now then," he greeted me, removing his pipe. "I wasn't sure you'd come."

He showed me into a room with a good fire in the hearth and two little boys playing on the floor.

"Betsey! Mr Armiger's here."

She came in, leaning backward to balance her prominent belly, holding on to the door-frame for a moment, and putting down an infant she was carrying. She was a small woman with the remains of fair prettiness and still with a spark in her eyes.

"My wife, Mr Armiger." His voice was affectionate. "Sal!" a big girl of ten or twelve appeared. "Take the bairn for Mam, and bring us tea."

"I don't need any tea, thank you."

"You won't refuse to sup with us?"

I saw I'd injured his pride. "No, that would be delightful, thank you."

When the whole family was assembled the room could hardly hold us. We sat at a table covered with a red rep cloth while the children crouched in front of the fire making toast. I looked around at the pottery dogs on the mantelshelf, a handful of fairings and seashells, relics of a trip to Grimsby or Cleethorpes, arranged on the dresser next to a short row of books.

"You've a fine family, Mr Thwaite," I said, sipping cautiously. The tea was hot and the cups old-fashioned ones without handles.

"Aye," he replied, a rueful note in his voice. "They're gradely but us can't seem to stop them coming," nodding towards his wife's belly. From the look of her figure, her time could not be far off.

She flushed but smiled and pulled the biggest girl towards her, an arm round her waist. "Our Sally's my great help, aren't you, lass?" she said fondly.

The girl stuck her chin up. "I'm Mam's help, and next year I'm going into service, after the new bairn's weaned."

Thwaite nodded. "I don't want my bairns going into the mill. It's all slave labour now, not like when I were a lad. Then my father were his own master, and I were, too, before the machines come along and ruined it for us."

"Hush, Tom," his wife said. "Mr Armiger doesn't want to hear about all that."

"On the contrary, Mrs Thwaite, I would like to hear about it, but I'd like to paint at the same time, if I may?"

I'd brought the large book, with good stiff wove paper, and showed her the drawing I'd done of Thwaite at the mill standing by the beam, pipe in his mouth, and she laughed and called the children to see it.

"That's the spit and image of him, Mr Armiger. That's wonderful. I'd know him anywhere, of course, but that's really him," she repeated, putting up a hand to wisps of hair escaping from her cap.

I asked for a pot of water and set up my paintbox on a bench. I had meant to paint Thwaite outdoors, but now I'd seen him among his family I liked the idea of capturing him in his natural setting. I got him to sit by the window—the room was dark and the sky low, but the light was enough.

"Are these your books?"

"Aye, they are."

"Would you like to take your favourite?" He picked up a worn volume, the dark blue buckram frayed on the spine, and opened it on his knee. "Perfect." I began to draw rapidly.

Sometimes I began a drawing hesitantly, not sure where it was going, or what I was trying to achieve. Then it either gathered force or petered out, or after some tedious work was just good enough. Sometimes I just drew away, noting down the details of the scene, accurately enough but dully—a job of work, that was all. At other times, usually when the subject was interesting and perhaps novel, the pencil could hardly leave its trace on the page fast enough to keep up with my thoughts, and every mark was right, every shadow, no matter how hurried, precise. So it was today. The children gathered behind me to watch the strange man draw Papa, but didn't disturb me: Thwaite puffed on his pipe, gazing out the little window, his hands holding the well-used book.

I drew and drew, then turned to the paintbox and began to apply washes, dark at first for the background, the cottage interior, recklessly wiping off pale patches to stand for the pottery dogs, the circles of plates on the dresser, the oval of his wife's face bent over the baby. A wash of scarlet for his waistcoat—good—slash over it, wet in wet, some darker colour mixed with umber for the creases. A touch of Prussian, and flick it into the wet shadows to liven them. Push a brushful of dark ochre over the ceiling; run it down the wall by the door. Scrape it with the end of the brush for planks. I'd washed his face and hands in with pale ochre mixed with a drop of Sienna; his hair was darker, as were the shadows on the side of his face where his teeth holding his pipe gave his jaw its characteristic shape. And while I worked he talked, first reminiscing about his early life, when he and his father had worked side by side in the finishing shop, then about his growing interest in politics since the machines came in.

"I were lucky, because our father believed in education, and taught me to read and figure. He wanted me to be able to be my own master, and not be beholden to any man."

"Is it so very different?"

He took the pipe from his mouth and looked at me. "Happen you'd rather work for a master, than for yourself? I don't know how it is in your trade—or—business—I don't rightly know what to call it, being a painter."

"Sometimes we work for ourselves, and you're quite right, I do prefer it. Sometimes we work on commission—that's when..."

He interrupted, and I was struck again by the pride of these men. "I know what commission is—when they tell you what they want, and you do it for a price. That's the same in our trade."

"Yes—the same. I make paintings to order. It's not often you can make a living out of doing what you like."

"But the way things are now, we have to work for the mill-owners, and they make money out of our work, and we make nowt—or very little. They grow fat, and we grow thin." There was sadness as well as rancour in his tone.

"How is it they have come to take over all the trade so quickly?" As I spoke I recognised it was a stupid question, and one I knew the answer to.

"Because they have money to buy engines that do the work of many men, and put them in mills, and the small shops can't compete with their prices."

"But you've told me that the work was laborious and took years to learn. Surely it's a good thing to have engines to do these hard jobs?"

"Aye, it sounds well enough, but then what work will there be for us? And our bairns after us?" nodding towards his children, "and who'll know the old skills?"

"Won't there be work for them in the factories?"

"You might think so. Look at scribbling, though—they were the first to come in, after the gig mills. A lad or a lass can produce in fourteen hours, with a mill, what took a man ninety or a hundred hours."

I must have showed my surprise, for he smiled ironically. "You didn't think it made so much difference? And scribbling's only one part of it. Spinning, that's been done by machine now for a long while. Then the gig mills came in."

"I thought they'd been invented quite a long time ago? Wasn't there some petition taken to Parliament about them"—ages ago, when I was at the Schools—"and they made them legal?" And I'd never thought then that, as a professional artist, I'd ever find myself drawing one, or have its workings explained to me, or be sitting in a tiny cottage painting a man who worked one.

"Aye, that were Gloucestershire cloth-dressers got up a petition to try to get 'em kept for coarse cloth—blankets and the like; but the mill-owners had brass, and influence, so Parliament did what they wanted, and now Hall's and Shirlow's and all of 'em have gig mills for fine cloth. So it's like scribbling mills—a man and two young ones can do in twelve hours what used to take a grown man ninety or a hundred."

"I can see why the masters like the machines."

"Aye, and machines don't break down—or not much—and complain, and want time off to see to their wives and bairns, or want more pay. So you can see why men get up combinations and institutes to speak for them, since the government is all for them as has brass, and don't care about them as don't." He patted a page of the book on his knee.

"*The Rights of Man*?" I enjoyed his surprise.

"Have you read it?"

"No, but I've heard of it, and I'm going to read it when I get home."

A tap at the door and the sound of voices. Mrs Thwaite

heaved herself up in some confusion, smoothing her hair, and looked anxiously at her husband. Sally ran to the door.

"It's Mr Somers and Miss, Mam."

Thwaite got up and his wife went to the door. The children left me and ran after her. Mr Somers came in, stooping under the lintel, followed by Miss Somers with a basket.

"How do you do, Mrs Thwaite? And Sarah? And the children? Mr Thwaite?" He put out a hand, which Thwaite took, ushering him towards the fire.

I too, had got out of my chair and put down my book.

"Why, Mr Armiger! I did not know that you were acquainted with my friend Thwaite. What a pleasure to see you again! But we have interrupted your visit," turning to Mrs Thwaite. "If it's not convenient—but Rachel had some things for you, and we thought we would drop in after the service."

The small room was full of awkwardness, people looking at each other.

"I can go—finish it another time," I said, putting my pencils and brushes in the box.

"Pray, sir, do not go on my account—our account," said Somers.

I took his hand, which was warm and his grip strong. "But I don't want to prevent your visit."

"You remember my daughter Rachel." We bowed. She had thick, waving, light brown hair and an open forehead.

"Don't go, Mr Armiger," Thwaite said. He rubbed his chin, looking at his wife for inspiration. "Mr Armiger is taking my likeness."

"Sally, take the children to the other room, and fetch some hot water."

Mrs Thwaite began to take cups from the dresser and, now that we were to stay, we all found somewhere to sit.

"No tea, please, Elizabeth—we have just had some." Miss Somers had a pleasant voice. She took a pile of white cloths out of her basket and handed it to Mrs Thwaite. "It is just a few things for the baby. I know you are short of linen, and I came upon these, which I thought would be useful. I've washed them..." and the women went into a huddle over the little garments.

"I remember you said you were painting some views, but instead I see you are painting Mr Thwaite." Somers' smile took any offence from the words. "May I see it? Or shouldn't one ask?" His manner was so engaging that I showed him the page, although I usually dislike anyone seeing unfinished work.

"It's only half-done."

"But very interesting, all the same—it isn't often that one gets to see a work at this stage of completion. I think I can see how it will be. But we have stopped you from working. Please go on."

I looked at Thwaite, who answered by taking up his seat again with the book on his lap. There wasn't going to be another opportunity, and I had been disappointed at the thought of leaving it, especially when it had been going so well. I took out my brushes again, wet them in the pot and began where I'd left off.

"I see you have your favourite book out," Somers remarked. Despite their disclaimers Mrs Thwaite had brought tea and he sipped as he talked. His hands were long and lean and I thought I'd like to draw them. He had the beaky profile that seems so often to go with clergy, when they're not meaty and florid.

"Aye, and we were just talking about it."

"Are you a disciple of Paine, Mr Armiger?"

"I hardly know. I have heard something of his ideas, but I have yet to read it."

"I have my reservations. You will understand that I have limited enthusiasm for an author who seems to advocate doing away with the established church, as the revolutionaries across the Channel have done."

"Aye, but when church and government are just for the rich, and them as own land, what are working men to do? And in these times—price of wheat's up again, and we can scarce get bread. And now Hall's and Shirlow's—aye, and Croker's, and the others, are talking of getting in new frames, and that'll be more men turned off."

"I know, and I know it is a great deal to bear. I heard there was trouble at the market the other day and some men were taken up. Rachel has been to see some of the wives. We are raising funds for a Soup Shop. It's only small at present, but we hope soon to be able supply a nourishing hot meal to all those in want."

"That's good news, Mr Somers, for them as can't work, but what us croppers want is work. We're willing, but what can we do when they bring in frames that'll do the work of six men?" Thwaite's voice was keen and his colour had risen.

"We must think of the consequences of our actions. Such uproar as there was the other day can't be good for anyone. It is not right to have violence and public disturbances."

I wasn't going to admit that I'd been there, but I wanted to say something about the market riot. I could see those glittering points and grimacing faces, very set and white, in my mind. Painting away, and keeping my eyes on my work, I said:

"The militia were called out and I know there's been talk of dragoons. It's a bad thing, I think, when the authorities feel that the right response to problems among the people is to bring armed troops against them. There must be a better way. The troops should be in Spain, fighting other soldiers, not old women and children." Reverend Somers smiled. "Do you hear that, Rachel? Here is an artist from London, who has sympathy for our poor. It's good to hear, sir, that you have a Christian conscience."

"Well, I don't know about that." I did attend church—usually—but would hardly rate myself an ardent believer.

Thwaite broke in. "What's to become of workers, then, who can keep a roof over their heads now and a decent home for their wife and bairns, and put bite and sup on the table? When prices go up and up, are we meant to do nothing, until we're starving?"

Miss Somers looked up from where she was sorting clothing by the dresser. Her voice was low but clear. "You mentioned dragoons. I hope they won't come, because although they control the crowds, I believe they make things worse. But I hope they won't be sent. Earl Fitzwilliam said the other day that 'outrage and conspiracy are the offspring of distress and want of employment fostered and rendered formidable by nothing but the want of trade'."

Her father nodded. "Yes, he's a good man. It is very encouraging to see someone in that station in society with those views."

"Who is Earl Fitzwilliam?"

"The Lord Lieutenant of the county. I'm afraid he is in the minority, but there are some good men, men of conscience. Let's just hope he can influence his fellows, and especially the magistrates. Is there much discussion of these issues in London, Mr Armiger?"

SHORTLY afterwards the Somers took their leave. He shook my hand warmly. "It was a happy chance that brought us together again, Mr Armiger. If you should happen to be in Rochford in the future, you would be welcome at the Rectory. You will always find me at St Saviour's." I promised that I would. He was an educated man, and kindly, and his daughter was pleasant. I'd enjoyed the meeting, too.

BY the time the Somers left the day was drawing in, the candles had been lit and I was packing my things away. I showed the family the finished study. I was pleased with it and we all admired it together.

"Thank you for the tea, Mrs Thwaite. It was a pleasure to meet you and your family."

Thwaite put out his strong hand. "It were good of you to come. You'll think on those things—what we talked of?"

I said I would, and meant it. His sincerity and passion had struck me deeply.

"Happen we'll meet again."

"I hope so."

Chapter Ten

Mr Hall's barouche took us to the ball in comfort. I had been afraid that Shirlow would have been asked to dine and make one of the party, but he wasn't. The Assembly rooms were freshly decorated in the Adam style, with tall pier glasses between the windows and sculptured plaster decorations girdling the ceiling and trailing down the pale pink walls.

The Halls had a wealth of acquaintance and I was introduced to fourteen or fifteen people in succession. I had never been less interested in meeting new people, which I found burdensome at any time and especially when I was never going to see them again. Then it occurred to me that if my hopes were realised, I would see a great deal more of these Ibbotsons and Crokers and McIlwraiths, and numerous other large red-faced men and well-got-up ladies in slightly out-of-date fashions, who almost universally greeted me with: 'So you're the young fellow Hall's got to draw his house'. I was not very pleased with any of this. If—when—we were married, we would of course live in London. I had not quite determined what we would live on, but Francesca had hinted more than once that her father would give her a handsome portion, whoever she married, which had reassured me immensely.

The orchestra had already begun and I claimed her for my dance. I spent the time thinking of how to approach her. It was divine dancing with her; her smiles and dimples were ecstasy. Her behaviour in the last few days made me certain she cared for me. I kept hearing her voice—'madly in love'. The idea that she could be mine by the end of the evening was a sort of exquisite agony. I wanted to crush her in my arms. The dance ended.

"Oh! I do wish it could go on for ever—don't you?" She looked up at me, laughing.

"Yes, I do. Perhaps it can.""

"How do you mean?"

We were standing in the middle of the floor, surrounded by people.

"We could go on..."

"I say, Miss Hall, I believe this is mine?" A pink young man in tight breeches offered his hand.

She relinquished my arm and took his. "Oh, yes, Mr Dawes, I believe you're right." The band began a country-dance and they walked off. She looked back at me, her eyes sparkling. I watched them out of sight, then went and danced with Mrs Hall and Miss Hall.

"I hope you have enjoyed your stay," Miss Hall said. She danced well, although without her sister's flair.

"I have, thank you. It has been most interesting."

"I hope you will come back to us some time."

"I expect to be back in three or four months, to draw the house again."

"Oh, that's right, I had forgotten."

How could she have forgotten? I had the impression again that she meant to say something else altogether.

The evening dragged on. I was waiting for the last dance. I was going to get Francesca alone if I had to abduct her. Either that, or make my declaration in the middle of the cotillion. I roamed about vaguely, dancing with the wives or daughters of people I was introduced to and hiding in the card-room or supper-room in between.

At last my turn came. I claimed her and we went to the middle of the room where the set was forming, but as soon as there were people around us I drew her to one side. There was a sort of alcove with palms in pots at one end of the main room, where ladies sat out. It would have to do.

She looked up at me, panting slightly from her exertions. The dancing had brought a high colour to her cheeks and neck and she had never looked more ravishing.

"Miss Hall, there's something I want to say to you."

"Oh, so solemn!" The orchestra began playing the quadrille. "Shouldn't we go? I don't want to miss it."

"In a moment—Francesca, please." It was the first time I'd used her name. I put my hand on her arm.

She stopped. "Yes, Mr Armiger?" Her eyes were cast down demurely, but she didn't take away her arm.

We stood together in silence for a moment.

"I have known you for some time now and ever since we met, I have..."

While I tried to frame the right words, Mr Innes appeared in the distance.

Francesca glanced up. "Oh dear, there is Mr Innes. Papa has probably sent him to find out where we are."

She did not change her pose, but the interruption threw me out.

"Please ignore him, perhaps he won't see us. Francesca, I was saying that..." The wretched man entered the alcove and came towards us. I gritted my teeth. "I must speak to you—please!"

She put her hand over mine for an instant and gave me one of her brilliant smiles. "Another time would be better. How do you do, Mr Innes?"

He bowed over her hand while I moved away a step or two. "Very well, Miss Francesca—how do you do, Mr Armiger? Your father wants you. May I take you to him?"

She went off on his arm while I gazed after them, furious, relieved and disappointed. She gave me one backward glance, which I couldn't decipher. I walked into the card room and drank a large glass of brandy. I wished Campbell had been there to confide in. Then I got another brandy, sat down, and tried to think.

It felt like the time I'd been out hunting and rushed towards a big fence, heart in mouth, the rest of the field at my elbow, ears full of the sound of the horns, baying hounds and galloping hooves, and just as I put in the spurs and rose to take the fence, the horse—a hack from a livery stable—dug his toes in and I went straight over his head, and all I knew for some time was the pain in my back and hoofbeats diminishing into the distance, while I lay alone in the stubble. I had lost her. I'd tried, and had lost. It was as bad as it had been with Belinda all those years ago, but worse, because I wanted Francesca so much more.

But was it really that bad? Perhaps it was the heat of the brandy or the calming effect of a cigar, but after a while I began to feel that perhaps it was not quite as bad. I reconstructed our conversation. She had not actually refused me. In fact—it took me some time to realise this—I had not actually asked her. In my heart I had, and my head was full of it, but in point of fact the words had not yet emerged from my mouth. Then I began to remember more hopeful things. She had not moved her arm away from my hand—I could still feel her warm soft skin under my palm. She had not objected when I called her Francesca. She'd let me speak. She had put her hand on mine! My fingers quivered at the thought. The words she'd used began to come back to me. Yes—she'd said 'another time'! 'Another time would be better'! I sat up, forgetting my drink and cigar. That was real encouragement! It was as good as telling me to ask again! Now I was too happy and excited to stay still, so I rushed out into the ballroom in time to admire her dancing vivaciously with an officer. In her silk dress she was the most beautiful girl in the room, and she had asked me to 'come again'. I could hardly wait.

For the next two days my entire being was focussed on trying to get a moment alone with Francesca. I got up in good time the morning after the ball and found myself alone at breakfast. The servants looked at me disagreeably; I think they had spent the evening in their own revelries, depending on the family coming down late, and were not pleased at having to attend me. I ate some toast, drank tea and read the morning paper. Eventually Mr Hall appeared, then Mrs, and Miss Anne. We enquired how each other had slept, and congratulated each other on a delightful ball. No sign of Francesca. At last I couldn't stand it.

"I hope Miss Francesca is quite well?"

Her mother paused, toast in hand. "She has a headache and is resting. She danced too much last night, I thought, and we stayed too late. We should have come away earlier, Mr Hall. You know I wished it."

He rustled his paper angrily. No doubt he had a headache too. I was not feeling altogether well myself, and if I had known Francesca wouldn't be down for breakfast I would have stayed in bed too.

"You're going back to London tomorrow, then," the maid observed with some satisfaction while she tidied my room. Perhaps she resented the extra work my presence—especially in the old schoolroom—had caused her, or perhaps she was hinting for a large tip.

I smiled brightly. "Yes, that's right, but I won't forget how obliging you have been."

She rewarded me with a smile, and when she turned away

I rewarded her by pinching her backside. She gave a squeak and ran out of the room.

It was the only diversion of the day. I hung about awkwardly all morning, then went for a walk. It was one of those crisp autumn days when the blue sky draws you outdoors, where you discover how cold it is and wish you had worn a muffler. I went to the George and Dragon and bought my ticket for tomorrow's coach, and took the opportunity to drink some brandy in the hopes of it improving my temper. Then I returned and packed up some of my things. Mr Hall was in his office; Mrs Hall was engaged about the house; Miss Hall was writing letters. I didn't feel like drawing, and had already written to Campbell and my landlady to tell them I was coming home.

Francesca came down to dinner after the bell had rung, looking a little pallid and downcast but as beautiful as ever. Dinner was *en famille*, so we didn't sit long with the wine, and spoke mainly about my journey tomorrow, the progress of the building works (which were going on at a great pace), and when I would come back to draw the finished house. When Mr Hall and I got into the drawing-room Francesca was doing her filigree-work and Miss Hall was rolling the papers for her. I sat by them and we talked about the ball, but after a little while she said she was tired and the ladies all went up. She did not seem very happy. I wondered whether it was my imminent departure or whether her father, who also seemed out of sorts, had been scolding her again.

Tomorrow would be my last day. The coach left in the evening. I had to speak to her tomorrow. I couldn't leave without knowing.

The coach lumbered over the moor, the wind whistling through the cracks around the windows and doors. I had brought a book, but it was too dark and I was too unhappy to read.

I had spent yet another day doing no work and effectively nothing at all. In the morning Mr Hall insisted on taking me out to Coldbrook to inspect progress on the house. They had pulled down the old farm. When we got back I went immediately to find Francesca. I heard her singing; she was in the drawing room—with her mother, sister and Shirlow.

When I came in she gave me a meaning glance, and when she finished her song she came over and put her hand on my arm.

"I am so glad you've come. I was afraid you would go without seeing you."

"I'm glad, too. I wanted to see you before I left." She pressed my arm lightly.

At that moment I almost thought we were engaged and I was ready to go to her father before I left.

"Francesca, my angel, come and show Mr Shirlow that Italian song you have the music for. We were just speaking of it. Which is it?" Mrs Hall was shuffling through sheets of manuscript by the pianoforte.

She ran back and began handing pieces of music to Shirlow.

"So, you're going back to London. I hope you've had a pleasant visit. Will we see you again soon?"

Shirlow was very affable all of a sudden. I hoped it had nothing to do with my going.

We discussed the progress of the house at Coldbrook and the possibility of riots until the bell rang for dressing, when I found that Shirlow was to stay to dinner. There was literally not a single moment when I could speak to Francesca alone. I was fairly sure Mr Hall had arranged it all on purpose. If so, that meant he knew of my feelings and opposed the match. Desperately anxious and furious, I was obliged to maintain a pleasant demeanour. I thought of coming out into the open, taking him aside, asking him straight out for her hand. But if he refused, I had nothing to fall back on. I had hoped that if I could secure Francesca's consent first, her happiness might override her father's concerns. But there was no opportunity.

As soon as dinner was over the footman came; my baggage had been taken to the George and Dragon; the coach was about to leave. I found myself outside the door in my greatcoat shaking hands with the whole family—and Shirlow—before I could think. Ten minutes later I was in the coach taking me away from Rochford. I had one memory to carry away, of Francesca pressing my hand in her little one.

Nothing had been settled.

My studio looked both familiar and alien, like a friend you haven't seen for a long time and has had his hair cut differently. Everything was cold and covered in dust, and smelt stale.

I was trying to create some sort of order the next day when Campbell arrived. It was good to see him and I needed to get back into the routine of work.

"I'm glad to see you. How was the north? Have you decided on your Competition entry? What did you think of mine? Did you get my letter about the Philosophers? How did you get on with Miss Hall?"

He threw himself down on the sofa. "I brought you a bottle of claret and some biscuits, since I thought you'd have nothing in." I lit the stove and gave him an edited version of my time at Rochford.

"Are these the sketchbooks you took? You don't mind?" and he started leafing through them. "This is the house? A great pile of a place, is it not?" He paused over some rough sketches of Francesca—sitting in the window, taking a turn around the drawing-room, and a few of her family similarly employed. "And how did you leave things with the beautiful younger Miss Hall?"

"I hardly know. I don't want to talk about it."

"Tchah. It was that bad?"

"Not necessarily. I really don't know. I'm trying to forget about it at the moment because I must get on with the Competition work. Have you started yours? Incidentally, Miss Anne Hall asked me to convey her compliments to you and hopes you are well."

He looked thoughtful. "Did she, now? That was kind. I hope she is in good health?"

"As far as I could see. A pleasant woman, although quiet."

"Aye, and with a great deal of sense—prudence."

"Has she? I hadn't noticed. A pity she doesn't have her sister's looks—it must be hard on her." As soon as I spoke I realised I'd put my foot in it.

Campbell had gone quite pink. "Miss Francesca is very beautiful, I'll grant you that, but 'beauty will wither and die', as the Scripture says. Miss Hall has more lasting qualities."

Well! I'd never heard Campbell speak so brusquely. "Er—yes, I suppose so." Campbell had no idea of beauty in a woman, if he could think that the difference between Francesca and her sister was unimportant.

"Aye. Aye. Well now, what think you of my scheme of the Philosophers? I have it well under way. I've written to them all to get permission to paint them and have begun arrangements. In the mean time, I'm working out the composition. Look, here's a sketch...," and he pulled a piece of paper out of his pocket and unfolded it.

We discussed his painting for some time. I found it hard to work up the required enthusiasm. The subject was worthy but I had the feeling that I'd seen it many times already. I always felt that a group portrait was an awkward thing. However elegantly you managed to pose the individuals, it was hard to make them look natural.

"It's like that Zoffany picture of the Royal Academicians in 1772. I never look at it without feeling that the *écorché* cast is about to strike Wilson, who looks as though he's had too much to drink, on the head, and as for Cosway standing in the foreground with his nose up and poking his stick in the belly of that female torso, it makes me wince."

Campbell sniffed. "It's old-fashioned now, I grant you, but it's a fine piece of work all the same. Ingenious. It's about time they had another one."

"A good commission for you."

He smiled, shaking his head. "After I get this finished! But I do want to imitate Zoffany in one thing—the way he's caught the character of each man—not just their features."

We talked about canvas sizes—he'd already bought one, three yards wide. "A large painting attracts the judges' attention and gives it importance."

"Agreed—provided it doesn't magnify its deficiencies!" I'd come to the same conclusion about my own entry. "Have you heard how everyone else's are coming on?"

Campbell nodded. "Aye. Quayle is being exceptionally secretive but the rumour is that he has his Dido well under way, and that he has consulted with the President several times. He's also been dining with Sir George Beaumont and someone saw him coming out of Angerstein's on Tuesday. No-one has seen Hallett at all, he's supposed to be in France, but that model of his is always hanging around Slaughter's. Alcock is said to be working on a conversation piece, but no-one has seen it."

All this made me feel as though I'd been away for a very long time, and was very behind-hand with my work. There had also been a heap of bills waiting for me.

THE next day I went to Middleton's and bought a canvas for Agamemnon. After inspecting what they had, I paid a guinea for a ready-made canvas a little smaller than Campbell's—about six and a half feet. It was expensive but I needed to get to work. His prepared canvasses were excellent, with two or three layers of lead white and chalk mixed with oil and separated by strata of gluc size. When I got it home I rubbed it back and applied another layer of size, as I wanted a really good surface, and not too absorbent, or the pigments would dry too quickly.

I unpacked the colours I'd bought and put them away. The studio was cold and empty. I thought of going down to Slaughter's or the John O'Groats for some ale and conversation, but discarded the idea. It would just be putting off the moment of starting. I tidied up a bit, looked at the canvas, got out the studies I'd done for it up north. Then I sat down and thought about Francesca. Work was impossible. I felt as though all the energy I'd had for work, and for this Competition, had been drained away by my feelings for her and the different experiences I'd had in Rochford. Images of Thwaite and his family in their cottage, clacking machinery, the dark mill, Miss Hall saying 'my sister is very charming' and a thousand impressions of Francesca herself, flitted through my mind. If only... no wonder I was so unsettled. I used to be a good worker. My short time away had completely disrupted me. But work was now an urgent necessity. Some of the fee I'd got from Hall had already gone on the two journeys, the new canvas, left-over expenses from Bath. And the Competition. I had to start soon to have any chance at all. I jumped up, put on my coat and hat and went out.

I wandered through the Park, thinking about Rochford and Francesca, drawing Thwaite in his little home and talking politics with the Somers. They were good people. I ought to write to Mr Somers, as he had suggested. The sky arched blue over the lawns, bringing brilliance to the avenues. At this time of year it was all massed russets, ambers and golds set against greenish grass. It was one of those fine days in late autumn when winter still seemed far off, although cold nights had already withered leaves and dried sap. The air held the acrid smell of crushed leaves. The pale afternoon sun lit the limes, gilding the knotted brown trunks and clear delicate leaves veined with green. They were still festooned with their odd brown fruits, each ball suspended from its single brown wing. I used to play with them as a boy. If you joined two together they became a bird's wings, with a ball for a head and another wing for a tail. I used to love collecting seeds and leaves of different trees and grasses, and thought myself an amateur of natural philosophy. I'd come home with my pockets full and arrange them in geometric patterns, until my room became full of scattered drifts crunching underfoot and the maid swept them up. I thought I knew even at the time that it was their shapes and textures interested me more than their classification.

My favourites were horse chestnuts, or conker trees, as I had innocently called them. There were still some shrivelled spiky shells on the ground under them now, and their browning leaves kept up a mournful rustling. I thought nothing of the sort in nature exceeded the beauty of a freshly-peeled conker, red-brown and glossy. The Guards clopped by. No sight evoked England for me as powerfully as the Life Guards trotting down the avenue in spring, scarlet coats glowing and black horses standing out against the bright green leaves and massed candelabra of white flowers. I had seen fine landscapes in Europe and elsewhere in England, but none seemed quite as English to me as a great park with ancient trees. The most impressive landscape, particularly in a sublime way, was

Alpine, massive distant crags covered with snow, plunging rocky chasms and so forth, but there were moods when soft rolling meadows or a lake at twilight were more to one's taste. That was one of the things I liked about Wordsworth.

These musings brought me to the park gate, and I returned home in a better frame of mind for work.

THE big easel's wheels rumbled as I dragged it across to the middle of the floor. I wound the ledge down and put the new canvas on it. Then I set up my work table at my right hand, laid out my studies, put on the old velvet dressing gown I worked in and took up a nice new Borrowdale pencil. I'd decided to draw straight onto the canvas, rather than enlarging and transferring my preliminary drawings. I wanted it to have a vitality I was afraid it would lose if I followed the usual method. I glanced at the sketches and began drawing out the composition in broad sweeping gestures. The pencil grated pleasingly on the canvas. Fine particles showered onto my hand. Here, the head of Agamemnon; a broad curve for the line of the bay; here, the rise of the hill; a scribble for the distant figures and the galleys on the beach. I stood well back, sketch in hand, checked the proportions and perspective, then went in and corrected them. After a time I took a piece of bread and rubbed off the excess lead, leaving only the pale outlines.

When I was satisfied with the outlines I rubbed it again and began to set my palette. During my long cogitations while I was at Rochford and in the coach there and back (an excellent place for thinking—there was nothing much else to do, and the rumble of the wheels and steady clip-clop led to a sort of meditation), I had decided that I'd treat the whole thing as though it was a watercolour. So instead of starting out with a coat of dead colour to set the tones, I went straight in over the creamy-pink size and greyish lines with thinned pigment in coloured washes, the way I would with a landscape sketch. Outside, the rain streamed down steadily. It didn't matter. I was on the beach at Aulis.

I planned to contrast warm and cool areas, as Wright of Derby did, which had worked well for me in smaller pieces, so I laid in great sheets of ochre tinted with Indian red over the central section (leaning to the left) where the hero would stand, spread out a yellower ochre along the strand and washed the sky and sea with Prussian blue mixed with a little umber. The colours were pale and bright, but no matter. There were many layers to go over them yet, and if they were too glaring when I finished, I'd put a glaze over them. Much easier to darken a bright area than brighten a dull one. If the layer underneath was too dark, it would still shadow through and drag down the lighter layers you paint on top, and I wouldn't have time for a lot of scraping back.

I worked steadily until the light started to go, then stood back and looked it over. The whole canvas was covered with colour and tone and the main shapes were blocked in. It looked all right. I turned it upside down and studied it again. It still looked all right. The composition was balanced, but not too obviously; the main lines were diagonal, which would give it movement; the tones and colours were well distributed over the whole canvas, and I could envisage what it would look like when the upper layers of paint, and especially the figures, were put in. The whole arrangement swirled around the off-central figure of Agamemnon, as I'd planned. At present he was only a looming mass against a bluish sky, almost one with the rock he stood on. He was the key. I must get him right. Tomorrow I would start on Agamemnon.

Chapter Eleven

When I was not working I was despondent, bad-tempered and fidgety. I needed constant distraction and anything I did in that way still left me irritable. The remedy was obvious, but one of the odd things was that I felt disinclined for work and did everything in my power to avoid starting. I tidied the studio; put my colours in order; cleaned my brushes; arranged my books—anything. The effort of will needed to begin was extraordinary. Time and experience enabled me to identify what was happening and to know how to rectify it, but had not given me the power to avoid it. I couldn't work consistently without getting into these ups and downs. I supposed I had got a little better at just getting on with it—advice that I always gave to pupils, while being acutely conscious that it was a glaring case of 'don't do as I do, do as I say'.

The secret was not to get deflected, not allow other things to intervene and take me away from the work. Once the thread was broken it was hard to restore, but I was easily distracted—one of my great failings. If I hadn't liked other things so much—going out, eating, the company of friends, walking in the park, peering into shops—I would do a great deal more work and perhaps be correspondingly famous and successful. It was my own fault. Sometimes I wondered if I was just not ambitious enough.

Best not to think about it, but to get a little piece of paper and make a bit of a sketch, or better still, take out one I had already started and touch it up a bit. With effort, and after a while, I would eventually be working away, humming to myself, filled with energy, ignoring meal times until I came to a point where I'd be content to break off for a while. Then I could hardly wait to get back to the work and sit down in front of the canvas again, still with a biscuit in one hand while I dabbed away with the brush in the other.

Usually it worked. But this time I knew what the problem was. It had a name: Francesca. I had made a good start with Agamemnon but after a day or two, while I worked away fruitlessly at it, making it rather worse than better, she interposed herself, all charm and gaiety. I went to bed thinking about the canvas and woke thinking of her. I tried everything I knew. I went to Vauxhall Gardens one night and got drunk on punch as a form of relief, and in the hope that it would upset my system and that I'd be able to return to work. It only gave me a headache and the feeling that I'd blabbed more of my feelings than I'd meant to. And not working in itself made me irritable.

After a fortnight of this I gave in and bought a ticket to Rochford. I couldn't really afford it and had no idea what I was going to tell them up there as to why I'd suddenly turned up. I was so dispirited that I hardly cared. The only consolation was a very cordial letter from Mr Somers, continuing some of the discussion we'd had at Thwaite's, recommending some reading and hoping that we might meet again. If things went well I might call on him.

THIS time I boarded the coach at the Saracen's Head in Holborn without any paraphernalia, only a bag with a few clothes and a book to read on the journey. Last time it had been the *Lyrical Ballads* and I had been reflecting on 'emotion recollected in tranquillity', but this time there was no tranquillity and very few emotions that I wanted to recall. Mr Somers had suggested Wilberforce's *A Practical View of the Prevailing Religious System of Professed Christians*, but it was far too heavy for my mood, so I compromised with *The Rights of Man* and Godwin's *Caleb Williams*, (also on my list of books to read for years), which I'd got from the Circulating Library. The coach was full, chilly and airless and it was hard to read. The weather forbade sitting on top and admiring the scenery, so I had to listen instead to a capitalist with a doughy face complaining about the progress of the war in Spain—'Wellington has done nothing, nothing at all, since Talavera. He has no conception of the effect the war has on business at home. They ought to have given the command to Lord Moira', *et cetera*, while the lady next to me in a wealth of black lace, on her way north to her mother's funeral, sniffed continually under her veil and poked me in the ribs with her multitude of umbrellas and baskets.

It was a relief to disembark at the now familiar George and Dragon. I bespoke a room and left my bag there. I still had no plan of attack; all I knew was that I couldn't leave Rochford without getting an answer from her. I had thought of writing to let them know I was coming, but since I didn't know what to say, I ended by simply arriving. I walked up to the well-known door with my heart thumping. The footman looked surprised to see me. I sent in my card with the explanation that 'I happened to be in Rochford'. I hardly cared. In a moment I would see her.

'The family are at home—that is to say, the ladies, if I would care to step in.'

They were all in the drawing room, but had their bonnets on and the maid stood by holding their pelisses. I had managed it badly. They were obviously going out.

'Oh! Mr Armiger! This is an unexpected pleasure', and so on.

They seemed happy enough to see me. Mr Hall was of course at the mill. I told them they were about to go out and they agreed, but invited me to dine and to stay. I thought this was a good sign. They were pressing, so I consented, and Jeffreys was sent round to the George for my bag. We were all still standing in the drawing room, so I suggested I should accompany them on their errands and carry their parcels. Francesca fluttered her lashes at me in the way I knew so well—it meant that she was pleased. She had of course said nothing beyond the polite greetings, but when we were out in the street she began to tell me about everything she had been doing since I had left, about more public disturbances, which had annoyed her father immensely, and how much my painting of her had been admired by her friends since it had come back from the framers. Being in her presence again seized me with the same palpitating desire as when I first saw her and I could hardly respond.

We went into one or two shops. The sky was pale blue and the town looked its best.

"Look at the trees, Mama," Francesca said.

We were passing one of the gardens that had been laid out with fountains and beds in the town centre. The trees stood in heaps of rustling leaves, being swept up by old women with birch brooms.

"Shall we take a walk?" I thought this was an excellent idea.

"I am too tired, my dear—another time."

"Perhaps you would care to rest on one of these seats, ma'am, and if you would permit me, I could accompany the young ladies while they take their exercise?" Things suddenly seemed to be going my way.

"If you wish. Is this place quite dry?"

We installed her on a suitable bench and set off down the long path. Miss Hall fell behind, I felt on purpose. I looked round and she was stooping to tie up her shoelace.

"I am so glad you have come"' Francesca said. She slipped her hand through my arm.

"I wanted to—I had the opportunity," I mumbled.

We walked on a little way. I had only one thought: to seize this moment. I quickly ran over my ideas—her beauty—charm—my feelings. I looked about. This was as good a place as any. At once fear swelled my throat. Now I was going to ask, and she would perhaps refuse. My hands trembled. If I didn't speak now, I wouldn't be able to.

"It is so pleasant walking here with you."

The pale sun lit her long dark lashes as she looked up at me. "Yes, I'm very happy," she replied, smiling, "especially as I have something very particular I want to tell you. I feel I can tell you anything, and I know I can rely on your discretion."

"Oh, certainly." I was too surprised to make more than the most general reply. It sounded intimate. Was this an unbelievable stroke of luck? Something 'very particular'! She settled her hand more closely in my arm and I pressed it against my side. Surely—no, impossible. Was she going to declare her feelings to me? "Please—say anything you wish." If she did, I was the luckiest man in the world.

"You won't mind my confiding in you?"

Already I was breathless. "Oh—no—please—do go on."

"Perhaps you have guessed already?"

Perhaps I had. My heart was pounding. I muttered something.

"It is not to be generally known yet, but I want to tell you. Mr Shirlow has made me an offer and I have accepted him. Mama and Papa are delighted. As you know, he has large business interests that run with Papa's, and they intend to bring them together. And we are to have a house in London, so I will be able to see all the exhibitions and wonderful things that you have told me so much about."

I reeled. I might actually have staggered. I may even have spoken. For a minute I couldn't take it in. "Mr Shirlow?" was all I could say.

She chattered on. "Yes, we have known each other for some time, and it is Papa's wish."

"I see." I instinctively loosened my arm and she withdrew her hand.

"And he has given me the most beautiful bracelets, which exactly suit my complexion. Do you like them?" and she extended her delicate, graceful wrists, which I had so often fantasised about kissing, to show me a pair of enamelled gold bracelets in the Etruscan style.

"Very fine," I managed to choke out.

"I knew you would like them, you have such wonderful taste in beautiful things."

"Thank you. Yes, they are beautiful." They were, and fifty guineas if they were a penny. I would never have been able to give her gifts like that, let alone a London town house!

She gave me one of those slanting glances and dimpled smiles that used to make my heart leap, and it lurched, but with a new pain. It could never be. She belonged to someone else now. She was gone, to be happy with someone whose main qualification, as far as I could see, was that he had a great deal more money than I did. And was that what was important to her? I thought of her trembling face as she came out of her father's study, and her voice saying 'it would be so wonderful to be madly in love'. She could not possibly be madly in love with Shirlow. Liking, perhaps, love—never. I would give her one try.

"And may I ask, is it your wish, as well as your father's?"

Her head drooped for a silent moment, but she raised it with a bright smile.

"Oh! Yes. I mean, I thought—once—but I have known and liked Mr Shirlow for a great while. He is everything I could wish."

Well! In that case, there was no hope for me at all. She looked at me expectantly. I had been remiss.

"In that case, may I offer my felicitations? I hope you will be very happy together." I managed to get the words out.

"Thank you, and I do hope you will come and call on us when we are in London—after the honeymoon. We can't go to Italy, of course, or Paris, because of the war, which is so annoying, but we will go on a tour of the Lake District and Scotland and we can go abroad after the war finishes, Mr Shirlow says."

I couldn't stand one more minute of this. Bowing to Mrs Hall, who was cruising up unhurriedly with Miss Hall, and to Francesca, I made off as fast as I could. The pain in my heart was excruciating. The only thing I could cling onto was that I hadn't spoken; I hadn't been refused; no-one knew my secret. Thank God I hadn't spoken before she did! That would have been embarrassing past endurance.

I walked around for some time, still reeling. When I got back to the house Mr Hall was just coming in from the mill and taking off his wraps in the hallway.

"Now then, Mr Armiger, it's grand to see you again. Have you had a pleasant day?" He took out his snuff-box and offered it to me absently as he always did, although I always refused. He glanced at me keenly. "Come in here a moment," and he led me into his study. "I can see you look disappointed, Mr Armiger, so I expect Francesca's told you her news."

I had to admit that I was disappointed, although 'shattered' would have been a better word. So he knew, after all! I supposed everyone knew. My embarrassment was complete. There was no point in denying it, except to salve my self-respect, and that was at such a low ebb that I didn't have the energy to pretend. Hall sneezed into his handkerchief.

"I'd thought she favoured me," was all I could say.

He shook his head. "Mr Armiger, you know I'm a blunt sort of fellow. I like you well enough and I like that you have ability and pursue it. But I wouldn't throw my Francesca away on a man who has nothing. I have no son, so all I have will go to my daughters and their sons. I always intended something better for her."

That was blunt, all right.

He glanced at me, not unkindly. "She were never going to take you. I could see what you were about well enough, and if I'd thought she were in danger, I'd have spoken to you."

My face must have showed my feelings, for he added: "Don't take it too hard. She has been half promised to Shirlow these six months and her mother and I were only waiting to see if they could like each other well enough. I wouldn't have her marry against her will, but she knows she's obliging me in taking him. His business is counterpart to mine and together we'll own half the woollens in Rochford."

His complacency was appalling. I had to put up some resistance, try to salvage a fragment from the wreckage. That her father had wanted her to marry Shirlow I could well believe, but had she cared for me at all? All those pressed hands, glances from under her eyelashes—did they mean nothing? And her 'come again' the night of the ball? Perhaps, despite his—and her—assurances, she was being forced into the match.

"What if the young lady had had her own ideas?"

He smiled, undisturbed. "Francesca's a good girl and wouldn't disappoint her father."

At that moment she came in and, as though in illustration of his remarks, went up to him. He put his arm around her and for an instant I saw the resemblance between them. It was not so much in feature as in a certain expression, a look, a way of holding the head. I wondered that I never noticed it before.

I bowed and left them, going straight up to my room where, happening to stumble across my valise, I kicked it across the room with all my strength. It struck the chimney-piece and a small ornament fell down and splintered in the grate. Then I sat down on the bed, my head in my hands. There was no way around it. It was over, and I had been mistaken, a fool, a damned, stupid fool. I had been completely taken in. Even now I could hardly believe it—all those looks and sighs! Could they really have meant nothing?

At first I was almost in tears, but as I began to think of it, I became angry. I had been such an idiot. The phrase that really stuck in my mind was 'half promised to Shirlow these six months'. That was before I had ever met her, and no-one had thought to mention it to me! I supposed that was because I was considered 'no danger'—otherwise I would have been warned off like a poacher! Perhaps I would have been packed off, even without finishing the pictures. But no, they could safely leave me to finish them, since poor wretched Armiger, the humble painter, represented no threat to the prize.

I had never felt so humiliated in my life. Campbell had been right, absolutely right, from the beginning. I should never even have tried.

But if all those smiles and looks meant nothing, what was she about? My face flamed as I began to think that it had meant nothing to her. It was her wish as well as her father's—she had assured me of it. She did not share my passion in the slightest. In short, she was just amusing herself with me. I remembered all the great mooning calf-eyes I had made at her and which she now, no doubt, thought a great joke. Perhaps she even laughed about me with Shirlow. I punched the bed several times in my agony. Then I jumped up and stalked up and down the room. Surely, surely she must have cared for me, even a little. Had I really misinterpreted every word, every gesture? She did like me—had liked me—or—or—she was the damnedest flirt in the world. I threw myself down on the bed and stayed there until the dinner bell sounded. It was the worst afternoon of my life.

It was only pride that got me through dinner. I would not appear to be overwhelmed by the news. Oddly, it actually helped. Having to look as though I didn't care ended by calming me. I ploughed through a quantity of roast mutton and potatoes while managing to restrict my intake of wine to almost ordinary levels. By the time dinner was over I had got used to seeing her and speaking to her as though she was anyone else—outwardly, at any rate. I went to bed early, pleading the fatigue of the journey.

The next day I called on Mr Somers. I couldn't possibly go back to London immediately, it would be far too obvious, so I alleged business in the town and walked out soon after breakfast. I knew no-one else in the place who wasn't connected with the Halls. I also particularly did not want to see Shirlow. I supposed he would be hanging about the house, and if I saw him I might have to hit him, which would be bad from a prudential point of view, although immensely satisfying in another way.

I wandered about vaguely for a while, then found my way to St Saviour's. It was a venerable stone church in the old part of the city. I reached it down winding streets of cramped dwellings and its square machicolated tower was only visible when I was almost in front of it. Then the street opened out into a little square, a graveyard on one side with a high iron fence and some ancient yews. On the other stood a large grey house with a garden in front, which must be the rectory. The church was a solid edifice dating from the time of the Normans, if its sturdy walls and round-arched windows were any indication. I was unaccountably pleased that it wasn't what I'd been dreading, a staring new red-brick box with a sharp spire.

The heavy oak door stood open, so I went in. There was a fine carved screen and a mosaic of dimmed colour slanted across the aisle. The church smell of old hassocks and prayer books, leavened with foliage, dust and extinguished candles, hung heavy in the air. There was no-one there. I sat down in one of the pews, looking about. It was very still. From where I sat I could read the brass and marble memorials on the walls, recording how 'She Hath Done what She Could' and 'Blessed are They which Die in the Lord'. This is what it all came to, in the end: all the effort, and striving, and longing, and failing. And the succeeding, and happiness as well as despair. 'She Hath Done what She Could'. I sat there for a long time, thinking and feeling comforted. Nothing really mattered in the great scheme. You simply did what you could. It was enough.

"Can I be of any assistance?" came a quiet voice. "Are you a visitor here? Why, Mr Armiger. How are you?" Mr Somers in his cassock had appeared noiselessly.

I got up and embarked on my tale about happening to be in Rochford.

"I'm so glad you had leisure to call on us," he said, brushing aside my apologies for not writing to let him know, and ushering me out of the church and into the rectory. "Rachel, my dear, here is Mr Armiger. Is there any tea?"

We were shortly sitting in the rector's study in front of a good blaze, drinking tea and eating muffins, which Miss Somers adroitly toasted at the fire.

"Have you had time yet to read Wilberforce's book?" His eyes were palest grey, almost transparent, the same colour as his hair. "It is such a pleasure to us that such a great campaigner against social evils represents our own county in Parliament."

I had to admit that I hadn't.

"I imagine you are very busy at your work, as we are with ours, but I'm afraid I know very little of the art world—although we both enjoy attending the exhibitions of the Rochford Society of Arts, and there was an excellent public viewing last month of some of the old master paintings in Earl Fitzwilliam's collection."

I told him something of an artist's life in London, conscious that I was supposed to be there at this moment doing the work I was describing, not sitting in his study being solaced with hot muffins.

"I do sometimes wonder whether—the things one hears—whether you would not encounter a lot of people of—how shall I put it? Rather loose morals?"

"I don't know that artists are any different from, or worse than, any other group of men in that respect," I said, although I had my own doubts on precisely that point.

"The artists themselves, perhaps, but other people that you would associate with. The young women—I have heard about 'models'—they can hardly be respectable." I thought of Hallett and his girls, and Alcock's 'very fine in front', but also of Campbell's disgust and Quayle's family life, which as far as I knew was exemplary. I didn't use models a great deal myself, but when I did, they were generally good girls.

"Like other people, they vary a great deal. Some artists are undoubtedly men of—unorthodox lives. I don't know whether they feel that their profession gives them licence to behave as they wish. Others are pillars of rectitude, or lead the most mundane lives, with wives and families just like other men. As for the models, those I employ are generally ordinary women who have fallen on hard times. You know they can make as much as ninepence an hour. I'd be surprised if some of the women you see in your Soup Shop would not—er—pose, for money, and they'd be none the worse for it."

He flinched, glancing at his daughter, who had finished toasting and had taken up a shirt she was sewing. "

"It is no worse than what many of them probably do to put bread on the table in hard times, surely, and if they comport themselves respectably it is a great deal better."

"Ninepence an hour! That's a great deal of money to these people. I hadn't realised it was as much as that."

I didn't tell him that an experienced top model with an extraordinary physique, such as old Strowger had been, could make double that at the Schools.

"But to expose themselves like that! To be seen by men who are complete strangers to them! And it cannot be good for the men themselves, to, to..." He was getting himself into a tangle.

I had trouble extricating him, because my own relationships with models were sometimes such that he wouldn't approve of. That was the way things were. All artists had liaisons with models occasionally—probably not Campbell, but everyone else. But mine were not many and I did not force myself on women nor take advantage of their poverty. Sometimes it was they who made the advances, and I'd turned down not a few. But how to explain all that to Reverend Somers, sitting in his study with his eyeglasses on the end of his nose, the firelight flickering on his books and his daughter stitching away on the other side of the hearth? I thought I would try another tack.

"I wonder whether the Rochford capitalists behave any better with the factory women, and with less warrant?"

Miss Somers looked up. "It is so—some of them, at any rate. Mrs Stokes, for instance, whose husband caught his arm in a machine and has never been able to work since."

She turned to me. "She has the misfortune to be young and pretty, and when she went to see the mill owner to try to get some sort of place for her husband, he..."

"That will do, Rachel," her father interrupted. "Yes, it does go on, sadly."

"It's not only the working people, father, the morals of the factory owners leave a great deal to be desired."

He removed his eyeglasses and rubbed his thin hand over his face. "It's true. The whole community suffers under a moral sickness. Wilberforce has said so many times. He may have been referring principally to the trade in human souls, but I think his remarks can be taken as having broader implications."

I asked myself what was worse, Hallett's surrounding himself with young girls who he later discarded, but who were eager enough to form part of his entourage? Alcock's unabashed fawning to ingratiate himself with the influential? My own paltry affairs? There were few in the art world who would even comment on such goings-on, let alone censure them. But all the same, I was often unhappy about them, including my own activities. I excused my own under the heading of expediency, but presumably that was exactly what Alcock did—except that I always felt that Alcock was the supreme pragmatist. Either his lobbying had the result he wanted, or not. That was his only ground for judgment. But compared with the actions of the Napoleons of the commercial world, whose decisions put hundreds, perhaps thousands out of work, all my colleagues' intrigues looked trifling.

"How are you getting on with the Soup Shop?"

"Well, I thank you. We have been able to open it in a limited way and hope to expand. There is enormous demand, as soon as the people understood that it was free. We try to give them a pint of wholesome soup—even once a day, it is more than some of them can get now at home."

He passed his hand over his face again. I thought he looked tired.

"Have you seen the Thwaites?"

His daughter answered. "I've been to see Elizabeth once or twice. I think they are all right, but she worries about her husband being so taken up with politics. He is one of those who are trying to negotiate with the mill-owners about the introduction of the new frames. I'm afraid it isn't going very well."

Her father sighed. "Some goodwill on the part of the owners would help, but they are rather unbending. They are not prepared even to delay bringing in the machines until trade improves, or perhaps our wars with the Americans or the French are over. Don't you think we live in such distressing times? Sometimes I wonder what has happened to the modern age. Of course the inventions—I mean in science and medicine—are wonderful, but..."

I had not expected to enjoy my day, but when I walked back to the Hall's in the dwindling late afternoon, I had—almost—forgotten for an hour or two what had driven me out of doors in the morning. Our conversation had been long and broad-ranging, and we had promised to continue it by correspondence. It was a pleasure to talk with a man of his education and thoughtfulness. And although entirely outside the world of art, he was pleasingly free of the usual prejudices.

The next morning I took my leave of the Halls with a reasonable degree of grace. I managed to farewell Francesca cordially and look Hall in the eye as we shook hands and agreed that I would come up again to paint the house as soon as it was finished. Next time I saw her she would be married. Please God she would be away on her honeymoon when I came again.

Miss Hall lingered for a moment. "I hope you will convey my best wishes to Mr Campbell, and tell him how much we like his pictures, and what a pleasure it was to have him here. We will be pleased to see him again at any time." She gave me an expressive look.

"I will certainly do that."

She put out her warm soft hand and I took it. "I am sorry your visit should have been so... unhappy for you, Mr Armiger. My sister..." she dropped her eyes and there was a pause, during which she continued to hold my hand, standing there on the chilly stoop. "My sister can be very thoughtless, although her situation is not altogether..." She stopped.

"I understand that your father wanted a good match for her. But I hope that she—that she will be happy."

She looked up. Her expression was sombre, but she gave me a slight smile as she said: "There's a saying in these parts"—she dropped into the local accent—'don't marry for money, but go where money is'. I think Francesca will be happy. She has known John Shirlow a long time."

"I hope so."

"But I hope you know that you always have a friend in this house." She released my hand; her expression was earnest. "And I hope you will not let this interfere with your painting, which is so important."

She turned back into the house and closed the door, leaving me standing there, somewhat surprised.

Chapter Twelve

The rain dripped irritatingly against the window-panes. Christmas was not far away. The sky was the luminous blue-grey that presages a rainbow—when the rain should stop. I was not in the mood for symbols of hope. I turned back to the easel.

I'd been hard at work on the Agamemnon ever since I got back to Town. My pursuit of Francesca had been a terrible mistake. For her, I had neglected my work and seriously injured my confidence. I still felt the same anguish of desire whenever I thought of her, which made me feel like throwing down my brushes and walking away. Calmer reflection had convinced me that she had cared for me, that I was not entirely mistaken, but that her father, as he had explained so candidly, had no intention of letting her marry a poor man. And Francesca? She had not had the courage to stand up against him, or—it was horrible to contemplate what the scene would have been like—she had done so, and he had overborne her, and told her she was to marry whom he chose. Perhaps she had not been just playing with me. Perhaps she had truly hoped, as I had, that it might be possible. If only I were rich!

Thinking of all this, and of her with that oaf Shirlow, made me mad with despair. I felt a terrible aching loneliness, an emptiness that no usual panacea such as going to Slaughter's, getting drunk or even the fairly desperate expedient of getting drunk and picking up a whore, could assuage. I'd tried all those in the past and they left me, after the moment had passed, and sometimes even during it, feeling sick and disgusted with myself, and just as lonely as before. I had failed with Francesca; I felt that I would pass my whole life alone, with no witness to my life and work, no companion to share my thoughts and ambitions and triumphs, no warm soft body next to mine in my bed, no tender arms around my neck when I came home tired or jaded, and no-one to pour out my love and tenderness and desire on.

So I had resolved not to think of her, by sheer exercise of will. I was behindhand with a number of small commissions, my rent was due and I had to get on with the big picture if I was going to enter the Competition. I had lit a fire in the stove and taken out all my pictures of her, sketches and secret studies I'd made at one time or another, and fed them into the flames, one by one. I couldn't look at them or I wouldn't have been able to do it. At the last minute I had snatched the best from the fire, scorching my hand, and patted it flat again. Then I'd put it under a pile of drawing paper in the bottom drawer of the press and turned to work. There is a well-worn saying that work heals grief. It had no instantaneous effect in my case, but at least it distracted me and I could stop reproaching myself with my idleness.

I finished a couple of small landscapes of Bath that I'd promised to an old customer and took them round. He was pleased with them, which was a fillip to my spirits, and the thirty guineas enabled me to buy some of the things I needed for the big picture. I never ran up a bill at the colourman's. It only got you a bad reputation among the art fraternity and you risked having supplies cut off at some critical moment. Paying cash on the nail made me popular with Middleton and he showed me new pigments he got in and gave me useful hints about their properties.

It was hard to get on with Agamemnon, but I still had confidence that the theme and the composition were good. I laid in more areas of colour, especially in important parts such as the rock in the foreground and the figure of the hero, although I wanted to work evenly over the whole canvas. It was an unconventional approach but I felt that one of the main problems with many works was the impression they gave of a collection of pieces stuck together onto one canvas, which were well enough in themselves but never quite joined in harmony. As a boy I'd had one of those maps of Europe made of coloured pasteboard shapes for the different countries, which I assembled to learn my geography. A lot of pictures were like that. One of the many merits of Richard Wilson's landscapes was that while the various elements were distinct, they seemed all of a piece, like Claude's.

My plan was to lay down colour and tone over the whole surface to create the general forms, tones and perspectives, then gradually focus more and more, through additional layers and more detailed painting, on the most significant parts, which would in this way emerge from and unite the whole composition. I was not using much oil or megilp at this stage, but I planned to build up thicker layers and glazes in the final stages, together with strokes of impasto, which would help define the forms. The great master, Reynolds, like Rembrandt, used impasto to good effect. I'd first seen it in Reynolds' portrait of Miss Gale, where the delicate white lace of her dress, which appears from a distance to be most detailed, is on closer inspection a medley of thick strokes dabbed on at the last minute. The effect was brilliant.

But that was a long way off. For now, wash after wash, carefully toned, must be drawn across the canvas.

The rain cleared and a faint rainbow followed. The late

afternoon sky was spotted with floating drifts of cloud like sea-wrack on a pale turquoise strand, violently coloured with brushstrokes of dull indigo overlaid on pale grey, pink and cream, with a few large masses lit into peach and coral by the lowering sun. The pigeons emerged again and began to flutter about, prosecuting their final squabbles before finding their roosts for the night. No more work for tonight, since the exact shades of colour and effects of light were too important to be undertaken by artificial light. I scraped my palette and cleaned my brushes, then went down to dinner. Another day gone.

Campbell called in with Brigstock. I hadn't been to Slaughter's nor the John O'Groats since my second trip to Rochford. I was too low in spirits. I'd only been out to Middleton's once, when I got something at one of the cook-shops in Porridge Island behind St Martin-in-the-Fields. I hadn't expected them, but was quite pleased to see them anyway.

"Well, here he is, working away! We wondered where you'd got to."

"Just working." I wasn't going to tell them about my abortive second journey. I couldn't bear to talk about it.

"Is this it? Let's have a look."

"No, no." I hastily draped a cloth over the easel. "It's early stages yet."

I usually didn't mind Campbell seeing part-finished work, but this time I felt that my new approach was opening a gap between my work and his. I didn't want to get involved in discussions about it until I was surer of my ground. I had some trouble deflecting him, but Brigstock picked up one of my sketchbooks that was lying on the table.

"Did you do these at Rochford? What's this?" He dived into it before I could stop him. He held up one of the first pieces I'd done in the mill. Campbell craned over it.

"It's the woollen mill my host owns. This is from near the entrance. This is what they call a gig mill. Look, you'll like this one, Brig." I turned up one of the big beam engine in its narrow room.

"Ah, yes. Now that's a steam engine, you see."

"I know, Brig. I was there."

"This is the main engine, while this is the shaft, or beam..." he really was preposterous. He went on to describe its parts and workings, mostly incorrectly.

While he rambled on, Campbell picked up the big book and began turning the pages. I suddenly wished they would go away. It was all too recent. Looking at the drawings took me back into the place, the din, the smell of wool and oil, and the Halls' drawing-room, her face, her voice, heard through the doorway, singing an Italian air...

"Why, what's this?" Campbell had found my study of Thwaite leaning against the beam, his pipe in his mouth. "What a quaint fellow! Is he one of the workmen?"

"Yes. What they call a cloth-dresser, or shearman."

Campbell turned the pages. "Here he is again!"

"Yes. Look at that arm. I thought he would make an excellent model."

Brig was interested now. "You seem to have spent a lot of time drawing people. Is this a new departure for you? I expected to see books full of the northern moors and such."

"Oh, I have them as well. Here's Hall's house."

Campbell glanced at them, but continued leafing through the large book. He came next on the study of Thwaite in his home with the book on his knee. "This is the same man again, is it not?" He looked at me keenly. "What are all these for? You're not going to put them in your Competition picture, are you?"

"No, of course not."

"You told me you were doing a classical subject, with landscape."

"I am."

"What are these for, then?"

"I thought they were interesting subjects. Life is quite different up there. You get a new idea of things. Some of these men are quite educated, and have their own ideas."

"Aye, so I see, by the way he's holding the book. And have they converted you to their views, then?"

Perhaps I was just in a bad mood, but his tone struck me disagreeably. He almost sounded like my mother.

"Not just him, there were others too. An uncommon sort of parson and his daughter, who are concerned about conditions among the working people."

"Factory hands and parsons! What a fine time you had!"

"They've given me fresh ideas, at any rate. About politics. The book the man's holding is Paine's *The Rights of Man*. Seeing and hearing about these new things was the most interesting part of my visit." I hadn't thought of it before, but it was true.

"Ideas you can't get in London? Aye, I can well believe it. The *Rights of Man*! Radicals, then? Can we look for you to become a Jacobin?"

He was still turning over the pages. I wished he wouldn't, but I didn't know how to take the book from him. He glanced round the room and his eye fell on the study I'd made of the beggar at Bath, which was propped on the mantelpiece.

"So you're giving up landscapes to become a portraitist to beggars and tinkers! Have these vagabonds got the money to pay you?"

"Not at all. I just thought they made good subjects."

"But the way you depict them it looks political—as though you sympathise with them. Art shouldn't be political."

"What do you call the 'Death of Wolfe'?"

"That's different. It's patriotic—celebrates heroic virtue."

"Well, this celebrates virtue too, only not heroic—or not military heroism, anyway."

"But this fellow—if he follows Paine, he's a revolutionary—an agitator. Wolfe was a general, doing his duty."

"Is that how the French and Canadians saw it?"

Campbell made snorting sounds, scowling. Brig was still turning the pages of the folio, oblivious.

"You're being deliberately obtuse."

"Can I have the book, please?"

Eventually they left. I wasn't sure whether Campbell had just been chaffing me or whether he was in earnest. All the same, there was something in what he said. People saw Wolfe as embodying generally-admired virtues—duty, honour, heroism. Thwaite didn't. But his virtues—fighting for justice, defending his livelihood—why weren't they recognised as duty and honour and heroism too, and admired? I supposed Wolfe was acting on behalf of his country, not on his own account, but the workers and their combinations were acting not just to save their own jobs, but to protest against the loss of work for whole communities through no fault of theirs. They had no voice but their own. To my mind there was something heroic about their struggle. But I knew that there were not many who would agree with me, and those who did were called radicals. I hadn't intended to, but perhaps Campbell was right and I had turned into one. Did it signify? No-one would care, but it would injure my reputation and therefore my income, and that mattered a lot to me. Success was what I had always desired, but did I have to abandon what interested me to get it? That wasn't success, in my lexicon.

Why was he so prickly, though? Perhaps he thought I'd been avoiding him. In a way I suppose I had. Now I was annoyed. He'd disturbed my labours at Agamemnon and reminded me of things I was anxious to forget. But what rankled most as I got back to my washes was that he had made me feel disloyal to Thwaite and the workers of Rochford.

A few days later I came to the end of the under-layers and thought it was time I made an appearance at Slaughter's. Besides, I was getting tired of the landlady's mutton. A large beefsteak with plenty of onions beckoned—and a pint or two of ale.

When I went in Quayle was sitting in the window, his glossy head immaculate despite the weather, looking as though he'd just left the ministrations of his manservant.

"The prodigal returns! Heard you've been away in the north. Useful commission?"

"Not bad. A bit more to come. How's Dido?"

He smiled paternally. "Very well, very well, thank you. Are you dining?"

"I certainly hope so."

We made our way to the chop-house at the back. It smelt strongly of wet dog, emanating from a couple of spaniels begging scraps from the tables. I wondered why he wanted to dine with me. I quite liked his company, but he did little without a purpose and I'd always thought that he regarded me as rather a small entity in his spheres of influence. He started at once without preamble.

"I'm opening a gallery in my house at Chelsea. I've built a saloon on the top next to my studio and I'm going to show my own work there."

"Good Lord!" The beef arrived, sizzling.

"Yes. I'm tired of only being able to show my work a couple of times a year, the Academy of course in June, and the British Institution, but those are nothing like often enough and I don't altogether trust Seguier to keep my work before the public, even though he does have Charles Long's ear, and all that Tory set, who are useful men to have about. No, I've been thinking about it for some time."

"It'll only be your own work? Will you have enough? Will it be open to the public?"

"I don't plan on promoting other people's work—they can do that themselves." He forked in some beef and tossed the gristle to the dogs, which tussled over it, growling. "As for open to the public, I'm not sure. Probably not. I don't want a lot of people just coming and hanging about and putting off genuine buyers. I'll be inviting connoisseurs and clients to special viewings."

I was impressed by his enterprise and amused by his unabashed egoism. His self-promotion never bothered me, perhaps because it was so artless.

"Poaching the British Institution's clientèle, in fact?"

He laughed, smoothing his hair. "Why not? Half of them are already my clients." He became more serious. "Now, this is what I want you to do." There had to be something. "Here's a card I've had printed, nothing so gross as a handbill, and I want you to give it to any of your clients you think would be suitable. Don't give them away by the dozen, they weren't cheap, but you have to advertise if you want to get ahead."

He really was shameless. "And what if I want to keep them as my clients, instead of handing them over to you?"

He pushed his lips out, making a 'pshaw' sound. "Our work's nothing like the same. You do your landscapes, I'll do my—well, whatever I'm doing at the time."

I relented and took a few cards, which he handed over as though they were precious stones.

"Since you mention it, I'm expanding too."

"Oh yes?" He signalled the waiter energetically.

"I met some interesting people up north and got a look at the world of industry. It's made me think about possible new directions in my painting."

To my annoyance Alcock appeared in the doorway, with Campbell and Hallett on his heels. Seeing us, they steered for our booth.

"Move up, you fellows. Give a man a bit of room. Good. What did you have? Where's the waiter?"

"New directions, you were saying?" Quayle went on. "Not giving up views? There'll always be a market for them, you know."

I hadn't seen Campbell since his visit to my studio and I would have preferred to meet him alone. I still wasn't sure what terms we were on. I asked him how he was.

"Well, thank you. Getting on with work."

"The twelve apostles?" Alcock's face was set in his usual expression of petulant anxiety, the nostrils pinched and the eyebrows a little contracted. When he opened his mouth to speak you felt instinctively that nothing pleasing was going to come out of it. Campbell gave him his 'dour' look.

"Aye. And you—you haven't told us what you're doing for the Competition yet."

"Oh, it's not to be generally known yet," Alcock muttered, "but it'll be very successful. Has Quayle told you about his gallery? It'll be splendid, don't you think? Just what's needed."

Now he was toadying to Quayle. It was almost worse when he put himself out to be agreeable. It was probably the contrast with his usual demeanour, but I had never encountered a man who was so obvious when he set out to please.

Quayle smiled noncommittally. "Elections for Associate next week, isn't it?"

Alcock gulped his ale and banged the pot down. "Yes. Lot of competition—like last year." Everyone knew he'd been passed over last time and was lobbying furiously to get in this time. He obviously didn't want to discuss it. "What were you talking about?"

"Armiger was just saying he's going into something new."

"Your radical politics, this'll be, will it?" Campbell turned his 'dour' look on me.

I returned it. I had nothing to be ashamed of. "When I was at Rochford I had some interesting conversations about working conditions and the changes the new machines have made, and about the effects of the war on business. I had no idea really of what it's like."

Campbell sniffed. "What is it like?"

"I certainly wouldn't want to be working in one of those mills. The noise, the stink, the dim light, the long hours—and they don't seem to get enough to eat."

Quayle raised an eyebrow. "Well, of course you wouldn't want to. You're a gentleman—you don't work with your hands. They're labourers. What else are they going to do? Besides, they'd be used to it."

"I can't help feeling that when they worked outdoors or in their cottages, their conditions were better. They had their own work and those who were good at it, or worked hard, could do well. But in the factories they're shut indoors all the time—you should see how pale they all are! And the factory owners can turn them off at a moment's notice."

"Of course they can." That was Alcock. "They're not charities. It's their business and I'm sure they know what they're about."

"But there are very large numbers of people dependent on them for work, which I think is a new thing. Before, manufactories were only on a small scale. Now one man employs hundreds."

"Surely that's a good thing?" Campbell asked.

"But now there's a trade depression, which I'm told is caused by the Continental Blockade and the war with the Americans, and men who've done nothing wrong will be dismissed in their hundreds."

"Well, you can't expect them to be kept on when the

mill-owners hardly have warehouses to store all the cloth they already have," Campbell remarked.

"That's exactly what Hall says!"

Campbell's face grew a shade pinker. "Aye, well. As it happens I had a letter from him yesterday."

"Another commission?" I asked.

He shifted in his seat. "Aye, generally..."

He was a hopeless liar and I knew him far too well for it to escape me. He was up to something. I frowned, trying to think what it could be. If it was just a new commission he would have told us all straight out.

Quayle wasn't interested in Campbell's commissions. "I suppose it must be inevitable—unfortunate, but inevitable. Nothing can be done about it."

"Some people think that the government should make regulations to make business proceed in a more... orderly, manner."

Alcock couldn't hide his contempt. "Now you sound like Godwin, or one of those fanatics. Parliament can't control all the unfortunate things that happen to people. They interfere far too much as it is. Things will find their own level if trade is allowed to continue in its own way. The men who are engaged in it know best how to manage it." He gave me his doggish leer and poured himself another drink.

I knew I was getting heated, but I didn't want to stop. It was the first opportunity I'd had since I got back to discuss my ideas. These were my friends, my colleagues. I wanted them to understand what I'd seen and felt up north. I knew what I was about to say would annoy them even more, but it expressed my own ideas exactly. I took a deep breath.

"Society ought to be for the benefit of the whole. It must be against the law of nature for it to be only for the benefit of the few, while ordinary labourers can't feed and clothe themselves and their families."

Hallett, who'd been inspecting and arranging the contents of his pockets, looked up for the first time. "*Voilà*! Rousseau in our midst. You've been reading his *Social Contract,* I take it."

"No—as a matter of fact, I read it in the *Political Register.*"

I thought there would be a cry of derision but I was taken aback by its virulence.

"Cobbett! Oh, really!"

"You're an artist, Armiger. What on earth are you reading that rubbish for?"

Campbell was silent for a moment, but gazed at me reproachfully. He took a letter from his pocket, smoothing out the creases.

"Mr Hall tells me that he's worried about his new frames, which have landed at the docks, because there have been new outbreaks of violence in the north. Forty frames were broken in one evening in Nottingham last week, causing immense loss to their owners. In some cases the homes of the owners, even the owners themselves have been threatened. Don't you think that people like Cobbett should be called to account for stirring up this violence? Look at what it led to in France!"

"Lord, yes," Quayle said, yawning. "Let's not have any of that here. People I know absolutely had to flee in the middle of the night when Robespierre started laying down the law. Unbelievably bad for business, too. I mean, who's buying art in France now?"

Hallett consulted his watch and finished his wine. "Must go, people are waiting for me. Mustn't disappoint them."

Quayle winked. "I thought that as the fellow in the play said, 'I don't mind disappointing other people, it's disappointing myself I can't abide'."

The others laughed and I tried to laugh with them. Hallett was no Tony Lumpkin, but Quayle had hit him off precisely. But I didn't feel like laughing. I got up to go.

Quayle tapped me on the arm. "Don't take that stuff too seriously."

But the trouble was, I was finding that I did, and the others' reactions disturbed me greatly. How could men who had pretensions to education and breeding spend their time so trivially? How could they care so little about important things?

I was so hurt and angry that when I got home I could only relieve my feelings by seizing paper and a piece of chalk and scrawling an immense caricature of all of them, then screwing up it up and throwing in the fire.

It was two days before I felt cool enough to see Campbell. He was my oldest friend. I didn't want to fall out with him and thought it would be a good idea to go and see him and talk about his Competition entry. He had, after all, called on me. Perhaps if we got back to discussing art it would return us to the easy friendship we'd had before, although I still didn't understand the coolness on his part. Perhaps I was over-sensitive, still yearning after Francesca, though I thought I was overcoming it. It was six weeks now and I was able to think of her with less emotion. I even succeeded at times in not thinking about her at all. Knowing it was futile helped.

Long shadows sloped between the oaks as I walked across the park. The few remaining yellow leaves stood out against the damp black trunks. The sky was grey and not many people were about.

Campbell answered the door in his painting overall. He greeted me and we went up to his studio.

"I wanted to see how you were getting on with the Philosophers, but I don't want to interrupt your work."

"Och, I can take some time from it." He sat down in an

old armchair. "Will you have some tea?" He got up, called down the stairs and returned.

"Not going well?"

He shrugged. "There's an awful lot of it. Perhaps I've taken on too much."

I'd been afraid of the same thing. Twelve portraits is a lot to embark on at once, especially when you have to fit it in between your paying work. He gestured to the easel and I went over and inspected the large canvas. He'd blocked in the whole composition and laid in his dead colour, and had got some distance with underpainting the heads and figures. The background was almost untouched, except for the furnishings sketched in in thinned burnt Sienna. The subjects had been grouped, three and three, four and two, and were depicted in a room with windows at the right, which I could see was going to provide light and focus to the right side of the painting. The pair of figures was near the windows, one seated at a table, the other standing and gesturing outwards.

"Who are these?"

"The one seated is Sir Joseph Banks. He's got one of the plants named after him in his hand, and his other hand's resting on a map of his voyages. He's showing them to the astronomer, Herschel, who in turn is pointing out the heavens to Banks. He's holding a telescope. Two men of science, you see, one exploring the heavens, the other the earthly sphere."

"I like the idea—a nice conceit. They make a good pair."

He brightened. "You really think so?"

"Certainly. They'd make a good group by themselves." The tea arrived.

I could see who made up most of the group of four in the centre of the composition, since Campbell was quite advanced with the faces. They were the men who represented the arts. They were in pride of place, showing each other various objects.

"Who's this?"

"Sir George Smart. He has some sheet music in his hand. Since he's an organist I could hardly paint him at the instrument. He's pointing something out to Mr Wordsworth, who holds a copy of one of his books."

"The *Lyrical Ballads*?"

"If you like. Then next to him, of course, Nash."

"Is that to be a model of one of his buildings? Good idea."

"Yes, I thought I needed something else, otherwise every man in the picture will be holding a piece of paper. Also, I plan to light it so that it brings interest to the centre front."

"How on earth did you persuade the President to sit for you?" West's face was almost completed and the upper part of his dark coat and white shirt-front sketched in.

Campbell grimaced and got up to rummage in a portfolio. "You've put your finger on the problem—getting all their permissions, and getting around the country to do them all. I'm catching Davy at the Royal Institution and going down to Bath in a couple of weeks to do Herschel." He came back with a print in his hand. "West gave me permission to include him, but said that at his age and with his engagements he had no time to sit, so I'm using Holloway's engraving of his self-portrait. Of course, I know his features and expression well enough myself, and I hope he'll be satisfied with the result. Also, he may have felt that it might look ill to be spending too much time in the company of one of the competitors."

Trust Campbell to think of that! He was so scrupulous. Some men would have included the President with the particular view of trying to influence him.

"I thought it looked familiar. But it's coming on well."

"Good." He seemed really pleased. "And here are James Watt, Humphry Davy and Dalton, each with some emblem of their work—Watt with a model engine, of course."

"That'll please Brigstock!"

He smiled. "Aye. And on the other side, all the others. I was going to have Dr Jenner showing Wilberforce his arm with the inoculation scar, and Bentham with a speech, but I changed my mind."

"Who's this smaller figure in front of them? He seems to be being pushed into the foreground?"

Campbell grinned. "That's what I think is my best idea of all—if it works. It's a wee laddie, do you see, whom Jenner has inoculated. He's showing the place to Wilberforce, who has his hand on the laddie's head, to indicate his benevolence. My landlady's son will be the model—perfect type."

"Not bad! And the boy represents the future of our race, our nation?"

"Exactly so! I thought you'd grasp it. The heir of all these modern advances, who will carry them on. What think you?"

I was more impressed than I'd expected. Campbell had really excelled himself in the range of his imagination. I told him so. The part that was still bothering me was the typically piecemeal approach, in which the background would be the last thing to be painted, and it would be hard to unify the lighting of the individual figures. The tonality was quite dark, too, as far as I could see from what had been done.

"I thought of having the Muses of the Arts and so on somewhere, perhaps in statues arranged around the room behind the main figures. They could be in part shadow, in umber, just visible. What think you? It would point up the allegory."

I thought it was a terrible idea. The composition was already quite crowded, and there was always the danger that the Muses would end up either looking like idle bystanders, or receding into the shadows so much that they became mere decoration.

"I wouldn't bother. You don't need it. I think people will

grasp your point from the principal figures and you'd just be giving yourself more work." It would also be old-fashioned and obvious, but I refrained from mentioning it.

All in all, we spent a pleasant afternoon. Artists always like hanging around each other's studios, inspecting their work and their equipment. I'd probably been wrong in thinking that Campbell had some animus against me. If there had been some momentary awkwardness, it had dissipated.

Chapter Thirteen

It was all right at first. I walked through the tunnel and although it was quite dark, I could still see—like being in the street as night's falling in winter. The tunnel was high and arched, the squalid brickwork of the roof disappearing into twilight. A disturbing, insistent sound in the distance was too remote for me to make out, but it was always there. Then the tunnel began to slope downhill and darken. It was harder to keep my footing. I wanted to go back, but when I looked behind me the slope was already too steep to climb. This was puzzling, as it had only just started to incline. There was nothing for it but to continue downwards, even though I was getting lost. It must end some time, and when I emerged into the light Francesca would be there, waiting for me. I had to get to the light. My feet grew heavier and walking was awkward. I tried to run, but something kept tripping me up. I looked down at my feet and they were encased in enormous wooden clogs studded with nails. I knew it was the nails that were making them heavy. 'Too many nails', I said, but no-one was listening. The tunnel spread out sideways into a huge room as it got steeper and darker, and in the gloom I glimpsed what seemed to be machines of some sort. Brig said 'it's the Modern Age'. I heard his voice quite distinctly, but I couldn't see him. In front the wall had been painted in blues and browns with a large hill rearing up and sea behind it. It was the Bay of Aulis. I needed to touch up the foreground.

I felt for my brushes, but the ground was falling away. As I began to career helter-skelter down the slope Francesca said 'I must show it to Mr Armiger', but she was too far away and I was falling too fast. The distant voices were laughing at me as I tried to grab the wall. Faster—faster—I was going to crash.

I woke up panting, my heart pounding and the sheets twisted around my body. Trembling, I got one arm free and groped for the tinderbox. At last I got a light struck and it was only then, with the candle flame before my eyes, that I was able to compose myself.

I often had large, colourful dreams and sometimes night-mares, but this was terrible. I disentangled my bedding and tried to understand. I was left with a frightening sensation of menace, of helplessness and humiliation. I was sweating, despite the chill air of my room. My body felt strange and I moved my feet surreptitiously under the blankets. I needed to feel that they were all right, my own naked feet. The sheets slid over them reassuringly. I felt my arms and chest and ran a hand over my face. Then I felt calmer. I put out the light and tried to go back to sleep, but the dream went round and round in my head and it was a long time before I succeeded.

WHEN I woke again in the morning, wan light creeping around the edges of the curtains, I thought mainly of Francesca. How real she had seemed in the dream. I would never see her again, or if I did, she would be Shirlow's wife. It was worse than Belinda, because I had nothing to reproach Belinda with except not loving me. Francesca had made a fool of me, perhaps to gratify her own longings, but with no thought of the effect on me. I couldn't think of her without a lump rising in my throat. I had mistaken her; I thought I had known what was true and what wasn't, and now I doubted my ability to tell. I wanted love more than ever, but I would never know it.

After breakfast I started dully on some landscapes that were overdue for a client—I needed to get on with some paying work. I hadn't made much progress before I heard feet thudding on the stairs. Campbell flung the door open.

"What?" I really didn't want to see him, or anyone, at that moment.

"Alcock's been elected ARA."

"What?"

"He's been made an Associate of the Academy. He's got in. All that fawning's paid off for him at last. I never thought he'd make it this time, what with all the applicants left over from last year's round."

"Oh. The names are out, then?"

"Aye. Raeburn, Westall and Bird got in. Well deserved, especially Raeburn." Raeburn was a Scotch portraitist Campbell had long admired. "The best man for a likeness in Edinburgh since Ramsay, and once he became President of their Society of Artists they could hardly leave him out. A lad of parts. Imagine Alcock in that company!"

"He's not in the same class."

"You're raving! He's nowhere near it!" Campbell threw himself onto the sofa.

I gave up on work for the time being—he'd obviously settled in for a good gossip. "Any news of Hallett?"

"He'll never say whether he went in for it or not, but mark my words, he put in for it. He's as ambitious as Alcock."

"He's just not prepared to do the work that Alcock does to get there."

"Work! You don't call that work!" Campbell pulled a face.

Whatever his faults, Campbell was a much better painter

than Alcock, whose pedestrian portraits, often of himself, attracted little interest from the critics or the public—except that he'd once been savaged by Hoppner in the *Quarterly*, but that was too common an event to depreciate his stocks.

"I don't mean his paintings," I said. "I mean all the dinners with Sir George Beaumont, running errands for Charles Long, painting the President's portrait, getting critics to say something about his work, and all that. I'm not surprised he hasn't much time for painting."

"You're in a sour mood!" But he laughed. "Aye, he's had to give up a lot to get his success. I agree with you—Hallett just isn't prepared to make those sacrifices."

"If he were really to produce a lot of pictures, he'd have to give a lot of things up, mainly his social life. 'Frivolity, thy name is Hallett'. Can't spend every night carousing at Vauxhall with some girl if you want to put in the hours at work the next day."

"Aye, as you say, it's a sacrifice he's not prepared to make. You have to concentrate on what you want to achieve. He'll never get anywhere in the long run if he doesn't."

Campbell was right—or at any rate, it was the standard that he and had I pinned our hopes to. Working hard at what you believed to be good painting, was how we hoped to get ahead. It had gone reasonably well up until now. Both of us were waiting to apply to the Academy until we felt more established in our chosen fields—unless one of us could win the Competition.

"I hope you're right." I felt despondent again. "But you know, the worst thing about people like Alcock and Hallett, and Alcock being elected, is that they make me feel as though I'm wasting my time. If that's how you become successful, I'm doing it all wrong." I was near to believing it, and if it were true, what did it augur for my future?

"Losh! You're down. Something amiss?"

I hadn't told him about the wreck of my hopes of Francesca, but in my low spirits I decided to unburden myself. I got up and poured us some madeira.

"Painting's not going so well." How could it, in my present mood? Every time I looked at it I felt more distant from it. "And it went badly for me at Rochford. You were right about how it would be." I didn't go into all the mortifying details, but it was a relief just to speak of it. I was surprised at how much better I felt after I had finished. All at once the pain seemed to slip away—not vanish altogether, but retreat into a more shadowy distance.

Campbell said very little, sipping his wine slowly, but there was not much he could say. "Will you go back there?"

"I'm supposed to paint some more views when the house is finished. Whether Hall will still want me is something else." It had been weighing on my mind, but now I thought it might not be too much of a burden.

He nodded, but there seemed to be something on his mind. "They want me to go up and paint him and—er—the younger lady, some time. To match the others." He was trying to be delicate.

I was pleased for him. "Perhaps we can contrive it so that we're there at the same time? Go up together?" If I had to be there at all, it would be good to have his support.

"Er—aye—we'll see. That is—I don't know when it'll be." All at once he was distant, fidgety. "Did you say you weren't happy with your painting? Let's have a look at it. Maybe I can help?"

His ideas about my painting were not likely to be particularly useful, but I grasped at whatever he was prepared to offer, and we sat down in front of it and discussed it for some time. I could see that he didn't really understand what I was trying to achieve in terms of technique, but I was confident about that myself. When it came to the subject, which was what was worrying me, he didn't see any problem.

"It's a grand theme and the way you explained it earlier, I think it has every chance of success, if you put in more detail in the figures and tone down the colour."

"That's exactly where I want to do something different, something new."

He shook his head. "You cannae be too forward with these things, especially not with a competition piece. There's nothing surer to put people off than novelty. You might get away with some of it with a client who likes that sort of thing. But you know you have to give clients what they want, what's in fashion now. You have to do what's expected—in this case, the sort of thing that the Academy's shown it approves."

In his own way, listening to Campbell was as disheartening as listening to Alcock or Quayle, even though he meant well and he was my friend.

"I believe I have to do what I think is good, or I couldn't bear to go on with it." I was conscious as I spoke that Quayle would think such a remark ludicrously sentimental. But I really did believe that an artist had to have faith that his work was the best he could do. I tried to make it sound more business-like. "If you do anything less, aren't you just giving the client inferior work? And when it comes to new directions in art, who'll show the way, if not an individual artist experimenting?"

"But then it's just one man's taste, there's no warrant for it. Don't you want to be successful?"

"Of course—more than anything! You know I want to do something grand, noble. But I don't just want to be following the dictates of fashion, toning things down a bit here, bringing them up there, doing the same themes as everyone else. I can't see how that's going to produce grand, noble art, and it makes me feel like a sheep—'bell-wether jumped over, and all the rest followed'."

Campbell shook his head. "You know what I think," he said, getting up to go. "It's the Academy that leads the way. That's what it's there for—as the arbiter of taste. You'll only go astray if you don't follow the rules."

We parted on good enough terms but my spirits were still low. Was doing what I thought important in art the sacrifice I had to make to get ahead? Should I give up all thought of innovation in favour of success on the Academy's terms? Somebody had to be the leader—why not me? I glared at the big canvas, hating it suddenly. If it was going to chain me to a subject and a style I abhorred, I'd rather throw it in the fire. Only the thought of how much it cost and how much work I'd put into it stopped me from breaking it up there and then.

I got my coat and hat and went out to Slaughter's. Halfway there it occurred to me that it would be full of Alcock and his cronies celebrating his rise to the Pantheon. I changed course and ended up at the Coach and Horses, a low tavern much frequented by ostlers and stable-boys, but whose landlord let me have drinks cheap in consideration of a signboard I painted for him last year. I took the opportunity of asking if he knew anyone else who wanted something done, which would enable me to get some money in. He did, and I took down the address. I spent the rest of the evening drinking porter and playing skittles with some coach-drivers from Stepney. No-one mentioned art.

THE papers were full of news from the north, none of it good. According to the *Times*, 'Discontents and other disorderly persons have assembled in a riotous and tumultuous manner and have destroyed or materially damaged great numbers of frames'. It made me uneasy enough to look at some of the northern newspapers. They were even more crammed with reports of violence, which they seemed to take delight in spreading over as many columns as possible, with much exultant detail and the headings in the largest type.

'It is with very great pleasure we state, that the destruction of frames this week has been much less than that of the last. On Monday evening a frame was broken at Croker's Mill, and carried clean away. On Tuesday the County Militia arrived here, in 30 wagons, they having left the barracks in Manchester, at 7 o'clock on Friday evening last. Yesterday two field pieces arrived, which belong to the regiment. On Wednesday two more troops of the Hussars likewise entered this town. We understand that the Magistrates have been using their utmost endeavours to learn whether politics have any connection with the present troubles in this neighbourhood; and we likewise understand they are convinced of the contrary. Committed since our last, for trial at the Assizes, Frederick Lowry, of Coldbrook, charged with having, in company with divers other persons at present unknown, wilfully, maliciously, and feloniously, broken, destroyed and damaged two frames.'

They spoke of one man being behind it all, someone called 'General Ludd', or 'Ned Ludd', and of assemblies of men on the moors to plan attacks on mills. I couldn't believe that all these widespread incidents were the work of one man, and thought of the shearman who spoke to me after the food riot at Rochford market, and Thwaite in his cottage with the *Rights of Man* open on his knee. I hoped they had nothing to do with it. Was this Frederick Lowry a cropper like Thwaite, perhaps put out of work by the new frames, or just some local reprobate? Coldbrook was very close to Rochford and I'd met Mr Croker at the ball. All those soldiers and two pieces of artillery, to set against unarmed men! One company of infantry, with their levelled muskets and bayonets, had been enough to frighten me witless at the market.

I wondered how the Halls were doing. Croker was a friend of theirs. Mr Hall was perhaps one of the magistrates who had decided that the disturbances weren't 'political', and I speculated on how they knew. His new frames must have arrived by now. I imagined Mrs Hall beside herself with anxiety, and Francesca—Shirlow must be just as concerned as the Halls would be, and his mill would be in as much danger. She might be in danger. According to the news, these men broke into mill-owners' houses and threatened the inhabitants. I suddenly felt that I should buy a ticket immediately and dash up there. For a few minutes I actually calculated the state of my finances and thought about the coach departure times. Then I realised I was being ridiculous. They were none of my concern, especially Francesca, and what could I do if I were there, anyway, that those who had more right would not be doing? A vision rose unbidden to my mind of my rushing to protect her from a band of ruffians, throwing my body between her and them, seizing her in my arms to wrench her away from an attacker.

It was an effort for me to return to reality, but I took hold of myself and realised I was being both alarmist and sentimental. I got paper and ink and wrote to Mr Somers all the same, expressing my anxiety, hoping that that they were safe, and asking him to let me know the state of things at Rochford.

When I went home I took up Paine's book and began to read. I needed to know more about the ideas behind this wave of unrest that had broken out in our country, that is, if it was 'political'. I thought that the magistrates were probably mistaken in thinking that there was no political dimension to the incidents. I could imagine that they would not enquire from the operatives themselves, or if they did, they would not tell them the truth. It occurred to me for the first time that I had been unusually trusted by both the man at the food riot and more especially by Thwaite, who had allowed me into his home. The thought warmed my heart. He evidently trusted the Somers, too, as Mr Somers seemed to know all about his radical leanings.

Paine's polemic stirred my mind. His ideas were extreme, but I found his arguments persuasive. I wanted to be up and doing something, something to change things for the better—not as far as Paine would go, but at least to express my concern at the turmoil. I was troubled, but had no conception of how to act in response to these events. I wished I could discuss them with Campbell or some of the others, but the few occasions when I'd raised such things I'd been derided as a Jacobin or as having been tainted by my time in the north. I was not going to expose myself to that again.

I'D allowed myself a day off from the Competition picture, but I had to get on with it. I hadn't been altogether happy with it for some time, but had thought I could put right by adjusting the composition. Now I looked at it with real loathing. It looked tawdry, obvious, mannered—all the things I hated most. I stood back and put my hand up to block out various parts of the canvas, a useful trick when you can't identify what's wrong. Nothing leaped out, but the part I most disliked was the figure of Agamemnon. I squinted at it, thinking. It came to me in a flash. It was Agamemnon himself that I didn't like. He was spoiling the picture. Oh, God! I sat down and stared at it.

It was a huge blow. There went my chances for the Competition; there went the possibility of coming to the notice of some influential patron. I needed to come to grips with what was wrong with Agamemnon. The whole concept was wrong.

Something Campbell had said struck a note that resonated with my predicament. I tried to reconstruct the conversation. It was when we'd been talking about Hallett. I could see Campbell sitting on the sofa, glass in hand, when he said it. He was laughing. 'Hallett wouldn't make the sacrifice—girls—Vauxhall'. Sacrifice—giving things up. That was it.

Iphigenia was the sacrifice and she was missing from the composition. Agamemnon gave up his own child to the goddess—for what? To make the winds blow, so that the fleet could set off for Troy, to recapture fair Helen—'the face that launched a thousand ships, and burnt the topless towers of Ilium'. Suddenly, it didn't make sense. Kill one woman to get another? His child, for his brother's wife? Impossible—ridiculous. Why would any man surrender something so precious? I squinted at the picture again. The fleet arrayed there on the beach—I was quite pleased with the way that was coming along—perhaps I could keep that and just change the main figure.

The real hero of the story was Iphigenia—she should be on the hilltop, not her father! She gave herself up so courageously for her father's victory. How could her father be so cruel as to accept? I'd been so intent on the idea of Agamemnon as the supreme leader that I had forgotten to notice the immense cost of his triumph: the life of his child and the lives of thousands of his people. In a rush of dismay I realised that it wasn't Helen he was taking the whole Greek nation to war for, it was power—power, and hubris. The lady was only the occasion.

It wouldn't be going too far to say I was appalled. I could almost hear my entire idea, my Competition entry, splintering like a shattered glass. I'd chosen Agamemnon as the symbol of all that was greatest about Britain today. If he symbolised Britain, what did that say about our country—about the 'Spirit of the Present Age'?

My first thought was to abandon the picture entirely. That probably meant giving up entering the Competition. I really needed to enter it, to at least be seen among the field, to bring myself to the Academy's attention, if I ever wanted to become part of it. If I didn't enter they—Farington, Dance, West, all the influential members—would think I wasn't interested. I ground my teeth in frustration. This was what happened when you got involved in the race for advancement. Every other artist became a rival instead of a friend, and you had to do things that you didn't want to instead of spending your life on work that had meaning. Everything was going wrong.

But it would be nothing short of ridiculous and feeble to give up the Competition. I looked at the picture. Iphigenia appeared as a small figure on the left, fading into an artfully-rendered mist. Now I saw that she must occupy the central position. She represented the strength of Britain today—the people who made the sacrifices. Theirs was the nobility. I grabbed a piece of paper and began to sketch her pose. She would take the place of her father on the hill. She was the real hero. The commander who called the Achaean army together was their destroyer, an example of a bad governor.

I drew frantically, determined that my painting would be a manifesto of the Spirit of the Age such as no-one else would produce. It might not win, but it would set everyone aback, make them think. That was what I wanted. I wanted to create something with real meaning, and this would have it. Real meaning! That was what I'd been looking for. I drew and drew, then, impatient, when I had the pose fixed, seized a palette knife and began to scrape down the father and sketch in in umber instead the pale, heroic, resolute figure of his daughter.

Chapter Fourteen

Iphigenia was drying and I needed some respite from the big work. I took down the study of the sleeping beggar, put a nice medium-sized canvas I'd prepared for something else on the small easel, and began to copy the drawing.

I had new colours to prepare, so laid out the oils on the workbench and put on an overall. When I could afford it I bought colours ready made up in pig's bladders the size of a walnut, but the price reflected the work that went into them and especially at the moment I needed to save money. Most men ground their own colours except when flush, although Quayle had an assistant to do his heavy work, while Hallett bought all his pigments and canvases ready-made from a mysterious man he had found in a back street, whom he claimed had secret recipes. Hallett had once remarked that there was no point at all in the labour of art, which as far as he was concerned included not only stretching canvases and grinding colours, but even drawing. When I heard him say that I knew he was no artist, for all his imagination. No man who doesn't like drawing is an artist, in my opinion.

I enjoyed working at the slab. I usually did it in the afternoons, as if I went on too long my wrist was unsteady for hours afterwards and my shoulder sore. I'd tried different mullers and ways of working them, but it made little difference, so I kept the ordinary heavy glass one I had started with at the Schools. I liked the sharp scent of the linseed or the sweetness of walnut oil. There was a meditative pleasure in the rhythmic circling of the muller, watching, almost without seeing, the gritty paste grow imperceptibly smaller and smoother, adding drops of oil, seeing the colour come up little by little until at last it had all transformed into a rich butter and there it was, ready for work. I often had my best ideas during the process and sometimes had to break off to make a sketch or jot down a note. I had plenty of ideas for the 'beggar', and since I'd never be able to sell him I would let myself go with broad brushwork, intense shadows and sketchy impastoed surfaces.

THE work went smoothly and I substantially finished him in a week. Goodness knows I'd spent enough time thinking about how I'd paint it—all I had to do was put my ideas down. It was amazing how quickly painting went when I didn't have to think about pleasing a client, creating a 'well-finished' surface with little brushes and all the rest of it. I used plenty of megilp, made the shadows rich by hatching a thin veil of indigo over Vandyke brown and illuminated the lights with dashes of Indian yellow. When it had dried enough I'd create the texture of the stone wall behind him by dragging a dry brush loaded with yellows and grey-browns over the stratum I'd laid in of thickish greys and ochres tinged with green. You'd be able to feel the roughness, not just see it. I'd given him a cloth-dresser's red waistcoat, just visible like a robin's breast in a thicket where his fustian coat fell open, and touched up the grass with a good green I mixed from indigo and the new yellow. The depths of the dog's eyes would be touched in with clear gold, and then the whole harmony of greys, browns and ochres would spin around that central point. Depending on how it looked at that stage, I might throw some glazes over salient parts to bring them forward.

Guilty at indulging myself with the 'Beggar', the next day I got smartly out of bed and began straight away on the landscapes for the spring show. I couldn't face the big canvas yet. I chose the best views of Bath from my sketchbook, squared them up and ruled up some large sheets of white laid paper. I got the main outlines transferred to the big sheets before breakfast. I'd paint them together; it saved mixing up the same colours all the time.

I hadn't made any plans for Christmas, although I had some money in my pocket now that my pupils had paid their fees. Campbell usually went up to Edinburgh to see his parents, although Scotland was the last place I'd want to be in this weather. Since I had no family it was a quiet season with me anyway, and I had too much on hand to be thinking of any sort of jaunt. People at the clubs were talking about the weather and speculating on whether the Thames would freeze over again, as it did last year. If it did, it would be entertaining to go skating on it. But I had a lot to do before anything of the sort could be thought of.

In the event I went to church in the morning, it being of course a Sacrament service. I had thought of going to St Paul's to see it in its Christmas finery, but it was too cold and too far to walk, and I was not minded to lay out the five shillings a hackney coach would have cost. I went to our parish church instead, and found it half empty. My landlady invited me for dinner, as she had the last two years. We put some green branches in the house and I helped her buy a goose, which was very agreeable roasted with bread sauce and a lot of potatoes and ale. The remains went into the kitchen where she held open house for the poorer neighbours.

I liked eating the special foods of the seasons as they came round. Now there would be Twelfth Night cake to look forward to. If I got the bean perhaps my luck would change for next year, and if it wasn't too cold I might go and see the Holly Man and the St George Play down by the river.

Last Christmas I had gone out with Laura. Of course that was impossible now. And I had hoped that this year I might have been with Francesca. Instead I was pottering about alone in the studio, wearing a flannel waistcoat under my working jacket and stuffing extra coal into the stove. I toyed with the idea of writing to Laura or going to see her. Writing would be better. She would probably be angry, but then we might settle back into the comfortable routine we had had before. Or she might refuse. I supposed it would depend on whether she had found someone else. I scratched at the frost-flowers on the windows. The sky was low and the sound of horses and carriage wheels outside stifled by snow. I thought about writing her a note saying I'd like to see her, but found I had no enthusiasm for the task. It wasn't her I wanted.

WITH nothing much to do, I had plenty of time to read. I got through some of Wilberforce and half of Godwin, but I liked Paine best. While I read, I kept recurring to Campbell's remarks about sacrifice. There was personal sacrifice, which people usually thought of as noble, but that was when it was to benefit another. In other cases it was just another form of self-interest. Alcock was more than willing to give up his self-respect, and if he knew it—and perhaps he did—the respect of a large number of his colleagues, in his pursuit of success. Hall didn't mind people making jokes about his name because he had power, in the form of wealth. Quayle didn't mind spending time being confidential and urbane with the Lord Arbuthnots and Sir George Beaumonts of the world. And when it came to sacrifice on a grand scale, the great advances that England was making today were at the expense of her poor and the sort of workers who were being displaced, probably for ever, by new machines owned by new men who had risen up from the communities that they now found it so easy to dispense with.

Disturbed, I wrote to Somers. There was literally no-one else I could talk to. In this, I was lonelier than ever in my life.

"Is this just the way of nature—the strong rise up and prosper? Isn't that a good thing? Shouldn't society be governed by the most able? But what if the most able are willing to trample on the less powerful to gain their ambition?" And I added what seemed to me the crux of it: "according to Paine, and I believe he got it first from Locke, human rights are bestowed by nature, not by laws made by governments, so no laws made by governments should be able to take those rights away?"

Somers' return came promptly, in his careful Italic hand. 'My dear Armiger… I do agree with you. I believe that human rights come from God. But I think perhaps Paine and I are of a like mind on the subject, except that Paine will not admit the name I call the Agency that generated those rights.'

Dear man! He was a comfort to me when I needed it, and I read his letters—for we exchanged several—in my studio where I was supposed to be working, in front of my stove, getting up to put coal on the fire or to open a book he recommended.

Because these ideas were disturbing. I was used to the age-old wisdom that some were born to rule and some to be ruled, but this tradition had taken a considerable battering lately in France and America, where men had declared that governments existed to serve their societies, not dominate them. It followed that if government oppressed instead of served and cared for its community, then it was a bad government. Certainly, if I pursued that idea I would soon come to the conclusion, like the shearmen I'd spoken to, that an authority that favoured the rights of some over the rights of others was a bad one.

Somers had written: 'There are more soldiers now stationed in the north to guard factories against workers and to keep the peace, than there are fighting the tyrant Bonaparte in Spain.' And those soldiers had been invoked against the people by the authorities in the various districts, instead of trying to negotiate with the workers to come to some settlement.

Thwaite didn't strike me as unreasonable; many of these men were skilled and educated, not an ignorant rabble of felons. Didn't they have the right to ask that their needs be considered? How could it be right to throw hundreds, thousands of men and women out of work, perhaps permanently, in order to help men such as Hall and Shirlow become rich, or richer?

At Slaughter's the talk was all of the weather, the snow, several feet deep, and of the continued troubles in the north. I thought Campbell would have been back, but no-one had seen him.

"Isn't he still in Rochford?" Brigstock suggested.

"I thought he was in Edinburgh?"

Brigstock looked confused. "Oh. Perhaps he is. I thought… perhaps not."

"What?"

"I don't know." He waved his hands vaguely.

He was sitting with Alcock and some men I didn't know. There was no-one else there I wanted to talk to, so I left. I'd hoped that some of the philosophers might have been there and I could have talked to them about what I'd been reading, but there were only a couple of mathematicians deep in a page of calculations. I went to the John O'Groats and ate a mutton chop in solitary state. The streets were full of slush.

When I got in my landlady was excited. "You've had visitors, Mr Edward—you missed them."

"Mr Campbell?" It couldn't be. She wouldn't be so agitated. The visitors, whoever they were, had impressed her. If it had been Campbell she would just have said 'Mr Campbell called'.

"No, sir, a gentleman and a lady—foreigners. They left a note."

By 'foreigners' she meant they were not from London. Could it have been the Halls? Francesca? I ripped the note open, conscious that I was flushing. A gentlemanly hand I recognised. 'My dear Armiger, I am sorry to have missed you...' Mr Somers. And his daughter, presumably. I read on. They had come to London in connection with their work and hoped to see me. Well, their company would be very welcome: in fact, just what I needed.

"Thank you, Mrs Mullins. I will not be in to dinner."

I put my hat back on and set out for Holborn.

At the Saracen's Head I had to make my way through crowds of passengers waiting to embark, porters heaving up trunks and grooms pushing horses into the shafts of coaches. Inside the bustle was not much less. I enquired for Mr Somers and was shown into a small dark parlour on one side of the corridor while they went to tell him. I stood over the meagre fire warming my coat-tails and speculating on what had brought them to London. In a minute the door opened, but it was Miss Somers who entered. It was months since we had met and she was taller than I remembered, wearing an indigo woollen dress with a lace collar. Her thick hair was dressed up in braids. I apologised for not being at home when they called and explained about the letter.

"I am afraid my father has gone out about his business. He

will be very sorry to have missed you—that is, unless you can wait a while for him?"

I assured her that I was at their disposal and we sat down.

"You are probably wondering why we have come to London. It's because the people are in a great deal of trouble at home. The new frames are about to arrive at some of the mills and it is said that the croppers have been meeting on the moors at night. Unfortunately, the mill-owners have decided that they won't negotiate with the men. There have been further uprisings, and even attacks within the town itself. Perhaps you would like to read this," and she handed me a folded paper, the *Mercury*. "You will see why we are worried."

The account the paper gave was certainly calculated to alarm. 'On Wednesday night, information upon oath was given to the Magistrates of this Town, of a conspiracy to destroy the Machinery of certain mills employed in the dressing of Cloth, for this purpose the members of this confederacy was to assemble in a certain place to be agreed upon, and from thence to proceed to the work of destruction. The Magistrates upon receiving this information immediately assembled and proceeded in person to carry them into effect. Near the Canal, a number of persons were found assembled, many of them with their faces blacked who dispersed on the appearance of the Magistrates, seeking their safety in flight, one of these persons of the name of Robert Danby, was taken into custody, and examined before the Magistrates and committed to Rochford Castle, under what is called the Black Act charged with disguising his person, and having in his possession several offensive weapons, we believe a hammer and chisel.'

"I thought the Black Act was designed to stop poachers?"

"It always used to be, but the authorities have started invoking it against the workmen." She was on her feet, walking about the room. "It's a clear misuse of the legal process. That's what things are coming to."

"Who is this Robert Danby? Do you know him?"

"Yes—that's the worst of it. He's a friend of the Thwait-es—you know them. He used to work with Mr Thwaite in his dressing-shop, but I believe he was turned off from Croker's mill for insolence some time ago. He is not a steady man and we think a bad influence on Mr Thwaite."

"I can see why you are concerned." Hall and Shirlow were magistrates. Presumably they were involved in the business.

"Yes—so men are in prison—Danby and others, who were taken up at different times. The frames that had landed at the docks in Liverpool were on their way to Shirlow's mill when they were attacked on the road and destroyed. The mill-own-ers are coming down on men who they believe to be in these combinations, or clubs, and refusing them work. So the bad feeling grows."

"The people seem divided? Some are informing on their fellows, by this account."

"The magistrates are offering fifty guineas to any person who informs on the frame-breakers, and have undertaken to try to procure the pardon of any man convicted of rioting who will give evidence against the others."

"Fifty guineas!"

"In some places I believe it is more—I have heard of two hundred guineas being offered at Manchester, and paid agents sent out to try to get the confidence of some of the agitators and induce them to turn informer."

"That's outrageous!"

"Yes. There is a terrible atmosphere of suspicion and unrest. Having troops stationed in the town only makes it worse. They are quartered in the Park so they can rush to any locality. It is like being in a town at war."

I tried to think of something to say. The latest news from

the Peninsula was that the Duke of Wellington was laying siege to the fortress town of Ciudad Rodrigo on the border of Spain and Portugal. In an arid land, columns of red-coated soldiers moved across the plain, dragging the matériel of war. Behind the tawny stone ramparts of the citadel, frightened townsfolk and blue-uniformed French peered out at the besiegers and trundled cannon into position. Hawks wheeled in the pristine sky while gaudy officers cantered about delivering orders. Two generals, Agamemnon and Hector, in cocked hats with plumes, stood on hilltops scanning the dispositions through their spyglasses. An arm was raised, the signal given, and a shot blazed out in a puff of smoke and ploughed into the ramparts, raising an answering cloud of fractured masonry. But that was war—war against an enemy of the country. Good governments go to war to protect their citizens from those who would enslave them. Bad governments go to war to enslave their own people. Could it really be that simple?

"There you are, father! How did you get on? Here is Mr Armiger. Come and stand by the fire."

Somers, his hat and coat dripping, looked drawn. His daughter took his umbrella, sat him by the fire and poured him tea.

"A pleasure to see you, Mr Armiger."

I expressed my own pleasure while he drank his tea and the colour returned to his face.

"Have you told Mr Armiger why we are here, Rachel?"

She shook her head. "I was about to—we were talking about the riots."

"So you know our sad state. It is becoming, I fear, desperate. Parliament is debating the Frame-breakers Act, which will bring in new laws against the workers. I have discussed the matter with some of our colleagues who work with the poor and unemployed in parish relief, and the result is that I have been deputed to come here, now that Parliament is sitting again and the potentates are gathered in London, and try to represent the condition of the working men of the north to the authorities. I know that Mr Wilberforce will give us a friendly hearing, at least, and I have introductions to some of the others. Earl Fitzwilliam has given me a letter for Lord Byron, who of course is from Nottinghamshire, so he will be acquainted with the situation among their lace-makers and the stocking-knitters, who this Bill is largely aimed at. Poor fellows! This afternoon I went to Westminster to try to get a sight of the members, and see when I might be able to make some appointments."

"Were you successful, sir?"

"I have made two appointments for tomorrow evening. The House sits at a quarter of four, and if there is no urgent business, which is thought likely, I should be able to make some progress then. I do not feel that many of the government truly understand the issues. They see only civil unrest, magistrates being called out, and so on. We hope to convince them of the very real problems the northern workers are facing. Which reminds me, Mr Armiger," he felt in his breast pocket and brought out some creased papers. "If you would look at these?"

I took the papers, which turned out to be proofs of tracts, or pamphlets, set in type, arguing the case of the woollen workers.

"They were written partly by me—with Rachel's help—and partly by Reverend Preston, one of my fellow-labourers in the vineyard at Rochford."

They looked useful, as far as I could judge, although I had no way of knowing whether they would convince the men who needed to be convinced. There were gaps here and there in the columns of letterpress where there was nothing but yellow paper.

"What goes here?" I had a sudden, premonitory lurch.

Miss Somers and her father looked at each other.

"It was my idea," she said. "I hope it is not to presume... I thought that the pamphlets would be more effective if the power of art could be harnessed to them—if they showed actual images of the people and their distress, not merely words, that can be scanned over without noticing." She lowered her head, then raised it and looked at me straight.

"You'd like me to draw something?"

Her father nodded. "If it would not inconvenience you, yes. We know of no artist who could do the work, then I thought of the drawings you made of our friend Thwaite and wondered... we feel it's essential that the work be well and professionally done, to convey the right impression."

"I understand. What are the subjects you want, and how many, and how soon? I suppose you need them immediately."

Somers bowed his head. "You understand it perfectly. I got these proofs from the printer today, and we hope to distribute the pamphlets as soon as possible—before the new Bill comes up for debate."

I didn't think about it. I knew as soon as I saw the blank squares that it was I who must fill them. "I'll do it. I'll begin tonight." I had subjects in plenty in my sketchbooks and in my head.

"I'm afraid there's something more—you may not wish to—about the fee..."

"I suppose there isn't one?"

"All our money has gone into the Soup Shops and Parish Relief."

I shrugged. It was inevitable, but I wanted to do it. I'd been looking for something to do, and here it was. I'd just have to try to do them quickly and then knock out a few inn signs or views to get some money in.

"I'll start tonight."

We dined at the inn and over the meal discussed the scenes that should be shown. The old woman grubbing on the cobbles for potatoes came back to me, and the farmer standing up in his dray brandishing his whip at the crowds of women, and they liked the ideas. I could do them from memory and my sketchbooks. Emaciated children I had seen in plenty, and they had other subjects they wanted me to include when they found I wouldn't make difficulties. After we had settled the drawings, I canvassed Mr Somers' views of Paine, and Wilberforce, and even talked to him about my problems with Agamemnon. Luckily I'd started on the revised version before this job came along.

"I thought of calling it 'The Sacrifice of Iphigenia'."

"An unwilling sacrifice, and a fascinating story," Miss Somers remarked. It seemed she read Greek.

"I have my pupils too, Mr Armiger, you see! And by the bye, speaking of art, I met another artist just before we left. I believe he too was staying with your friend Mr Hall—a Mr Campbell, a Scotch gentleman. Rochford is becoming quite the place for artists! Are you acquainted with him?"

Campbell in Rochford! Brigstock had been right. I felt hurt immediately that he hadn't told me he was going. I supposed he was painting Francesca. He could have told me—but then, he hadn't wanted me to travel with him when he mentioned the commission. I discovered that I was more annoyed by Campbell's secrecy than by the thought of his spending time with Francesca. I must really have recovered.

Somers saw my expression. "I hope I haven't spoken out of turn?"

"Not at all. I know Campbell well. I believe he is painting the portrait of one of the young ladies."

He smiled. "Excellent. I was afraid for a moment that I had stumbled into some professional jealousy."

"We are in quite different lines of work—he a portraitist,

I in landscapes. We were at the Schools together."

"Which reminds me, my dear—there is an exhibition of pictures that we want to see, isn't there? Mr Armiger will know where it is, I'm sure."

It was a warm, sociable evening, despite the indifferent food and execrable ale, and I walked home with my head buzzing with Iphigenia and Rochford, ideas for drawings and thoughts about Wilberforce. I hardly noticed the snow and when I got inside, late though it was, I went straight to the studio, threw some coal into the stove and started leafing through my sketchbooks.

Chapter Fifteen

The exhibition the Somers wanted to visit was the British Institution's February display. They had seen the widespread advertisements of West's picture of 'Christ Healing the Sick', universally proclaimed the *chef d'oeuvre*. With any luck its publicity would bring extra customers to the show, who might be satisfied with a lesser work to take home. I'd sent a few things in to it before Christmas—a landscape by an up-and-coming man at fifty guineas would be an excellent choice, I hoped. There were four of my favourite vistas of St James' Park: avenues winding back into the distance, appropriately framed by groups of trees in the foreground and staffed with a few pedestrians in the front to give scale. I'd treated them in the manner of Richard Wilson, but with the looser brushwork I'd been developing lately. The tones softened into the furthest distances and in one I had introduced a glimpse of St James' Palace, in another a view of the red-brick front of Lord Apsley's house in the hope of interesting its new owner, the Marquess Wellesley, in a larger commission.

When we got to Pall Mall at ten a fashionable crowd obstructed the entrance to number 52.

"It appears we have come on a bad day," Mr Somers said. "Do you think we will be able to get in?"

"No, sir, it's only because we're early. If we wait a few minutes they'll open the doors."

We occupied ourselves with looking in the window of the bookshop opposite until the porters opened up and the mob streamed in, a solid mass of feathered bonnets, beaver hats and dripping umbrellas.

I had the shillings ready in my hand for the doorkeeper before Mr Somers could notice the entry fee, and we climbed the staircase to the three large rooms that formed the exhibition space. It was an impressive place, as it well might be, having been purpose-built only a few years before for the Shakespeare Gallery. The Directors of the Institution had bought it smartly when poor Boydell went bust. It formed a useful addition to the exhibiting possibilities for artists, particularly as it didn't admit portraits. That upset Campbell and his colleagues, but gave the rest of us a welcome lift.

"The Institution is quite separate from the Royal Academy—or not?" Somers inquired as we made our way into the North Room.

"Yes. It belongs to a committee of connoisseurs—patrons—not artists. The Earl of Dartmouth is the head."

"Even though the Prince Regent is the Patron? I do wish I could admire him more, since he is our monarch, but his treatment of poor Princess Caroline makes it very difficult, even though her own behaviour is... It is such a bad example to others."

"If he didn't like her, he shouldn't have married her," his daughter observed, frowning, "but having married her, and taken her away from her own people, he was bound to treat her with respect as a wife. You mustn't mind if I take her part, Mr Armiger—she is a woman, and I'm bound to stand by her."

I liked her outspokenness. "I agree entirely. Perhaps the Prince's patronage of the arts is the best of him."

By this time we had arrived at West's picture. It was not hard to find, since the entire crowd had gravitated to the same spot. The ceiling lights in that part of the room had been dimmed and the immense gilt frame draped with green and purple silk. The picture itself was more than twelve feet wide and nine high, the President plainly subscribing to the view that important pictures should be big. I thought of the Agamemnon, which I had done no work at all on since the Somers arrived. I'd been entirely taken up with the drawings for the pamphlets, which were now finished. I had to get back to Agamemnon tomorrow. There were only two months left to the closing date for entries.

Mr Somers took off his hat. "It is so beautiful, Rachel. See the expression of pity on the Saviour's face—how he holds his hands out to the crowd around him. He wants to include everyone in his healing." He looked quite radiant as he gazed at it.

"Yes, indeed." She studied it for a few minutes. "It's very fine, but I do wonder at the expense of such a size. I imagine the materials must be quite dear?"

"Yes. Only artists of the stature of the President can afford pictures of that size, although of course this was a commission."

"I read about it—and that it cost three thousand guineas." Her expression suggested that she could think of other uses for a sum like that. "However, I can see that it is full of life and feeling, and sincerity. I think that's especially important in sacred paintings, don't you, Mr Armiger?"

I hadn't thought about it before, sacred art not being a field that I'd had much to do with. "I think all art should be sincere, but insincere and self-parading sacred art must be worst of all."

"You must show me some art that you think insincere, and see if I can tell the difference."

We set off around the room, leaving her father still engrossed by the masterpiece. I pointed out a few people I knew in the crowd—Prince Hoare, talking to Farington and Dance; Reinagle, the Secretary of the Academy.

"Now there you have really successful artists—members of the Academy. I'll show you their work in a moment."

She stopped in front of a painting by William Collins, depicting some peasants carousing outside an inn. "What is it called?"

"'Mayday'." I'd provided myself with a catalogue.

"I see. Now please explain to me what is good, or bad, about it. I want to understand."

"I like the clear light and the perspective, especially of the background. But I think the best part of it's the sky." Collins had painted feathery clouds lit by afternoon sun drifting sideways across a low horizon, and the effect of a fine summer day was convincing.

"Don't you like the people? But then—you're a landscape painter." She gave me a sly look, but smiling.

"They're well painted, and the variety of figures and types has been praised by the critics, in particular the bedizened dancer, but I'm afraid there's always something about this sort of painting that I never quite… the artist seems an onlooker… of course, he must be, but..."

Miss Somers studied it for a few minutes while I tried to specify to myself exactly what it was I didn't like about common-life paintings.

She saw me frowning. "The artist and the people are separate in a way that they aren't when the artist paints people of his own level of society. I think one feels that quite distinctly in this picture, don't you?" She was absolutely right.

"Yes—when artists paint people above them like the nobility, they tend to look up to them, and when they are working people, they look down on them." But was this just a political view? Perhaps it was inappropriate to apply this sort of opinion to art? We moved on.

"This is the same artist, isn't it?" she asked. "'The Weary Trumpeter, or Juvenile Mischief'."

In an interior, a group of children were playing with the accoutrements of soldier who'd collapsed with fatigue on a chair, oblivious to the horn being blown in his ear.

"It's got the same problem. My instinct's to feel sorry for the soldier, who deserves his rest after what's obviously been a long day, but the artist wants us to be amused by the children's antics instead."

We gazed at it, side by side. "Actually, the best part of it is the scarlet of the soldier's coat and the white of his breeches, which Collins has handled well, which contrast with the dingy colours employed in the rest of the work. They also suggest that he's come from somewhere else—that he doesn't really belong to the other people there—that his life is more exciting, 'brighter', if you like, than theirs. That's quite good. I like that. But all that could be done without the necessity to make guys of the other people in the picture. That's even more true of the 'Mayday'." Amazing how explaining things to other people clarified them for oneself. I'd been grappling with this exact matter for some time in the back of my mind.

Miss Somers nodded. "Yes—I feel that he's making a point and wanting me to agree with him. But I had imagined that pictures were supposed to be like that. They don't make other people uncomfortable, do they?" I didn't think so. Like her, I'd thought it was an idiosyncrasy of my own.

We found Mr Somers again, standing before the lovely Veronese of St Nicholas that the Directors had bought. I thought it twice as good as the West, and at half the price a great acquisition.

"Ah, there you are, my dear. Are you enjoying yourself? Look at this—fascinating. Of course they are Papists, but we must not let that influence our consideration of the painting. What do you think of it, Mr Armiger?"

I was taking the opportunity to inspect the surface, but the conversation I'd just had with his daughter was still in my mind.

"It's a fine work by an Italian master—and a Venetian, so a great colourist. I wish I could get a green like his! The blue I suppose is ultramarine. Those pinks are exquisite. But it's the way he brings them all together, united and scattered by the duller hues, and at one with all the other compositional elements. And of course the quality of the drawing. The perspective of the angel, twisting backwards and up, is magnificently done."

"I like the way the artist shows St Nicholas catching up his surplice as he begins to kneel," Mr Somers remarked. "How often have I done exactly that! You feel his knees sagging. And the way the bishop leans forward on his crozier, his hand already out. It is the moment, to the life."

Miss Somers had been looking from one to the other of us and at the painting.

"Yes—all of that, and even more, what we were just speaking of, Mr Armiger. Here the figures—I was going to say 'characters'—seem oblivious to the artist, to the viewer, whereas in those other paintings they seemed to be posing. They seemed self-conscious and made me aware of what I was thinking about them. These people—the saint, the bishop, the angel—all seem caught up in their own concerns. I don't feel like the sort of observer I did with Mr Collins' pictures, and I don't feel I'm above or below them."

"You'll have to explain all that to me, my dear. But if it's so, why is this work so different to Mr Collins', and so much better—it is better, if I understand you, Armiger?"

"There really can only be one explanation, sir, much though I don't like to malign a fellow painter, and the President. Veronese is a much, much better artist than Collins. You can tell, not just by analysing his picture, but by the effect it has on the viewer. In the presence of great art you look without being aware of yourself, or it. You are taken into the artist's vision without self-consciousness. And here's a heresy," they leaned forward as I lowered my voice, "Veronese's a much, much better painter even than Mr West."

After inspecting the rest of the rooms they were exhausted, but they insisted on being shown my landscapes, having noticed them in the catalogue,

"So, this is the sort of painting you usually do?" Somers said. "They are delightful, really delightful. And I am glad that our demands on you have not taken you entirely away from your proper work."

I had forgotten that they had never seen my work apart from what was in the sketchbooks. Miss Somers said little, but examined them intently.

On the way out we passed Quayle and Hallett, who tipped their hats. I didn't stop to introduce them, but when I looked back Hallett had swivelled round and was staring.

I saw them back along the Strand. They were going to spend the rest of the day making up the pamphlets into bundles to distribute to various people who had promised to help them—some for members of Parliament, some to go in booksellers' windows or coffee houses, some for London parishes which were helping with the work.

I was satisfied with my drawings. The engraver had done a good job and they looked well set into the smudgy printed columns. One was of the old woman, crouched and looking up with the pleading expression I remembered well, while reaching for some potatoes; others were of children working at a scribbling mill and a version of Thwaite leaning against the beam, the machine in the background. I'd had to simplify the drawings, and rely on light and shade to get the effects

I wanted, but my mill sketching had come in very handy. I'd enjoyed thinking about Hall and Shirlow while I was working and pictured their annoyance when they saw the pamphlets. I was sure I could rely on some obliging friend to draw their attention to them. I hadn't signed them and didn't know whether they'd know me as the author or not. I'd decided I didn't care. It was unfortunate that the work wasn't paid, but I'd finished some medium-sized landscapes I'd been working on and the client had paid up with amazing promptitude and commissioned two more, so I felt quite justified in taking the time off.

Mr Somers was anxious to get the pamphlets out quickly as Parliament was shortly to begin debating the new Frame-Breaking Bill. This was largely directed against stocking-frames rather than the shearing frames used in the woollen industry, but its provisions were causing alarm throughout the industrial counties. The current penalties for smashing frames and causing damage were considered onerous enough by the Somers and other opponents of the bill, and I agreed with them. Transportation for fourteen years to a penal colony! But the alarmists in the Government, spurred on by the capitalists, thought that only the ultimate sanction would deter such destruction, and wanted the death penalty. There were of course those who opposed the Bill, including the young Lord Byron. He was going to speak in the House for the first time soon, and I was going with the Somers to hear him. The conservative newspapers had done their bit by raising the spectre of the Revolution in France. Our factual information about starvation and unemployment in the north, and the justice of the workers' demands, was sorely needed. I was happy to have been able to help. It gave me the feeling that my talents could do something other than ornament rich men's drawing rooms.

But I had my real work to do. After I'd left the Somers I

went to the John O'Groats, ate a chop and drank some ale, then went home and got on with the Agamemnon. I was still calling it that to myself, even though it was now Iphigenia. Her figure, and especially her face, still eluded me in detail, although I had more or less finished the background. A month and a half to go. I could do it.

On my way to Slaughter's next day a shabby figure accosted me in the street. He wore a dilapidated brown coat and his lank greying hair was tied in an old-fashioned queue. I would have passed him by if he hadn't spoken.

"Good Lord! Babbage!"

We'd been at the Schools together and he was younger than me, but he looked ten years older. I put out my hand but he shook his head, hands thrust deep into his pockets.

"No, no. How do you do, Armiger? I suppose you're getting on all right." His tone suggested that I'd once done him a great wrong but he was prepared to overlook it. I remembered that he'd always been snappish.

"I'm well, thank you. Haven't seen you for years. How does your work go on?"

He scowled. "You might well ask. Of course everyone is against me. I was to do a commission for Sir George Beaumont, but he changed his mind about it and so I withdrew the work. It was near finished, but as a man of honour I had no alternative."

I recalled having heard something about it. Sir George had wanted some alteration, nothing great, but had insisted. "Well, that was bad luck. What else have you been doing?"

"It's impossible to get work. Napoleon has made sure of that." He sounded as though the Emperor's sole aim in invading Europe had been to interfere with his prospects. His expression snuffed out the joke I had been about to make.

"No more commissions?"

"Sir George will have gone round and told all his friends not to employ me."

"Surely not. I wouldn't believe that of him."

He frowned darkly. "You'd be surprised. The fact remains that I can get no work, no work at all. I have not had a brush in my hand, except to amuse myself," his laugh was mirthless, "for several months—even years. And of course that means that I have no income. You see that I am virtually in rags."

I was shocked. He was a painter of more than average ability, producing portraits and scenes from literature—Othello, and so on. He had been well-regarded early in his career.

"Look here—I'm just going to Slaughter's. Some of the other fellows will be there. Why don't you come too?"

"I can't possibly afford that kind of luxury."

"Of course I'm inviting you."

He shook his head. "It's all right for you. I suppose you're well in with everyone—everyone who matters." His square face crumpled and reddened. "You and all those other 'fellows'—you get as much work as you want. You're comfortable. You don't know what it's like to be out of work." His voice was rising. A couple of passers-by cast glances at us. He went on without noticing. "No-one wants me—and I was a Medallist!"

It was true. He had won the Gold Medal the year we did our Diploma pieces.

"'Beware of envy', my father said to me when I took it home. He was pleased, of course, but he knew it would make me enemies, and it has. The penalties of success!"

He gave his grim laugh again. I began to wish to be away from him. He exuded an atmosphere of almost tangible rage. His fury, mixed with despair, was distressing. I wanted to take him by the arm, but was afraid he would strike me if I touched him.

"Look—come and have some coffee—or wine. Have you heard about the Competition? There would be a great chance for you—the premium's a thousand guineas and there's a commission to follow."

"I've heard of it," he snarled, "and of course I'm working on a piece for it—that's if they allow me to put it in. I expect they have already decided to exclude me—they'll find some excuse. Perhaps they'll 'lose' it. They're against me, because I spoke out against some of their decisions. It was my duty to do so when they were in the wrong. I can tell you now that I won't win. Don't you know what it says in the Scripture? 'To those who have much, much will be given, and to those who have little, even that little they have will be taken away.' No, I won't win. Success goes to those who are already successful, surely you've noticed that?"

I put out my hand, but he shook his head again and stumped off, hands still in his pockets, growling to himself. I went on to Slaughter's, shaken. I could overlook his offensiveness to me—I felt he hardly knew whom he was speaking to, that this diatribe was going on in his head all the time, and burst out upon anyone who chanced in the way. But it was appalling to think that a man of his ability had come to this. At a time when his contemporaries were still climbing towards a peak of achievement, he was on the scrap-heap. His resentment had obviously been festering for some time. His anguish was more disturbing than I could say. It took some time to restore a degree of inner tranquillity.

In the coffee-house I told Campbell and Brigstock.

"D'you know who I've just seen? Babbage."

Campbell raised an eyebrow. "It's been a long time since I've seen him. Wasn't he down in Kent somewhere, painting a series for a country house?"

"I thought so, but it must have come to an end, and now he's in a bad way." I related the gist of his tirade. "What can have happened? He seemed to be doing so well. I was thinking of him only the other day, about the Competition."

"I always thought he was hard to get on with," Brigstock remarked, dropping pieces of sugar into his cup.

"Aye, that's it. I introduced him to a collector I was painting a year or two back, I mind me, thinking he might get something out of it, and he immediately began arguing with him about a remark he'd made about art, I don't recall what."

"Well, now he's quarrelled with Sir George Beaumont."

Campbell groaned. "Some people have the gift of getting on with everyone," he didn't have to name Quayle, "but others..."

I finished it for him. "Babbage has the gift of antagonising everyone who could possibly be of use to him. It's more than accidental. He must do it on purpose."

"Aye—his sense of honour is so sharp that he sees slights everywhere and can't ignore any, and he has a very high idea of his own abilities."

"You're right." It was terrible how a man could be destroyed by such idiosyncrasies. "I remember he would always make a point of correcting me if he though I was wrong about anything, and one doesn't want to be taken up in that way all the time. But he was friendly when we were students together. He helped me move into my studio. We used to go out for drinks."

"Did he mention the Competition?"

"He's going in for it but he says the Academy won't let him win. He thinks it's because he's criticised them publicly."

"Nonsense. Lots of people have done that. Look at Hoppner. About the Competition, though, have you decided yet..?"

But it was a long time before Babbage's angry, despairing red face faded from my mind.

A few days later, at four o'clock, I met the Somers in Old Palace Yard. It was raucous and teeming with traffic as members and the public assembled. I was excited, never having been in Parliament when it was sitting, and having a personal interest in the issue—even more so, when a woman standing by the doorway pushed a pamphlet into my hand.

"Starving workers, sir—no death penalty! True facts!" It was one of ours. I gave her a smile and thrust away a man who was offering one of the other side's—*A Factual Account of how French Radicals are Destroying our Industries.*

"Absolute rubbish," I said loudly. Then I left our tract in a conspicuous place so that someone else might take it.

Mr Somers had got tickets for us so we had little difficulty getting in. An attendant pointed out the door. The Lords met in the old Court of Requests, their numbers having grown too large for their own chamber. It was a spacious airy room painted white, with lunette windows along the top and splendid three-tiered brass chandeliers suspended on red velvet ropes. The lords, magnificent in their finery, were seated along the sides under some enormous marine paintings. We were in a crowded gallery at the back, facing the dais, on which a jaded-looking Lord Chancellor sat next to the empty throne.

"Can you see Lord Byron?" Miss Somers whispered. It was very pleasant sitting there together.

Her father peered along the rows of nobles. "No—unless that's him," indicating a dark young man near the front.

I was unable to make out anyone except the bishops, by their dress. After a few minutes the gentleman who had been speaking sat down and Lord Liverpool got up and introduced the Bill. Lord Eldon, the Lord Chancellor, then called on Lord Byron and a different dark young man got to his feet, bowed and swept his gown back with a decisive air. Somers nudged me and we leaned forward.

"The subject now submitted to your Lordships, for the

first time, though new to the House, is, by no means, new to the country."

The poet was slight, with curling black hair and a pale complexion which coloured as he warmed to his subject. He was said to have a lame foot, but it was not evident from his posture. He spoke superbly, everything that I expected from such a writer, and with a dramatic air which I thought well suited to his theme. Some ladies behind us made disparaging remarks, however, suggesting that he wished to draw attention to himself with his gestures, would be better off at Drury Lane, *et cetera*. Two dingy men next to me, whom I took to be from the newspapers, scribbled down every word. I had my small book out too and drew him as he stood there, lit from above.

He seemed in command of both his subject and his audience, although this was his maiden speech. He spoke of alarming outrages, but said that it could not be denied that 'they have arisen from circumstances of the most unparalleled distress', and how 'nothing but absolute want could have driven a large and once honest and industrious body of the people into the commission of excesses so hazardous to themselves, their families, and the community'.

"He's right there," one of the newspapermen nodded, scratching away.

Both the Somers were fixed on the speaker, but I noticed that some of the noble lords were reading papers, whispering to each other or writing. I thought it rude, but I supposed they had to listen to speeches all night. All the same, this was an important Bill and I wished they would pay attention. My heart sank a little. These were some of the men we had to persuade with our pamphlets. If such an orator as Byron couldn't move them, how could we expect to?

He went on in a fine vein, saying how he had seen the distress at first hand in his own county, and although he had been in Spain and Portugal during the present war, and had travelled in Turkey and other infidel places, they were nothing to the wretchedness he had seen in England. He pointed out that the frame-breakers were guilty of nothing worse than having children they could no longer feed, and that they had not begun destroying machines until they started putting them out of work. Then he turned to the Bill itself, and told the Lords that the sword should be the last measure to be used, not the first, and that the government should negotiate with the men and the factory-owners instead. I was nodding at his every sentence and had to stop myself, or I would have looked a fool, but everything he said thrilled me. He put into words all the ideas I'd only half-understood, half-articulated to myself. And seeing and hearing him speak in the greatest assembly in the land showed me how serious our cause really was. I couldn't take my eyes from him.

The Chancellor became restless under Byron's attack, as were some of the members, who began muttering, turning round in their seats and calling out remarks. The poet had obviously anticipated criticism, for with all the coolness in the world he told them that the 'mob', whom the Bill would oppress, were the people who manned the army and navy, worked in their fields and provided their servants. He finished with a fine flourish, saying that the Government had been forward to help the Portuguese suffering under the French onslaught, but their response to distress in our country was to bring in a Bill condemning the workers to death. I thought he was brilliant.

I supposed he spoke for half or three-quarters of an hour, but it seemed only minutes. When he sat down half the gallery rose in applause, but the other half looked at us with annoyance and the Lord Chancellor suppressed the clapping. Some of the members also applauded. I understood this was customary when a man gave his first speech, regardless of the content. Some people began leaving.

"We should go, too, father. You don't look well. Are you in pain?"

Mr Somers did indeed look pale. We struggled out again and found our way into Palace Yard where a throng of carriages and hackneys was disgorging late arrivals. There was nowhere for him to sit down. He leant on my arm, breathing heavily.

"I think we ought to go back to the inn immediately. Father, we'll go back straight away."

Miss Somers managed to find a nook in the wall and he leant against it, coughing slightly, as people tramped past. I didn't like the look of him at all. I'd noticed before that he tired easily, but thought it was just overwork and his age. I saw a hackney cab discharging its passengers and ran up, securing it.

"Miss Somers—over here."

We got him into the cab and drove off. By the time we got to the Saracen's Head he seemed rather better and went up to his room unaided.

"If you will excuse me, my dear Armiger? It has been a great day, but I'm a little tired. But a great day. I am very glad to have heard such a speech. It gives one hope."

I detained Miss Somers for a moment. "Does he need a doctor?"

"I don't think so—not at present. He has these attacks occasionally."

"You'll let me know if there's anything I can do? If I can recommend a medical man?"

She pressed my hand. "Thank you. Although my father doesn't often mention it, we are both so happy to have a friend like you in London, where we're strangers—someone who shares in our work. And I know he enjoys your discussions about politics and art and so on—as I do." Her eyes shone sea-green in the dim light of the hallway. I clasped her hand in return.

"It's a pleasure for me, too. I hope your father improves. Let me know how he does."

"I will. Now I must go and see to him." But when I looked back from the street she was still standing in the doorway.

WHEN I got up next morning, my head was still filled with Byron and the excitement of the debate. I wanted to see what the morning papers said, but I was keeping away from Slaughter's, so I went to Rainbow's instead. I didn't want to hear about other people's progress with their big pieces, let alone enquiries about mine, and I wasn't interested in Hallett's tall stories or Alcock's gossip about his friends' love life and careers. I wanted to work.

At Rainbow's they had the *Morning Post* and the *Morning Chronicle* as well as the *Times*. I'd have to wait for Sunday to see what Leigh Hunt had to say in the *Examiner*. The *Times* had the speeches we'd heard and Lord Holland's, which followed Byron's but which we'd had to miss, but was along the same lines, Lord Holland being, some said, the younger man's mentor. There followed some words from the Lord Chancellor and speeches by Lords Lauderdale, Harrowby (in favour), Grenville *et cetera*. The *Chronicle's* coverage was more extensive and I read the debate with interest. Many thought the people deluded about the effects of the machinery on their employment, and wanted more enquiry as to whether 'hanging them as an experiment' was the right way to correct their misapprehensions. Despite what I thought were some very fine speeches, an attempt to get it adjourned was rejected, and the Bill was read for the second time and sent to Committee. So it looked as though it would pass despite determined opposition.

Poor fellows. It remained to be seen whether fear of death if they were taken up would overcome the desperation that had driven the workers to frame-breaking in the first place. Like Lord Grenville, I thought it unlikely.

Chapter Sixteen

Attending the debate had set my zeal on fire. I had to do something in this emergency. The pamphlet drawings had given me a taste for it, and seeing them in print, distributed to people who might read them, and who might make a difference to the workers, inspired me. I felt eager and restless, and wanted more. I wanted to influence the politicians to understand the condition of the workers and be more generous in spirit towards them, but I couldn't see how. Perhaps there would be more pamphlets to come. In the mean time, I had to get on with my work.

I got out my large sketchbook and turned to the study of Thwaite in his parlour. It had really come out well. I thought about working it up, but I was satisfied with it as it was—a good-sized water colour. I leafed through the book, past the scenes in the mill and a few landscapes, until I came to the one I really wanted, Thwaite standing in the mill, the slanting light modelling his brawny arms and catching the machinery behind him. I had known from the moment I saw him like that, that it was the subject for a large canvas. Who would ever buy it, I didn't know, and likewise where I could exhibit it, but I wanted to paint it.

I looked at the Agamemnon. I still hadn't been able to get the right expression on the face of Iphigenia. I'd hired a couple of different models who I thought might do, but I couldn't make them look anything but prettily vacuous or sullen. Perhaps I wasn't cut out for a portrait painter. I should stick to landscapes. I could make a tree look like whatever I wanted. But the Thwaite pictures had gone well; my studies of Francesca—I flinched at the memories—had gone well, and so had some sketches I'd done of Somers and his daughter.

I stared at the big picture, disliking it. What was wrong with it? Nothing, apart from the heroine's features. Why did I have to persevere with it? On a purely practical basis, because I'd paid a lot for the canvas and the colours. I could use the colours on something else. And then there was the Competition. I had to enter it to be taken seriously. Everyone agreed on that. Even bone-idle Hallett was rumoured to be at work on a huge triptych which would amaze the judges. Goodness knows what the subject was, but it was sure to include several of the pulchritudinous nudes he specialised in. Just thinking about the Competition made me tired. All the lobbying to get it hung well at the exhibition, to get it well spoken of by the critics—I simply couldn't work up the requisite enthusiasm. I knew that when I'd started the picture I'd been full of energy, but it seemed an immensely long time ago.

I thought of the exhibition at the British Institution and the conversation I'd had with Miss Somers about sacred art, and the superb Veronese, and the difference between the Veronese and West's *tour de force*. Sincerity—that had been the issue. A sense of authenticity of emotion that had its own force and truth and removed the work entirely from that sense of posturing, of parading false emotions, of displaying well-approved ideas before an admiring public who got precisely what they expected. Not that West's was not a great picture in its own way. God knows he might have felt exactly what the picture showed, but did it have to look so pleased with itself? There was more truth in one of Constable's skies. No-one could contest their absolute sincerity.

The Agamemnon said nothing to me, nothing at all except some passages of colour and texture that I was pleased with. The composition was all right. But the subject was nothing. I was only still struggling with it because of the Competition. If I gave it up I had to give up the Competition—there wasn't time now to do anything else. But what was the point of going on with something that I hated, didn't believe in? How could I expect anyone else to believe in it? But it was so strange. I knew, distantly, that I had believed in it, sincerely—unless I had been deceiving myself all the time. I remembered how I'd read the Potter and the *Odyssey* and how excited I'd been by the story. I frowned, gazing at it. I could still trace the elements of my enthusiasm in it, but they no longer spoke to me. The story was the same. I must have changed. I couldn't go on with it, Competition or no Competition.

I took it off the easel and put it in the corner, face to the wall, behind some half-finished views where I couldn't see it, and went down to dinner. I felt guilty but relieved.

I went to Middleton's and bought a couple of nice medium canvases, nothing ostentatious, but a good size.

"How is your Competition entry coming along, sir?" enquired the assistant. I'd made the mistake of telling him about it when I bought the big canvas. "All the gentlemen are very excited. Mr Farington was in here the other day discussing it with Mr Reinagle. Do you know who the judges will be yet? And of course the Annual Exhibition is not far off. We've just made up a large parcel of colours for Mr Lawrence. I'm sure he will impress us all again with something exquisite. Have you seen Mr West's 'Christ Healing'? A very beautiful and inspiring work, just what we expect from the President. Oh! Will that be all, sir? Can't interest you in this new mastic?"

I escaped with my purchases. The streets were damp but

the sun was out. I had an irrational holiday feeling, like a boy at half-term. I got a pork pie in Porridge Island then went home, put one of the canvases on the easel and started transferring the drawing of Thwaite. I could do what I liked now. The only troubling thought was how I would make a living.

EATING a chop at the John O'Groats and conning over the papers, the word 'Rochford' caught my eye. A meeting of the principal inhabitants had been called with a view to preparing a Loyal Address to the Prince Regent, 'expressive of the strongest assurances of their attachment to his Royal Person and support of his Government', in emulation of those made at Manchester and Leeds. The meeting was to be held in the Exchange Building. I remembered it well, an imposing Palladian structure in the centre of the town where the merchants gathered to talk business.

In the mean time, according to the *Mercury*, 'several most inflammatory hand-bills were posted up in the town. Instead of leaving the discussion of the question to the well-informed part of the inhabitants, no pains were spared to work upon the passions, and to mislead the judgment of the lower orders'.

I pulled a face. The lower orders, as I had discovered, thought the upper orders singularly ill-informed about their real conditions. I wasn't surprised that they'd decided to take some action. The *Mercury* printed one of the bills. It urged those who 'do not wish for an Increase of Taxes and Poor Rates, an Advance in the Price of Provisions, a Scarcity of Work, and a Reduction of Wages, to go to the Meeting on Wednesday morning next, and express your detestation of the conduct of those Men who have brought this Country to its present distressed State, and are entailing Misery on Thousands of our industrious Mechanics. Speak and act boldly and firmly, but above all, be Peaceable'.

Having seen the men and their poverty, I wondered whether they were finally being pushed too far. When men have nothing, they have nothing to lose. But the manufacturers had not responded well to the evident distress shown in the food riots, not only in Rochford but all over the north, and even among the tin-miners in Cornwall, according to the *Political Register*.

The morning of the meeting, thousands of people (probably an exaggeration) had gathered in St Paul's Square outside the Exchange and the public meeting was called off. However, 'one of the town demagogues'—I wondered if it was Danby—read the Resolutions out to the acclamation of the crowd. Whatever their grudges against the masters, they wanted the Prince to know they were loyal Englishmen. Then things went bad. Some of the mob broke open the door of the Exchange and took forcible possession. 'Matters were thus proceeding', the *Mercury* remarked with some satisfaction, 'when suddenly arrived from the barracks the regiment of Scotch Greys, and the County regiment of Militia. The Riot Act was immediately read. Never did soldiers perform their duty with more propriety. They were frequently provoked to acts of violence, but conducted themselves, with great moderation and forbearance towards the rabble. No lives were lost but several were wounded by the sabre'.

I shuddered. That 'rabble' was men and women driven to despair. I thought of the boy I gave the pie to, who could hardly grasp that it was for him, and wolfed it down in case I grabbed it back. Was he one of those 'wounded by the sabre'—or the old woman at the potato riot? I felt sick. And surely this couldn't be the end of it. The people would be angrier than ever. I folded the paper and put it back on the rack, then ordered coffee—strong, and plenty of it.

I applied myself to the painting of Thwaite with additional energy. I was sure he had been at the Square with his colleagues. I wanted to do something that was not sentimental, but showed that these men weren't the ignorant mob the papers thought. I liked the drawing too much to spoil it so I didn't square it up for transfer, but traced the main contours on thin oiled paper and drew the rest in freehand. It was something I was good at, having what is called a 'good eye'. The painting would be mainly an essay in tonal values with a limited range of subdued colours, as with the Sleeping Beggar. I still called him that, even though I now believed he was a shearman. The new canvas was exactly the same size on purpose. I hadn't forgotten my idea that they formed two halves of a story, perhaps the beginning and end, and I saw them as a pair. I propped the Beggar by me as I worked so as to co-ordinate them. It is a great mistake to start a painting separately and then try to bring them together by little alterations later. They should be together *ab ovo*, as it were, and grow up together. I hummed as I worked. The sun was out and my holiday feeling persisted. Now that the weight of the Competition had slipped from my shoulders I felt amazingly free.

True, my pupils had returned, but their fees were welcome, and the disagreeable doctor's son had persuaded his father to withdraw him—or *vice versa*. In his placc was a silent, fair-haired little boy who had a good hand and whose mother wished him to acquire the accomplishments of a gentleman. Tomorrow the Somers were coming to visit. I'd invited them as a result of some hints they had dropped after our visit to the Institution. It hadn't occurred to me that people who were neither artists nor clients would be interested, but they were. Mr Somers had recovered from his indisposition—no more than a slight chill, he said. I would have to tidy the studio and bespeak some tea from Mrs Mullins.

Feet on the stairs; Campbell's voice. "I'll go straight up, Mrs Mullins."

I reached for a cloth to cover the painting, then put it back. This is what I was painting. If people didn't like it—well. But I did turn the easel away a little.

"Morning, Armiger. Just thought I'd call in. Brigstock was saying yesterday we hadn't seen you for a wee while."

"No, I've hardly seen you since you got back from Rochford. How did you get on? Portraits finished?"

An extraordinary expression crossed his face that I'd never seen before. I couldn't quite identify it, but he was definitely pleased about something. It was almost smugness.

"Aye, aye—well—they're finished, aye."

"And your philosophers?"

"Aye, coming along well." He sat down on the sofa. "I got behindhand while I was away, but now I've caught up. I'll have it finished by the fifteenth."

"How's Brig?"

"Well." We talked for a few minutes about mutual friends and the Institution exhibition. I told him about the Somers, but only as friends who were visiting London.

"And how goes it with your Agamemnon? I can see I've disturbed you in the middle of work."

I was pottering around as we spoke, cleaning my hands on a rag and covering my brushes and palette.

"But that canvas looks smaller than I remember." He twisted around on the sofa. "Aye, much smaller. Have you started on something else? Have you finished the Agamemnon then?"

He got up to look at the canvas. He took in the drawing of Thwaite, the Sleeping Beggar and the sketched beginnings of the new painting. He scowled.

"Are you still on these? Man, that's no way to be going! What's happened to the Agamemnon? Is it finished?"

"No. In fact, I've given it up. It just wasn't going well. I tried a few different things but it wasn't working, so I've given it up."

His eye roved around the studio as though he meant to find the painting and force me to finish it. "Nae, nae, that can't be right. When I was here before it was well on the way—it was fine. Let me have a look at it."

"No, I'm sorry, Campbell, but I've really given it up. You'll see—it gives you more of a chance to win! You should want everyone to give up."

He clearly wasn't in the mood for joking. His earlier smirk had vanished.

"So you're abandoning the Competition altogether? You're not thinking of putting these things in?" He pointed at the new works.

I shook my head.

"What are they for, then? You're not going to tell me they're a commission. I mind me, that's the mannie you drew at Bath."

"Yes, I'm abandoning the Competition. I was spending my life working on something I didn't like, just in the hope of winning. I probably wouldn't have won anyway. Now I'm painting things I like—that I'm interested in."

"But we agreed that even if we didn't win, we had to enter to be seen as a coming man. What chance have you got with these things?"

Referring to them as 'things' was beginning to annoy me. "Why worry about it so much? I'm touched by your concern," I wasn't, but thought an exercise of tact useful, "but really, I'm happier as I am."

"Well! I never thought I'd see you just giving up like that. I thought you wanted to make a career in art."

"I'm giving up the Competition, yes. Giving up art, not at all. But what I want is a different kind of art. I suppose it's being true to myself, as Shakespeare says."

He was getting red in the face. I didn't know why he was taking it so personally. He was behaving like a jilted Miss.

"But there's no market at all for these things. They're completely outside modern taste. No-one wants pictures of beggars and such."

I mentioned Hogarth's 'Shrimp Girl', Gainsborough's rustic poor, Murillo's street urchins. He brushed these aside.

"You don't need to pay attention to taste, to proper standards? Perhaps you're too good for the Academy now?"

"Hold on! I can paint what I like, surely? I don't need the President's permission to daub a few canvasses for my own amusement?"

I wanted to stand up for what I believed in, but it was hard when Campbell was a good friend. I didn't like confrontations. God knew what he'd say if he found out about the pamphlets.

"Look here—there are two sides to every question. Many perfectly respectable people are interested in the problems of workers and the urban poor. Wilberforce, Lord Holland and so on—Lord Byron spoke against the Frame-Breaking Act in Parliament the other day, and he was not the only one."

"Pah! Whigs! You've been too much influenced by the low sort of folk you seem to have taken up with in Rochford. You had every opportunity there, but instead of getting to know proper people like Shirlow and the Crokers and McIlwraiths, you put yourself out to associate with rogues like this." He pointed to the drawing of Thwaite. "Don't you realise these people are undermining the economy? Just when trade's so bad and the factories are full of cloth they can't sell and the situation with America gets worse every day, these scoundrels are going about destroying machinery and mills. Half of them are radicals who'd like to see a revolution here like in France—is that what you want? And the other half are just feckless rogues." He was breathing heavily and glaring.

I stared at him, bemused. He sounded just like Shirlow. This wasn't the Campbell that I knew. I scratched my head while he stood there glowering. What on earth had happened to him?

"Why do you say I'm associating with rogues? What do you mean?"

"Why, everyone's seen those scribbles you did in that pamphlet—I won't call them drawings—Cruickshank would be ashamed of them. We recognised your hand straight away."

So the proverbial fat was on the coals. "Who's 'we'?"

"Well, Mr Hall, and John Shirlow. We all recognised your style, and the picture of that man in the mill. I told them I'd seen it in your sketchbook. You can't credit how angry they were. They'd given you their friendship and hospitality, and this is how you repaid them!"

"I'm obliged to you for having pointed me out to them as the author." I could hardly put enough sarcasm into my voice. "And the people connected with the pamphlet are very respectable indeed."

"I don't call people 'respectable' who incite the labouring class to violence." He was breathing heavily.

"Why does it matter so much? You associate with the people you want to, and I'll choose my friends."

His expression transformed dramatically. "Well, in point of fact—speaking of associating—I suppose it is bound to be known some time—but between ourselves …"

I had a strange feeling as though I almost knew what he was going to say, but it was still a shock.

"Miss Anne Hall has done me the honour of agreeing to become my wife."

The smug look had returned. It would not be going too

far to say he looked like the cat that had got the cream. The change was astounding.

"I may not be in London much longer. We'll probably live in Rochford. Anne's father's in a position to bring me a great deal of patronage."

"Well!"

"I hope you're happy for me. It's a great step."

Everything was becoming clear with great speed, but it was taking me time to assimilate this startling re-alignment.

"Er—yes, of course. Happy, and all that."

He smoothed his chin, smiling. But it was my turn to be annoyed. Furious, when I thought of it.

"You told me to keep away from Francesca, and that her father would never allow it—but you went after her sister!"

He shuffled his feet, sniffed.

"And without telling me! Why didn't you tell me you were courting her? You knew how I was placed."

"It's not as simple as that. To start with, I wasn't at all sure of my reception."

"But I told you about my situation when I wasn't sure either. Not at all sure!"

Campbell shuffled. "One shouldn't speak about a lady behind her back."

"Oh, really! I'm not suggesting you made her the toast of the regiment! Only that you should mention to a friend…"

"And then, we were not at all sure of her father's approval. It was only the other day that he gave it. In fact…" he fell silent.

"In fact, what?" He shook his head.

"What?" I was getting angry—angrier.

"Well, since you insist! It was only after Francesca's engagement to Mr Shirlow was decided, that her father was prepared to agree to Anne marrying me. Anne advised me to wait to ask him, as she thought it might turn out like that. I've always admired her common sense. So I waited, and she was right. He hummed and hawed for a bit, but ended by giving his permission."

I flinched. Sly, the pair of them! But I saw how well Anne's character chimed with Campbell's. He'd always been prudence personified. I thought of her remark about 'going where money was', and thought I understood it all.

"Why did that make any difference?" I wanted to hear it from him.

"He wanted to make a good match for his daughters. As he has no sons, you know, he must leave his fortune to his daughters and sons-in-law and his grandsons."

"Yes, thank you, I'm aware of all that." Could I ever forget Hall's expression as he explained that he wasn't going to 'throw Francesca away' on me?

"Having got one daughter married well—he was very pleased with the marriage settlement he's made with Shirlow, who has come down handsomely, very handsomely—Francesca's fortune is in trust for her sons—he felt he could indulge Anne. Of course we will have a great deal less than the Shirlows, but Anne is prepared to accept that. So you see it has worked out well for us."

"Yes, I see, all right—I see that by selling one daughter for an excellent price, he can afford to be a little generous where the other is concerned. Perhaps Miss Anne was not quite such a valuable commodity!"

"Look here, Armiger!" He was dark red.

"I wasn't good enough for Francesca. You've benefitted from my being sacrificed!"

"I can't help it if you resent my good luck."

"You would too, if you were in my position."

"It's not my fault. What did you want me to do, refuse to pursue the woman I love because you had been rejected for her sister? Be reasonable."

That did give me pause. Was that really what I expected of him? But although it wounded me in the sorest of places, it wasn't my main objection.

"I don't want to quarrel with you, Campbell, but what hurts is that you could go on like that behind my back, knowing about my hopes, and when I'd trusted you—that's not much like a friend, I think. When were you going to tell me? Or was I going to read your wedding notice in the *Times*?"

He had the grace to look shamefaced. "I didn't know how to tell you. I knew you'd be displeased."

"Well, I am. You come here and tell me that the sort of art I'm putting my heart into isn't good enough, and the people I like aren't good enough, and I'm turning into a radical, and then it turns out that it's all because you're marrying the daughter of a rich man. Damn it, Campbell! Well, good luck to you!" We stared at each other.

He picked up his hat. "I suppose I will see you somewhere about."

"I suppose so."

"I'm away then."

"Yes." I heard his footsteps slowly diminishing, then the front door slammed.

I was still nettled by Campbell's visit the next day when the Somers were to call. He had opened the wounds made by Francesca and I felt lonely and rejected, as well as in severe doubt about my new paintings. I had defended them to Campbell, but perhaps he had been right. I wavered between confidence and complete self-doubt, and at moments was near to giving the new work up entirely. What if he were right about the Academy? Perhaps my enthusiasm was leading me astray—I'd always distrusted it. It might be better to stick with what was generally approved. I had gone to bed confused and unhappy and woken the same.

I was looking forward to some congenial company, and the Somers were that. My spirits lifted as soon as they walked in. He looked pallid but otherwise his usual self. Miss Somers was wearing a green woollen dress that matched her eyes and complemented her tawny hair. There was something different about her appearance.

"You've done your hair in a new style."

Instead of all being put up at the back, she had allowed some to fall on her neck in loose curls. She coloured and put her hand up to it.

"I hope it is all right."

"It suits you very well."

"Well, so this is what an artist's studio is like!" her father was saying. "Fascinating! It's a privilege to be invited into your inner sanctum, Armiger."

"You're very welcome, sir—Miss Somers. Now, what would you like to see?"

Everything, it transpired. I showed them my presses full of papers and pigments and they tested the odours of ochre and turpentine. I let them try the walnut, poppy and linseed oils, and they were intrigued by their different uses—how linseed darkened light colours, so walnut or poppy had to be used instead, and how they dried at different rates, so that I used one if I wanted the paint to dry slowly and another if I wanted it to dry fast. Miss Somers dabbed her finger in the raw pigments I'd been grinding and exclaimed when they stained her hand.

"Hold still—I'll fetch a cloth." She wasn't annoyed, but laughed as I wiped her hand with a turpentined rag.

"Now what we really want to see is your paintings, if that's permitted?"

Somers was looking fatigued by this time and coughing a little, so I sat them on my old sofa and called Mrs Mullins to bring the tea. When they were settled with cups and plates I put the small easel and some chairs in front of the sofa and arranged a selection of my landscapes in oil and water colour on them. They were interested in those of Bath, where they'd never been.

"I like the way the light slants in to this interior—the Abbey, I suppose?" Mr Somers studied it. "I have a real sense of the volume of the place. And I feel that silence that one gets in venerable places of worship. You have really evoked it. I believe St Dunstan was there. We must travel more, my dear. I should like to see some of these historic places before I'm too old."

"As soon as you're better, father—in the summer." She smiled affectionately.

After we'd been through the best of the landscapes I showed them some pages of my sketchbooks that they hadn't already seen. My plan was to leave my new paintings until last. I wanted them to see what I'd done earlier, before moving on to my recent work. I wanted them to know my evolution.

I put the Beggar and Thwaite side by side on the easel. They were in different aspects, one horizontal and one vertical, but when I stood back and looked at them I thought they matched well. Miss Somers got up and went closer.

"Oh, I do like these!" She was silent for a while, examining them, her head bent, eyes serious. "They are just what I thought of when we were looking at those pictures by Mr Collins at the exhibition. Sincere—and you don't look down on the people. There isn't that feeling of distance, of standing back from them, that I felt with those pictures."

"Yes, I agree," Somers said. "It's our friend Thwaite, isn't it? It's very like. I can see this is where you got the drawing for our pamphlet. But these paintings—they're unlike anything I've seen before. Do I detect the influence of Rembrandt?

There is something about the shadows, the figures emerging—and if I may say so, Rembrandt's compassion, that is so evident in his works."

"You couldn't say anything that pleased me more, sir. I admire him greatly."

"And your style is so unusual. I like these effects—is that the word?"

"I've been experimenting with what we call loose brushwork—where you can see the actual strokes of the brush, and the colours aren't altogether blended, but sit side by side. I like the feel of the paint, its texture, and I want the viewer to feel them too."

Miss Somers was still studying them. "Who is this man?" She indicated the Beggar.

"I don't know. I saw him at Bath—that's the Abbey behind him—and something about him struck me. I don't know who he was, but now I've made up a kind of story that he was a cropper. He was wearing the same sort of clogs that you have in Rochford."

Somers looked at me, considering. "And that's when you first pictured the plight of the poor?"

"How did you know?"

"Your painting shows such thought. I congratulate you. These are fine works, if I am any judge."

His daughter nodded. "I do agree! Have you done many?"

"No, these are the only ones so far. I'd like to do more, but I don't quite know—I don't think they would be accepted by the Academy, or the British Institution. The subject matter is considered unsuitable."

"I'm sorry to hear that," Somers said. "I'd have liked to hear what the critics thought of them."

"Oh—father," Miss Somers exclaimed. "We almost forgot! Have you got the paper?"

"Here it is, my dear. We weren't sure whether you would

have seen this? We were so pleased when we read it." He offered me the latest *Literary Panorama*. "There—where it says 'The Winter Art Exhibitions'—halfway down the page."

I hadn't seen it and began to read a review of the British Institution exhibition, wondering why they wanted to draw my attention to it, unless they kindly thought that I'd be interested in anything about art.

Miss Somers pointed. "I've put a pencil mark next to the important part," she said, stressing 'important'.

I found the place. 'Among the landscapes is the work of an artist who has not gone unnoticed in the past, although he has not so far ascended high. We confidently predict, however, that if he continues the development which he shows at present, he may eventually rank among our foremost exponents. I refer to Mr Edward Armiger. We have seen many representations of the parks of London, but none that convey a more pleasing display of the richness and delicacy of our Royal gardens. 'St James' Park, with a view of the Marquess Wellesley's Residence', is no mere portrait of a gentleman's house, but a composition worthy of the late Mr Richard Wilson. The colours are delicately rendered with lightness and truth, and are animated by a kind of classical charm which characterizes the whole composition. 'St James' Park—the Lodge' is excellent. Nothing is abrupt, nor is there any passage without interest; the colouring is pure and natural, and the pencilling free.'

"Now, isn't that nice? We were most impressed that we know such an important artist."

I was impressed, too, and taken aback. I'd never received such a review before. I read it through again. It plainly hinted that great things were expected of me and that I should be in the Academy before long. But would the critics be as complimentary about Thwaite and the Beggar?

"There is no name to it. Do you know who wrote it? Obviously a man of discernment," Somers said, smiling.

"It could be anyone, but Hoare often writes for the *Panorama*, and it reads something like his style. Whoever it is, I'm immensely obliged to him." I continued to gaze at the page, resolving to rush out and buy a copy as soon as the Somers left. There is an enormous charm in seeing one's name in print, especially when it is coupled with such flattering remarks. "It will do me a great deal of good, I'm sure. It's very obliging of him, whoever it is."

I rubbed my hand over my chin. To get such a notice! It was wonderful. But just when I was giving up landscapes? It threw me aback.

"Are you all right, father? Some more tea?"

He was leaning against the cushions, coughing into his handkerchief. There were hectic spots in his cheeks.

"I'm sorry, sir—caught up with my own concerns. I've tired you out. Is there anything I can get you?"

"No, no, I'm quite well, thank you," waving away my solicitations. "But perhaps it is time we went. Rachel, where is my coat? It's been a most pleasant afternoon—fascinating—and I feel I've learned so much about art. It has been very good of you to show us your work. I've enjoyed it thoroughly. And I feel quite the man of the world, visiting artists' studios!"

I left him with his daughter getting his coat on and winding his muffler around his neck and came back with the water colour of the interior of Bath Abbey that he'd admired, packed in a piece of pasteboard. I'd been going to put it in the Water Colour Society's spring show, but it didn't matter.

"Please take this—you said you liked it."

"My dear Armiger! It's very good of you, but I couldn't possibly. You have already given us a delightful afternoon."

"Please do—if you like it. I've enjoyed your company so much. I'd like you to have a memento."

“In that case—it certainly is a very lovely work. We’ll treasure it, won’t we, Rachel?”

“We will—you can be sure of that, Mr Armiger. Thank you again. I hope we’ll see you soon.”

“That’s a nice young lady, Mr Edward.” Mrs Mullins had been gossiping with Miss Somers while I went into the street and procured them a cab.

“What were you talking about?”

“She complimented me on my griddle cakes and promised me a special recipe of her mother’s for spice bread. There’s not many that’d take the trouble. She’ll make some fortunate man a good wife.”

I was used to her broad hints, but this time there was real warmth in her tone and a wistful look in her eyes as we stood on the doorstep and watched Miss Somers’ womanly figure walking away. In my eyes, too. I had held her hand as I cleaned off the pigments. It had been firm and warm, and her laughter came back to me, and the shape of her eyes when she smiled, and her good humour, and I began to feel that it would be very pleasant indeed to see more of her. I pressed my hands together, still feeling the print of hers.

I saw her again sooner than I’d thought. The next morning I had a note saying that her father had been taken ill in the night. The doctor had been called and felt it might become serious if not attended to. They were returning to Rochford, where she could nurse him properly, on the next coach. She hoped to see me to say goodbye.

Chapter Seventeen

It was a relief to get to the Rectory at last. The journey in the coach had been cold and gloomy. We had brought plenty of rugs and shawls to keep Mr Somers warm, and taken it in turns to get down at the inns and procure tea and hot bottles. It was 'we', because I couldn't let Miss Somers take the burden of getting her father home alone. He was too ill to do anything but lie in his bed coughing feverishly. I was determined to help.

When I got her note I had gone straight round to the Saracen's Head.

"Oh, I'm so glad you've come!" had been her first words. She had bitten her lip.

I saw she was distraught and had offered at once to do whatever I could.

She had hesitated. "I don't know how I'm going to get him in and out of the coaches and up the stairs of inns."

"I'll come with you."

She nodded, then put fingers to her lips, unsure. We went up to see her father. He was ill and anxious.

"I am sure you can manage, dear, but if Mr Armiger doesn't mind," he had turned his head away for a moment, "I think it would be best."

I had assured her that I was happy to help, that my students could look after themselves for a week or two, and that I had nothing particularly pressing on hand. Now I'd abandoned the Competition, it was true. After a few more words she had agreed and I went down to buy the tickets. Then I had gone home and put a few things into my valise, which by now was acquiring a well-travelled look, packed up my painting things and left notes for Mrs Mullins to send to my students. We had taken the coach the same night.

In the warmth and rest of his home Mr Somers seemed easier. His doctor visited every day and sounded his chest. He was not happy with his condition, but applied a course of leeches and left strengthening tonics and strict instructions as to diet. By the end of a week Mr Somers had improved enough to sit up and take soup and arrowroot without difficulty. Fortunately a curate had been doing the duty of the church while he had been in London, and stayed on while he was needed. Some of the other clergy visited and their wives sent calf's-foot jelly and other appurtenances of the sick-room. I could do little but keep Miss Somers company and read to her father when he was well enough.

"Mr Croker has had one of those warning letters from General Ludd, according to Mr Robson," Mr Somers announced after one of the clergy visits. "I am sorry to hear it, but I cannot say I am surprised. He has the reputation of being a hard man. Deputations have attended on him asking him to delay the introduction of the new machines until the depression of trade lifts, but he is adamant. A wagon-load of his new frames was destroyed coming over the moors last month, but he has persisted and expects a new load this week. I am afraid for him, more than for the other mill-owners, because the people seem to have singled him out as the focus of their troubles. But I suppose it's nothing to wonder at after that incident with Robert Danby."

"What was that?" Miss Somers was writing at the table in his room, while I was at the other end working on a new set of drawings for the next pamphlet. We were going to include one of Lord Byron giving his speech.

Mr Somers shook his head. "I can hardly credit it, even from such a man as Croker. Thwaite told me that Danby was on the moor near those cottages outside Coldbrook when he saw a woman lying fainting by the road. He knew her for the wife of a cropper who'd been turned off from Croker's last year. She had a baby with her. Just as he stooped to pick up the bairn, and found it quite dead—from hunger, Thwaite said—Croker rode by. Danby lifted up the babe to show him—no doubt he shouted out some unpleasant remarks, as he is hot-blooded in the extreme—and Croker slashed him across the face with his whip."

"So that's how he got that scar! But it's a terrible story. Can it really be true?" Rachel got up to stand by his bed, her face clouded.

"I don't know, my dear. Thwaite believes it, and so do the people hereabouts. Violence, and more violence, is what their present hardship is breeding. Danby's brother Luke has been terribly angry ever since Robert was taken up. I wish I could speak to Croker, but he is one of Robson's flock and both of them would take it amiss if I did."

"What is he doing as a result of the letter?" I asked.

"Gone to see the magistrates to ask for help, and has sent to the garrison at York for soldiers. But you know last time, General McKinnon said that he didn't have enough men to send troops to every house and mill that was threatened all over the county." They looked at each other. "In the mean time, I suppose he has got his sons and his own men on guard."

Miss Somers sat down again. "And all we can do is write, and make pictures, and speeches—no offence to you, Mr Armiger, we are grateful for your work. But it seems so slow, and events are moving so quickly."

She took up her pen and began to write again. I saw she was disturbed and wished I could comfort her. I watched her for a minute. The pale light, coming through the lace-curtained windows at a low angle, modelled her features and picked out the contours of her hand, moving rapidly across the page in fine swift script. Where the sun struck it her hair was the honey gold of beech leaves in early autumn. She looked up and saw me looking at her and I bent over my drawing again.

The pamphlet was addressed to the mill-owners and magistrates of Rochford. She had a gift for prose of this sort, recapitulating the various arguments more concisely than her father, and with a warmth of appeal that he found it hard to generate—not that he did not feel it, but his classical education got in the way. Since his illness she had taken over the work almost entirely, and as I was there I was able to do the drawings as she went. Her competence on a variety of matters was remarkable.

THE next day I went out on some errands and retuned in time for tea, to find that it was laid out in the parlour and a visitor was installed by the fire, a young man in clerical black.

Mr Somers was downstairs, well wrapped in shawls. "May I introduce Reverend Arthur Crosland? We were not expecting a visit, but it's a pleasure to have him here."

I assumed he was some colleague of Somers' and greeted him politely. We all sat down. Miss Somers had her head bowed over the teacups, but I thought she was blushing. I suddenly felt that something was up.

"Mr Armiger. It is a pleasure to meet you. Rachel has told me about your work."

'Rachel'? What the devil did he mean?

Somers saw my expression. "Arthur and Rachel are engaged to be married," he said. "I should perhaps have mentioned it earlier."

Engaged? Miss Somers engaged to be married? God Almighty, was every single woman in Rochford engaged? Was not one of them unattached? It seemed as though the streets abounded with attractive women, but when it came to the point, they were all taken, every one. I was surprised at how put out I was. I had no business being annoyed. What was it to me, anyway? Rachel Somers was a friend, that was all. She smiled at me, pink but encouraging. I realised I was scowling and pulled my face into a more appropriate shape.

She poured the tea, handing the cups first to her father, then to Crosland, and last to me.

"Arthur was my curate when first I came to St Saviour's," her father was saying, "and was of great assistance to me. At present he is acting as *locum tenens* for an old school friend of mine in Devon."

"I'm happy to be of use, of course, but it is unfortunate that it is so far away. I was able to take advantage of a friend of Sir Perceval, whose living it is, coming here on business and offering me a place in his carriage. They are very kind people there altogether." Crosland took a tea-cake and began eating it. He had a round face. He would turn into one of the meaty clergy when he was older. I could picture him now, rubicund and genial, his waistcoat rather tight around the middle.

"We hope that his current employment may lead to something better," Somers said, "but would have preferred that he was closer to us here. Still, we must take what we can get."

"Is your post a lengthy one?" I had to find something to say.

"Six months in the first instance, but it may well be longer if Canon Marshall is delayed in his travels."

We passed on to other subjects. They seemed to get on

well, although he was not the sort of man who I thought would have attracted her.

In my room before dinner, I sat down on the bed to think. I didn't know why I should have been so annoyed by this piece of news. Nothing could be more natural than that a woman of her age, if not married, should at least be engaged, but it had not occurred to me for an instant. She hadn't told me she was engaged. I dwelt on that for a while, rankling. But why should she? What did it matter to me if she was engaged, or to whom? But turning it over in my mind, I understood that I had imagined her as always at the Rectory with her father, a snug pair, united in work and disposition. Now she would go away somewhere with the curate—younger than I was, and somehow seeming a great deal younger—and leave her father alone.

'Of course it cannot be for some time,' Crosland had said, glancing at her. 'I must get a better place, which we hope will not be too far from here, so that we can visit regularly.'

They would not marry soon, but marry they would. Already Crosland was completely at home in the Rectory and I felt like an outsider, just when I had begun to fancy myself an intimate of the family circle. Damn him, and her. No, not her. Never her. She was too good, too kind, too clever for him. He had mentioned something, when we were discussing the pamphlets, about her giving them up after they were married. 'She will be far too occupied with the house and children', he had calmly remarked. She deserved much better—someone who would really appreciate her unique qualities.

I got up and stared out the window at the bleak churchyard and the tall yews, black in the dim light. The scene was familiar, but everything else had suddenly changed. I ran headlong, with a smack in the face, into the cause of my vexation. In an indistinct, half-unconscious way, I had seen myself eventually becoming part of the family. It was not at all like with Belinda so long ago, when I was just a boy, or my infatuation (I couldn't call it anything else, now) with Francesca. I had had no realistic plans to marry her, but I resented someone else taking her away.

"Damn! Damn, damn, damn!" And perversely, now I knew that she was spoken for, she seemed even more alluring.

EVERYTHING was as usual at breakfast, but everything was different. Crosland was not present and Miss Somers and I made rather awkward conversation. I hardly knew how to address her, and stumbled over every little exchange—passing the sugar, asking for more tea. For a while I'd been afraid I was going to be evicted from the guest room to make way for Crosland, but fortunately that wasn't necessary—he was staying with his family. But it seemed a good idea to keep out of the way as much as possible during the few days of his visit. I didn't want to talk to him and I wasn't happy about being in the same room as the pair of lovebirds. I snarled to myself as I thought of the phrase. Lovebird! One of a pair—a pair for life. It looked as though that would never be me. Belinda, Francesca—and now Rachel—I was fated always to fail with women. I couldn't even claim one as a close friend and companion, let alone wife. It was something in me. I just wasn't good enough.

What did Crosland have that I didn't? It was all a mystery to me. I'd never understood why some men attracted women and I couldn't. I wanted to love, and to be loved, sometimes so badly that it hurt. But I was condemned to a life of loneliness.

I couldn't stop in the house all day while Crosland was there. It was too painful. I'd wanted to make some studies of Coldbrook Manor since I saw it from the top of the coach on my first trip north. What an age ago that seemed. The journey was now so familiar that I was on friendly terms with the garrulous coachman, and every time we passed the Hall he pointed it out to me again and told me the history of the Ashbys, the old family that owned it. That gave me an idea. At the George and Dragon I found out that I could get a lift on the London stage in the morning, get down at Coldbrook, and pick up the Rochford coach in the evening. That would give me a long day at the Manor. It would be dark when I returned, but I didn't mind. The longer I was out, the better.

This was the ideal moment. I packed up my sketchbooks and paintbox and boarded the coach. At Coldbrook I got down and strolled through the village, a pleasant higgledy-piggledy street, up and down with a patch of cobbles outside the inn, a tiny ancient church set back from the street surrounded by the gravestones of earlier Coldbrookians, and a coppice of fine alders. I got some bread and cheese and a bottle of tea at the inn to take me through the day and set off for the Manor.

The day was chilly but I had my greatcoat and muffler, both of which I took off after walking a little. It was good to get away from the Rectory. I needed time on my own, to think. The sun gradually burned the dew and mist from the grass and by the time I reached the Hall it was a fine day. The house looked shut up and the innkeeper had told me that 'Squire's away', but it didn't matter. I found a good vista and began to draw. It was a long time since I had had a day in the country and, as always, I wished I spent more time there. The smells of grass and trees, the country sounds of sheep and cows that populated the meadows below, birds and the distant clank of a forge or wagon, calmed my spirits and brought Wordsworth and tranquillity to my mind. I drew away and got out my paints, filling my waterpot at a little brook that bubbled down the hill. The water was icy enough to make me gasp, but diamond- clear and clean.

I spent much time thinking as I worked about Miss Somers, and Crosland, and the revelation of my feelings. The serenity of the countryside worked on me as I had hoped it would. It was good to have the time to consider the future quietly. I resolved at last that I could do nothing. I thought—no, knew—that she liked my company, but there was nothing more than that. She was engaged.

It was an enjoyable day and I made two good studies of the dignified old house, one in morning light and the other in the afternoon with the sun warming the bricks and firing the latticed windows into shards. I took plenty of notes so that I could work them up into oils at home. In between I stretched out on my greatcoat on the grass and ate my bread and cheese, and contemplated Wordsworth, and the power of nature to soothe and revive, and how all things must pass in the end, and of spring coming, and the lives of animals compared to the lives of men.

I worked until the light began to go, early in these northern hills, and needed to get on my path back to the village. I had left it a little late and had trouble finding the track I had taken. I went up one hillside and down another, carrying my gear in a satchel on my back, then found myself near a small farm which I certainly had not passed on my way in the morning. It was twilight and I began to worry. I called out and the dogs barked; a man came to the door and told me that I had taken completely the wrong road and must turn around and go back to the Manor, then strike out in a new direction. He gave me detailed instructions, but a great deal depended on my recognising 'the old crooked oak', 'the new fence' and other local landmarks.

"Can you give me a light?"

He sucked his teeth for a minute, then went into the house, reappearing with a horn lantern. "You're better off without it, master. Moon'll be up soon, and you'll have plenty to see by."

I took it all the same, and gave him a shilling.

He watched me thoughtfully as I walked away. "Don't you forget now, left at old oak, then straight on."

He was right about the moon, which shortly appeared on the horizon, huge, a glowing orange disc. It rose with amazing rapidity as I walked over the moor, paling as it went until it was a yellow circle in an indigo sky, diffusing a radiant halo and brightening the sky around it. I shuttered the lantern.

I went back the way I had come, looking for familiar and unfamiliar points. I thought I recognised trees I had passed and the shape of a hilltop near the Hall. Moonlight lent the landscape an eerie bluish appearance, the tops of hills and trees luminous, their shadows ink-black. Now the sun had gone down I was glad of my coat. My feet rustled in the grass and a faint mist was rising.

After a mile or so I thought I heard voices and made for them. I thought I must somehow have come on the village from a different side, although I had not found the crooked oak that marked my turning point, according to the farmer.

Then it reared up black against the sky, a vast dome half-blasted by some storm. The voices were louder. Men were gathered under the tree—many men. There must have been thirty or forty of them. They spoke in low voices; some carried shuttered lanterns, which gleamed fitfully on metal. I was suddenly glad that I had covered mine, and stopped in my tracks. Whatever these men were doing, I wasn't sure they would be pleased to see me. I crept closer in the shadows. Then I saw that their faces were blackened like poachers, and many wore neckerchiefs over their faces and caps pulled down low. In their hands they held muskets and pistols, and some had hatchets and hammers. They muttered together then divided into groups, according to their weapons. For the first time I heard a voice distinctly.

“Us won’t wait any longer. Let’s be off now.” And they moved off with the regularity of soldiers, but they were not soldiers.

I had stumbled on a meeting of frame-breakers.

My heart raced and instinctively I thrust the lantern under my coat. They mustn’t see me—who knows what they would do! They would think I was spying on them—they’d never believe I was merely lost. I remained crouched in the dark, thinking to wait until they’d gone before making my way back to Coldbrook and the coach. But as the tail of the column disappeared over the hill I was seized with a burning curiosity and the thought that I might see sights that would make paintings such as no-one had done before, and before I had come to a decision I was after them.

We tramped for ages across the moor. Their attention was all on the task ahead, although they stopped from time to time and looked about them. I followed a good distance behind and dodged behind gorse bushes and trees when they looked around. Once I stumbled into a sleeping cow which lurched to its feet, bellowing, and once I saw a light moving in the distance and the sound of wheels and realised it must be the main road. After two or three miles I began to see a lighter haze in the sky ahead. It could only be Rochford. Another half hour and dark shapes loomed against the haze and the moon, breaking out of cloud, illuminated a huge black rectangle with a huddle of smaller buildings around it.

I had no idea what their destination was and hoped it wasn’t Hall’s mill. I didn’t recognise this building, but everything looked different in the dark. If it were Hall’s I would have to give the alarm, since the family lived alongside it. I couldn’t imagine how I was going to do it without being discovered, but I couldn’t leave them to whatever depredations were planned. It may have been ignoble, but I felt that if it was Shirlow’s I might perhaps leave Mr Shirlow to look after himself.

As we came closer the men went into a huddle and there was more muttering—orders were being given. I didn't know the place, which in darkness had the look of a fortress, but thank God it wasn't Hall's. All silence was at an end now. A group of men armed with muskets spread out at the front of the mill; they banged on the house door, demanding entry. Lights went on and I crept closer, looking for a vantage point where I could hide but still see. I was so excited that I had forgotten that I was supposed to be back at the Somers, almost forgotten who I was. I believe if the authorities had come at that moment and tried to drag me away I would have kicked and struggled to stay.

Looking about, I saw a stable on the far side of the mill yard, with a hayloft above. Quick as I could I scuttled through the blackness to the wall. I could hear the shouts and blows as the men demanded entry. The warm smell of horse sweat greeted me as I opened the door a fraction and eased through it, and they whickered sleepily as I passed them. Up the ladder and into the hayloft and I rushed to the front, falling over bales of hay, and looked out the loft door. I was not twenty feet from the house.

The yard was a blaze of torches which the men had lit. The house door stood open, a yellow rectangle, and three men, fully dressed and armed with pistols, stood in in the hallway. They were instantly confronted with muskets aimed at their heads and laid down their arms, which were seized by the guards.

"Who are you?"

"General Snipshears, come to pay a call." Some of the men sniggered.

"Frame-breakers, I suppose." It must be the owner. I was impressed by his coolness.

"You may say so. Open the mill doors!"

"Never!"

"There'll be no violence against you if you do what we want," the leader said, "but if you get more frames in after this, we'll be back to finish the job."

The cold-blooded warning shocked me. The owner opened his mouth, presumably to protest, but said nothing. Perhaps he was afraid that if he complained they would finish him then and there. The man who confronted him looked capable of anything.

Some men were beating at the mill doors with hatchets and hammers, but the leader shouted at them to stop. He presented a pistol at the head of the owner, grabbed him by the arm and forced him down the steps and up to the mill doors. I saw by the torchlight that the doors had been strengthened with iron bars. Other men took hold of the men from the house, preventing them from following, and tied them together, laying them on the floor and standing over them with pistols.

While they were doing this the reluctant owner, pistol at his head and swearing dreadful oaths, had produced a key and was opening one of the doors. Men streamed in, hammers ready, only to return a minute later.

"Them's scribbling mills! Us don't want 'em!" Two men gripped his arms and his pockets were searched; the keys were found—I heard them jangle and clank as they fitted them into the locks. The bars were wrenched away and the men again rushed into the mill, leaving a guard on the owner and lookouts on the corners of the buildings. I was amazed at how well-orchestrated and disciplined they were. I had heard it said that there must be some military mind behind these attacks, as common workmen would never be able to organise them so well. Someone had even suggested that they were being trained by French officers on parole. I didn't see anyone in the crowd who fitted either description, and thought that the gentry underestimated the mental power of these men. At the same time I was frightened by their violence and crouched well down in my eyrie.

Loud crashing, shouting and shattering sounds suggested that the men had found the shearing frames. Pieces of apparatus crashed through windows onto the cobbles. There was loud laughter and oaths, but the men in the yard were silent, listening to the work of destruction. I could see little that went on inside, but suddenly a glow began to light the windows at one end of the mill. There was a babble of voices and the sounds of destruction stopped, then men began to emerge from the building. The owner, bound as he was, writhed desperately on the ground, raving and swearing at the top of his voice.

"Oh, you bastards! You'll destroy everything! Fetch water! Let me go! Let me go!"

The orange light spread and flames leapt from the windows. It was a magnificent and horrifying sight. I was transfixed. I had never been so excited and terrified at the same moment. Now I really understood what 'sublime' meant. I wanted to race down and join in the commotion in the yard, to shout and rush about with the others. Then I heard hooves, and one of the horses below me neighed.

An answering whinny came from up the street. A moment more, in which every head in the yard turned in that direction, and with an immense thunder of hooves and clatter of harness a squad of dragoons burst onto the scene, sabres drawn, the firelight turning their crested helmets to flame. They did not pause for a second but rode straight into the crowd, slashing all in their way. Men scattered like leaves driven before a gale, but I saw at least one go down, bleeding, to lie on the cobbles. The men with muskets fired while others simply ran, tossing away their hammers. The dragoons returned fire with their carbines. The banging ricocheted around the yard. Men screamed. There was a frightful din. I clung to the door-frame, horror-struck, petrified. The fire in the mill increased in intensity. Orange light flickered over everything. Through the hullabaloo I noticed that the owner had got free from his ropes and was running into the mill, pistol in hand, perhaps intent on capturing some of the breakers. Firing continued for a few minutes more, then the yard was empty save for the dragoons—except those who had galloped after the fleeing men—and some bodies sprawled on the cobbles. Flames overwhelmed the building.

I came to my senses. I had to be gone. It only took a moment to tie the lantern to my satchel, slip down the ladder, back through the horses. Oh God! There were soldiers in front of the door. I looked about, terrified. Was this the end for me? There was a small grimy window at the back. I ran up to it, setting the horses neighing and plunging in their stalls, dragged up a bucket, set it by the wall and jumped up, but it was still too low. Almost weeping in my panic I found a wooden box, set it on the bucket, scrambled up, smashed the window with my arm, dropped the satchel through, tumbled after it, fell heavily into a pile of muck, got to my feet and ran away as fast as I could.

I got safely into a street behind the mill, where I struggled into my satchel— but had hardly paused for breath before I heard steps behind me. Not steps; hoof-beats. I pressed myself against the wall; they got louder. Two, at least. A horse whinnied.

"I'm sure I saw one going this way, Jack."

I didn't know whether to stay still or run. I held my breath. All was silent. I ventured to move a foot or two and instantly the night burst into the clatter of hoofs and jangle of harness.

"Down there! There he goes!"

I ran, dark lantern in hand and satchel thumping on my back, the cold air burning in my throat. The hoofs were louder, closer. The street was straight and narrow: nowhere to hide.

My eyes darted from side to side as I ran but I saw nothing but house fronts hard against the road.

"Stop there!"

I turned, appalled. Two dragoons were not ten feet away. Their faces were hidden under the peaks of their helmets and their white breeches and belts stood out wraithlike in the moonlight. Their sabres bounced against their horses' flanks and the moon glinted on the carbines in their hands. They sprang forward and I felt, rather than heard, the discharge of a flintlock, and something struck me hard in the left shoulder like the kick of a horse. My arm went limp. I staggered but ran again, sobbing in pain, and they came after me, until a narrow alley opened suddenly between two houses. I slid into it and heard them jolt to a stop. Looking back, I saw them leaning down over their horses' withers and peering in. I stumbled on and found myself in a yard filled with pieces of wood and broken-down carts. I leaned against one for several moments, trying to get my breath and holding my arm. A light flickered in a window overlooking the yard and a man leaned out.

"Who's there? You—what are you doing?" and a dog set up a great barking.

One of the dragoons had dismounted and was leading his horse into the alley. I wriggled under a broken cart and found the door of a small outhouse, which I slipped into as silently as I could. Judging by the smell, it had been used for pigs. The dog knew I was there and started barking again. The damned thing would have me killed. The horse's feet echoed on the cobbles. I thought I was going to die there, in that shed, and almost fell to my knees in despair.

Then, miracles of miracles, I saw in the darkness a little gleam of moonlight like a pencil. It came through a small door of rough boards. I put my eye to the crack and made out bushes and weeds—a little piece of waste ground. Perhaps the owner had let his pigs out there. I eased the door open quietly. No-one was there. I almost crawled through it, crept hunched between the bushes to the fence, and slipped into a rutted path lined by trees.

After half a mile I felt safer and stopped to lean against a wall and recover my breath. I looked about me; I was in the outer parts of the town, but I couldn't recognise where. I listened, but heard no pursuit. I was in a street of low houses, empty except for a prowling cat which regarded me suspiciously. I thought it was safe to light the lantern and struck a flint. I surveyed myself: I was covered in straw and dirt, the sleeve of my greatcoat was cut where I had smashed the window and my boots were covered in mud. My arm and shoulder throbbed, but had recovered some movement. I couldn't see what was wrong until I could take off my coat. I pulled out my watch and held it up to the light: it was half past one. What must the Somers be thinking?

I kept walking without much idea of direction, hoping to see a church spire or the tower of the Town Hall to give me some idea of where I was. It seemed to be a region of small houses, nondescript and without identity. They could go on for miles. I came to a cross-road, hesitated, then struck out at random. I passed a church and a few shops which gave me no more information than the fact of their existence. I was completely lost for the second time that night. There was no-one to speak to, no-one to tell of the exhilaration, horror and fear I had just experienced. I felt like a ghost ship drifting rudderless across the empty ocean, ever slower and more frail, until sheer exhaustion brought me to a halt. Then I would collapse little by little, my sails yielding, mast toppling to the deck, timbers breaking up, till I sank gradually from human sight.

At last I saw a man at the end of the street, limping slowly along. There was something about his hunched look that made me reluctant to approach him—that and the knowledge of my own dishevelled appearance. But I was exhausted, and I didn't want daylight to find me wandering in a strange part of town. I pulled some of the straw from my coat and increased my pace. A few yards from him, he turned and watched me approach with an air of extreme reluctance.

"Hallo there! Would you be good enough to tell me my way?" I lifted the lantern.

His cap was pulled down over his face and I wondered, as he no doubt did about me, what he was doing about the streets at this time of night. He stood well away but answered civilly.

"Where is it you want?" There was something familiar about his voice.

"St Saviour's church."

He started slightly and turned away. His voice was muffled. "It's not far. See that turning? Down there, keep straight along until you see a warehouse on your left. Turn down by it, and you'll be behind the church graveyard. You can go through it, or round, if you mind the spirits."

"Thank you."

He muttered something and began to move away. I walked after him and as I got nearer I saw that his clothes were of fair quality but soiled and torn. I crossed the road to the turning he had pointed out and held up the lantern: as I did so he turned his head slightly and our eyes met. It was Thwaite. His face was blackened and he had a neckerchief over his mouth, but I had no doubt that he had recognised me as I had recognised him. He too, had been at the mill. For a moment we stared at each other, then he went on rapidly, dragging his left leg a little. Then he was out of sight.

When at last I arrived at the rectory I was beyond fatigue. Even in my condition, I couldn't bring myself to rouse the house. Everyone would be sleeping and I didn't want to get Somers out of his warm bed on this cold night. I stood shivering by the door for some time, considering what to do. My shoulder hurt now, a wound like fire, or a hot knife probing my back. I put my hand up under my coat and it came away wet with blood, but I could move my arm. I clenched my fingers and shifted my arm about, and although it made me flinch in pain I seemed to be whole. I was also famished, having had nothing but a bit of bread and cheese since breakfast. I tried the door of the church, a forlorn hope. Then I trudged around the back of the house, through the back gate and into the kitchen garden. The hen-house was too small for me, but there was a lean-to behind the scullery where they kept firewood and garden implements. It would have to do. I crept in, groaning to myself, my shoulder already stiffening and my body aching, laid down on some sacks and gathered my greatcoat around myself. Then I waited for dawn.

Chapter Eighteen

At first light I was walking up and down in the yard, trying to get warm and waiting for someone to wake up. I would do anything for a cup of hot, strong tea and something to eat. I had spent a lot of the night nursing my arm and thinking about hot soup, beefsteaks, macaroni with cheese sauce, toasted muffins. At last the scullery door opened and the maid came down the steps with a bucket. She started on seeing me. I must have been an awful sight. She dropped the bucket and ran inside.

"Miss Rachel! He's here!"

Following Maisie in, I all but collided with Miss Somers, running into the kitchen.

"Edward—Mr Armiger! We had given you up! Where have you been? Look at you! What on earth have you been doing? We have been so frightened. How dare you cause my father so much anxiety, ill as he is? We were up half the night worrying about you. It was thoughtless—very thoughtless! I would have thought better of you!"

She was red and breathless. I'd never seen her in such a state. I'd been prepared for awkward explanations, but not for being rated like a schoolboy caught stealing apples. Before I could speak she whisked out of the room.

"Lord, sir, you do look bad. Sit down and I'll get you a piece." Maisie bustled about the kitchen and I sank gratefully onto a chair, holding out my hands to the stove.

"I hope I didn't frighten you, Maisie."

"I was never scared of nobody, Mr Armiger. Drink this."

I'd never relished tea more. By the time I'd warmed myself, drunk the tea, eaten a piece of pie Maisie found in the larder and struggled out of my filthy, battered greatcoat, Miss Somers had returned. She was calmer, but still flushed.

"I am so sorry to have caused you so much trouble," I began. "I really couldn't help it. It was so late when I got back here—past two—that I didn't want to wake you."

"Where have you been all night?"

"In the lean-to, with the spades and shovels."

There was a moment's silence, while we all looked at each other. Then, to my surprise, both she and Maisie began to laugh and after a moment I joined in. I knew I presented a ludicrous sight, my boots muddy and scarred, a day's growth of beard, my hair on end, and the vision of myself crouched in that horrid den struck me, too, as ridiculous.

Miss Somers wiped her eyes. "I'm sorry for what I said just now. We were very concerned—you may imagine." She avoided catching my eye, but her tone was quite different. I was relieved. "Are you all right?"

"Yes, thank you. I'm sorry," I repeated.

"I've told father you are safe. What can have happened? Were you set upon? "Oh Heavens!" Her hand went to her mouth. I had turned away to the fire as she was speaking and she had caught sight of my back. "What has happened to you?"

I tried to twist round to see it but the effort brought the pain stabbing. My left arm was stiff and sore. The women between them got my coat off, with a hole in the back. There was a great blotch of dried blood on my coat and my shirt was stuck to my skin.

"Maisie—hot water—soap!"

Sitting in front of the kitchen fire, Miss Somers sponged

my shirt until she could pull it away. The whole shoulder was throbbing and inflamed but felt better exposed to the air. Exhausted as I was, I tried to tell her my story, but she wouldn't let me give her more than the barest sketch.

"You're too tired to tell me about it now—but how did you get this wound? It seems like a bad cut, but I don't think it's deep. Perhaps we had better send for Dr Soames."

"No, don't do that." How could I explain being shot? The fewer people who knew, the better. I had meant to inspect it in the privacy of my room, but she had been too quick for me. She peered at my back and employed the sponge more briskly. A tiny clink, and something fell into the basin. She picked it out and held it up. A flattened musket ball. I held out my right hand and she gave it to me. I closed my fist around it.

"Good Heavens! How on earth..?"

Maisie was at the stove, pouring more hot water. I put my finger to my lips. "Perhaps I can tell you later." With the fatigue and the injury, I was feeling almost feeble.

"I'm sorry. You are quite pale. What am I thinking? You must have a bath and a rest. Maisie…"

She applied some lint and a linen bandage and soon I was lying in a hot bath, followed by a clean nightshirt and blessed, blessed sleep.

I slept until late morning. When I got up and dressed, pulling on a clean shirt and a fresh coat with some difficulty, I went with Miss Somers into her father's room. We sat by his bed and I told them all about it, how I'd got lost and then followed the men to the mill. I had hoped not to mention being pursued by the dragoons, but her discovery of my wound made it a necessity. I thought of glossing it over, but decided to come clean. I tried to make light of it, though, suggesting obliquely that it was all somewhat of a mistake on their part and that I had unluckily got in the way of a stray shot, but I wasn't sure I was convincing. I concealed my meeting with Thwaite, however. He had made it plain he was incognito. His secret was not mine to betray. Miss Somers sat silent, listening, her eyes on her lap, but I saw her flinch when I spoke of the shooting and the fire, and of my escape from the barn. Her hand went to her mouth more than once.

Somers was dismayed by the violence and my recklessness. "I cannot believe that you were engaged in any violent action, Edward, but I wish you hadn't been there at all."

I assured him that I had been a witness, nothing more.

He sank onto his pillows, coughing, then raised himself again. "I am sure of it. But I'm sorry that the men take matters into their own hands in this way—and to set fire to the mill! That was a terrible crime, and will be a great loss to the owner."

"I thought it might have been an accident—a dropped lantern, perhaps."

"Yes, that's true. We mustn't think the worst of people. I'm sorry that the authorities thought it necessary to set the military on the people. It can't do any good in the long term, it'll only bring resentment. I know these people—they aren't bad, only desperate. Earl Fitzwilliam agrees, but the magistrates prevailed on him. They have no Christian conscience. The world is generally a wicked place. But it seems to me today more than ever, that so many who are educated enough to know better, make a god of money, or progress, or success, or looking impressive in the eyes of others. And you see what terrible violence results."

"People in high places need to start the reform," Rachel said. "They should set an example."

Her father sighed. "I think so. But they are the hardest of all to reach. People think that the poor and uneducated are the hardest to preach the Gospel to, but in my experience it's those who think they have everything they need, and have created it themselves, and have no need of salvation, or want to help those worse off than themselves."

He ran a thin hand through his hair. His words were affecting and his evident sincerity even more so. "Edward, I do wish you hadn't been involved. No good can come of it. When we are tempted by evil, we should turn away from it."

It was the first time he had ever rebuked me and it made me unhappy. He was older than me and wiser. He was probably right. I felt bad about upsetting him and his daughter. I was surprised by how angry she'd been—there was no other word for it. But there were parts of the episode, even so, that I gloried in having seen and done, even, mad though it might seem, in having been shot at—since I had survived. I had run, it was true, but I hadn't capitulated. Perhaps at my age I should have known better than to want something thrilling to happen. Was it so wrong?

After dinner we went to sit in the drawing room. Rachel took up her work. She was always sewing when she wasn't writing. This time it was one of her father's shirts.

"I'm so sorry you were injured. How is the shoulder now?"

I moved it experimentally. It burned, but no worse. "I think it's well. Thank you so much for your ministrations." I felt the tender touch of her hands as I spoke.

"I am so glad."

"It could have been much worse—I couldn't understand how it wasn't. But when I looked at my satchel I saw that the buckle on the strap was broken through. It must have taken the force of the ball."

"Thanks be to God for that!"

I concurred, fervently. If it had struck me plain it would

have broken my shoulder-blade, and I would be a wreck, if not actually dead.

She stitched on for some time in silence. I looked at her profile. She had a short upper lip which was often slightly raised. When she was concentrating, she caught the bow of her full under-lip in her front teeth in the most attractive way. Her green eyes were fringed with dark lashes.

"I must say, despite everything, it's good to have you here, Mr Armiger. With father the way he is…"

"I wish you'd call me 'Edward'. 'Mr Armiger' sounds so formal, the way you say it, and I think we're good enough friends, don't you?"

I spoke on impulse, but it was something I'd been thinking of—despite Crosland. Her attitude to me had subtly changed since last night—first angry, then—I wasn't sure, but I suspected. A kind of consciousness. It was a way of trying her out.

She smiled faintly. "All right, then—Edward. You've been a good friend to both of us."

That was pleasing. Not only wasn't she still angry, but there seemed to be a new warmth in her manner. Perhaps... "How is your father this evening?"

"Dr Soames thinks he might get up in a day or two, with the weather getting warmer, although the nights are still so cold." The fever had abated and some of his colour had returned, but he still looked frail.

I could see she was troubled. She sewed, while I laboured on, one-handed, finishing the drawings for the pamphlet. I had made one of Lord Byron giving his speech—we hadn't his permission to include him, but I reasoned that the speech was a public event which had been in the public press. The work was nearly complete and Rachel was going to take the manuscript to the printer's as soon as I was done and her father had corrected her text.

After a while she put her work down and I asked her: "What do you think will happen about the attack?"

"The owner will pursue the trouble-makers, there's nothing surer. It will be transportation at the least for anyone involved. But there is something so unfair about it all. What they did was wrong, but it's because of the owners' decisions that so many men are out of work—skilled men like Thwaite. It's hard for them to see their families suffering and do nothing." Her voice was firm but the candlelight quivered on her hand.

"You really like these people, don't you? It's not just 'good works'."

I had come to like them too, but I would never have her easy familiarity, her instinctive knowledge of the right thing to say or do. The best I could manage was a sort of awkward *camaraderie*.

She took up her work again but looked at me. "Yes, I do. It's not their fault they're in a different station in life, it's what they were born into. Certainly there are reprobates among them and some who waste their money on drink, and fight, and beat their wives, but they are not many, and for every one of those there's ten—twenty—good men and women who work hard and try to live a good life, even if not many come to church. We must go to them, father says, if they don't have time for church. Mr Robson doesn't believe so, but then I sometimes think that when churchmen are hard-hearted, that's when people go to the Dissenters."

"Do you think they should stay in the Established Church?"

"Mr Crosland does, but I tell him he has an interest in the subject, so he can't be impartial." She laughed.

It was good to see warmth in her face. But Crosland. How could he be made to go away, disappear somewhere?

She was still speaking. "Of course I would never join

them, but I have heard some of them preach and I thought they were sincere men and women and their words touched my heart. What do you think?"

"I haven't thought much about it, but if they are doing no harm, I think people ought to be able to worship wherever they want to. But did you say you had heard a woman preaching?"

"Yes—once."

"A virago, all boots and black bonnet and screeching?"

"For shame, Edward! Not at all. Can't you believe that a woman could be quiet and feminine, and still be educated and thoughtful, and speak well on a subject close to her heart?" She was in good spirits again and glanced at me, smiling.

My own heart warmed. "Yes—I can." 'And she is in this room', I wanted to add, but didn't.

THE eldest Thwaite girl burst into the room while we were eating breakfast next morning, the maid behind her with her hands in the air.

"Miss! Miss! Our Dad's been taken up!"

Rachel sprang up, throwing down her napkin. "How? Why?"

"They come first thing this morning and took him to the prison. They say he killed someone. It weren't him, Miss!"

"Killed someone!" Rachel turned to me. I shook my head firmly. I knew nothing of any killing.

"Where's your mother?"

"She's home with the little ones—she sent me—she wants to go to the prison. She asked for Parson to come. What are we to do, Miss?"

Rachel was already looking for her coat and bonnet. "Mr Somers is sick, Sarah, but I'm coming. Maisie—put some food in a basket—the pie from last night and some of the soup. Edward—could you tell my father—gently—and tell him I've gone to Mrs Thwaite? Don't let him get up, please. He'll want to be doing something, but he mustn't."

"Of course. But isn't there anything I can do? What would your father do if he were well? Shall I go to the prison and see what's to do? Perhaps I can speak to the magistrate?"

She was hurrying about the room, putting things in a basket, tying on her bonnet.

"That would be useful—thank you. It must all be a terrible mistake. Is this to do with the attack on the mill last night, Sarah?"

The girl was jigging from one foot to another, twisting her hands in her pinafore, wanting to tell her story and wanting to be home.

"They said so, Miss. It were Croker's. Mr Croker's killed, and they said our Dad were there."

Croker killed—murdered! And I'd been there! I remembered the figure darting into the mill, silhouetted against the flames. Perhaps it was just at that moment. I'd almost witnessed it. The murderer was one of the men I'd followed. I felt suddenly weak at the knees.

Rachel glanced at me, horrified. "Killed! But surely your father wasn't there? Didn't he tell them that?"

"Aye, Miss, but they said someone told on him, and his leg..." she faltered to a halt.

Rachel looked at me. I shrugged and tried to look nonchalant. Her eyes narrowed for an instant then she turned away, leaving me cursing myself.

"Let's go, then. Edward, if you could send me a message as to what you've found out. Tell my father I don't know when I'll be home, but I'll send word," and she was gone, the child running ahead. I went slowly up the stairs to the Rector's room.

'Whereas on Tuesday Night last, about Eleven O'Clock, a great Number of Men, armed with Pistols, Hammers and Clubs, entered the Dwelling-House and Mill of William Croker, of Rochford... wantonly and feloniously broke and destroyed Shearing Frames... and did then maliciously and feloniously murder the said William Croker...'

The town was disfigured with bills on every wall, advertising in big letters a reward of £1000 for information leading to the arrest of the murderer. A further £200 was offered on conviction to 'any person who will give Information of any Person or Persons wickedly Breaking Frames'. This was even extended to anyone 'actively engaged in Rioting, who will impeach his Accomplices, who shall, upon Conviction, receive the same Reward, and every Effort made to procure his Pardon'. It made me sick in the stomach. It was revolting to see a price offered for a man's life and incitements to men to betray their friends and associates. A gentleman's life hinged on notions of honour and duty, and informing on your friends for money was antagonistic to every quality I had been brought up to value. I supposed the authorities thought that common people would not have the same views, but I thought—hoped -that they were mistaken. I thought these men had as strong a sense of honour in their own way.

But I began to wish that I had never been so crazed as to become involved. I had thought on the impulse that it would be exciting. It had certainly been that, but it was also stupidity incarnate. It was a criminal enterprise for which the penalty had recently been raised to death on the gallows, something I had known perfectly well but which, oddly, had not crossed my mind for an instant on that night.

In retrospect I couldn't imagine why not. Campbell, for instance, would never have come within a mile of doing something so idiotic. Perhaps that was part of it. I rebelled against the idea that I should always be calm and rational—and dull.

And I sympathised with the frame-breakers—they had been hardly treated and the mill-owners could well afford the loss. Setting fire to the place had scared me, but I was willing to believe it had been accidental. Being shot at by dragoons—my shoulder ached in sympathy—I had been secretly excited by, after the fear, and the fear of a mortal wound, was past. This morning's news, though, was horrifying. I looked at a bill and the letters leapt out at me. Persons 'actively engaged in Rioting'—was that me? Had someone seen me? The dragoons had. I felt again the horror of that awful pursuit through the silent streets. Could they identify me? Oh God! What had I done? I stopped dead in the street.

I had never felt in so much danger in my life. I looked furtively at the people hurrying by me. I didn't know the men who'd been at the mill—except one. Did any of them know me? Had the dragoons seen my face clearly? Was someone, even now, making his way to the magistrates to say: 'There was a gentleman there—I didn't know him, but here's his description, and I could identify him for you'? Or, worse still—'it was Mr Armiger the painter'. And if they did, the wound in my back would tell its own story against me. An immense desire to be out of Rochford seized me and my heart thudded. I had to get back to London and the safety of my studio, and stick to my painting and never get involved in anything like this again, and speak to no-one about it. Thank God no-one knew.

Except the Somers. They knew the whole story—almost. This morning I'd told Sarah Thwaite's news to Somers before leaving the house on my errand. He had been disturbed enough by my having been at the mill when it was only machine-breaking. Now it was murder, what would that quiet, good man think of me when I came back? And he knew I'd been shot at!

They wouldn't give me up, surely? It was an index of

my fright that I could even think of it. No, they were too upright, too honest, too loyal. I could trust them. But I suddenly thought that although they might not betray me to the authorities, they might never trust me again—trust me not to be involved in something mad, even criminal? They would expel me from the house. I would go back to London all right, but it would be never to see them again. At that moment I realised that they were my best, my dearest friends. An enormous desolation swelled in my breast and I leaned against the wall. I would never see them again, and it was my own fault. 'Them'—I was fond of her father, but it was Rachel I cared for most. I had begun to love her, I realised, but had not understood it until I found out about Crosland. And now, since the other night, I was almost sure she cared for me too. She was engaged to another man, but if she truly loved me... I had watched them closely and I could see that there was a good understanding between them, but I couldn't see any spark of passion—any of the fire that would be there if I loved a woman, or if she loved me. I knew now that I didn't just want to be with her, I wanted to gather her in my arms, press her body against mine until I could feel every contour of her figure, her full breasts, her narrow waist, and I wanted to kiss her and kiss her without stopping. At the thought of losing her—all that she was, womanly, caring, inspiring—and through my own fault, I was overcome. It was all I could do not to weep.

Some time had to pass before I was able to go on my way. There was nothing I could do at present, but I dreaded going back to the Rectory when its occupants would have had time to digest my role in events. It might be the last time I was ever there. Now I felt the full value of what I had come to take for granted—their friendship and esteem. There was nothing I could do about it but hope. And fulfil the tasks I had undertaken on their behalf. At least I could do that.

I made little headway at the prison. It was deep under the Castle, a horrible place, as might be expected. It was the last place I wanted to be, almost thinking that at any moment someone would point at me, crying: 'That's him!' and I would be clapped in a cell myself. But I braced myself. It would be unforgivably cowardly to sneak off leaving Thwaite to his lot and his family in ignorance. I had to go on with it.

No-one could tell me anything, but they led me through ancient corridors to the cells. I had not been five minutes in the place before I was crawling with vermin. A dozen men, some in irons, lay on the straw in each stone-walled cell or leaned against the grimy sides. There was little noise but their oaths, the clank of the shackles on stone, the screech of keys as one or another cell was opened. Small high windows in the thickness of the walls allowed a ray of pale light into the rooms and permitted a tiny glimpse of sky. When they heard our footsteps some ran to the iron bars and stared at us, some with longing or expectation, others calling out insults or demands to the turnkey.

I hardly knew what I was going to say to Thwaite. When we got to his cell he jumped to his feet and came over to the bars.

"You can have five minutes, no more." The turnkey moved off to converse with one of his colleagues.

"How are you?" It was a feeble beginning, but not altogether inappropriate. He looked worse than when I'd last seen him. Perhaps he'd been roughly handled by the police.

He was surprised to see me and looked at me somewhat shiftily, I thought.

"I'm well enough, thank you, Mr Armiger, but I don't want

to be here. It's nowt to do with me. How's my wife?"

"Miss Somers is with her now. I'm sure she'll look after her."

"She will, I know that. She's a good woman. But what will become of 'em while I'm here?"

It was hard to speak with the warder loitering ostentatiously in a corner and four other men in the cell considerately looking away. What I really wanted to know was whether he had had anything to do with the outrage. He'd been at the mill, I was sure, but what part had he had in the murder? He probably wanted to know what I knew, what I was going to do. We looked at each other for a minute.

"Do you need anything? Is there anything I can do for you?"

"Nay—I'm all right." He picked a flake of rust away from a bar with his fingernail and watched it fall.

"I'll go and see the magistrate and find out exactly what the charges are and when you'll be brought before them."

"Thank you. And will you tell 'em I had nowt to do with it?" He looked me straight in the eye. His fingers clenched on the iron grille.

"Nothing at all?" I raised my eyebrows.

He shook his head vigorously, still holding my gaze. "No. It weren't me."

"Even though…"

"It weren't me."

"All right. I'll tell them that." I indicated the men in the back of the cell. "Who are they?"

"Other fellows they picked up. No mates of mine."

There didn't seem anything else to say. "I'll come again and let you know what's going on."

"Aye, do that, if you will. And tell Betsey—I'm sorry."

He watched me away down the corridor, accompanied by the turnkey. I couldn't tell what he was thinking.

It was a relief to be in the open air again. I made my way to the courts, hoping with all my heart that the magistrate would be neither Hall nor—even worse—Shirlow. Ideally it would be someone I'd never met. My position was ambiguous. Was I there as an advocate for the prisoner, or on behalf of Somers? I tried to put myself in his place, but being a parson gave one a certain standing as well as experience. I had neither.

When eventually I was shown into his room the magistrate, seated behind a mahogany desk littered with bundles of papers and quills, turned out to be Shirlow. He grinned, sticking his chin out and reminding me again of a bulldog. I drew myself up, prepared for an acrimonious encounter, but he behaved as though we were old friends. And now I'd seen him, I didn't mind him quite as much as I had thought I would. He was still irritating, but my desire to hit him had lessened.

"Ah, Armiger." His tone was full of innuendo. "I hope I see you well? What can I do for you today?"

I told him.

"Thwaite. Ah, yes. One of Hall's employees. No longer, of course. Somewhat of a radical, I've been led to believe." He shuffled through some papers.

"May I ask who led you to believe that?"

"I can't divulge the sources of information, but I understand he's well known as an agitator."

"Is that why he was arrested?"

"That was on the basis of information."

"Given by?"

He smiled again, shaking his head.

"Someone who came forward for the reward? Can you trust such information?"

His smile faded. "What exactly is your interest in the case?"

Again that tone, which I disliked but could not interpret.

Did he know something about me? Had I been informed on too?

"I am enquiring in lieu of Reverend Somers, who is sick at present, on behalf of the Thwaite family. Mr Thwaite states that he had nothing to do with Mr Croker's murder."

"I see." He toyed with his pen-knife. "The man Thwaite was arrested on information. He was seen at Croker's mill. When he was taken up this morning he had an injury to his knee and was in possession of a neck-scarf such as the attackers wore as disguise, and could give no adequate account of how he came by either."

"And is that the extent of the case against him? It seems both slight and circumstantial."

"And he is a known agitator, and a member of one of the croppers' combinations, which are of themselves illegal. Seditious literature was found in his house."

"Do you mean *The Rights of Man*?" I was getting annoyed.

"Among other things."

"Well, on that basis, half the gentlemen in some parts of London would be traitors. The book is not prohibited."

"Yes, I'd heard that you were democratically inclined yourself. You should watch your step. It hasn't done you any good here in Rochford, however fashionable it may be in your London circles."

Now we were glaring at each other like rutting stags. I tried to calm down. I didn't want to prejudice the case by my dislike.

"I am convinced of Thwaite's innocence."

"Are you?"

I tried not to hesitate. He had been at the mill, but surely he had had nothing to do with the murder? I couldn't imagine it. "Yes, and so is Mr Somers."

"Well, you're entitled to your opinion, I suppose." He made it sound like a major concession.

"You will oblige Reverend Somers by informing him of the date of the trial, when it is set, and of any relevant intelligence which comes to hand."

"I will do so."

I reached for my hat. "I'm very obliged to you, sir," I said, with all the sarcasm I could muster, and bowed myself out.

I felt I had achieved nothing, except to let him know that Thwaite had friends interested in his case. I hated him more than ever.

RACHEL had spent her day arranging assistance for Thwaite's family. Luke Danby was also suspected, but they couldn't find him. On my way home I'd seen new posters advertising for information as to his whereabouts.

We sat down to dinner with Mr Somers, who was strong enough to come downstairs well wrapped-up. He said nothing about my part in it all but he was plainly unhappy. He said Grace in a lengthy murmur and I knew he was praying for everyone involved in the attack on both sides. I felt a complete hypocrite as I sat with head bowed.

"I've settled for them to be supplied at the Soup Shop and collected some food from the parish and a little money," Rachel told him.

"Good, my dear." Somers paused. "But the real hardship will strike when their rent next falls due, on Lady-Day." The 25th of March. It was not far off. "With the men out of work they'll have no way of paying it and they'll be turned out in the street. It's beyond what I can raise or the parish can afford. It's one of the drawbacks of being in such a poor part of town, Edward—there are few wealthy parishioners I can call on."

"What were you able to find out from the magistrates?" Rachel asked me.

"It doesn't look very good. They seem determined to prosecute. But Thwaite insists he's innocent."

"I can't understand someone informing against him. The people hereabouts are disgusted by the murder, but they feel the authorities aren't their friends, in fact there's a lot of antagonism. Usually they protect their own, as they'd say. And the Thwaites are well liked, and the Crokers are not."

"But murder is a capital crime."

"True, but I think people—people like the mill workers—feel that it is up to the magistrates and the police to find out who did it without their help."

"What about the reward? Have you seen the handbills? It's an enormous sum." My personal concern gnawed at me.

"They offered the same reward for information about the attacks at Leeds and got no response," her father remarked. "I think it will be the same here. The people won't give up one of their own for participating in the raid. I don't know whether it's right to do so in such a case, but they stand by each other staunchly. Thank the Lord at least that Thwaite is innocent of any crime—he wasn't even there. We must see how soon we can get him back with his family. It has obviously been a terrible mistake."

I grimaced and unfortunately Rachel noticed. "Is something wrong?"

"No, no. Nothing."

She gave me that searching look. I ate some soup.

"Did they say who informed on him?"

"No, just someone who said they knew he'd been there."

"That looks very bad for him, then," she said. "But he must be innocent. I think he's too sensible to get caught up in such violence."

I wished we could get away from the subject. "Yes. Will you be going to see Mrs Thwaite again tomorrow?"

"Probably, if father is well enough."

He smiled at her. "Yes, dear, and as soon as I can I'll go to see Thwaite myself and find out exactly what happened. We must get him out of there as soon as possible."

When dinner was finished Mr Somers climbed back up to his bed. When she had seen him settled Rachel came down and sat by the fire sewing. The firelight glowed on her tawny hair as she bent over her work. I could tell she was thinking. After a while she looked up.

"Edward, you seemed rather reticent about father's plans for getting Mr Thwaite out of prison."

I should have known that I wouldn't be able to lie to her. "I hope he does."

"But you don't think he will be able to?"

"No."

"Is it something Mr Shirlow said?"

"Not precisely."

"Is it something you know yourself?" She was an acute questioner.

"Don't ask me, please."

"Then you do!"

"I can't talk about it."

We sat in silence for a while. I tried to think what was best to do. I thought I had to protect Thwaite. In the face of the evidence they already had, the authorities wouldn't release him, regardless of his protestations. The more I thought, the more I didn't know why I didn't tell Rachel. During my cogitations she sewed without speaking, but from time to time lifted her head and looked at me. Her eyes were bright with concern. She was entirely trustworthy. Her father had not mentioned it to me beyond last night's rebuke, although I could see how distressed he was. She had said nothing to me at all about my involvement. Then I understood at last that they were my friends and that I should trust them.

"I saw Thwaite that night when I was wandering the streets. He was on his way home. His face was blacked and he was limping. I didn't see him there, but I'm sure he'd been at the mill. He knew I saw him—he saw me." It was a burden lifted.Rachel started. "You really saw him?"

"Yes—not far from here—when I was coming back."

"You're sure it was him?"

"Yes. I saw him plainly, and he knew me."

"Then it is very bad." She thought for a few minutes. "And so he has been lying to everyone about it. To his wife, to the authorities."

"I'm afraid so, but I can see why."

"Yes. It would go very badly for him if the authorities knew."

"I know—that's why I'm afraid."

"They mustn't find out. They mustn't know that you saw him."

"No, of course not."

"Do you believe he did it?" We stared at each other.

"I don't know—I really don't know. I can't imagine it. But he might know who did."

Another pause.

"Edward, when do you go back to London?"

We were both thinking the same thing.

"I should go soon. I was waiting for your father to be well."

"Perhaps…"

"Shall I go tomorrow?"

She rested her chin on her hand, thinking. "If anyone finds out you were there, they'll want you to give evidence. They might make you identify Thwaite. Can they do that?"

"I believe they have the power to compel me." I had only vague knowledge of the subject, but I didn't want to find out more by being arrested. "A subpoena, I think. They could force me to give evidence in court, tell them about the men's *modus operandi*, everything."

"One of the men might be able to identify you, too. What if Danby knows who you are?"

"I don't think anyone saw me. I was hiding. But…" I was thinking. Shirlow's inquisitorial stare was in my mind. "I don't know if Mr Shirlow suspects something—about me. He doesn't like me. If he found out I'd been there, he wouldn't hesitate..."

I couldn't lie on oath, but be damned if I was going to help them send Thwaite to the gallows. About the others, I didn't know. I didn't know them and I didn't know their involvement. I couldn't save a whole movement, but I could do what lay in my power to save the one man I knew.

"You should go." She was definite. It was a novelty to have my actions decided by a woman.

"I'm frightened for myself, too, if they say I was involved." I couldn't leave as a paladin who was only concerned for others, when I'd known abject fear today and was still afraid, a dread that wouldn't go until I was well away.

"Even more important for you to go—go before anyone starts thinking, talking. You can't do any good by staying. It's better for you to be out of the way."

Her thoughts ran in tandem with mine. But leaving meant leaving her—them. And Crosland was still here. I hesitated. If I went away, when would I see her again?

"Rachel…"

"What is it?"

No, I couldn't do it. It was wrong. She was betrothed to another man. What could she do if I spoke? I would be placing her in an invidious situation. She could only refuse me, tell me to go away, never to speak of it. I would be wronging Crosland, too. His wife-to-be should be safe from such advances. She cared for me, I was sure she did. But she could never declare it while she was engaged, and I had no warrant for believing that she cared more for me than for him—perhaps much less. To leave her in these circumstances was agony, but I must leave.

"Nothing. Tomorrow, then."

Before I left, my bag packed, I went to Mr Somers' bedside to farewell him.

"I don't know when we'll see each other again," he said, "but I will write and let you know what happens to our friend Thwaite and his family."

"I'm sorry for any trouble I've caused." I didn't know what Rachel might have told him this morning, or what he knew about my feelings, or hers. His clear grey eyes looked steadily into mine.

"The Lord forgives sins that only he knows of," he remarked. I saw, not for the first time, that it was a mistake to underestimate his insight. "Now let me give you a blessing, my boy." His hand moved over my head. "'The Lord bless you and keep you. The Lord make his face to shine upon you and be gracious unto you. The Lord lift up the light of his countenance upon you and give you peace, now and evermore.'"

Chapter Nineteen

"How was your holiday, Mr Edward?"
"Eventful."

Mrs Mullins took my coat and gave me my letters. I'd hardly been away a fortnight but it felt like much longer. The familiar odours of boiled mutton and cabbage hung about the hall, superseded as I climbed the stairs by oil and turpentine. It was good to be home. I had felt my fears falling away the further south I came, and by the time I got into the studio, put on my old coat, lit the stove, tidied up a bit, sent notes to my students that I was back and set out some work for them, I was at ease. My left shoulder was till sore, but the wound was superficial and was healing well, thank God! There was a nagging in a corner of my mind about Shirlow. Could they still arrest me in London? Would they go that far? Even so, I was tolerably light-hearted.

For the next week there was nothing in most of the papers about the attack at Croker's. I formed the habit of going to Rainbow's on my walk, for coffee and to look at the news. There were some reputable men there, although not the same number of philosophers and artists as at Slaughter's. I discovered some fellows I'd known at the Schools, and talked once or twice with a doctor who knew Humphry Davy. I wondered how Mr Somers' health was and thought about Rachel. I missed her, especially in the evenings, when she had written or sewed while I drew or read, and we had talked about what interested us or the work in hand. Now I worked or read alone, thinking of her warm presence and trying to work out how we could be together. Crosland must be back in Devon by now. I hoped with all my heart that he would stay there. I turned it over again and again, but came always to the same conclusion: I couldn't speak while he was Rachel's affianced. Then I fell to thinking about accidents that might befall him, and pulled myself up short. Or perhaps he might meet some eligible young lady in Devon. But even then, would Rachel want me? She had said nothing, hinted at nothing. I knew she had far too much propriety to even think of encouraging another man while she was engaged, but was her composed demeanour towards me a token of that, or of the calmness of her feelings for me?

I'd hoped to start some new paintings, but with all this on my mind I was restless and couldn't settle. I was happy with the drawings I'd done for the tracts—not great works of art, but I wasn't ashamed of them, and they were for a good cause. But all that seemed to be over now. Rushed through as an 'emergency measure', the Frame-Breaking Act received the Royal Assent before the end of March. Our efforts in London had failed and there was no call for any more—at present, at least.

I'd sent some landscapes in to the Society of Painters in Water Colour exhibition before I'd left and there was nothing particular to do. I hadn't thought what I might send in to the Academy's annual Exhibition, now only a few weeks away, but couldn't work up any enthusiasm for going through my landscape oils to see what might do.

I dropped in to Slaughter's for a chop and a pint of ale. The place was full of men discussing the worsening situation with America and the likelihood of outright war. It also seemed that Bonaparte was moving his army eastwards, his destination presumably Russia. At the back the usual people were sitting in one of the booths eating beefsteaks. Campbell looked at me sourly. I gave him the sort of nod one reserves for slight acquaintances.

"Haven't seen you for ages." Quayle nodded genially. "Have you really given up the Competition?"

Alcock was his usual satirical self. "Saw your review—very good! How much did you have to pay Hoare, ha ha?"

"Heard you're on a new tack," someone else remarked.

"As a matter of fact it's quite true. I'm trying something that hardly anyone has tried before."

"What—your beggars?" Hallett asked, his lip curled.

"That's part of it." I paused to give full weight to my pronouncement. Hallett inspected his reflection in the window glass. Quayle smiled, eyebrows raised in anticipation. Alcock merely looked cynical, Campbell glum. "Gentlemen—I'm painting pictures that I particularly wish to paint, for no other reason than that I wish to paint them."

"We all do that, Armiger," Quayle said.

"All the better for you, then," I replied, knowing it wasn't true. Or it might be, in his case. What he wanted to paint usually coincided exactly with the wishes of his patrons.

Alcock was at his most boorish. "You've never been the same since you took up with radicals. It won't do you any good."

"I'm obliged to you for your concern." He'd always disliked, not to say hated, me. I really didn't know why we saw so much of each other.

Quayle was curious. "How are you going to make a living?"

I'd been worrying about that myself. "I suppose I'll just have to try to paint good pictures and hope someone likes them. Everyone has to get known for something in particular, or there's nothing to make him stand out from the crowd—how often have I heard you say that?"

He laughed. "Certainly. But you don't want to get known just for being eccentric."

"I'll have to take that risk."

It was a gamble, but then painting had always been a chancy business. Alcock devoted his time to ingratiating himself with the wealthy and influential, but apart from getting him elected, it hadn't done him much good. No-one I knew thought much of him as an artist and apart from his cronies, he was not respected. Quayle at least was a good painter who worked fairly hard and knew his trade well. His urbanity stood him in good stead, too. He was liked by those who didn't mind his palpable ambition. Hallett had the lowest rate of production of anyone I knew. Occasionally he turned out a small work, not without interest, but he was idle and unreliable to a degree. I had no idea what he lived on, but he was always in debt. His output was so meagre it was hard to tell whether he had real talent or not. The vigour that should have gone into his work was drained by his social life.

I was suddenly tired of them all. "Will you excuse me? I have to get on with some work."

"I suppose we'll see you at the Exhibition?"

"Undoubtedly."

As I walked away I heard them laughing. It might not have been at me, but I felt sure it was.

THE Water Colour Society's exhibition opened at last, a sign that the season was getting under way. It was at their rooms in Spring Gardens, the last house on the right next to the gateway into the Mall. I'd been a member since they started in 1805, so that my career had to some extent run side by side with theirs.

I usually went with Campbell. When Brig found that I was going alone he insisted on accompanying me. It was kind, but he had the most conventional taste and was not a lover of art or of an aesthetic sensibility, although he felt that he was. It was awkward to refuse.

I was a little before time and began surveying the works. Then I spotted a greying figure examining some Heaphy portraits, his long nose leading the rest of his face, full lips pursed as he consulted his catalogue. I walked up behind him and took his arm.

"How do you do, Hoare?"

He turned and greeted me civilly.

"I'm glad to see you," I added. "Some very obliging fellow wrote a notice in the *Literary Panorama* of my work in the British Institute exhibition, which was of material assistance to me. I don't suppose you know who it was?"

Hoare smiled modestly. "I'm sure it was well-deserved, anyway. I liked them a great deal."

"Well, if you see him, please thank him for me. His encouragement was particularly useful to me at that moment." Encouragement, and income—I had had a hundred and fifty guineas when the committee divided up the proceeds.

He bowed. "Attendance seems down this year, don't you think? I just saw the Secretary, Reinagle and he was quite worried."

"It does seem a bit sparse." I looked around. "But surely it's too soon to tell?"

"Is it the quality of the works or the French wars, do you think? People aren't spending money on art. But last year someone complained that there were so many landscapes that it was like travelling around Britain on a coach, and just like a coach trip, after a while the scenery begins to pall."

"I know that feeling only too well, especially the scenery between Holborn and Rochford."

"What do you think of these?" He pointed to some paintings depicting sheep scattered over verdant pasture with

Snowdon or some cognate crag looming in the distance.

"In my opinion they should bar all paintings which include sheep that look like dogs."

"Now that you've spent so much time on the moors, I suppose you're an authority on sheep."

"I certainly am. I saw thousands of them while I was there, although admittedly it was mostly through coach windows. I have also seen a number of dogs, and if you ask me, those are woolly dogs."

We moved on to a group of animal portraits.

"Does your ban include dogs that look like sheep?"

I was about to answer in the affirmative when I saw Brigstock making towards us.

"Good-day, Armiger—Hoare. I hope I see you well."

Brig and I set off around the room. There were many really interesting works on display and this was the only place to see them, since the Academy refused to show water colours. That was why the Society had been formed. Walking round the rooms full of pictures, many of them excellent, I was struck once more by the idiocy of the Academy's position.

"Don't you think it's odd, Brig, that the Academy still won't accept water colours when there are so many people painting them? Look how many there are here—two or three hundred—and it's the same every year."

"Yes, but amateurs paint in water colours. Professionals use oils."

"I know that, but many men do both—me, for instance. And they're very popular. The Academy could easily restrict their entries to professionals, if they're afraid of lady amateurs." And gentlemen amateurs, I might have added. Brig had towed me to a corner where he pointed out a set of studies of great cathedrals.

"What do you think? I did them on my summer tour. It's the first time I've had anything in."

"Congratulations." I inspected them. The style was laboured and the colour pedestrian. For a minute I couldn't identify what was strange about them. I looked from Norwich to Ely to Peterborough before I realised what it was. Despite their considerable dissimilarities of architecture, shape and scale, he had somehow contrived to render them so that they all looked the same. It was amazing.

"Well, what do you think?"

"Amazing."

We moved on. I'd forgotten what it was like going to exhibitions with Brig. As we walked about I could feel him bristling with urgency, which increased if I spent more than a minute examining any one work. This intensified if we happened to get into a part of the room populated by works of a more modern tendency, or which he did not like for some other reason.

My own contribution of my three best medium-sized landscapes of Bath, one of Coldbrook Manor and two of the moors, was quite well hung—not in the best positions, but near the line and in a good light. Better than last year. Perhaps my success at the British Institute had influenced the hanging committee. I amused myself by standing in front of them, saying: 'these are very good!' and walking away. Then I looked back to see how many people gravitated towards them. It was a childish trick I'd often played with friends, but Brig wasn't amused.

After we had been there half an hour, which was hardly long enough to skim a dozen works, he got more impatient. While I was practically fainting with delight at the exquisite colour in one of Turner's latest productions, he was fidgeting and yawning in such a way as to make it impossible to enjoy it. At moments like that I resolved that I would never go to an exhibition with him again. Then, on leaving, he started questioning me about how such things could properly be called art. It is a particular form of torture, not generally recognised, to be in the presence of things which are greatly affecting, in the company of the indifferent. Brig was a good man, but he was not aesthetic.

The London papers were mostly silent on the mill attack, but the *Morning Chronicle* had daily accounts, reprinted in the main from the *Mercury*.

'On Tuesday night last, the extensive cloth manufactory of Mr Croker, of Oatlands, near Rochford, was surrounded by a large body of armed men, who, after securing all the approaches to the premises, proceeded to break into that part of the mill appropriated to the dressing of cloth, where they completely destroyed all the shears and frames; the former were not merely snipped, but absolutely broken in pieces, as if actuated by the most diabolical frenzy'.

'Diabolical frenzy'? I supposed it had been that, but there was no mention of the circumstances that had motivated the attack. The next day's *Chronicle* concentrated on the fire and the murder.

'The Gig Mill was discovered to be on Fire and the flames extended themselves with so much rapidity, that notwithstanding the exertions used to check their progress, about half the upper part of the building was consumed before they could be extinguished. The damage to the premises and stock, both of which are insured in the Norwich Union Office, is estimated at about £500.' It went on to describe the 'dastardly Murder' of Croker while attempting to defend his property and to say that some ten of the ringleaders were later arrested during scenes of unrest in the town and taken to the castle.

The trial date had been set for a fortnight's time. The murder, Croker's influence in the town and the concerns of his fellow producers had probably brought the date forward.

The article suggested that 'the apprehension and hanging of the Malefactors would give a stern lesson to other rogues and prevent further Outrages'.

Reading it gave me pangs of anxiety and guilt. I did not like Thwaite's chances. The family in the cottage, with its rickety furniture and treasured keepsakes, would soon be without a father. How would they manage then? He had been a good father to the children. Now they would be on the street. Mrs Thwaite would not be able to work because of the little ones, and she had not looked strong. The older children might get employment in the mills, but would anyone want the children of a condemned agitator—or a murderer? How could Thwaite have been so insane as to risk his life and their welfare for the sake of—what? Demonstrating his political views? A gesture, that could only halt the progress of mechanisation for a year or two, if that? I had thought he was a serious, solid man, and I still thought so, but there was another side of him. His passion for his cause had brought his whole family down.

I wondered, though, what I would have done. Would it have been better for him to confine himself to reading, and speaking only to a close circle of friends? How would that have changed the injustice and hardship that not only he but all his fellows, were facing? Wilberforce and the Earl of Shaftesbury and Lord Byron were admired because they made a stand for what they believed in, to right injustice. It was all right for them, because their livelihoods and families would not perish by their actions. But it was not just because Thwaite was not of their class that he was in prison, but because he had engaged in criminal violence. Shaftesbury and the others didn't have to resort to such means, because when they spoke, people listened. Breaking the hated new frames was all that the croppers could see to prevent their livelihoods disappearing. Was killing Croker accidental, or deliberate—a way of halting the progress of the machines, even warning other capitalists? I fervently hoped it was an accident, or at the very least, that Thwaite had nothing to do with it.

I turned these things over and over in my mind, and they gave me a great deal of anxiety. I came back always to the same question: what would I have done? Not killed, I was sure of that, but smashing the frames? It was hard, because I had never known their desperation, nor their poverty. I realised that without that experience of life, any conclusions I came to were baseless. And I could still feel the rage and exhilaration and ecstasy of that scene in the mill yard, and how enthralled I had been, how eager, and how afraid. At that moment, I had been one with Thwaite.

A day or two later I had a letter from Somers.

'I have been to the prison and spoken with that poor fellow. He confided to me that he had in fact been present at the mill on the occasion of the attack, but had nothing to do with the destruction or the murder of Mr Croker. He went along with his friend Ackroyd, he says. I must say that it was most ill-advised of him to have anything to do with such an undertaking. I told him that we looked to him to lead the men away from such things, not participate in them. I think he is ashamed. The trial date has been set down and we hope Luke Danby may be captured by then. It appears that he was the leader, as we thought. He may also have been the perpetrator of the unspeakable crime against Croker, perhaps in revenge for his brother's imprisonment. So one act of violence leads to another! NB—We have still been unable to discover who betrayed Thwaite to the authorities. He is certain that it cannot have been any of his friends.'

He said nothing about my involvement, which was kind, nor about my sudden departure, although I expected Rachel had told him the reason. I writhed inwardly. I just wanted the whole thing over with and me out of danger. The abjectness of my situation provoked me even more. I hoped Somers understood that I had fled, not from cowardice, or because I feared involvement, but so that I wouldn't be forced to give evidence that might send Thwaite to the gallows. Here was just such a situation as Byron had described in his stirring address, and I could do nothing, nothing at all, to help. It made me mad to think of it, but at least I wouldn't be helping the prosecution.

The whole attack had been insanity on the part of the men. How could they have hoped to escape? At the same time I couldn't help remembering the magnificence of the scene. One day I would paint it—many times.

I started a couple of landscapes in oils. I had done so well out of the British Institution and Water Colour Society exhibitions that I felt it would be a mistake to give them up altogether. I had been approached for some commissions and the Marquess Wellesley had bought my small view of his house—that was a connection well worth having. Work, in short, was prospering surprisingly. If it went on like this I ought to have an open day. I groaned at the thought of the labour that would involve: cleaning up the studio, getting in flowers and refreshments and drapery and chairs, arranging the pictures. Next thing I'd be building a gallery, like Quayle's. The thought made me grin. He was doing well out of it and it had become one of the fashionable places collectors liked to visit. Any minute now someone would invent private galleries, where artists could exhibit their work and clients go to choose paintings the way ladies did bonnets, poring over their fancies in one shop after another. Anything was possible today—especially if someone could think of a way of making money out of it.

I got out my Bath sketchbooks, which reminded me of my ideas about grand landscapes, not like poor de Loutherbourg's—who was on his deathbed, I heard—but giving humble nature the importance and passion that Wordsworth brought to his poetry. It was strange going back to them after the industrial scenes. It seemed a long time, and after what had happened I felt a different person. The man who had sat in the Rectory at St Saviour's drawing the poor for tracts and discussing politics, let alone witnessing riots and fleeing from soldiers, seemed to be another person from the London me. I would have to try to fit myself back into my old mould if I was to get any work done. It would be a relief when the trial was over and I could stop agonizing about my part in the affair. But for poor Thwaite and his family, the end was likely to be tragic.

The weather was improving although March, like February, was still unseasonably cold. Primroses were appearing under the elms in the parks, even though the early flowers were nipped by the dry frost. I could go out soon and do some sketching, which might inspire me.

I'd written to ask Rachel what she thought about my keeping on with landscapes. I was much more interested in the new work. My experiences in the north had intensified my desire to do something related to them. Despite the confusion of my feelings about him now, the painting of Thwaite at the mill was still my favourite and occupied the best place on the chimneypiece, but I'd never be able to make a living out of them. It seemed indulgent. I knew that was what Campbell had thought.

'What should I do?'

Rachel had been characteristically direct. 'You should do what you feel called to, as we would say in the church.' Her advice proposed painting as a vocation, not just a profession. Was that indulgent? Sentimentalising a skilled profession?

But it was true that the best artists had always been men for whom painting was life, not merely a trade to take up. She'd also asked: 'Why does it have to be one or the other?'

It had been hard to explain. On the face of it she was right. I replied, telling her about wanting to work at things that were important to me.

'I understand—I think I do. It is a sort of imprisonment—a voluntary one—to do what you don't believe in for money and advancement, if you have the opportunity to do otherwise. Many people have no opportunity, but you and I do. Writing tracts and working for the poor are things that I have the ability, education and inclination to do, and it would be poor stewardship of my talents if I didn't use them when I could. The same is true for you.'

I hadn't yet decided, but her words stayed with me.

News of the outrages at Rochford dropped from the papers in favour of stirring intelligence from Spain. General Wellington had moved south after his success at Cuidad Rodrigo and was investing the fortress city of Badajoz. Our army was continually strengthening its position and we were getting the upper hand over the French. It was excellent news, but this would be a hard nut to crack. It was a strong place garrisoned by five thousand French under General Philippon and it might be a long siege. New recruits were being forwarded to the Peninsula; the shortages of food and work were spurring many men to enlist. At least in the army they had food, clothing and pay, however meagre, guaranteed. But for skilled men like the croppers, carrying a musket and pack and standing in the line of battle was a poor exchange.

I saw Campbell in the street and we barely exchanged nods. It was very uncomfortable. At home I mused on friendship and concluded again something that I had thought before at the lowest times in my life, that there was no real friendship, only convenience, proximity and habit. Friendship was a contract that lasted as long as each party got value from it. If something happened to disrupt that, for instance, if one party got more benefit elsewhere, he would repudiate the contract. You thought someone liked you, then there was a difference of opinion and they were off. I was uneasily aware that the breach between us had been partly my doing. I couldn't accept the way Campbell had changed his ideas and the things he valued because of his new allegiance. It felt like betrayal, but I knew that pride came into it too—my pride. I really didn't know what true friendship consisted of.

ALL the talk in the coffee houses was about the Competition and the Annual Exhibition. Only three weeks were left before entries closed. The Hanging Committee for the Exhibition was to consist of Farington, Dance and Smirke—it was their turn this year. I thought they would do it well, although whatever they did, there would be complaints and allegations of favouritism and paying off old scores. I heard hints that Alcock was using all his influence, or his father's, to secure a good position for his entries. He was already trying to work up to applying for full membership. And of course, everyone was wild to know who would be the judging panel for the Competition. At least I didn't have to worry about that now—I was out of it.

Although I tried to convince myself that I was well out of it I was dogged by a sense of loss. I felt at a loose end and part of me still wanted to be in it. And I had yet to find, or make, something for the Exhibition. A month. It was probably too late even to think of it. A few of the landscapes would do.

But I wasn't altogether happy. In previous years I'd sent in my 'brightest and best' and I felt I was letting myself down.

At last the trial began. I read the news at Rainbow's. A Grand Jury had been constituted. Baron Graham and Sir Simon le Blanc presided and Serjeant Butt was for the Crown. The prisoners Luke Danby (they had finally captured him), Thomas Thwaite, Jeremiah Ackroyd and half a dozen others were indicted for Riot and Frame-breaking, and the first three also with 'having entered the premises of William Croker on the night in question and discharged a pistol at the said William Croker with intent to murder him.' It was as bad as I'd feared, and I could only thank God that I was not there to testify against him.

Somers had written to say that he would attend the trial and would stand as a character witness for Thwaite, 'but I am afraid that Garrow himself couldn't get him off.' Since the passing of the Act they would all hang, even if found innocent of murder, if it could be proved that they took part in the attack on the mill. Crosland was in Devon. Rachel was spending much of her time with the families of the prisoners. I wanted so much to be with them—with her. I fretted about possible dangers she might be in, if some of Thwaite's associates were as villainous as the press made out, or from the antagonism of the townspeople. If only I could have been there to help her. I imagined discussing her work with her. Perhaps they might get out another tract to argue the croppers' case? It would probably be too unpopular and might even inflame opinion. I itched to be doing something, and above all I longed simply for her presence.

The evidence was summarised in the *Times*. Two constables deposed that they had searched Thwaite's home on the day he was apprehended and found a neckerchief covered in blacking and seditious literature. One of Croker's sons had heard Thwaite call out 'damn your eyes, smash away' when Croker protested. Elizabeth Thwaite stated that her husband had been at home when the offences were committed and had not left the house all night. Questioned as to whether she would have noticed if he had gone out after she was asleep, she said she would, but the court was not convinced, as on questioning she admitted that she was often so tired that she did not wake up when the children cried in the night and had to be woken by the eldest.

I looked at my pictures of Thwaite. Had this man really killed someone? I couldn't believe it of him. Our discussions came back to me, his eager expression as he talked about Paine and workers' rights, his tender regard for his wife and children, his earnest look as he told me about his father's skills that he'd passed on to his son. I felt in my heart that he was an intelligent, passionate man who might have been led into damaging the machines that had taken his living, but no more. The evidence given in court gave no impression of the real motives of the men at the bar. The prosecution had presented them as rogues, rioters, disaffected radicals and scoundrels who had needed little incentive to smash, break, burn and even murder. They could not afford to pay for advocates and had no opportunity to tell their stories. But how could a right judgement be made unless their stories and the effect on their families were made known?

The next day I rose early and hurried to Rainbow's. I seized the *Mercury* and found the heading 'Frame-Breakers Sentenced at Rochford'. I skimmed through it, looking for Thwaite's name. It came near the bottom of the column, after a long disquisition on the seriousness of the crimes. The judge in his charge to the jury commented that 'in a lawless assembly the act of one person became the act of the whole'. The jury, who had not needed to leave the courtroom to consider their verdict, then convicted Thwaite, Danby and Ackroyd of frame-breaking and acquitted two men whom I did not know. It was then the turn of who had fired the fatal shot: Baron Graham put it to the jury 'whether Thwaite was the man who had shot Croker'.

From the testimony of several of the men, he was adjudged guilty 'of aiding and abetting, but not of firing the pistol'. The learned Judge then remarked that hanging was the penalty for the crime committed, but in consequence of marks of contrition, sentenced him to fourteen years transportation. Danby had probably been the felon, but there was not enough evidence to convict him.

Thank God! At least Thwaite would live—and I was off the hook, too. I had a celebratory bottle and went home to write to the Somers.

I got up the next morning with the word 'transportation' filling my head. I could see the prison at Rochford, Thwaite's broad hands clenched on the bars, the dark cell, the verminous straw. He would be held there until he was sent to the hulks, I supposed, to wait for a transport to New South Wales. I imagined his wife and children visiting, weeping, each trying to comfort the others. I was almost in tears myself at the thought.

Someone had to tell their story. The thought gnawed at me. Almost without thinking I went into the studio and looked around for a spare canvas. There were one or two in a corner; I picked them up and put them down again. They were too small. My eye caught the Beggar and Thwaite at the Mill; the same size, a good pair. The beginning and end of a story, I'd thought. No: they were two of the stages on a man's road. The end of the story was a frame-breaker in jail, awaiting transportation. It was the subject of my lifetime. It needed a really big canvas, which would complete a triptych. It must be a big picture, imposing, a grand subject, a heroic painting of modern life. I could see it now, clear as the light streaming in my studio window. It would show the real Spirit of the Age, an age in which wealthy men divided themselves from the communities that had raised them up, starved poor men of food and work, took away their dignity, stifled their protests, forced them into direct action and then triumphantly sentenced them to exile or the scaffold.

My eye fell on a large canvas turned face to the wall. Just the thing! A couple of strides across the room and I turned it round. Agamemnon. Dust clung to the canvas and it had sagged a little.

I held it up for a moment, caught in indecision. It was nearly finished. What if I went on with it? It was quite good. I could still send it in to the Exhibition. If I painted the piece that had seized hold of me, I'd never be taken seriously again. But…

"Damn it all!"

I carried it to the easel, pushed away everything else I'd been working on, grabbed up a palette knife and began scraping. If I worked like a fury I might just get it done in time.

Chapter Twenty

I worked every hour of daylight and into the night, the studio flaring with candles. In a day I'd scraped off Agamemnon and put down a new layer of gesso. I could hardly wait for it to dry, but filled the time by making studies for the composition. It came all at once: the picture was already completely formed in my mind. I rushed out and hired some models for the poses of Thwaite and Betsey, and for Betsey's face—Thwaite's I had studies of already. Next door's would do for the children. I'd used them before when I needed them for staffage. This time, though, the figures would be the whole subject.

The warmer weather was in my favour. The gesso dried quickly, I rubbed it back and put on some size, laying it on carefully with a flat brush. I didn't have time for extra layers. It would have to do, and all it needed really was to cover the shadowy remains of Agamemnon. I hammered some keys into the back of the stretcher to tighten the canvas. Now it was ready for 'A Luddite: Awaiting Transportation', as I'd decided to call it. The others would be 'A Shearman at the Mill' and 'Out of Work', as I'd renamed the 'Sleeping Beggar'. I'd send them in as a group: the skilled cloth-dresser in his prime; brought into passivity and despair by unemployment; and finally the terrible results of his desperate actions. I thought about whether to use the word 'Luddite', and resolved that since the whole thing would be so completely unpopular I might as well make the point I wanted straight out. I had crossed the Rubicon with the subject: there was no point in shilly-shallying over details.

I went straight in with the pencil, sketching the composition and main figures from the studies I'd made. It must be exactly right on such a large canvas to create the effect I wanted. Far from being central the main figure, that of the Luddite, was placed on the extreme left, so that the eye had to search for him. His hands were clenched on the bars of his cell, while a thin ray of light came over his shoulder and illuminated the features of his wife, who stood left of the centre. He faced the viewer but I'd placed his wife in a back three-quarter view. Her attention was all on him. In her skirts huddled a little girl who gazed out at the viewer, the only figure to do so, while another stood towards the foreground, back to her father. I decided to leave the whole centre of the canvas empty to draw the viewer into the atmosphere of the work and into the prison itself. A grim turnkey stood by the bars, half lost in shadow but a menacing presence, while an older girl (in a light dress to draw the eye), cradled a baby in her arms. The composition sloped up to the right and back, where a group of prison officers and visitors hovered in half shadow. Light and colour would bring all the attention to the left foreground and the group of man, wife and children, eternally separated by the bars between them.

It was a bold composition which broke many of the classical rules. It was asymmetrical; one of the leading figures had her back almost to the viewer; the centre foreground was occupied by nothing but floor. It was filled with emotion, but if there was one thing I laboured to avoid, it was sentimentality. These people were poor and oppressed, but not in a charming, quaint, Murillo-urchin way. The children were not delightful scamps. They were grimy, tattered, with trodden-down clogs and running noses. They were not particularly appealing. My neighbour's little girl was just right, neither plain nor pretty, her dark eyes peering up from under her fringe. I put her clinging awkwardly to the mother's dress, one foot at an angle away from the bars, half hiding her face in the skirt. I painted her again from the opposite angle as another daughter, in a draggled dull-brown skirt and bodice too large for her, the sleeves rolled up like a scullion's, her hair under a scarf. Thwaite himself I had no trouble with. I could se him still in my mind's eye as he had been at Rochford Castle, his strong frame dropping sideways a little as he leant forward, his forehead furrowed, one hand up and one down on the bars. His expression was all-important and I leafed through my sketches, looking for the right one. At last I painted him confused and anxious, gazing into his wife's face. The whole emphasis must be on the consequences of his actions, themselves the result of what had happened to him.

The main figures were all women, because I had come to see that while men led in politics and took up arms in violent action, the consequences fell heavily on the women. They rarely appeared in this kind of trial, but when the men were imprisoned they had little recourse but to accompany them to a penal settlement or to stay at home without their man and try to manage as well as they could. The woman in the picture looked poor but respectable, but of the class that so often ended on the streets when struck by hard times. I wanted the figure of the eldest girl cradling the baby to suggest the all-too-frequent outcome—girls little more than children themselves giving birth in jail or the workhouse.

The four or five dark figures in the farthest corner were deliberately ambiguous. They were decently dressed—visiting the prisoners with tracts and comforts, perhaps, but also representatives of a class that condemned the unfortunate and supported penal legislation and the influence of the wealthy. The people who saw it would identify with them—'our sort of people'—and I hoped their presence in the prison would make viewers reflect on the gulf between the two groups depicted. But I wasn't going to preach. The picture must be a manifesto, but it was not going to seduce with charm nor persuade with oratory—not obviously, anyway. I wanted it to have the feel of the flaking rust, the grubby faces, the worn-down wood of the clogs, the gritted floor and filthy straw. I wanted it to touch their hearts, not have them admire its charm.

I went all out with my new techniques and worked faster and with more vigour and boldness than ever before. I felt newly confident, dragging washes across the canvas almost recklessly, slashing patches of light and dark, setting up a whole composition of ochres, yellows, greys and browns to cover the entire huge surface with a pattern of nuanced tones before I began on the figures.

I was part-way through and pleased with my progress when it all came undone. In my hurry I'd taken up whatever pigments I had on my shelves and ground them rapidly. I wasn't happy with the white lead after grinding up a lot of it to use in the under-layers. It had a chalky feel and the colour was weak. I remembered I'd bought it some time ago from a man I didn't usually go to. Fuming at the loss of a morning's work and the cost of the materials, I threw it away and rushed out to Middleton's to buy a proper lump of flake.

"That's the way, sir," the attendant cheerfully remarked. "We prefer the lumps, then you know it's all pure. You can add starch yourself, if you think it needs it."

"Yes, thank you." I hesitated, looking around. Since I was there, I might as well stock up to save another journey. "How much is the vermilion?" I planned to touch in the cheeks and some passages in the clothing to bring them forward.

"One and eightpence the ounce, sir." I winced. Red lead was a quarter the price.

"And the mastic varnish?" I had particular plans for that.

"Sixpence a phial, but it's very good."

"Dries well?"

"Definitely, sir. Much better than the fourpenny."

"All right, then. The flake white, an ounce of the vermilion, a phial—no, two, of the varnish, two phials of that superior drying oil, the one that's sixpence, and…" my eye roved across the shelves, thinking. "And some of the Antwerp blue." It was what I had in mind for the mother's dress, and would perfectly complement the vermilion. Ultramarine, while being exceedingly expensive, was also too purple for vermilion and too obvious and luxurious. Madder was what went with ultramarine.

"A shilling a bladder, sir. We have some already made up."

"All right."

"Will that be all? I'll put them into a parcel for you."

On the way home I dropped into my favourite framer's, Leeuwen's, in the Strand. I knew he'd be busy with the great influx of works for the Exhibition. It was a good place to see people's works in advance and as I expected, canvases of all shapes and sizes were stacked up in their ranks along the walls of the workshop waiting for attention in strict order of precedence. I hadn't come to inspect them, however, but to seek a favour. I hoped Leeuwen would help me.

"I need frames for these two." I unwrapped them and he raised a wheat-coloured eyebrow.

"Unusual. Would these be for the Academy?"

"They would indeed, and there's another to go with them. I want them all framed the same, nice gold frames but nothing too ornate." A big gold frame was *de rigueur* but I thought I'd make part of my point with the style of frame. Besides, I didn't want them looking like mastiffs dressed up as lapdogs.

"You don't have the other work with you, sir?" he asked, glancing at my empty hands.

"No, but I do have the exact dimensions." I pulled out a piece of paper with pencilled figures.

Leeuwen's round pink face was concerned. "I have a great deal of work on hand, as you can see, sir, and I prefer to have the work here. The work is very rarely perfectly square, as you know," he glanced at the numbers, "especially a canvas of that size. Bring it in, and I'll see if I can fit it in."

"That's exactly the problem." The work was nowhere near finished, I explained, and wouldn't be until the last minute. "I'll get it to you as quick as I can, but I won't pretend that it'll be anything but a couple of days beforehand. I thought that if you could make the frame while I'm working on it, at the same time as the others," I wheedled cunningly, "I could bring it in and you could just fit the frame on."

It was essential that he agreed. I couldn't exhibit it without a frame, and I'd never get one made in time.

He rubbed his chin. "I suppose it would be possible, although it's not the way I like to work." He was weakening. "What if it's not quite the right size?"

I'd thought of that. "I measured it very carefully, you can see from the diagram, and I thought perhaps you could make it a trifle larger all round and then pack it out to fit where necessary."

He smiled ruefully. "I can't promise anything, but I'll do my best." Victory! That was what he said when he meant to do it. "Go through and my son will show you the new mouldings. Tell him what you want."

I went home whistling, with my parcel of supplies under my arm. I'd chosen some very nice frames, large enough to give the works importance but not over-ornate. The amount I'd spent at Middleton's was nothing to the gigantic cost of the framing, which came to over sixty guineas. It was always the way, but usually I comforted myself with the thought that I'd recoup the cost in sales. This time I couldn't expect any sales and it would fall squarely on my shoulders. But I was still happy.

WORK went well now I had the right colours. The most frustrating part was waiting for the layers to dry. Time pressed. The under-layers were done and drying. I used the minimum of oil and only fast-drying varieties, but it was still taking too long. I sketched the figures lightly in thinned Sienna and began to block their lights and shades. It would never dry in time. I was beside myself. The picture was consuming me. I kept testing the surfaces. I had to take my mind off it. In the end took an afternoon off and went along to Slaughter's.

Quayle was there with Alcock and Hallett and a few people. They called to me and I went and sat with them.

"Not working?"

I affected nonchalance. "Nothing in particular." Everyone else lied about their output and pet projects, why not me too?

"Campbell was going to be here but he's putting the finishing touches to his twelve apostles," Alcock remarked. He had got puffy-looking and red in the face.

"How's yours progressing?" I asked.

"Oh, sent it in already. Don't believe in leaving it to the last minute."

"Quayle?"

"Oh yes, my fellow took mine down last week. Have to get on with a few other things for Lord Arbuthnot and I'm going down to Hertfordshire next week to meet some people."

"But you'll be back for the opening?"

"Of course, mustn't miss the dinner. Are you going?"

The Royal Academy's Annual Banquet was the biggest social event of the artistic year. Last year the Prince Regent had honoured it with his presence and had ordered an enormous bronze chandelier to improve the lighting. One hundred and twenty invitations were issued every year to the great and good. I wasn't one of them.

"No. Who's doing it this year?"

"Simpkin from the Crown and Anchor, same as last year," Quayle replied, screwing up his face. "He wasn't bad last time. I seem to recall some excellent lamb and the Committee thinks he's quite cheap. Thirty shillings a head with wine." That would keep me in dinners for a fortnight—with wine, although not of the class that was presumably served to the Prince Regent. "You're coming, aren't you, Hallett?"

Hallett looked up from the letter he was writing on the edge of the table. "Oh yes, wouldn't miss it."

Curiosity overcame discretion. "How did you get an invitation?" 'And how can you possibly afford it?' I managed to refrain from adding.

He smiled, pulling down the extravagant ruffles on his cuffs. I noticed that they were trimmed with lace, the only man I knew who could get away with such a thing. "Oh, I always like to be at these things. You meet such interesting people. Last month I was at a rout in Brighton and there were..."

Alcock interrupted. "I say, did you see my notice in the *Courier* the other day?"

I hardly read the papers now that the Rochford trial was over, and I certainly hadn't kept up with the exhibition notices. The *Courier* wasn't something I'd normally bother with anyway.

He pushed a copy over. Its smudgy column was full of encomiums about Alcock's portraits: 'a new Lawrence... rivals the master Sir Joshua himself... delicacy of touch...' I turned to the end but there was no name. I couldn't imagine who had written such trash. Alcock's work was nothing like either

Lawrence or Reynolds and although some thought it had its points, I'd never heard anyone refer to it as delicate.

"Very good. Who wrote it?"

He smirked. "No idea."

I turned to the front. The proprietor was a man better known for his conservative politics and society tattle than his knowledge of art. Quayle looked abstracted; Hallett had gone back to his letter. I handed it back.

"Most encouraging for you." He folded it and tucked it away in his breast pocket, then got up to go.

"See you fellows later on, I expect." We watched him go.

"Who on earth wrote that?" I asked.

Quayle sniggered. "No-one knows, but if rumour is correct, the author has just left us."

"Surely not!" Even Alcock wouldn't sink to that.

Quayle pulled a wry face and Hallett grinned. "He wants to get noticed. I suppose he thought he'd get the ball rolling. Speaking of which, distributing those cards was a good idea. People are putting their names on a list to attend my Open Days. It's doing very well. I've put another assistant on, a young fellow with a very good hand for drapery. You should drop in some time." He smiled benevolently.

Hallett looked up. "Have you heard about Wilkie?"

Quayle nodded. "He's having an exhibition—I heard something about it."

Wilkie was a Scotch artist, a young man who'd done well with his common-life scenes—'Rent Day', the 'Blind Fiddler', that sort of thing, and had recently been admitted to the Academy. I'd had an argument with Campbell about him—he admired Wilkie's detail, which he considered amazingly true to life, while I found the works sentimental and too dark brown. I think I'd used the expression 'painted in gravy', which had infuriated Campbell. But he had been widely praised.

"Yes, in Gainsborough's old house in Pall Mall. The Council's furious."

Quayle raised an eyebrow. "What's it got to do with them?"

"Wilkie's show will be on at the same time as the Annual Exhibition and he's not sending anything in to that. And they think it'll draw people away from the Academy show."

Quayle pursed his lips. "Bad, very bad. There's no need to snub the Academy just because you're doing well."

He would never do that—no wonder he was concerned.

He smoothed his hair. "Well, best be off." He got up and I with him. I'd had all the gossip I could listen to in one day and needed to get back to the studio, work and sanity.

THE work I'd done so far was dry—that is, it wouldn't be completely dry for months, but it was what might generally be called dry. I'd used thin pigments with little oil on purpose. Now, with only days left, I decided to paint the whole remainder *en premier coup*, without waiting for the paint to dry. I mixed in extra oil and set to work, picking up exactly what I needed from the palette with each brushstroke and laying it precisely in position. Normally I would have laid in a dark blue, probably Prussian, on the wife's skirt, for example, and touched it up in the lights with Antwerp and the shadows with Vandyke and black. I would have put a middle flesh colour on the face and hands and added shades and colour later. That took months of drying, though, or the upper coats would crack over the wetter undercoats.

So I painted away, leaning on the maulstick, working one area at a time, more rapidly than I had ever done and I felt, with a surer hand. First the wife, then the girls: the baby, hardly visible in its wrappings, a scrape of ochre for the hair, Naples mixed with flake for the shawl. I laid in shadows and lights as I worked, a single layer over the canvas, leaving the coloured grounds to show through where there were no figures. The blocking I'd done in the under-painting shone through and gave the forms solidity and roundness, as well as pulling the disparate parts of the composition together. The overall theme was greys and ochres and yellows, as with the two earlier works, but I brightened it and brought focus to the figures with dark and light and judicious use of reds and blues. There was little green. This was no fertile pasture.

I had no time to adjust the other two paintings to conform to the new work, but I had a card up my sleeve for that, with the new mastic varnish in reserve, and to put the final touches to the 'Luddite'.

It went against the grain to paint such a big work with no landscape at all in it, and I still had no idea what my future in art would be. In token of my first love, nature, at the last minute I painted a square of blue, a hint of cloud, a fragment of a branch, in the window high behind the prisoner's head. It stood too for a tiny flag, a signal, an emblem of the freedom he had lost.

Then it was done. I went out to Rainbow's and triumphantly drank a great deal of ale, then staggered home to bed, light-headed with liquor and achievement.

THERE were still a few days before the closing date for the picture to dry a little. The studio was a chaos of discarded grubby cloths, clogged palettes, open jars, empty phials, dirty glasses, cups and plates where I had eaten as I worked. I had forbidden Mrs Mullins to clean up until I had finished; the increasing debris had formed a kind of nest from which the work emerged. I should have tidied up, but instead did nothing but knock together a wooden case so I could transport the picture to Leeuwen's without damaging the surface.

I wished with all my heart that I could show it to Rachel

and her father. I wanted to know what they thought of it. She had given me so much encouragement. She was in my thoughts constantly while I had been painting—how lovely she was, and so kind and caring. She was my imagined audience. I wondered what she was doing, up there in the grey stone Rectory. She would be comforting the families and working to find them the necessities of life. How could they live, now that their men were gone?

And at home, at night? In a very short time I had become so used to her presence that my evenings in the studio, seemed empty without her. And I had thought about whether there was a future for us together—where we could be, and what we could live on. That was supposing Crosland was out of the picture, but every letter I had from Somers mentioned him. The wretched man obscured any happy vision I had of Rachel and me together. And I still had no notion of her feelings towards me. I pondered how I could find out, but could think of nothing. She was too loyal to let slip the slightest hint. All I could do was wait.

By way of showing them my great painting I made a water colour sketch and sent it up to them. They had seen the other two completed, and I hoped could imagine them together. It made them seem closer.

Rachel wrote back by return, saying she thought it would be magnificent and congratulating me on having found my vocation. Her father's health had improved and they wished me every good fortune for the exhibition. I had pleased her, at least. I had to be content with that.

I hoped the critics would be kind, but was sure they would take it badly. I was more afraid of the Hanging Committee. I didn't know whether a work had ever been rejected as unsuitable for public display, but I didn't want mine to be the first. Quayle's words 'you don't want to be known just for being eccentric' sounded in my head. People were already importuning the Committee about the hang of their works. Everyone wanted to be in the Great Room; everyone wanted to be on the line. Many people had special reasons for their work being hung, or not being hung, next to some other particular work. Wilkie had bowed to the pressure and agreed to send some work in to the Annual Exhibition, but he had caused a great deal of ill feeling. And the news came that a room was to be set aside for the Competition works, which would be judged during the Exhibition. The verdict would be made known on the last night.

At last I took one final look at the picture on the easel, put it into its box and with the help of a neighbour carried it downstairs, where I loaded it onto a borrowed handcart to wheel it to the Strand.

I hadn't even had time to visit Leeuwen's to see my other works framed, or whether they were ready, although I had written a note to tell him when I would come. I was relying on him and didn't think he'd let me down. As I trundled my cart through the streets, followed by some mocking little boys, my excitement rose, overriding my fears. When I got to the framer's and we carried the box in, he had the big frame ready. Empty, it looked enormous. His assistants helped extract the picture from the case and Leeuwen himself came to fit it into the frame.

"Be careful, please! It's not dry."

He regarded me, blue eyes twinkling. "It is not alone in that, sir. I think I've done nothing this past week but handle wet paintings. Now..."

He flapped me out of the way and disappeared into the workshop. His son emerged a moment later to show me the smaller works. I had the usual moment of delight in how well they looked framed, followed by the usual surprise in how different they looked from what I remembered, then the moment of panic in which I decided that the frames were quite wrong for the works. Then, as usual, it all settled down and I spent some time admiring them. I had never got used to the phenomenon that once framed, they didn't seem to be mine any more.

Half an hour later two assistants carried the big picture out. Leeuwen had done a splendid job. The frame was just right, neither too ornate nor plain, and fitted with a minimum of packing.

I had never seen all three works together and the assistants indulged me while I set them in a row and looked at them. On the left the sleeping beggar—'Out of Work'; 'Awaiting Transportation' in the middle and 'A Shearman at the Mill' on the right. I was quite overwhelmed to see them like that. They worked—I was sure they worked. I had a qualm. It wasn't too late to change my mind. I could still take them home. I could keep them for myself and put nothing in the show. But it only lasted a minute. I had already made my decision back at the studio.

Chapter Twenty-one

I had been right to abandon the Agamemnon. I knew it as soon as I arrived at the Exhibition. Row after row of classical scenes and classical allegories large and small, some well painted, some badly. I paused in front of Quayle's gigantic 'Dido Embarking for Carthage'. The Tyrian queen posed gracefully on the quayside, gesturing to her exotically-robed attendants. None of these works had anything to do with life today. They were all of the past, a foreign past that had nothing to do with England, or people one knew, or the conditions of life. I had been right to reject it, whatever the reception of my new works. At least they were of now, and they were true.

It was the first day of the exhibition and hundreds of people were crammed into every room. Many had been waiting on the steps since early morning to get in. Why, was a mystery, since no especially grand works had been promised and in fact the collection was much the same as in previous years.

I didn't have to rush to see my own pictures, since I'd spent the entire day there last week on Varnishing Day, when the works had been hung and artists had been allowed in to apply a final coat. This was what I'd been planning when I bought the expensive mastic, when I knew that I'd barely get the work finished by the closing date. I'd arrived before the doors opened with all my paraphernalia, the colours I'd need freshly mixed and put up in bladders. I had had a word with old

Strowger, the porter, and secured a ladder. I had passed the day perched on it, ignoring cries of annoyance from tardier exhibitors trying to get at their own works lower down.

First I went over the two smaller pieces with touches of the Antwerp blue and vermilion, as well as some shadow to slightly darken the tonality of the Beggar to bring it into line with the other two. I had planned some alterations to the compositions, too, to make them into a proper triptych—nothing startling, which in any case I couldn't bring off in the course of a day, but some modifications to the backgrounds—the angle of a wall, and in the case of Thwaite at the mill, the introduction of a patch of bluish shadow in the wall behind him to echo the window in the prison cell. Finally, I took a new round brush and a clean palette, mixed some colours with varnish and went systematically over all three works. I modified the vermilion in places with a madder glaze and the blue with touches of Prussian, Vandyke and black. I glazed passages that I wanted to bring forward, introduced hints of colour in shadows to pull compositions together, scumbled glaze across duller areas, and used it to bring freshness to the faces and hands. Last of all I went over all three with the end of my brush, even my fingernails, scraping lines and scribbles into stone, wood and clothing to bring texture and variety to the surface.

It had taken me the whole day without stopping for food or drink, but when I got down for the last time, took away the ladder and stood back into the room to look at them I was well pleased. They were not perfect, but considering the time I'd had to do them, I was satisfied. I had been anxious about the Committee's reception of them and had been half expecting a note asking me to take them away. I had offered no excuses nor special pleading, but simply a short note asking for them to be hung together, and in what order. I couldn't expect a good place, but it seemed that someone had sympathised. They were not in the Great Room, of course, nor on the line, but they were together just as I had wished in the second room, and not so far above the line that they were invisible. You could see them well as you turned to the left after coming in the door. There was only one row of smaller pictures—landscapes—between them and the best paintings on the line, and nearby were works by some of the Academicians. Now, as I studied them, the glazing caught the eye and they pulled together well. I had done it. All that remained was to see what the reaction would be.

THE painting of the exhibition was undoubtedly Turner's 'Snowstorm: Hannibal crossing the Alps' hung in the new room after some argument between the artist and the committee. If he'd taken it away, as he'd apparently threatened at one stage, it would have been a great loss. Although large, perhaps nine feet by five, it was by no means the largest. Its subject was interesting but not immediately striking. It excelled simply on account of the grandeur of its conception and the absolute mastery of original technique that it demonstrated. Seeing it took my breath away. It was incredible that it had been painted in the same twelve-months as West's 'Christ Healing', let alone any of the numerous lesser works in the genre. Next to it, every other work in the room looked antiquated. I inspected the application of paint. I had never seen anything like it for originality, delicacy and effect. It made my own efforts look crude and half-finished. At the same time I felt vindicated, no longer alone in my desire to break free from the strictures of academic finish and compositional canons. Ostensibly of a classical subject, nothing could have been less classical in style. It breathed freedom and despite its subject, it was a work for today. Just as well Sir Joshua was no longer with us. He would have been aghast.

There were some pretty views of Oxford of Turner's hung not far from my own works, with others by Ibbetson, Arnald and others, but my attention was taken by Westall's New Holland landscapes, which he had sketched while on his voyages with Lieutenant Flinders. He'd been at the Schools with Turner and Constable, about the same time as Campbell and me. I'd envied him the opportunity to travel, to see new lands and have new experiences. He had been to many countries and was likely to do well out of his illustrations to the *Voyage to Terra Australis*, now in production. But his 'Part of King George III's Sound on the South Coast of New Holland' was traditionally Picturesque in its composition and terribly brown in its colouring. Some natives, who I thought looked remarkably like the Indian in West's great painting of the 'Death of Wolfe', crouched in the centre foreground, while a curving isthmus stretched away behind. An extraordinary tree with a tuft of grass at the top instead of leaves was the only interesting thing in the picture. If that was what New Holland was like, I might as well visit Cornwall.

I searched out Constable's major piece, 'A Watermill'. It stood in bright contrast to the Westalls. The scene was commonplace but everything in it was fresh and glittering with reflected light. His application of many shades of green—I had to find out how he got them—and little flickering brushstrokes was fascinating. The whole work glowed with light, and what I liked most was his interest in the application of paint. His approach was completely different from Turner's, but just as new. These were the men of the future, at least as far as landscape went.

My tour of inspection was broken by Brigstock, who appeared at my elbow.

"Haven't seen you in an age, Armiger. How do you do?"

"Well, thank you." We exchanged compliments. I remembered what it was like going to exhibitions with Brig, but there was no getting away from him without being rude. In truth, I was glad of his company. I felt as though I had spent a great deal of time alone lately. I had to just steer him away from the 'Snowstorm'.

"You didn't put anything in to the Competition in the end, did you?" he asked.

"No."

"They're what I really want to see. They're in here."

We worked our way through the crush. A placard by the doorway announced 'Entries in the Competition for a Work Representing The Spirit of the Present Age'. I was full of curiosity, as well as pangs. If I had been more advanced in my thinking—if I hadn't wasted so much time on the wretched Agamemnon—if I had had more confidence—my works could have been there too, and perhaps...

"Look, there's Campbell's!" Brig pointed to a collection of group portraits clustered at one end. The Hanging Committee had obviously decided to arrange the entries by genre. It was hard to say whether this did the works a favour by enabling the viewer to compare like with like. I scanned the ranks.

"Which?"

"There!" He pointed upwards.

"No, that's surely not his." It wasn't his style, and unless he'd changed the composition radically... I checked my catalogue. "Number 43—no, that's Alcock's."

It was a huge canvas representing the leading men of the age. He had obviously tried to include everyone of influence: the Prince Regent occupied the centre, flanked by Viscount Wellington, the Prime Minister, the Marquis of Stafford (President of the British Institution), the Earl of Egremont, the Duke of Bedford (as a leading Whig, presumably to balance Mr Perceval and Lord Wellington), the President of the Academy of course, *et cetera*. It suffered from a flat woodenness as well as betraying too much the fact that the likenesses had been painted separately then assembled. It would have looked better on a smaller scale, when its deficiencies would have been less obvious and it could have been pulled together better, but men like Alcock always thought that they could convince with mere size—like raising your voice when you were losing an argument.

Campbell's, which I was keen to see, was a little further along. It was much better than Alcock's in technique and more imaginative in its selection of subjects. The great philosophers and explorers in the arts and sciences did far better with the theme, and he had excelled himself with his brushwork. There really were almost touches of Lawrence here and there. But the very fact that we had to pick his out from the collection told its own story.

"His is definitely the best. Perhaps he'll win. Let's look at the others." We moved on.

"I must say I'm disappointed there are no paintings of engines," Brig remarked, looking slowly around. "Let me see your catalogue." He inspected it carefully, turning the pages and finally handing it back with a dissatisfied expression. "I really think they might have included an engine. I made some excellent studies of the one at Abercorn, did I tell you? It was magnificent."

"Yes. Or a balloon—that would have been a brilliant idea," I suggested. "It could have included a panorama of England stretched out below."

"But you would have to go up in one to know what it looked like. You couldn't just imagine it."

"I could imagine it, and I've always wanted to go in one. But I'm not sure it would do for 'The Spirit of the Age'.

Brig was absolutely right, however. The whole room was full of works that might be dubbed 'the mixture—as before'. I felt I had seen them all on other occasions, or if not them, works so similar as to be indistinguishable. Whatever my misgivings about Barry and the 'Triumph of Navigation', I began to feel that some machinery and allusions to modern progress in the sciences and the industrial arts, would have been very welcome. Wright of Derby would have done something grand, I was sure. Our age was one of change, radical change, in politics, industry, philosophy. Even in the arts, a book had just come out about the theory of colour and completely new colours themselves were appearing constantly. It was a revolutionary age, and not just with reference to events in France. Would Europe ever be the same after Napoleon's depredations? Cook's explorations had expanded the boundaries of the known world. Science was changing our understanding of everything in nature, and there was hardly a town now but had its philosophical societies and reading groups. The theme the Committee had set was full of exciting possibilities, but they had been laid aside in favour of variations on the same old ideas.

We arrived in front of a large group that might have been headed 'Allegories of Progress'. For a moment I thought they had seized the subject by the reins, but no. Some of the ideas were there, but the techniques were traditional. References to military and naval power, industrial and commercial greatness abounded. Cornucopias flourished in corners, the gods of sea and land, even of the air, lounged holding their tridents or sceptres, their feet subjugating continents personified by elephants, costumed foreign maidens, Indians, palm trees and pyramids. The King's flag unfurled over panoramas of English landscape peopled by fat herds, spreading towns, magnificent architecture. Philosophers stood triumphantly on pedestals holding astrolabes, sextants, orreries and all manner of scientific instruments. Muses of the Arts and Sciences proffered their attributes to Britannia, seated with her feet on sleeping lions and globes of the earth, gazing out at future dominions.

Everything that had ever appeared in any work of the sort had been gathered into one colossal effort by at least fifty different hands.

Brigstock was moving his head about. "Where's Quayle's 'Dido'? I was looking forward to that, I've heard so much about it."

"It's in the other room." I was confused, too. Surely 'Dido' had been his Competition entry? I searched the catalogue, then spotted his piece—the largest work in the place, an enormous gold frame, hung on the line in the centre, everything else arranged around it. "That's it." It wasn't 'Dido'.

Brig looked hurt. "He didn't say anything about it to me!"

"Nor to me either, nor anyone else, as far as I know."

Typically sly! He'd let everyone think the 'Dido' would be for the Competition, when it had been promised to Lord Arbuthnot all along. He'd left us with our assumptions, working away in secret. No wonder he'd employed another assistant. Looking at the huge work, I thought I could see evidence of several hands.

"What is it of?" Brig peered at the title plaque. "Oh—'The Spirit of the Present Age: an Allegory of Britain's Greatness'.

Nothing new there, then, but I didn't expect it of him. It encompassed all the standard motifs and individuals gathered artistically around his Royal Highness in the centre, wearing his robes as Prince of Wales but holding the royal sceptre. The King tactfully appeared behind him, gesturing towards his son; hereditary peers and military leaders occupied the middle distance, Admiral Nelson among them as a ghostly presence, together with Edward the Confessor and goodness knows who else. The emblems of the arts and sciences and of the various countries in which England had planted her flag littered the corners. It was adroitly done, more so than many of the others clustered around it, and was a clearer statement of what it set out to say. In case of any doubt, there was a

Latin epigram inscribed on the frame:

'Tu pias laetis animas reponis Sedibus uirgaque leuem Coerces aurea turbam, Superis deorum Gratus et imis.'

Brig peered at it. "What does it say?"

"It's from Horace." I read from the catalogue:

'Thou lay'st unspotted souls to rest; Thy golden rod pale spectres know;

Blest power! by all thy brethren blest, Above, below!'

I couldn't help smiling. If one were to believe Quayle, Britain's greatness consisted entirely in its aristocratic history. He may have been right. But 'the spirit of the present age'? I didn't think so. It was a Tory manifesto, nothing more nor less, and ignored everything that made the present age one of superlative interest. But he would probably win. It was just the sort of thing the Academy liked.

I heard a discreet cough behind me, goodness knows how, in the bustle. Perhaps it had a familiar note. I turned and saw Laura not far off, her hand in the arm of a tall gentleman who was looking in the other direction. I couldn't tell if it was Captain Tennison, as he was not in uniform. Our eyes met and she lifted her hand, fluttering her slender fingers. I raised my hand and an eyebrow: she smiled and shook her head slightly, crooking it towards her companion. I smiled back and she turned away. She hadn't forgotten me, nor I her. She was as comely as ever, but I didn't feel inclined to renew our relations, even if she had signalled that she wished it. But I was glad that we were friends, and she looked happy.

Brigstock was pulling my sleeve. "Have you got anything here?"

"Not in the Competition but in the Exhibition, three pictures—a sort of triptych. They're in the second room."

I could hardly avoid showing them to him, but I knew he wouldn't like them. I had braced myself for adverse reviews, but hearing criticism in person was something I'd hoped to avoid. I wasn't sure that I was strong enough to bear it with the required indifference. They were my darlings, and hearing them denounced by a friend would be extremely painful. My stomach tightened and I had a constricted feeling in my throat. This would be the first time any of my art friends had seen them. My heart began thumping unevenly.

We arrived in front of the works. There was not a great crowd.

Brig looked about. "Where are yours?"

I pointed wordlessly.

"Oh! I though it would be landscapes."

"No, these are my new things."

He stared for a while and moved up to read the titles. I tried to look away but found it impossible. I couldn't swallow.

I heard a woman in the crowd say, "Disgusting—really disgusting."

Her companion replied: "The one on the left's not too bad."

"They really shouldn't allow such things in," I heard as they moved away. "Now, that one's really good!"

I turned to see what had met with their approval. It was a genre work by Craig of a jolly cook in his cookshop. Of course. The happy worker. I flinched.

"You showed us some of the sketches for these, didn't you, when you came back from Rochford?" Brig was saying.

"Yes." I tried to prepare myself.

"I like that one." He pointed to 'Out of Work'—the beggar. "I think you've done the wall awfully well, and the dog. I really like the dog."

I revived slightly. At least he didn't hate them all on sight.

"And the way the little girl's holding onto her mother's skirt—that's very good. It's a strange composition, isn't it, but I quite like it." He smiled engagingly.

I felt I could kiss him. "You like them?" I could hardly believe it.

"Oh, yes. They're a bit—advanced, I suppose—for me, and I would have done them quite differently, if it was me, you know, but they're very—I don't know—convincing? They look a bit half-finished, you won't mind my saying that, but I suppose that's the new look. You could do more work on them, but I do like them." He pointed. "I like the woman, I suppose she's the wife. Nice colour. And the strong man smoking his pipe. Is it the same man? I suppose it is. No, I think you've done well, although it's not what I expected."

I almost threw my arms around him. "Brig, you never fail to surprise me. I thought you'd loathe them."

He smiled modestly. "I'm trying to become a bit more up-to-date. But you know I always like your work. We're friends, aren't we."

I was flabbergasted. Brig was the last person I had expected to approve them, but he'd taught me a lesson. He had not been interested in (or even perhaps understood) the subject, but he had made a real effort to find things about them he could appreciate. I had underestimated him. Of everyone I knew, he was the real friend.

"Thank you. I'm really touched. It's very good of you." I hardly knew what to say.

He was already studying some sketches by Fuseli—'Ulysses addressing the Shade of Ajax', 'Lady Macbeth seizing the Daggers'.

What a good fellow that old gnome had been when I was a student. His work continued just as individual as ever. You could pick it out a mile off—it was nothing like anyone else's in the room. I was glad to see that he was still working, still exhibiting, resolutely sticking to his own style. I had probably been more influenced by him than I had realised. We never know what we owe our teachers until years later.

Brig moved away. "Let's go and get a drink, I'm tired. We can come back another time."

"Of course. Have you got a ticket?" Exhibitors got in for nothing, but others had to pay a shilling.

"Yes, Campbell got me one."

I felt remiss. Brigstock was a good friend, one of the few I had. I should have thought to get him a ticket. I'd been so enveloped in my own concerns that I'd neglected him.

"Come on, I'll buy you a drink."

We made our way towards the door. The grand staircase was thronged. I never went down it without thinking of Rowlandson's entertaining lampoon of the 'Stare-case', with plump pink ladies tumbling down, legs in the air, and dirty old gentlemen looking on with enthusiasm. We narrowly averted causing a similar incident as several ladies tried to push past us on the way up.

I caught sight of a familiar figure and heard a familiar voice. I would have recognised her a mile off. My heart stopped and I felt I had gone pale.

"Oh, Mr Armiger! Fancy seeing you here! Oh, no, of course, this is just the place to find you! How nice to see you again."

I bowed, trembling. "Mrs Shirlow. I hope I see you well? My friend Mr Brigstock. Mr Shirlow, Mr Brigstock."

"Good day, Armiger."

Shirlow looked self-satisfied but in a bad temper. I recalled he didn't like art. I expected Francesca had dragged him along. She was as staggeringly beautiful as ever, but marriage had changed her. There was a certain hardness to her features that I'd never noticed, and a little frown marred her perfect forehead.

"Do come along, John, we are standing in the way. Where is Papa?"

"I am doing my best, my love," he said, moving aside a little, but his tone grated.

Now I had time to look at her, my trembling subsided.

She was very pretty indeed, nothing could change that, but somehow she was not the girl I had been in love with. She had altered. I had not noticed her temper before, but now I thought of it I recollected how she had—charmingly!—always insisted on her own way.

"Now then, Mr Armiger," Mr Hall boomed in my ear.

He had not altered in the slightest. Mrs Hall was beside him, and as the crowd thinned a little I saw Campbell and Miss Anne coming up. The whole family was here. Brigstock immediately started talking to Campbell, who bowed frigidly to me.

Hall took out his snuff-box in his usual leisurely manner. "I'm happy to tell you the trouble up home has settled down since we hanged that rogue Danby, but business is even worse now we're really at war with the Americans. But I've finished my new place—Madam here is very pleased with it."

She smiled happily. "Yes, indeed, Mr Armiger, and it is so nice to have both of our daughters settled! It is such a worry for a mother, although I don't expect you to understand that, but now we have our beautiful new place, we will have Anne's wedding breakfast there, they are to be married at Coldbrook church, of course Francesca was married at the Cathedral, but that was quite different..." She stopped suddenly, perhaps recollecting why that was quite different and my involvement.

Her husband took the opportunity to continue. "I had to cut down those oak trees, you know, as they got in the way of the view, and I got a very good price for them. There's a great demand for timber with the war and the expansion of commerce. You may turn your nose up, young man, but business must go on, war or no war, and now the view is grand. You can see all of Rochford from the terrace. I've called it Prospect House."

They passed on and I escaped with Brig to a chop-house in the Strand.

"Who on earth where those people?"

"Campbell's future in-laws."

"I didn't really like them."

"No. I suppose they are all right. They're just not our sort of people." That was probably exactly what they were saying about us. I was glad we hadn't met in front of my pictures. I particularly didn't want to know what they thought of them.

"Mrs Shirlow is very pretty, but I didn't like her husband much."

"Me neither."

Brigstock didn't know the half of it. Seeing Shirlow had been distasteful, quite apart from Francesca. I had had a letter from Somers with the happy news that he and Rachel were coming to London for a brief visit. I couldn't help speculating that it couldn't be entirely coincidence that it was just at this time. At least I would be able to show them my work. And I would see her, and spend time with her, and perhaps glean something of whether she cared for me at all, or whether I should give up all hope. But I had previously determined that I would not do that until I saw her walk down the aisle on Crosland's arm. Until then, I hoped.

And Somers had had a bombshell to throw. He had at last found out who had informed on Thwaite. Thwaite had maintained all along that none of his friends would have done it, although privately I had thought it was probably one of them, for the reward. God knows they were poor enough. But it had been Shirlow who had given the information and claimed the money. He hadn't seen Thwaite himself, but one of his employees, a well-known poacher, had 'happened' to be at Croker's at the time of the attack, had identified Thwaite and passed the knowledge on to his master. The talk was that he had got half the reward.

'Shirlow denies it, but the man has been boasting about it and spending a lot of money in the village.'

Somers had wondered why Shirlow would protect the man, but had been told that he used the man for work that needed discretion and willingness to undertake unsavoury tasks. 'I gather that at the time the man was spying on Croker's factory, and on the frame-breakers—pretending to be one of them. Shirlow paid him for the information. This time he caught a much larger fish than he expected.'

So that was how poor Thwaite had been taken up—by the treachery of someone he trusted, employed underhand by a rival mill-owner. Now he was in the hulks with his family, rotting on the Thames at Woolwich, not a couple of miles from Somerset House. It seemed typical of the new era that had stolen up on us. I was not a paragon of virtue, but the world today, with its emphasis on money and greed and display—I loathed it. What had happened to morality? Fairness? Duty, dignity and self-respect? Lasting, worthwhile things!

These new men, despite their money and houses and carriages, were not gentlemen. Lord Arbuthnot was a gentleman. Lord Byron was a gentleman, whatever the rumours about his activities at Newstead. Reverend Somers was one, and not just by virtue of his cloth. Benjamin West was a gentleman, and so was I, and Campbell—it was just that some of us were more down-at-heel than others. But Hall and Shirlow were not. Shirlow's behaviour proved it, if there was any doubt. He was without honour. These new men were on a level of their own, just as their workers were, and shopkeepers. The old orders were breaking down. I supposed that the new men would make their own place in society eventually, but it would be a long time before they understood the principles of the old. They probably thought that if they had enough 'brass' it didn't matter. That was what the modern world was becoming.

Dr Johnson had said something to the effect that the rage for trade would soon be over, that it was like gambling and there was no point in it if everyone went in for it, because then there would nothing to be won. It was new in his time, this 'rage for trade' as he called it, but since then it had expanded immensely, and had done so on the backs of poorer men, and there was no sign of it diminishing. It probably never would, now, but would keep on swelling and destroying the value of everything that was not involved in making money, until there was nothing at all left but greed and rapaciousness, and a man would be valued not for his character or diligence but for the size of the funds at his bankers. Never had a great man been so entirely wrong.

Men advancing by their merits I had no objection to. It was men whose claim was that they had made a great deal of money by exploiting others, and gave nothing back, and thought everything and every man had a price, and that good could only be measured in terms of whether it was good for business, and whether money could be made from it. They did not value or understand the traditions of our civilisation. With them it was all show and display.

Of course there had always been show and display, but at least when it was on the part of those who inherited wealth and position there was real substance behind it—education and taste and service. These were the men who governed the country and led our army and navy, and were the great patrons of the arts and culture—men like the Prince himself, the Earl of Egremont, Sir Joseph Banks and the various nobles who assisted the work of the Royal Society and the Academy. With these new men it was all and only to raise them in the estimation of themselves and the community. There were good men such as Boulton, or Herschel, or Davy, who had advanced not by wealth or influence but by their merit. But they were gentlemen too—not landed, as in the past, but men of honour who put service to their country before comfort, and certainly before empty show. None of them would pay a scoundrel to spy on men and cover up his crimes because he was useful to them.

I grinned ruefully. I sounded like my father. I must be getting old. But if I had become old enough to know what was important in life, I was happy.

Chapter Twenty-two

Two days later, when the crowd had receded a little, I went back to Somerset House. I had not half got round everything I wanted to see and study. I ran immediately into Hallett and Alcock with a congeries of followers.

"How do, Armiger?" Hallett looked worn but cocky. His hair was dressed in a new style, curled up with a great deal of pomade. "Have you seen my 'Muses'?"

He steered me to the work, an immensely long canvas depicting several nudes in a variety of attitudes placed in a forest. The attributes of the arts were hanging from branches or propped against tree-trunks. I studied it for a few minutes while he chattered to his friends. Its finish was uneven, parts being highly worked up and others quite sketchy. I recognised the features of the girl who was always hanging about Slaughter's. His friends were talking about the Academy dinner.

"I was introduced to the Earl of Egremont and he passed me the wine after dinner," Hallett was saying. "He was sitting opposite. We spoke about his collection. He was most interested in my opinion."

"Did his Royal Highness attend?" Alcock asked.

"No, he couldn't come this year, but he visited yesterday. He stayed two hours. The Duke of York came with him, and they put baize carpet on the floor and he had a guard of soldiers."

"Which pictures did he like?"

"He looked mainly at the portraits. I suppose a lot of them were people he knew, the Marquess of Stafford and so on. I met the Marquess too. They were all at the dinner. The Prince asked if there was anything of Thomson's and they showed him the 'Infancy of Jupiter'."

I'd seen it, a horrid picture, although well executed in the usual style, of the ancient god with the goat Amalthea looking over his shoulder. God help us if that was the sort of thing the Prince liked.

"Big picture, Hallett," I remarked, pointing to his 'Muses'.

"Ah yes, size isn't everything, but it goes a long way, in my opinion. Of course the shape is daring, but I like to take risks, you know."

"The execution is rather varied. You won't mind my asking if you had an assistant on it?" It was a lot of canvas for Hallett to have covered by himself.

He scratched his cheek, looking a trifle self-conscious. "Well, I'm so busy at present, what with one thing and another, that I had to get someone else on it or I wouldn't have got it in in time. Actually I've got a few young fellows who've come out of the Schools in the last year or two. I'm giving them a step up, don't you know, by letting them practice—giving them a bit of work. A helping hand. I like to help the younger men." He had entirely recovered his self-possession.

"I see." What I saw was that although the composition showed the signs of his fertile imagination, he'd probably hardly put a brush to it himself.

Alcock was sniggering to a crony. "Bad luck about your beggars, Armiger."

"What do you mean?"

"I heard the critics are giving them the thumbs down. Someone told me Hunt was here this morning. I told you it was a mistake. People don't want radical politics shoved down their throats. They want something elegant and charming—

tasteful. They don't want to look at ugly rogues."

Hallett nodded. "Yes, bad luck. I mean, I can see that they have some merit—some passages of colour in the main one—but you should have stuck to the landscapes. I really quite liked one of the views you had at the Institution, it wasn't bad at all. But the stuff you've got here—no. No, you made a mistake there. Shame. Never mind," and he strolled off with Alcock and his friends, a loutish girl hanging on his arm.

My heart sank into my boots. I hadn't expected praise from them, but this was very bad. I walked on around the room, feeling more dejected by the minute. I went to look at my works, which I had loved so much on Varnishing Day. There was hardly anyone looking at them. I still loved them, but with a hopeless feeling, as though I knew they were going to die. I saw Quayle in the distance; he lifted a hand in greeting but quickly turned away. He certainly wasn't going to congratulate me.

After half an hour I was so miserable I had to leave. Looking at the work of successful artists was beyond me. I almost felt that the Committee was going to come and ask me to take them away. 'A mistake has been made, Mr Armiger—the space is required for other works...'

I slunk home, fretted by doubt. Perhaps they were right. Had I been completely wrong? Over-reached myself? Lost my judgement?

I hadn't felt so bad about my work since I graduated from the Schools. But after spending the day agonising, I decided I would take a stand. It didn't matter if the Halletts and Alcocks of the world didn't like them. I liked them; Rachel and her father approved (quenching the voice that said 'but they are not from the art world'); they were what I wanted to do; people will dislike anything new. Perhaps the critics would understand. Perhaps...

I pored over the close-printed columns.

'The artist has handicapped himself by choosing a disagreeable, not to say revolting, subject... injudiciously exposed to the general Public... they may be very correct as to resemblance; but are far from excellent as pictures...'

'Mr Armiger purports to give us Common Life but gives us instead nothing but the most Common Art. The brushwork is slovenly and insufficient attention has been paid to composition... wants more carefulness of execution...'

So much for the *Morning Chronicle* and the *Times*. I groaned, poured a large brandy, swallowed it in one gulp and reached for the *Morning Post* and the *Literary Panorama*. The *Examiner* wouldn't be out until Sunday.

It was worse than I had thought. I had been afraid the notices would be bad, but now I would gladly have settled for being ignored. It seemed that the entire artistic and critical establishment had got together and agreed that my work was rubbish. I ploughed on, still hoping for something favourable.

'It is to be regretted that Mr Armiger, whose work in Landscapes we recently had occasion to admire, has abandoned his former carefulness and firmness of handling... crudeness of Effect...'

'The sobriety of colour is well suited to the subject, which is, however, by no means a favourable one...'

'Soon after the founding of the Royal Academy, Sir Joshua Reynolds admitted to concern that its Annual Exhibitions would tempt artists to abandon classical subjects and idealism in favour of pictures of Common Life. He described such artists as those who 'express with precision the various shades of passion as they are exhibited by vulgar minds'. We are sorry to say that Mr Armiger's paintings fall into this error...'

'In what may be called Common Life, there are several well-executed performances... Mr Craig's 'Cook' is a picture from the life, full of truth and good humour... Mr Armiger's

'Awaiting Transportation' is a masterly performance. We feel it as though it were a scene from real life.' At last! Someone liked it! I read on. 'As a picture, it deserves to be engraved, but as a subject, we should be glad if it were buried in oblivion.'

Oblivion. That summed it up. There was nothing now but to creep away and resume my landscapes. If I were lucky, in about a hundred years people would forget about my foray into 'disgusting' paintings. It would take at least that long. A good review is forgotten in days; a much-praised painting haunts you for years—everything that Turner produced from now on would be compared to his 'Snowstorm'; but a bad review stays with you for the rest of your life. 'Isn't he the fellow who painted those disgusting scenes...?' The woman at the exhibition's words ate into my heart like acid. I drank another glass. I had not expected outpourings of admiration, but I had thought that some might see what I was trying to achieve. The glowing notices of Turner's 'Snowstorm' and the qualified approval of Constable's picture had given me hope, but it was not to be. I had got it all wrong.

My cheek sank onto my hand. Brigstock had liked my paintings, and Rachel and her father. One or two other people had commented favourably to me. They were the only ones. Everyone who had criticised them—Alcock's sneers, Quayle's pity—they were right. I had over-reached myself. I had made a bad decision, lost my power of judgement, been carried away by enthusiasm. I should have stuck to Agamemnon. I wanted to paint modern subjects, experiment with technique, introduce new ideas, make something truthful and sincere; but despite my longings I would have to leave all that to others with more ability. The spectre of Babbage rose in my mind like Banquo's ghost. Would I end up like him, embittered and lonely, wandering along the street ranting to myself?

I had failed.

A week later the Somers arrived, relieving the low spirits that had overpowered me. I hadn't been back to Somerset House and felt I would never be able to set foot there again. It was 'a brief visit, I'm afraid, my dear Edward, but we felt that we had to see your splendid paintings in their glory.' I wasn't sure about the glory—ignominy seemed more appropriate—but I was delighted to see them, happy to be with friends and more than happy to be with Rachel. She greeted me with her usual unaffected warmth, pressing my hand in hers and exclaiming how tired I looked. Her father seemed well enough and I was glad he had felt up to making the journey. They lifted my gloom and I took them round the Exhibition, explaining the virtues of Turner and Constable and pointing out the famous and infamous in the crowd, since *tout le monde* was there. They inquired about the notices.

"I'm afraid, sir, that they have been very badly knocked about by the critics. They have taken exception to the subject. Perhaps it was the wrong time to bring it forward—but the present events made it exactly the right time, I had thought."

"Did no-one at all like them? I am very surprised. I think they are magnificent—quite like the Paul Veronese in their directness and effect, and the colour."

Rachel, good, dear woman, was energetic in their defence, but she really did like them. I knew her well enough now to know that she would never tell a lie, even to console a friend. Her father was musing, stroking his chin as he stared up at them.

"Do you not approve, sir? Please tell me if you don't. I would rather have your true opinion."

He turned to me. "Approve? Of course I approve. They are what we have been trying to show people, made manifest in paint. I never thought it could be done. You say people do not like them. That is their business. They do not like our tracts, either, but I persist in believing that they are worthwhile. I feel the works are rough—you will forgive me if I do not have the right language to describe my ideas—they do not have the exquisite polish of Mr West's works, but they are very moving, and beautiful too, in their own way. But I was trying to think of Dr Johnson's remark—ah, yes: 'every thing that enlarges the sphere of human powers, that shows man he can do what he thought he could not do, is valuable'." I think your works fall into that category. They are like the steam engines and gas lights—I saw the lights in the street when we went to our lodgings last night, and I was amazed by them, truly amazed. It was as clear as day."

"But how are Edward's paintings like gaslight, father?" Rachel smiled, linking her arm in his.

"Oh, yes—I digressed. I meant to say that the new things make a glare, and smoke, and rattle, and everyone exclaims how noisy they are and how they disfigure the landscape, but in a few years you will see that everyone will say they cannot do without them."

I was far too unhappy to venture to Slaughter's and hid at Rainbow's when I wanted to consult the papers. Brigstock found me there and told me that the talk at Slaughter's and in the print shops was all of the Competition and the Commission that went with it. It was the same everywhere, even Rainbow's, but at least there I didn't have to listen to Hallett and Alcock crowing or Quayle commiserating with me. Pushed into the background by the effort and excitement of preparing for the Annual Exhibition, the Competition now occupied the centre foreground. The Exhibition had been opened, the dinners eaten and the reviews written, read and discussed. Now the insatiable hunger for novelty was focussed on the Competition.

"People are saying that you'll have to give up painting, or

at any rate get on with landscapes again," Brigstock told me, raising his shaggy head as he drained a tankard of porter. "Until the public forget about the Luddite things."

"I'd come to that conclusion myself." Whether I could or would do it, was something else. I was too low even to think about starting something new.

"Campbell's getting his Competition picture engraved. I thought it was awfully good."

"Yes. Perhaps he'll win. Is Mrs Humphrey doing it?"

"I think so. He thinks he'll make some money out of it. Hallett didn't put anything in the Competition, in the end. I suppose he was too busy with that big picture of the Muses."

"Or going to routs in Brighton."

"What do you suppose the Commission will be? Hallett says, a portrait of the Prince Regent."

"Another one? Isn't Lawrence doing one now?"

"I don't know—is he? What do you think it will be, then?"

"Can't we talk about something else?"

It was the same at Leeuwen's, where I went to pay my bill, which completely cleaned me out. No more visits to inns or coffee houses until I had got some money in.

"Who do you think will win the Competition, sir? Sorry your works were not reviewed more favourably. I though they looked very well in those new mouldings."

I scurried away, and resolved to shun Middleton's and all my other haunts until the whole thing was well over and London life returned to normal. But that was not until the end of June, when I would also be able to carry my pictures home and conceal them from public view. In the mean time I should be working up some sketches or, since the spring weather had at last arrived, going out and doing some more. Instead, I was loitering about uselessly at home, in between more inspiriting visits to the Somers.

At last there was a glimmer of approval, a struck match in a stygian cave. I ran into Robert Hunt in the Strand, who engaged me in a long and enjoyable discussion of the technical aspects of my pictures.

"I can't say I'm carried away with enthusiasm over the subjects, though I don't mind them half as much as the *Post* and the *Chronicle* seem to, but what they've missed altogether is the freshness of your application of paint and your colour and tonal values. I think the time has passed when 'finish' is all that's required. There is a great deal of tired old work in the show, and that spirit of emulation that always seizes the human race. After the triumph of 'Christ Healing', we'll be plagued by similar stuff for the next five years. So I was pleased to see a bit of inventiveness and originality, such as you've displayed. My notice will be in the next *Examiner*. Bye the bye, I heard that Turner commented favourably on your glazing." He tipped his hat and went on his way, leaving me positively rejuvenated.

Uplifted, I decided to take the plunge that I'd long been contemplating. I settled with myself to speak to Rachel. They were to return to Rochford soon and I didn't know when I might see her again. I wasn't sure what I was going to say. She was promised to Crosland, but I couldn't go on like this. I wanted her to know my feelings. I could do nothing more; I had nothing to offer her at present. Despite my debacle at the Exhibition, I felt the time was right. I didn't think that failure or my lack of income would weigh with her. The trepidation I felt was altogether different.

Having made up my mind, I decided that nothing was going to happen to change things, that one day was as good as another and the earliest opportunity the best, so I walked over to Holborn and called on the Somers at their lodgings. A servant let me in. There was a curious feeling of agitation in the house, palpable in little flurries in corners, Rachel whisking out of sight, the lady of the house eying me oddly before disappearing after Rachel, leaving me alone with her father. He took me by the arm and we went into the dim parlour.

"My dear Edward, I am very glad to see you," he said. "There is something very particular I have to say to you."

I had a momentary echo of the last time someone said that to me—Francesca, and what it presaged. What a long time ago it seemed—in another life. We sat next to each other on the worn plush of a sofa.

"It is about Rachel. She is my jewel, Edward. She is so important to me. I always knew that one day some man would take her from me, and it is right that it should be so. She must have her own life, and I have worried greatly (and I know she has too) as to what would happen to her after I am gone. I can give her nothing. She must have had to go out as a governess. Neither of us wanted that."

I thought this was my moment, and tried to say something, but he stopped me.

"Hear me out. When Arthur Crosland asked for her hand I was happy. He is a good man and would take care of her, and it relieved my mind greatly that she would have a home after my death. I came to think you cared for her, and of late I have felt that she cares for you, too. I will not attempt to influence her in her decisions. She is a good, sensible girl who knows what is right and I believe, rightly or wrongly, that I should not interfere. She must make up her own mind."

I was touched by his confiding in me, and what he said verified what I had believed was her situation. But I was at a loss to see where it was leading.

He held up his hand. "You wonder why I am telling you all this. It is because she came to me only yesterday and told me that she wrote to Arthur last week to break her engagement to him. I am telling you this because although she has said nothing to me, I believe it is because of you. I have seen your behaviour towards her and believe that you truly love her. You have behaved honourably by her, and I respect you for it. Now you must do what you think best. I trust you not to hurt my girl. God bless you."

RACHEL was in the hall when I emerged.

"It is a beautiful day. Shall we go out into the park?"

She took my arm in silence. She wore a close bonnet and I couldn't see her face. All the trees were in bud or leaf, which the bright day lit into a dozen different greens. Constable's work had made me even more conscious of their delicate hues. Above, a skylark made its quick repeated trills and I heard the rattling call of a missel thrush. In the distance the Life Guards clattered past and I shuddered involuntarily. The sight of heavy cavalry could never be a pleasure again; the memories they evoked were too painful. We wandered down the paths while I tried to think of how to approach her, for approach her I would. It was my time.

"Rachel, I can't tell you how good it is being here with you."

She smiled. "Father and I were thinking the same thing. We enjoy your company so much."

We went on a little. I longed to keep her near me, for always, but I didn't want to risk another rebuff. I thought it would be all right, but I could not be sure. She had only just broken her engagement. I should leave her alone for a while, but I wasn't going to. I had to know whether I had any chance. Her father, good, dear man, might be quite wrong about her feelings. What I was certain of was that if she could not or would not take me, she wouldn't hurt me. She wasn't capable of malice. We would always be friends—but I yearned for a great deal more than that.

She was talking at random, of politics and the recent

events that had displaced all else from the news. "Now that Lord Liverpool is Prime Minister and we are actually at war with the Americans, there will be a great deal to do. Some of the mills are speaking of closing until trade improves or the war is over. The price of bread is still rising and poverty is very bad in the north."

"Shall you go back soon?"

She hesitated. "I didn't want to trouble you, but Father is thinking of resigning his living. His health is not as good as he would have you believe, and his advocacy for the workers, especially the Thwaites, has made him unpopular in some quarters in Rochford. He can't get the support he needs for us to run the Soup Shops and the school for the children. I'm afraid that people like the Crokers and Shirlows have turned the Town Council against us."

"I'm very sorry to hear that."

Despite my firm intention, I didn't feel I needed to hurry. I felt surprisingly calm, but closer to her than ever, more bodily aware of her presence, her warmth, her supple figure. It was almost as though we were already united.

"But it is essential that the work goes on. I was speaking yesterday to one of our colleagues from Hackney. They have started a Ragged School for the children of the district, despite some opposition, and have already fifty children coming of an evening after they finish their work. The need is there."

"And you must go on with your pamphlets." If she was not to be Mrs Crosland, there was nothing to stop her—I certainly wouldn't. "If you need me for any drawings, you know I'm more than willing."

"Thank you, Edward. I know we can always rely on you." We skirted one of the great elms, now clustered with pale papery bunches of seeds. Rachel stopped and picked some. She loved trees and everything to do with them. I watched her graceful movements. The sun lit tiny gold hairs on the back of her neck. I felt myself tremble. She buried her face in the posy.

"I always expect them to have a scent. We don't see many elms in Rochford. It is mainly oaks and alders."

I stopped in the path and swung round to face her. "Rachel, I don't know if I should speak now, or say these things. Your father has told me—about your engagement—I don't want to be indelicate, but..."

She looked down at the leaves, moving them about in her hands. "I am glad he has told you. I wanted you to know." She halted.

"A difficult decision for you."

I was panting in my eagerness, but was afraid of putting her off by some word or sign.

"Yes. But I could not allow it to go on when I did not love Arthur as a woman should love the man she marries. When she…"

Released!

I seized her hands. "Rachel, can you love me?"

The bunch dropped to the ground.

"I love you. I want you to be mine."

Her hands were warm and firm. Her clear green eyes looked into mine. I clasped her waist and pressed her to me, heedless of everything. I felt her body trembling. She tilted her face towards me and I kissed her again and again as I had longed to do. I felt as though some great chasm had been filled.

THE scandalized stares and coughs of some passers-by made us draw apart, and she straightened her bonnet with a smile.

"I have nothing to offer you, you know that."

"We will manage somehow. You will become famous one day."

"Not very soon, I'm afraid."

We walked on, not caring where, her hand in my arm.

"I was longing to ask you, but could not while you were engaged."

"I know."

"Can I ask what made you change your mind, just at this time?"

"Arthur wrote a week ago to tell me that he had been offered the living of the place he is at in Devon, so we could be married immediately. I had thought it would be years away. As soon as I read his news, I knew that I could not go on with it. It would be wrong."

"Because you cared for me!"

She nodded, smiling shyly.

"Say it. I want to hear you say it."

A short interlude under a tree, broken again by people coughing angrily.

Rachel smiled at me, shaking her head. "I am afraid my behaviour has not been very like a lady."

I took her hand again. "I promise I won't reproach you with it."

Back at the lodgings, I announced my joy to her father and we all sat down together for dinner. It was the happiest evening of my life. We talked of everything and nothing, except to determine that they both would come to London, and I would look out lodgings for them. Everything else could be settled then.

At home I reflected on my fortune. I had gained the hand of the woman I desired, the most wonderful woman in the world, but how different it might have been. In the first place, if I'd never gone to Rochford. Strange to think that in a way, I owed my happiness to Francesca and Mr Hall! But things could have gone seriously wrong. Following the men on the moor—they might have discovered me, and—would they have killed me? Danby had killed Mr Croker, shot him in cold blood. If he had seen me? I shivered. When I thought of it I had been in danger any number of times during that terrible night. The shrieks of the men, the walls of the mill black against the flaring furnace within, cracking glass, the sound of the hooves of the dragoons on the cobbled yard. I felt again my anguish as I'd tried to get out of the stables, and the breath raw in my dry throat as I'd run, stumbling down the narrow streets with the soldiers behind me. God! I never wanted to go through such a thing again. I had thought I was going to die. And if it had not been for the buckle of my satchel, I might have. God! To die there like that, shot, writhing in agony in the icy, dirty street. What an end that would have been, and it was nearly mine. I had had no idea what I might have lost. And I might have been arrested, tried—condemned? It could be me, as well as Thwaite, lying on the filthy straw in the old Warrior at Woolwich, packed in with all the other felons. And there would have been no Rachel for me, no warm and lovely companion for my life.

My relief was so great I got down on my knees and made my thanks in proper form.

"Have I the honour of addressing Mr Edward Armiger?"

I was back at the Exhibition, having some business with Reinagle, and to see if there had been any interest in my work. As he spoke the gentleman doffed his hat. He was about my height, dressed in black broadcloth, with a pleasant round face, eye-glasses and thick greying hair. I bowed.

"I am Thomas Baxter. I understand that you are the author of these works? I was told that you would call in and have been waiting here, hoping to meet with you."

I was taken aback. He didn't look like a collector, nor a critic. He looked well-to-do, with some of the air of a clergyman. His name conveyed nothing to me.

"Yes, they are mine."

"They are very fine. Permit me to congratulate you."

Well! That was welcome, whatever else he wanted. I bowed again.

"Forgive me for appearing inquisitive, but I have seen works rather similar in some tracts which appeared recently on the subject of the Frame-Breaking Act. The artist was not named, but I felt that the hand was the same."

"You're very perceptive, sir. They too were mine—earlier essays on the same theme."

He looked about. "Is there somewhere we could sit down? I would like to speak with you."

I took him to the coffee house opposite. He insisted on treating me.

"Have you heard of Mrs Elizabeth Fry and her work in female prisons?"

I shook my head. "The name is vaguely familiar."

"You are not by any chance a member of the Society of Friends?"

"No." It was hard to understand where all this was leading.

"You haven't read Mr John Howard's *The State of the Prisons in England, and An Account of the Principal Lazarettos of Europe*?"

I was still entirely in the dark. I sipped my coffee. I began to wonder whether this stranger was some kind of lunatic, or was going to try to convert me to some unorthodox sect. But he did look very respectable, and his manner was calm.

"I'm afraid not."

The man smiled. He took off his eye-glasses and began polishing them with his handkerchief, which was fine lawn. "Forgive my inquisition. I am one of a group—several groups—inspired by the work of the late Mr Howard and of Mrs Fry in attempting to ameliorate the atrocious state of our prisons. I am myself a Member of Parliament and do what I can to advance the cause there. I was most impressed by your work. Mrs Fry has gone so far as to spend some nights in the female prison at Newgate. I wondered whether you had undertaken something similar?" He leaned forward.

"No, I haven't gone so far. That was painted after I visited someone I knew in the prison at Rochford Castle, in the north. It was a terrible place—I haven't shown the half of it. Very cold, dirty and squalid. There were women in the cells there, too. It was hideous."

"I felt that they were born of experience. They neither preach nor mock nor sentimentalise. I was struck by how they simply present the situation and leave the viewer to make his own judgement. But I can see that your sympathies are with the prisoners and families."

"Thank you. That's exactly the effect I wanted to produce. The man is—was—a cloth-dresser..." I found myself telling him the whole story, my relationships with the Thwaites and the Somers, our work on the pamphlets, the injustice of the treatment of the cloth-dressers. He listened intently.

When I had finished he leaned towards me again. ""What you tell me endorses the opinion I had formed from seeing your work. You have a rare talent, Mr Armiger. There are few in your profession today who concern themselves with such things, or perhaps who are prepared to take the risks that you have."

This was a new view of myself. A risk-taker? A rare talent? I had thought of myself more as irresponsible, wayward and wishing for adventure, and I thought that was the view of most of my acquaintance. But I liked this idea very much, and Baxter certainly understood my work.

"I am a banker by profession—or trade, some might say,"

he smiled, "and I do what I can, with my friends, to support the cause. Prison reform is long overdue in this country and now the long struggle to abolish slavery is in the main over, we are concentrating our resources on this social evil, as well as trying to improve the conditions of the weavers of London and relieve their poverty. It is not exactly your own field of interest, but I wonder if I could prevail on you to join us?"

"How? I have to tell you, I'm not at all well-off."

He laughed. "I did not for a moment think so. No, your wealth is in your talent. I hoped to purchase your paintings for my own house. They are for sale, I believe? By hanging them at home my visitors, including my fellow Members of Parliament, will see them, and I thought that with your permission we might have them engraved. I think there would be an audience for them—I am determined to create an audience. Sir Samuel Romilly saw them yesterday and was also struck by them. Did you see his piece in the last *Quarterly Review*? Pity—it was excellent. And I hoped that I might prevail on you to visit the weavers and see if their situation inspires you in the same way as the cloth-dressers. I feel that your paintings might reach men who are left cold by arguments. Art has been underestimated as a way of reaching the public. All they see of politics is patriotic works—the 'Death of Nelson', and so on—or portraits of the nobility. Or Mr Cruickshank's and Mr Rowlandson's lampoons. They are useful in their own way, but I have in mind something different—more personal. What do you say?"

It was just as when Mr Somers had asked me to do the first drawings. I spoke without considering.

"Yes. Thank you. I know nothing of weavers and prison reform, but I can learn. Thank you."

On the final afternoon of the Exhibition, the winner of the Competition was to be announced. I took up a post on the fringes of the crowd. A podium had been constructed at the end of the room. Members of the Council ranged themselves on either side of him on little gilt chairs. Their faces gave nothing away but a complacency that I associated with having completed a wearisome task.

The President rose to his feet and with much bowing and scraping and complimenting the Council who, it appeared, had jointly judged the works, began to outline the ideas behind the Competition and its evolution.

"A grand subject was required… there was, of course, much debate among the members as to what exactly that should be. Some believed that… others insisted… classical theme… allegorical… restrictions on subject… historical…"

He read from an immense sheaf of notes and quoted extensively from the Founder, whom he named in reverential tones. "Sir Joshua believed that… landscape not suitable… eventually it was agreed that a subject representative of the momentous times we live in, was the best possible…"

He went on so long that it seemed he was going to canvas the entire history of European art and ladies (the wives of exhibitors—next year, my lovely Rachel would be among them) began fanning themselves.

At last he got to the announcement. I had my eyes fixed on Quayle's face, having long ago decided he would be the winner. When West named him his expression, rather than broadening into a great grin, as mine would certainly have done, contracted into a modest smirk. There was a cheer of congratulation from his friends and polite applause from the audience. I don't know how many were surprised—not many, I suspected. Alcock looked glum. If there was one thing that irritated some people more than losing a prize, it was one of their friends winning.

The President continued with a speech of praise, which recapitulated the merits of Quayle's work and mentioned how impressed His Royal Highness had been with it. But there was something that everyone was still waiting for and perhaps conscious of increased fidgeting, he drew his speech to a close.

"It now remains for me to announce the Grand Commission which the Council has determined the winner of the Premium will execute, and which will be permanently displayed in the Academy's rooms. It has been forty years now since Mr Zoffany so ably executed the fine portrait of the members of the Academy with which we are all familiar. Over the years it has been suggested that, with the passing of time and the departure and arrival of many members, the time has come for a modern-day version. The Council has determined that the time has come. It offers its felicitations to Mr Quayle and is assured that the Commission—a portrait of all current members of the Royal Academy—is in safe hands. Mr Quayle, we are at your disposal."

I was still watching Quayle. As the President spoke his urbane smile vanished and an expression of absolute dismay crossed his face. It was only an instant before the smile reappeared, but there was something fixed about his expression as he received his friends' felicitations.

When the crowd cleared I went over. "My congratulations. I'm sure it's richly deserved."

He grinned, a little glassily.

"How will you enjoy painting all your fellow members? I do agree, as the President says, the occasion is well overdue for another portrait. You'll be able to spend a lot of time with them all. Forty members! But I suppose it won't take you all that long."

He couldn't prevent himself flinching. "Two years if it's a day, and just when I've got so much other work on hand! I only entered the damned thing because I thought it'd look good for my clients. Now it'll make me behindhand with all their commissions, which I can tell you are worth a damned sight more than this!"

I'd had my mischief and thought I'd console him. "Still, the portrait will go up in the entrance, I suppose, and for all time to come, whenever the Academy is spoken of, your picture will be referred to. Your name will become synonymous with theirs."

He brightened. "Yes, that's true, very true." He clapped me on the shoulder. "You're quite right. And I'll put my fellows on to it. No need for me to do all the draperies and so on. No-one will expect that, will they?"

I nodded. "Still, forty heads, and you'll have to do at least part of the clothing and hands."

He grimaced.

"Shovelling coal." I added.

"What?"

"It'll be like shovelling coal, I expect. But I'm sure you'll manage. Good luck."

I sauntered off, leaving him grimacing. He would manage, nothing surer. They'd given the prize to the right man and he would produce something which would please everyone. But now I knew what the 'big Commission' was, I was even gladder that I had escaped the whole thing. It would be a work of enormous tedium which said nothing new about anything, and would have shackled me to the Academy for years, on their terms.

I left Somerset House and strolled through the park, still glowing with late sun. I was to dine with Baxter at his club in St James, and then to see Rachel. The blue sky and white puffy clouds were reflected one shade darker in the gently rippling water: heavens, clouds and light, all joined in one composition scattered in a thousand glittering fragments.

The summer breeze blew snowflake blossoms from the trees, whirling around me until they settled on the verdant grass, opening and closing like butterflies' wings. And I felt myself floating too, light as air, far away from all that ballast of expectation and conformity, rivalry and pretence.

I hadn't won the Competition, but I was free.

THE END

Historical Note

The book is based on historical fact, although some events have been modified or moved in time. Individuals such as Lord Byron and the members of the Royal Academy mentioned are real, as is Byron's speech. Words and actions attributed to other real characters, such as the President of the Academy, Benjamin West, are fictional. The Royal Academy Exhibition and British Institution Exhibition of 1812 included the works of art described. The Competition is wholly invented.

The Luddite and food riots depicted are based on actual events of the period, as are the newspaper reports and trial.

Edward Armiger and his friends and associates and their works of art are entirely fictitious. However, the composition and many details of Edward's major painting 'A Luddite: Awaiting Transportation' are based on the fine work by Frank Holl, 'Newgate: Committed for Trial', which helped inspire the writing of this book.

Lightning Source UK Ltd.
Milton Keynes UK
UKHW020626181119
353752UK00012B/1530/P